FREEDOM
is a
FEAST

FREEDOM
is a
FEAST

A Novel
Alejandro
Puyana

LITTLE, BROWN AND COMPANY

New York Boston London

Little, Brown and Company
Hachette Book Group
1290 Avenue of the Americas, New York, NY 10104
littlebrown.com

First Edition: August 2024

Little, Brown and Company is a division of Hachette Book Group, Inc. The Little, Brown name and logo are trademarks of Hachette Book Group, Inc.

The publisher is not responsible for websites (or their content) that are not owned by the publisher.

The Hachette Speakers Bureau provides a wide range of authors for speaking events. To find out more, go to hachettespeakersbureau.com or email hachettespeakers@hbgusa.com.

Little, Brown and Company books may be purchased in bulk for business, educational, or promotional use. For information, please contact your local bookseller or the Hachette Book Group Special Markets Department at special.markets@hbgusa.com.

Book interior design by Marie Mundaca

ISBN 978-0-316-57178-4
LCCN 2024933873

Printing 1, 2024

MRQ

Printed in Canada

To Teodoro Petkoff,
whose real story I couldn't tell because no one would have believed it

Cuando se tiene un hijo, toda risa nos cala,
todo llanto nos crispa, venga de donde venga.
Cuando se tiene un hijo, se tiene el mundo adentro
y el corazón afuera.

—Andrés Eloy Blanco, "Los hijos infinitos"

PROLOGUE

2002

On a normal day María would have walked to the open window, and from the clothesline just beyond it she would have unclipped the dress: cotton, pink, knee-length, with a lacy white apron that began the day clean and accumulated stains as she cooked for the Romeros. She had two other dresses just like it, one mint-green and one baby-blue, all of them given to her by La Señora when María had started cleaning at Casa Verde four years ago. The bad year. The year her mother died. After taking the dress from the line she would have folded it and packed it in her workbag with a bar of Savoy chocolate for a midmorning snack. But La Señora had called the night before, asking her to stay home. They were going to wait and see what happened with the opposition march first, she said. Señor Romero had heard things were going to get rough.

María woke up at her regular hour nevertheless, the lazy light just crawling over the mountain, stretching thin on the zinc roofs of Barrio Cotiza. She had lived in the barrios on the west side of Caracas ever since she could remember. First in an apartment building in Catia—when her mom still lived with family—working-class but sturdy, made of concrete and iron, with an elevator that wended its way up to the fifth floor shakily and slowly, and a bus stop right outside the building. When her mom started cleaning at an office building, they'd moved up the mountain, to a rented room that was a five-minute walk from the street through sets of concrete steps. Then, when María was a teenager, they made another move—farther up the mountain and down the poverty line—to their first rancho, no more sturdy walls, no more dependable utilities. Her mom was both disappointed and relieved when María insisted she needed to work, that school could be something she thought about later. Finally, they got here, to the highest part of Cotiza, her mother already sick by then, María's son, Eloy, already a boy without a father. The burden of work sat heavily, and solely, on María's shoulders. There was no more barrio above them, only mountain, and in this city none but the poorest lived this high up.

She brushed her teeth and checked on little Eloy, sleeping on the couch wrapped in Disney sheets—hand-me-downs from the Romeros.

At noon she was still home. That never happened except when the Romeros took their vacations: summer visits to Miami, Christmases in Whistler. But she was thankful not to travel across Caracas to Casa Verde today. The protests had been making public transit impossible. Fewer than half the buses were operating, they all charged more, even if it was against the law, and you had to fight your way on. With schools closed for days, figuring out how to keep nine-year-old Eloy occupied while still getting to work had been taxing—for her; for Magali, her best friend; even for her neighbor Jacinto.

But it felt wrong to be still. On weekdays the only people who weren't up before the sun and on their way to work were drunks and criminals. Even though La Señora herself had asked her not to come, María couldn't help feeling she was disappointing someone: her dead mother? herself? her son? She wasn't sure.

She crossed the tiny living room of the rancho, winking at Eloy, who was lazing on the couch, and walked past her folding table covered in flowered contact paper to the kitchen at the far wall. Her two-burner countertop stove and her small fridge had grown patches of rust, and sported numerous dimples and bumps. Her concrete floor had cost her a year's savings to install, and she was proud of it. On the wall to her right, the only one made of brick (the others were corrugated zinc paneling), one door led to the bathroom and the other to the sole bedroom in the house.

She opened her last bag of Harina P.A.N., a quarter full. She would have to figure out how to make it last, since she most likely wouldn't have another for days, maybe weeks. The stores had been out of stock for a while now (though you wouldn't know it from the pantry at Casa Verde, where María stacked the bright yellow bags one atop the other, like bricks in a wall). There were countrywide shortages of basic goods, including arepa flour, sugar, coffee, rice, even pasta. She made the arepas smaller than usual, leaving some flour for tomorrow, and placed the disklike corn cakes in a black skillet. While the arepas cooked she walked to Eloy, who lay reading a book, a blanket with a Donald Duck pattern wrapped around his skinny legs.

"It's almost ready," she whispered in her son's ear and stroked his hair. When she kissed him, Eloy rolled and nuzzled his face into the cushions.

María went back to the kitchen and considered turning on the news. She had been avoiding it, knowing it would be more coverage of the march, more news about people hating Hugo Chávez or people loving Hugo Chávez. Why Chávez was the worst thing ever to happen to Venezuela, why Chávez was the savior of the people and the only way to Bolívar's promise. Her own mind was a mess of contradictions, of memories of her mother and her devotion to the president, of her own feelings about him. On one hand, she liked him, the way he spoke to her and to her struggle in a way no other politician ever had. The way he looked: a strong, handsome man—but not in the way TV told her a handsome man should look. How could she not have fallen in love with Chávez, seeing him through her mother's eyes? Seeing bits of Eloy in him—someone in power who looked like her son, his brown features devoid of European influence — made her feel good, gave her hope that her son could become someone important too. But Chávez also loved a fight, pitted people against one another. Four years since his election, and even though the magic of that day had not left her — it never would — he was starting to feel like just another politician. She wondered if her mom would feel similarly. The answer was no. She'd be out there with her red shirt and her beret, marching and carrying signs. Maybe she would have been able to prevent the thought of Chávez from turning rancid in María's mouth, like old ham.

María decided to turn the TV on anyway. News about the day's opposition march snowed in and out. She fiddled with the antenna until the picture fizzed into place. Men behind podiums had been calling for marches against Chávez most days now. The noise of people banging their pots in protest had become a nightly occurrence, even here in the barrio — a metallic concerto to lull Eloy to sleep. Still, what she saw now on the TV was unexpected: a mass of people so large that she had trouble making it fit in her mind. A helicopter flew overhead, following the highway from one side of the city to the other. The mass was like a snake so large it seemed poised to swallow the city whole — each marcher another of its infinite scales. There were so many people that they couldn't all fit on the highway, some of them overflowing into side streets. How many times had Magali told her that it was just a bunch of sore losers crying over the power they used to have? Just white people horrified that someone unlike them held the presidency. Enraged that the revolution couldn't be brought down by sifrinas and their rich husbands.

But the last few days had not looked like rich ladies throwing a tantrum. It was a country up in arms. People like La Señora, sure, but also people like Magali. Like her mom. The announcer said the horde was heading to Miraflores, the presidential palace. The sound the masses made — a tumult of whistles, clanging pots, and chants calling for Chávez to leave — got under her skin and made her hair prickle: "MI-RA-FLORES! MI-RA-FLORES! MI-RA-FLORES!"

As Eloy zombied through the confines of their small house—looking for a shoe here, a crayon there—María cut open the first arepa, the crust toasted and crunchy, but inside as soft as a pillow. Steam rose from the opened corn cake, and her face blushed at its warmth. She filled the arepa with yesterday's tuna salad. Eloy was already sitting at the table holding a card.

"I tricked you! You thought I would forget!" he said as he handed it to her.

Sometimes his smile was so big, his light so bright, that María didn't know if her body could hold all of it. She marveled at each small freckle on his brown face, one of the only things he'd inherited from her. He looked so much like his father otherwise: the dark skin, the tight curls, the sharp jaw already squaring. He fit in Cotiza, unlike her. Her light bronze skin packed with freckles had shone a spotlight that turned her inward and made her easy prey for playground bullies telling her to go wipe the stains off her face.

"¡Qué gafo!" she said.

The card read "Feliz Cumpleaños" in red. She imagined Eloy making it in secret while she was at work, all his colors out on the floor. Eloy's attempt at cursive handwriting, unpracticed but still quite beautiful, read "Te quiero mucho mami" and was punctuated by a drawing of an orange bird.

María reached across the table and grabbed Eloy's face in her hands. "Gracias, mi amor. I love it."

"You like the bird?"

"It's very good," María said. "Maybe next year we can have our birthdays together. What do you think? I know they're a few days apart, but we could be birthday buddies."

"Can I still have my own cake?"

"Of course, mi amor, you can have your cake."

The sound of gunshots on the TV interrupted their sweet moment. The voice of the announcer came into focus for her again: "We are getting footage of marchers encountering the president's supporters close to Miraflores Palace. The first protesters have reached Miraflores and have been met with stones, tear gas, and now gunshots. We are confirming that two people are dead, one of them a reporter. Again, this is live footage from Avenida Baralt, close to the presidential palace in Miraflores."

Avenida Baralt went south to north on a hill. At the top of the hill, Chávez supporters roared; at the bottom of the street, opposition marchers did the same. Dividing them was a no-man's-land wrapped in a cloud of gray tear gas—with rocks, bricks, and debris of all kinds arcing above the smoke. One wall of officers in blue uniforms, Metropolitan Police protecting the marchers, stood their ground with masks and anti-riot weaponry, preventing a clash against the pro-Chávez mass. Another wall of army forces, in green uniforms, did the same with the Chavistas protecting the palace.

"What's going on, Mami?" Eloy asked.

But María was mesmerized by such a big thing unfolding in such a small square. It felt to her like it could explode out of the TV and suddenly she and Eloy would be placed there, in the middle of it. Then the announcer broke in again: "We've just received footage of the first confirmed death. Warning, the images you're about to see are graphic. We can confirm that photographer Jaime Soto has been shot dead by what seems like fire from pro-Chávez counterprotesters. Again, journalist Jaime Soto is dead from a gunshot wound to the head. Peace to his remains."

Before she could even think to turn away, or shut the TV off, or cover her son's eyes, María watched the footage. A man, wearing a multi-pocketed vest, aims his long-lensed camera toward the top of the hill, and in the next moment he is felled, as if by some invisible, godly ray. The man's limp body is carried by other men to some sort of safety. María wondered if the people helping him thought there was still hope.

The footage kept jumping from skirmish to skirmish, to the people far away from Miraflores still marching and protesting, to opposition politicians calling for change. Different streets, different people screaming, different clouds of tear gas swirling in looping variations. But all of the same rage exploding in the sounds of banging pots and gunfire.

And then she heard another shot, but not from the TV. It was much louder and echoed inside her rancho. Then another, and then a few more in succession. She dropped to the floor, under the table, pulling Eloy with her. The floor was cool against her cheek and the scent of dust filled her nose.

"It's okay, Eloy. It'll be over soon," she whispered.

She wondered if the protests had reached them here, but of course not. Why would protesters be this high up in Cotiza? It was just gunshots. They heard them every day here, regardless of politics. Actually, the barrio had become safer during the recent turmoil. As the city had slowed down with the protests so had the gangs of malandros.

"Lots of plomo, Mami," Eloy said as the gunshots persisted. His eyes were shut tight, his nose scrunched up.

María could still hear the news on the TV, the march happening far away: "Miraflores! Miraflores! Miraflores!" people chanted. "Not one step back!"

"Stay down," she said.

She crawled over to the front door and opened it a crack. Across the street she could see Don Jacinto's house, with his myriad hanging ferns, the only green things in sight. She had always admired them. It was rare to find anyone in the barrio willing to dedicate time and money to something as ephemeral as plants. This was, after all, a very pragmatic place. You lived here because you had to. Spending money on something without the expectation of a return was considered frivolous. More than once María had heard Magali comment on the ferns: "Does he think he's better than us?"

Don Jacinto was crouched behind his motorcycle, a clunking old Honda, taking refuge from the bullets, clutching a rag so tight that María wondered if the motor oil it had absorbed throughout the decades would suddenly start dripping back out.

"Vecino!" María yelled.

"Señora María! Are you two all right over there?"

"Yes! What in heavens is going on?"

"Gangs! Some sort of turf thing. And today of all days!"

"I know, it's crazy!"

Magali came down the road toward María's rancho with the languid pace of a Sunday promenade. Fearless. Unbothered by the commotion. She wore her red MVR shirt, Chávez's face next to his party's logo on her chest.

"Hermana!" Magali said. "What are you doing on all fours? Those gunshots are coming from way down the mountain. Get up, mujer."

María did, feeling ridiculous. This was the power that Magali had on her. María could somehow siphon her friend's confidence and make it her own for a while. She dusted herself off, but still, with every gunshot she ducked her head.

"I'm going down," Magali said, matter-of-fact. Like she was announcing a trip to the bodega.

"For what?" María said.

Don Jacinto had also stood, no longer behind his bike, and looked at Magali with disbelief.

"To defend what's ours, coño! I should have been there already. Fucking escualidos."

"Maga, they're killing people. What are you going to do down there?"

"Protect the revolution, catira!"

It was her nickname. No one outside the barrio would ever have mistaken her for white, much less blonde, but still, *catira* had stuck, and as far as nicknames went, she had suffered much worse growing up.

"They're taking it away from us," Magali said. "Today! They hate that one of us is president, and we're not going to let them kill him. Come with me!"

"I've got Eloy here, I can't leave him. And it's too dangerous down there. No way."

"María, get your head out of your ass, we need everyone to show up. If we don't defend Chávez, no one will, and we'll be back where we were before, or worse." She turned toward Don Jacinto. "Viejo," she called. "Will you look after the boy?"

"Stop!" María said. "I'm not going."

"Coño, comadre, está bien. I'll do the fighting for both of us. But in this new Venezuela we're going to need balls. I'd start growing a pair if I were you."

María gulped down her response. She couldn't stand up to Magali. Magali who lived with her nose in the newspaper, who went to barrio meetings and played dominoes with the elders, talking about Marx, Fidel, and Mao as if they were buddies who hadn't visited in a while. If María's mom had met Magali they would have been close. Maybe that's why María gravitated to her; she saw her mom in her friend.

A new cascade of gunshots popped, so near this time that the bullets seemed like whispers whizzing by their ears. An engine revved up the crest of their narrow street, tires screeching, and a black jeep appeared. Then a shirtless man with half his body out the window shot his pistol at two motorcycles following the car. María saw him so clearly, a large mole on his left cheek, the tattoo of a cross on his left shoulder, his hair cropped tight to his head. She had never heard a gunshot so close before. It sounded like it was coming from inside her body. Even Magali joined María on the ground now. Glass exploded somewhere and then the vehicles passed them, gone in a cloud of dirt, the scent of gunpowder seared into the air. María stood up and brushed the dirt off and saw the broken windowpane, and below it a single tiny hole in the zinc panel that acted as one of the walls for her home.

She ran inside. The light coming in through the hole in the wall made a thin beam filled with galaxies of dust and floating particles. She followed the beam through her little rancho—she'd never known the space could feel so big—all the way to Eloy, who held his crimson belly with both hands and looked at her.

"What's going on, mi amor?" María said, even as she already knew the answer.

ELOY FELT WARM. Like when he rolled himself tight in the blanket and rested his head on his mother's lap while she read him stories. Like when he ran from third base to home plate and his friends all slapped him on the back. It was like someone had taken all those feelings and compressed them into two red dots, one in his belly, one a couple of inches off his bony spine.

Everything moved slowly, everything sounded far away. He could see his mom screaming but it was like the noise was lazy and didn't quite reach him. He couldn't understand her face, had never seen her move this way: her eyes wet and skipping, like she was looking for something important that was lost; her chest going up and down so fast, like his own after racing his friend Wili up the barrio stairs. When she finally reached him, and hugged him, and picked him up in her arms, he felt her vibrating, like her whole body was a heart. BOOM. BOOM. BOOM. An earthquake in each beat.

His mom carried him outside, and his madrina shouted, "Jacinto, the child is shot!"

His neighbor took him from his mom and flipped him around, lifted his shirt. It made a wet sound as it came away from his skin.

"El plomo went out the back," Jacinto said. "That's good."

"Viejo, what do you mean?" his madrina said.

"The bullet isn't in there—the doctors won't have to go digging for it—but he's bleeding a lot. We don't have much time. Magali, get me some towels from the house."

His madrina ran into the rancho and Don Jacinto rushed him and his mom to the Honda. Eloy loved that bike so much. He would sit with Don Jacinto after school and help him work on it. It's where he had learned most of his cusswords. Hija de su gran puta was used for the motorcycle in general, whenever she would not start. But there was also the coño e' su madre carburetor, the pendejo clutch, the brakes de mierda, and the engine of los cojones. When his mother wasn't around, Eloy was allowed to jump on the bike and pretend he was driving it. Jacinto would bring his radio and they would listen to the baseball games together as Eloy made *vroom* sounds from inside the big helmet.

His madrina ran back to them now with the towels.

Jacinto, astride the bike, was struggling with the ignition. "Hija de su gran puta," he muttered.

Eloy's mother picked him up and squished him between Jacinto's back and her body.

"Señora Magali," Jacinto said, "have María put pressure where the bullet went in and out."

At first it didn't hurt, he just felt something leaving him, like when he was little and peed the bed.

"Mujer, listen," Magali told his mom. "Go to Vargas Hospital. That's the best place for treating bullet wounds. Don't stop for nothing, you hear?"

Don Jacinto was still struggling with the bike, one kick after the other with no luck.

Magali applied deeper pressure on Eloy now, holding his mother's hands with hers. "Like this, María. Hold the towels like this."

Then a sharp pain traveled from Eloy's belly, half of it down to his toes and the other half up to his head. He screamed, loud and high-pitched, and his mom kissed him on his crown as the pain radiated outward, through his mother and his madrina and Don Jacinto, through la hija de su gran puta, through Don Jacinto's green ferns, through the million ranchos and the million bullets flying through them, through Cotiza and down the mountain.

At last, the Honda sputtered to life—the mechanical whirr seemed to echo inside him—and his madrina placed the helmet on his mother's head.

MARÍA WRAPPED HER ARMS around Don Jacinto's waist, squishing Eloy's thin frame in between them. The blood pooled, soaking the towels held in place against his belly and back. With every bump on the road her shirt squished like a wet mop. The blood was warm, but the rest of Eloy was cold, though she could still feel his small torso expand against her with the effort of his breathing.

In the frantic ride downhill she caught glimpses of the barrio. How as they descended the buildings became more solid. There were actual walls that could stop bullets, colorful paint, barred windows, porches and balconies. There was dignity in every cement block, in every metal door. Still, it was a different barrio today, with businesses shut down, the porches of the houses empty, the plazas and basketball courts lifeless. People were marching down in small groups, dressed for a fight. They carried sticks, bats, the occasional gun. They wore Chavista garb, berets and red shirts, singing and chanting as they made their way down the mountain to protect the president.

María held tight to Don Jacinto, pressing Eloy between them.

Don Jacinto was having trouble navigating through the increasing mass of people making their way to the presidential palace. They were the opposite of those on the TV, who had called for Chávez's resignation, removal, or death. This was the other side. "¡UH, AH, CHÁVEZ NO SE VA! ¡UH, AH, CHÁVEZ NO SE VA!" they chanted in defiance of the multitudes on the TV screen. María wished for the protesters to vanish, to let them pass unimpeded.

Then the motorcycle squealed, the back wheel skidding back and forth, and somehow, without throwing the three of them off, Don Jacinto managed to halt before a burning barricade. People were tossing things into the fire: rubber tires, pieces of wood. A blue plastic pupitre, the kind Eloy sat on in class, flew into the pyre. A line of men carried items out of a preschool—chairs and desks—and two others pushed a bookcase into the blaze, the books falling from the shelves like teeth from a rotten mouth. A short, hairy man hurled a blackboard still marked with chalk. Everything, sacred or not, was food for the fire. The smoke, thick and black, vomited into the gray sky. Through the rubble, María could see the gathering of men in blue uniform—Metropolitan Police tasked with protecting anti-Chávez marchers—on the other side.

"Get off, Señora María," Jacinto said. "I can't get through here. Let me talk to some people...see how we can get to Vargas Hospital."

On a normal day it would have been only a couple of minutes more, but their path was blocked. María placed Eloy on the ground and applied pressure to his belly. He was unconscious now, but still breathing. With her free hand María gripped her necklace, the black jet carved into a fist that had been her mother's, had seen them both through so much. Under her breath she asked her mom for help.

Don Jacinto was arguing with some masked men. All of them brandished weapons—bats and lengths of oxidized rebar—and two boys gathered and piled rocks while other masked men, with T-shirts wrapped over their noses and mouths, threw the rocks over the barricade and at the police with the expertise of years of sandlot baseball.

Don Jacinto turned from the men to walk back to the motorcycle and it seemed he moved in slow motion. He wore an old pair of slacks nearly black with oil stains and a white T-shirt now all but crimson. It was as if she had never looked at him, not before he wore Eloy's very life on his clothes. He was tall, his skin the color of coffee with too much milk in it, and balding, but with enough white hair remaining to comb some long strands over his bald spot. His was a strong old age, a fibrous one, with wiry muscles, scruff on his cheeks, and callused hands. He was kind, she knew. He was a good man. He was trying to protect them.

"Vámonos," he said. "We're not going to get through here with the bike. We have to walk." He lifted Eloy from the pavement gently, like something already dead, and went to an alleyway littered with rubble and debris.

María couldn't stop coughing. Neither could Don Jacinto, whose cough was deeper, scratchier, tobacco-haunted. Smoke from the barricade mixed with tear gas made her eyes water and itch. But she did not hear Eloy cough as he lay on Jacinto's shoulder, and it terrified her. She walked behind them clutching the azabache necklace. Emerging from the alley, she saw the police officers on the other side of the barricade. They wore black helmets and carried tall shields, shotguns, and tear-gas launchers, buzzing around each other in unorganized fashion like wasps around a nest. One of the men, his body half-obscured by wisps of rolling tear gas, noticed them.

"Hey. Hey!" he screamed. "Stop right there, coño!"

Flanked by two other men, the officer ran at them with his shotgun raised. María and Jacinto froze. For once the only thing that seemed to move was Eloy, his little body coming to life with a squirm.

"What do you have there? Drop it!" the cop screamed at Jacinto.

The glint of the shotgun's metal hypnotized María.

"I can't!" Don Jacinto screamed back. "It's a boy, it's a boy, it's a boy!" he cried, sobbing through his words, his left arm up, his right arm still holding Eloy.

The policeman flipped up his visor, then cocked his head, like a curious dog. He lowered his weapon. With his hand he motioned the other officers to do the same. "It's a kid," he said, and ran toward them.

"My son's been shot," María said. "Please. We need help."

"Come with me," the cop said and tried to take Eloy from Jacinto's shoulder.

Jacinto recoiled.

"Okay," the man said. "Easy. It's okay, you can carry him. I have a car two minutes that way. Let's get your boy to the hospital."

ONE

1964

1

It was merely day one, and the only thing worse than the mosquitoes drinking Stanislavo for lunch was the July humidity. The thick of rainy season promised no reprieve, even though today the sky was untroubled by clouds. He didn't understand how insects could fly in that soup—Stanislavo practically had to push the air apart as he walked. Everything was hot: the air he breathed; the sweat weighing down his clothes; the back of his neck, already lobster-red and sprouting new freckles by the minute.

The northeast of Venezuela had become a center of guerrilla activity, spurred mostly by the lack of military police and the zigzag coastline—remote coves, islotes, morros, and tropical forest. But with the election of President Leoni the year before, the guachafita that had existed under his predecessor ended. Leoni immediately began operations, both open and covert, in any place that had guerrillas, to keep the Movement busy, tired, and spending its limited resources.

The Movement had assigned Stanislavo to lead a yearlong mission to secure shipments of weapons and ammunition coming in from Cuba, to organize the militia in the area, to recruit new members from nearby communities, and to create a reliable system of trails that could accommodate possible new camps. By then Stanislavo had grown sick of university activism: meetings, marches, debates. Revolution from Caracas apartments. The assignment felt like a chance to prove something to himself—better yet, to prove something *of* himself.

"We must be close now, right?" he asked Molina and Nunzio as he wiped his face with the soiled handkerchief, his machete stabbed in the dirt. But the sweat kept pouring down his face, gathering in his thick orange mop of a mustache.

The Mochima camp was supposedly tucked into a forested foothill an hour's trek from the beach, according to their boat driver. It would be a tiny clearing swallowed up by jungle and abandoned banana crops. But the three of them had been at this for two hours, confounded by a web of game trails and innumerable shades of green.

"We are as close to it now," Molina said, "as we were when we took a right at the split cacao tree, which looked exactly like this one right here."

He leaned against the cursed thing, from which a spotted branch hung broken in the exact same angle as half an hour earlier, and wiped his eyeglasses—round and gold-rimmed—with his sweat-soaked shirt, showing off his belly. Molina looked out of place in the jungle, but then he looked out of place everywhere—except maybe sitting at a table with a napkin tucked into his collar.

"How about we take a left this time?" he said. "Isn't that what a good communist should do anyway?" He inspected his glasses against the sky.

Nunzio, who rounded out Stanislavo's threesome of city guerrilleros, walked behind Molina, twice as tall, it seemed, and thrice as skinny. He stood hunched, always—as if the world had trained him to bend so he could interact with it. His sharp, Roman nose flared with each breath. His father had come to Caracas from Bologna over twenty years ago, with a pregnant wife and a duffel bag full of books.

"Left sounds good to me," he said.

They were all tired of going around in circles, and Stanislavo felt responsible. He read the pen marks on the map again: the beach where they had been dropped off, the location of the camp, and the distance separating the two *X*'s, no more than the width of three hairy fingers. He adjusted his pants—mindful of the revolver bruising his hip—and walked left of the cacao tree, southwest. His hand hurt from holding the machete so tightly, every awkward swing a reminder of his inadequacy. It bruised his pride to be so lost, so soon.

"You do it," he said, offering the machete to Nunzio.

Frustration had always gotten the better of Stanislavo, his body a vessel filling with the bile of it. He couldn't suffer ineptitude or indecisiveness in others, but he especially hated them in himself. It had been like that since he was a kid growing up by the oil fields of Maracaibo with his twin brother, Ludmil. Every task a sport, every errand a race. At the time, his parents were both doctors with Caribbean Petroleum, tasked with treating workers at the Mene Grande oil field.

Nunzio hacked, but his arms were so long that he didn't have room to maneuver, and he made excruciatingly slow progress. Even the normally jolly Molina was cranky now.

The path became wider, more manageable, the farther they advanced southwest. It was the afternoon, and what had been a clear day was now gray and menacing with fat drops starting to come down. They donned their rain jackets, the thick material making them even hotter and more miserable. Nunzio grew more adept with the machete as he went—better than Stanislavo, at least. Molina finished the water in his canteen, dribbling the last few drops down his stubbled chin. Then a *thunk* sounded to Stanislavo's right, like a ripe melon crashing onto kitchen tile. He heard the low buzz before seeing the hive, brown and rough and appearing to writhe as its residents were expelled, first only a handful of hornets, venturing out as if dazed and sleepy, then pouring out of every hole: infinite, fast, and angry.

"¡Avispas!" Stanislavo screamed. Then a stab in his right cheek.

He ran into the trees, ducking from the cloud encircling him. As he struggled through the forest, his face pulsed with pain at every heartbeat. Branches and thorns cut his arms—or were those the stings of more hornets? He kept moving until his own trampling was all he could hear. He could see only a slit of light out of his right eye. When he touched it he found a meaty lump. He glanced down at hornets crawling on his poncho and slapped himself until five brown corpses lay curled at his feet. Two hot welts had already bloomed on the back of his left hand.

Molina reached him, out of breath, followed closely by Nunzio.

"Are you both okay?" he asked.

Although there were no visible stings on either of his friends, a thin red line was slashed across Molina's forehead.

"Fine," Nunzio said, catching his breath.

"I'm good," Molina panted. "One fucker got me in the ankle." He skipped toward Stanislavo and stared at his face. "Well, at least no one will call you a pretty boy once we get to the camp."

They had run out of the thick brush and onto an open path. Footprints, not theirs, were fresh in the dirt.

"It only took a swarm of hornets to send us the right way," Nunzio said. He crouched, his knees sticking out like a stork's.

The path led to a small clearing that held a farmer's hut made of rough adobo walls and a palm-frond roof. The forest lapped at its walls. Two bony mules stood eating rotten plantains by a stone firepit. Next to it a green tarp propped up by branches gave shelter to a group of young men sitting around a wooden table. The rain pounded on the tarp, and the water sluicing off its edges gave the gathering the dreamlike blurriness of a painting. The men passed around a half-empty bottle, the aguardiente so raw that Stanislavo could smell it from ten feet away.

One of the boys stood up, gripping a pistol, and stared at them.

Stanislavo raised his hands and stepped forward, seeing nothing out of his swollen right eye.

"Tucán!" the boy yelled in the direction of the hut. "They're here!" He sat down, dirty and bored, and took a swig of the moonshine.

A spindly, bare-chested guerrillero with the biggest nose Stanislavo had ever seen lazed forth from the hut. A revolver stuck out of his fatigues. His abdomen bore a bullet scar like a second belly button.

"Stanislavo Atanas con Jaime Molina y Nunzio Guelfi," Stanislavo said, walking up to him. "You must be Tucán."

"Muchachos, this is our new boss," Tucán said to the group with a half-smile and a full stretch. "What are you doing sitting down? Show some respect."

The boys stood up with no sense of urgency, one of them leaning on the chair, half-drunk. Another one, his torso all ribs, no more than sixteen years old, looked out into the forest and covered one of his nostrils with a finger, shooting snot into the dirt.

Tucán pulled a backpack from the hut and tossed it in their direction. "Alfredo was here two weeks ago and left this for you." He stared at Stanislavo. "Mierda, what's wrong with your face?"

"Oh, he's just ugly," Molina said. "He gets that all the time."

The boys looked at one another, unsure if it was a joke, but as soon as Tucán started laughing, they all joined in.

The afternoon rain had stopped, giving way to a clear night. The tension around the dwindling fire felt like petting a growling dog. The three of them sat alone, next to the large tent Alfredo had left for them with Tucán, while the rest of the men rested either in the hut or underneath the makeshift shelter. Stanislavo could hear half-whispers from the men under the tarp, resentment toward these city boys, who were as green as the banana plants that surrounded them.

Stanislavo removed a small silver flask from his pocket and sipped warm rum. He read the letter Alfredo had left in the backpack among supplies and pieces of a radio that Molina had already begun to assemble. He wondered why Alfredo hadn't come with them to smooth out this meeting. It would have been so easy: Alfredo and his imposing frame, Alfredo and his booming laugh, Alfredo and his way of drawing everyone in. But all Stanislavo had to do was read to find his answers. *I don't want this to be my thing,* Alfredo had written. *This is the way you get ready for what's to come. It's the way you get to know what revolution really is.*

Alfredo had already gone through that himself. When Stanislavo followed him like a puppy into the Cause—as a young writer, all of nineteen, for the Communist Party's newsletter—Alfredo had been the one leading organizers of the general strike of '58 that put an end to Marcos Pérez Jiménez and his atrocities. Alfredo had spent six months as a mole in the cement factory, turned the machinery off the morning Pérez Jiménez fell, the lack of smoke signaling all other factories in the city to start the strike. The letter reminded Stanislavo that his experience of the world, of Venezuela, of the Movement, was limited—filtered by his own reality and his privileged upbringing.

The day Stanislavo went to Alfredo and asked—no, demanded—to be posted somewhere else was the same day his father had invited him to lunch at El Carso. Stanislavo hadn't been wearing a jacket, his hair was long, and his mustache unruly. At first the waiter by the door had prevented him from coming in, but Eduardo, the maître d' who had worked at El Carso for years, spotted him.

"That's Dr. Atanas's son, vale," he admonished his waiter and led Stanislavo inside.

"Your mustache keeps growing, I see," his father said, and motioned to the seat in front of him. "And you're working on the beard too. You trying to be the redheaded Fidel?"

There it was, the first punch of the afternoon.

Eduardo came by the table rolling a cart, handed Stanislavo a Dewar's and club soda, and started working on a steak tartare for his father. "Should I prepare one for you, Stanis?" Eduardo asked as he angled the silver tray at them, the meat cut into small cubes, fresh and crimson.

"No, Eduardo, gracias. I'm not staying long." Stanislavo met his father's eyes, green like his. Cold too. "Why am I here?" he said.

All around them were suited men, sipping their own scotch and sodas, talking business in the dark of the restaurant. Lunch at El Carso was both industry and pleasure. The new Venezuela was being forged in places like this just as much as in banks and company headquarters.

Eduardo placed a spoonful of the meat in a glass bowl, then scooped mustard from a ceramic container and mixed the two.

"I've been hearing things," Stanislavo's father said. "Your name has cropped up in conversation." He looked at his son, then at Eduardo, who cracked pepper on the mixture with a mill the size of a child's leg.

"So?" Stanislavo said.

"Your name is my name, Stanis," his father whispered, somehow raising his voice at the same time. "Your name, therefore my name, is in the mouths of certain people."

Eduardo, averting his gaze, arranged the neat tower of beef on two slices of tomato in front of Stanislavo's father. With a silver teaspoon he sculpted an indentation on the top of the meat, then lopped off the top of a quail egg with a swift slice and slid the raw egg onto the tartare. He folded a cloth napkin over his forearm and, with a half-bow, asked, "¿Algo más, doctor?"

"No, Eduardo, we're good here."

Eduardo pushed his cart away, leaving Stanislavo alone with his father's disappointment.

"What are you so worried about? That General Marcano will stop bringing his friends in for their regular checkups?" His father had moved so far from the days of treating roughnecks for Caribbean Petroleum. Stanislavo gripped the armrest so tightly he thought it might tear. "I'm worried about my friends being tortured and you're worried about my name in someone's mouth?"

Stanislavo's father inspected his plate. His voice lowered, he said, "Some mouths, Stanis, when they say your name, it's as if they're crossing it out with a red pen." His anger from before had been replaced by so much concern that Stanislavo's body softened. "Your mom is worried too. She's terrified of losing you. How could you do that to her, after what happened to Ludmil? It's so cruel."

That one stung. His brother's death was a subject no one touched. They didn't speak of the car accident. Of Stanislavo, unscratched, while his twin sat dead beside him. The whole thing was so buried under layers of grief and guilt for all three of them that it took otherworldly strength to dig it up. Under the surface was this: Everything Stanislavo did he felt he had to do double. Fight twice as hard, care twice as much, lash out twice as sharply. He wanted to tell his father he was doing this for Ludmil, too, but couldn't conjure the name to his lips.

"This is not about you or about Mom or about our family," he said. "I'm not rebelling against you. I'm rebelling against *this*." Stanislavo lifted his hands as if pointing to everything surrounding them: the businessmen plotting in their booths, the ice clinking in their scotch glasses, the waiters in their crisp red blazers, coming and going.

"What about working within the system?" his father said. "People are open to change. Things are better than they were before. I remember Marcos Pérez Jiménez, son. This is not that. Leoni is no dictator. His presidency is different, there's room f—"

"Tell that to my friends getting rounded up by his hunters. They shoot first and ask questions never. Two of my friends have disappeared already. You call that democracy? It's all happening again and you're here eating fucking tartare!"

The people having lunch around them turned and watched.

"If you keep going the way you're going you'll end up just like them!" his father screamed back. "There's nothing I can do to help you, Stanis."

"No, Dad. There's nothing I can do to help *you*."

His father regained his composure, as if suddenly aware of the scene they were causing. He cleared his throat and pulled down on the lapels of his blazer. "I don't want to fight with you, son. I love you. What happens when you get thrown into a cell somewhere—or, even worse, what happens if you get shot out there? What happens to your mom?"

Those words, *out there*, bounced inside his head. At first they were hollow, like echoes caroming off the walls of a canyon, but instead of losing volume as they ricocheted, they became louder. Out there. Out there. Out there.

Stanislavo wasn't out there. La Universidad Central de Venezuela was not where the revolution would be waged. It would not be in the streets of Caracas, nor even in the streets of Petare, Guarenas, or Los Teques. No, this revolution had to be waged Out There. In the mountains.

"Tell Mom I love her," Stanislavo said. "I love you too, Dad."

And with that he had walked out of El Carso and gone straight to Alfredo. "I want to go to the mountains," he told Alfredo. No half-measures. Being there completely was the only way to truly understand what they were all fighting for.

The boys are decent, passionate, Alfredo had written in his letter. *They'll come around once they know you.*

The letter sang him a lullaby there in Mochima, and he fell asleep beneath the stars.

2

MORNING CAME with the smell of coffee brewing on the fire. Molina and one of the boys, the youngest-looking one, chatted easily. Tucán poured himself a cup and sat silent, his menace diminished by morning eye-crust.

"Tucán, you're with me today," Stanislavo said.

Alfredo's letter had described how Tucán held sway over the other boys. He'd gained notoriety inside the Movement not only by remaining conscious when he'd gotten shot but also by managing to capture a soldier even with a hole in his side.

Tucán blew on his coffee and looked up. "Where to, jefe?"

Stanislavo wanted to get to know some of the villages and caseríos of the area, to start building a network of allies, informants, and, eventually, recruits. He also wanted to get situated, so as not to feel so hopelessly lost. Tucán suggested San Ignacio, a small farming community close to the camp. A woman there, Tomasa, had emerged as the lead organizer of the region, deftly bringing in people ready to collaborate with the Movement.

They took off walking southeast, toward the caserío. It had started to rain again and every surface in the jungle was suddenly transformed into a musical instrument. Tucán, swinging the machete rhythmically, as if he'd been born with it for a hand, became some guerrillero conductor.

"Teach me, Tucán," Stanislavo said, pointing at the long knife.

"It's not power," he said.

Stanislavo could almost hear the man's thoughts — *Now I have to teach this city boy how to swing a machete?*

"It's speed and angle," Tucán continued. "See how I keep the blade pointing away from me? See how I snap my wrist?"

Tucán also focused mostly on just one side of the path, Stanislavo noticed, instead of on both sides as he himself had, thereby conserving energy while still making the path wide enough for them.

"And the mules can get through?" Stanislavo asked.

"Have you seen how thin they are?"

Eventually the path they opened took them to San Ignacio. The caserío consisted of eight mud houses, and a few conucos mostly growing root vegetables: yuca, batata, ocumo, and all sorts of bananas and plantains. Tucán led him to the biggest house and introduced Stanislavo to Tomasa, a large woman, maybe a few years older than he was, descendant of the thousands of African slaves brought to this part of the country to farm cacao.

"Another catire," she said to Tucán, and embraced him. "Did this one bring me any books?"

"Books?" Stanislavo looked at Tucán.

"Tucán didn't tell you?" Tomasa said.

"No," Tucán said, and put his knapsack down on a plastic table. "I forgot."

"I cook you food and give you a bed," Tomasa said, "you bring me a book. Why don't you bring me two next time?"

Stanislavo didn't smile often — it was rare to see his teeth under his thick, orange whiskers — but he grinned now as he browsed one of the rows of spines that brought the insides of the hut to life. He saw a few Spanish authors, mostly from the Generation of '27. Rosa Chacel, a couple of Lorca collections. Neruda's first book, *Crepusculario*. The caserío was called San Ignacio, but from that day on, Stanislavo thought of it as Alexandria.

He picked out *Razón de amor* by Pedro Salinas and thumbed through it. "My mom has this one at home."

"She must be a romantic," Tomasa said.

Hardly, Stanislavo reflected. His mother was as rigid as a tree trunk. She had escaped the rise of the Nazis in Europe, fleeing Poland after graduating from medical school. Had been the first working female doctor in Venezuela, treating workers at the oil fields in El Batey and then Mene Grande, where she'd met his dad, and given birth to him and Ludmil. Venezuela had been the first port she'd landed in, after a long journey across the Atlantic, and as with many other immigrants, she'd stayed. Why keep going? Was Caracas going to be that different from Bogotá, or Lima, or Buenos Aires? It's not as if she had family waiting anywhere. Her only sibling, a brother, was dead. She never told Stanislavo how, but it was obvious that the death had marked her—had perhaps even been what spurred her parents to give her everything they had to make the trip, promising to join her later. But in a couple of years the war started, and the dream of her parents coming to join her was replaced by her hope merely for them to make it through. They didn't.

He could not remember her smiling since the day Ludmil had died, almost ten years ago now, when they were just sixteen. He had never put an image of his mom and the word "romantic" in the same thought. And yet...he chuckled.

"What's funny?" Tucán asked.

"I guess she is," Stanislavo said. "Deep down." He'd always considered love unimportant, distracting from the Movement. So why did he love these poems so much? Perhaps he was a romantic too. "Don't worry," he reassured Tomasa. "I'll bring you books next time I'm back."

He spent the rest of the afternoon browsing.

Stanislavo noticed a big change in Tucán when he was around Tomasa—every time she looked at him, Tucán both retreated into his own body and puffed his chest out. It was some sort of play-ground love, and Tomasa liked toying with Tucán: a tousling of his hair, a sweet comment.

Tomasa had a meat stew going on the woodstove, chicken bub-bling in a pot of crushed tomatoes, ocumo, yuca, onion, and garlic. Next to it stood a tower of topochos, small but fat green plantains, which Tucán was helping her peel.

"C'mon, Stanis, stop reading and come help," Tomasa said.

"I'm useless in the kitchen," he said, putting the Salinas poems down.

"Nonsense. All you boys are the same. How can you be good at something if you never do it? Come here next to Tucán and cut the topochos." She handed Stanislavo a rust-spotted blade. "You see my fat finger? I want the slices this thick." She walked by Tucán and massaged his shoulders. "Muy bien, mi vida," she whispered.

Tucán yanked the green skin off the plantain. He and Stanislavo fried the slices in hot oil, flattened them into round disks with a board, dipped them in a mixture of water, vinegar, and garlic, then fried them a second time.

"Salt them as soon as the tostones come out of the hot oil, Stanis," she told him, and he did. Tomasa sat, bare feet up on the table, read-ing *Razón de amor*, sometimes aloud, while the two men fried plan-tains. "Now this is the life!" she said. "If the revolution happens while men cook and women read, the world will indeed be better."

Stanislavo ate two bowls, dipping the tostones into the thick sauce until they were gone. He had always been able to put food away. Stout and strong, he was a recipient of the thick bones and healthy appetites of his Eastern European heritage, combined with being the son of a Jewish mother who had narrowly dodged the Holocaust and always kept a full pantry at their house.

"I'm watching my figure," Tomasa said, more measured in her appetite, when Stanislavo offered to get her more.

When Tucán unbuttoned his pants and slouched, Stanislavo saw pride in Tomasa's face.

After dinner, the three of them sat on rusted chairs under the stars. Stanislavo shared rum from his flask. They talked about starting a small school, and Tomasa gave Stanislavo the name of two men—one a fisherman and the other a foreman for a cacao farm nearby—she thought were ready to be recruited. Later, Tucán and Tomasa sang Cuban revolutionary songs with voices that belonged in church and not in the jungle.

Stanislavo didn't want to ruin the moment by talking Cuba—Fidel, really—with his opinion having soured in the past couple of years. Cuba had done something incredible; a few bearded men woke up a nation, and then another, and then another. All of a sudden, an alarm clock had gone off in the world. Yes, there was violence, there had to be. But it had been used in the pursuit of something truly special. Stanislavo's problem with the current Cuba was that the violence that had once been a means now seemed to be the goal. Jailed journalists, murdered dissidents, the rounding up of critics—even those who had been invaluable to their victory. Fidel had turned to revenge. And he didn't strike Stanislavo as someone who would ever be content.

"I noticed you don't have anything by Miguel Hernández in your library, Tomasa," Stanislavo said. The rum made his face warm and his cheeks red, breaking down the typically guarded temperament he blamed on his stern mother. It made his tongue limber. And while he could not carry a tune or follow rhythm, he possessed a prodigious memory and a deep register of voice that made him great at reciting. He owed his new comrades this, something in return for the music. So he recited "The Winds of the People," stopping after his favorite verse:

Who said they would throw a yoke
round the neck of this race?
Who has ever yoked or hobbled
a hurricane,

who has held lightning
prisoner in a cage?

"That's Hernández?" asked Tucán.

"They say Franco walked him into his Madrid jail cell himself. Do you know what Hernández's last words were, scribbled on the hospital wall by his deathbed?"

"What?" Tomasa asked. She held Tucán's hand, lust in the shapes she drew on his skin.

"Goodbye, brothers, comrades, friends: let me take my leave of the sun and the fields."

Tucán and Tomasa looked at each other, and Tucán kissed her on her full lips. Stanislavo glanced away and up into the stars and he was at peace.

As Stanislavo and Tucán walked back to camp the next day, feeling easy with each other now, he wondered how Molina and Nunzio were doing—if they had managed to make inroads with the rest of the men. When they arrived, Molina—his mind always in motion, cunning and kind, with an idea or a solution for anything—was leading a domino tournament, the men joking with him as if they'd grown up skipping stones on the same creek.

Stanislavo could see it was true what Alfredo had written in his letter—that the group would soon become a family—as well as what he had implied: that Stanislavo would never believe in what they were fighting for until he lived it himself.

3

INDUSTRIOUS STRETCHES of time always passed quickly for Stanislavo. Even in the thick of rainy season the camp was a hub of activity as days turned into weeks. Tomasa started to come more frequently, and Stanislavo met a few other regular visitors. An older gentleman wearing a dirty Magallanes baseball jersey, obviously beloved by all the men, brought supplies from Puerto La Cruz every week. He was often accompanied by Emiliana Rodríguez, a tall and slender woman with black hair that reached the small of her back. A nurse who checked in on the men, Stanislavo learned. She was india—a descendant of the Caribe people, the Indigenous tribes who for centuries had ruled most of the Caribbean, including the northern shores of Venezuela, until the Spaniards decimated them. Given the generations of mixing among Africans, Indigenous people, and Spaniards, it was an uncommon sight—that angular face, the burnt bronze skin. She was older than Stanislavo—in her thirties—and beautiful. He was distracted, pleasantly so, whenever she was in the camp, and found himself inventing reasons to talk with her as often as possible.

Weeks became months, and the camp thrived, forming a strong connection with the San Ignacio caserío. With Molina and Tomasa leading the way, two other villages in the area, Arapito and Bananal, were brought in. Together these villages served as a warning system for military activity, which allowed the men to avoid skirmishes with government soldiers. Nunzio and Tucán established routes to different coves, identifying drop-off sites for supplies, ammo, and weapons, and Tucán led their biggest mission so far, clearing a small landing strip a few miles from camp, after almost two months of back-and-forth with leadership about where it should go. They became the logistical center of the Movement in the area, effectively isolating themselves from any martial action. Alfredo wanted to keep them away from conflict for now, he said.

In time the rains left, making way for the clear December sky, and the early mornings, while never chilly as in Caracas, had a crispness that made the floral coffee they drank even more electric. Of all they'd accomplished, what most excited Stanislavo was the education program they had created at the San Ignacio caserío with the help of Emiliana and Tomasa. Lately he'd been spending more time there than at the camp. The program covered everything from literature and philosophy to math and animal husbandry. Emiliana was there every week now, sometimes even staying the weekend at Tomasa's house. She taught women's health and first aid classes to the locals, some of whom came from the neighboring caseríos. She brought whatever medicine she could steal undetected from the military hospital she worked at in Puerto La Cruz. On pretty days she would take a group of them—a few soldiers, along with members of the neighboring communities—through the tropical forest on botany expeditions, relying on the beneficial flora her mother had taught her to identify when she was a girl. San Ignacio had become such a gathering place, with new people arriving all the time, that Stanislavo, Molina, and Nunzio had to move the guerrilla camp, and the military training, to a different site, a click and a half farther away, so they could adequately, and safely, store weapons and munitions, and conduct their training.

The new year came, and with it a sense of promise Stanislavo hadn't felt since the summer of '58, after Pérez Jiménez had fallen.

Stanislavo and Emiliana had settled into a routine. At the end of any day they were together at the camp or the caserío, they would walk alone up the trail to the stumps by the small araguaney tree, its fallen yellow flowers scattered at their feet. At first their conversations were just about what they could do to make things better for the people here, how they could use some of the things they'd implemented in San Ignacio as pilot programs for other communities. But eventually they left the day-to-day talk of camp and revolution behind, and spoke instead about themselves.

"You're Caribe, right?" Stanislavo asked.

"We call ourselves Kalinago," she said. "*Caribe* is what Columbus and his serial rapists called us, and it stuck. By all rights we should call it the Kalinago Sea." Her mom was really the only person around, she told him, who knew or cared about their previous way of life, and even that was only a fraction of what her abuelos had known. "There are more of us out there," she said, "but we're disappearing. In a sense, we're already gone."

Stanislavo shared his own family history, how his mother had escaped the rise of the Nazis, making it to Caracas alone with her doctor's diploma and a bag filled with a few clothes, all her mother's jewelry, and two gold candlesticks.

"You're lucky," Emiliana said.

"She's never talked about it much, but the rest of her family died during the war," he said. "But yes, she's lucky she made it out when she did."

"I mean as a people. They tried to do to you what they did to us. But you survived."

Stanislavo had never thought about it that way. And he didn't necessarily want to. It was hard to think about his parents at all here, especially his mom. She had endured all of that as a young woman, and then the death of Ludmil. Now, when she had finally set the worst of her sorrow aside, here Stanislavo was in the jungle trying to get himself killed. Hers was a grief he couldn't face, so he pushed it aside.

Emiliana hoped for the new Venezuela, the one they were building with the Movement, to have space for her culture. She wanted to rediscover it, she said. To honor it. There was already an effort underway to preserve Kalinago heritage, started on Dominica Island.

People were so strange, Stanislavo thought. Here Emiliana was, blowing with all her might to rekindle a fire that had been extinguished a hundred times over. His mother, on the other hand, in hiding from the Holocaust, had also buried her Judaism, escaping not only the Nazis but also thousands of years of her own customs and heritage. He and his brother hadn't been brought up Jewish. His parents were not religious at all. His mom was a fighter — she was the strongest person he knew — yet she had hidden that part of herself. He could understand why but found it profoundly sad. The only thing that remained from his mother's past was food. The challah bread on the weekends and the Thursday-night dinner of chopped liver, which he loved but had been embarrassed by any time a friend came over. Being with Emiliana made him miss his mom. He wished now that he could ask her about what had happened to her family back in Poland.

"Are you okay?" Emiliana asked.

"I had a twin brother," he said. "Ludmil." And it surprised him, that it was his brother whose name came out of his mouth and not his mom's. "He died when we were sixteen."

Emiliana placed a hand on his shoulder.

He explained how his parents had worked as doctors for Caribbean Petroleum. "The company had movie nights," he said. "For the executives and their families. They would show movies in a theater at the club, and Ludmil and I loved to take Dad's car to impress the executives' daughters." Stanislavo could still remember what Ludmil had been wearing, the starched white shirt, the pleated brown pants. "That night it was *City Lights*, with Chaplin. Have you seen it?"

Emiliana shook her head.

"It was dark on the way back and I swerved to avoid hitting a big tortoise in the middle of the road. Suddenly the electrical pole was right there." Stanislavo cleared his throat of the knot that had lodged there. "It wasn't even that hard. No big crash, no broken glass. I was fine. But my brother had a huge welt in the middle of his forehead. I tried to wake him up, shook him. When we were little, we would spend hours looking at each other's faces, trying to find differences. Our noses would come so close together. I hadn't held him so close since those days. It was like looking into a mirror. I pried his eyes open, willing them to look at me. But he was gone."

Emiliana reached out and held his hand. Both their hands, clasped, slightly swayed, like the branches of the araguaney tree above them.

"I'm sorry," Stanislavo said. "I haven't talked about that since the day it happened."

He paused for a moment to collect himself, feeling Emiliana's hand in his. A few months after Ludmil died, he said, was when Alfredo came to speak to the workers at the oil fields. He'd heard his parents arguing about the Movement in the weeks before the accident. His mom had wanted to attend meetings, but his dad was worried about what management would say if they found out. By the time Alfredo's meeting actually came, it was moot.

"I lived in a house with two ghosts," Stanislavo said. "When I asked my mom if she wanted to come with me, she said nothing. Just stared past me."

"Her boy had died," Emiliana said, and squeezed his hand.

Stanislavo only nodded. "Have you met him yet?" he said. "Alfredo?"

"At one of the Puerto La Cruz meetings," she said. "We've talked about the hospital a few times, how important it is to have me there."

"Then you know how electric he is. How imposing. I heard his speech that day. I looked at the other faces in the crowd, hoping I wasn't alone in what I was feeling. Maybe it was just that for the first time in months I felt something other than empty. Life came into me again. I'll never be able to repay Alfredo for that."

"That's what got you into the Movement?"

"It was. We moved to Caracas not long after that. We all needed a change. I tracked Alfredo down and have been following him ever since."

Emiliana was about to say something else, but then they heard the boys coming back. Molina had them all in stitches, telling the one about a rabbi and a horse in a bar. Embarrassed, Stanislavo let go of Emiliana's hand. He avoided her eyes and stood up.

"Molina!" he greeted them. Nunzio was there, and Tucán too.

"Look what I have!" Molina said. "Tomasa got it for us." He hoisted a Polaroid camera above his head. "Emiliana, will you take our photo?"

Emiliana rose from her tree stump and grabbed the camera. "All together," she said. "Closer. Tucán, you've got to scooch closer."

They pushed into each other, Stanislavo squished in the middle. They all stank of jungle and guerrilla.

"Say *whiskey*!" Emiliana said.

"*Whiskey*!" they all chanted.

The flash went off, and then the camera stuck out a tongue, like an impish child.

Every morning, over the black and smoky and sweet coffee he'd fallen in love with, Stanislavo met with Nunzio, Molina, and Tucán to discuss objectives. Tucán had a dog he called Titi, a wiry yellow mutt that came and went as she pleased and brought a smile to everyone's face when she curled by their feet, thumping her tail on the dirt. Nunzio, who had grown up with dogs and was an excellent trainer, bonded with Tucán over the animal. In a few weeks Nunzio had transformed the dog. Soon she flanked Tucán whenever he whistled and sat attentive whenever he asked her to.

Stanislavo woke up one dark February night with a need to relieve himself. The crescent moon appeared in the sky the size of an eyelash. On his way to the trees, Stanislavo spotted Titi asleep, nestled in a tangle of roots. When he bent down and petted her head, she startled awake and pounced instinctively. Though the dog quickly realized it was Stanislavo and did not bite, one of her claws caught him where his eye met the bridge of his nose. He wiped at the sting on his face and his fingertips came away wet with blood.

Titi yelped in apology, her head down and her tail between her legs, and Stanislavo appeased her by stroking her back. "Shhhh. It's okay, girl. It's okay. Sorry I scared you."

At the edge of the trees he relieved himself, then went to the hut where Emiliana slept whenever she was staying the night. She lay sideways on the thin cot inside, her hair so long it fell like black water, pooling on the ground.

"Emiliana," he whispered from the threshold, not wanting to scare her. "Emiliana, wake up."

She moaned softly and pulled her head up. "Stanis?"

"Sorry to wake you at this hour. Titi got me in the eye with her claw. I think I'm bleeding."

"Come, come. Let me see."

Emiliana stood and stretched her arms up and out like sprigs of wheat. She turned on the kerosene lantern and the hut lit up in amber. She inspected the wound and told Stanislavo to sit down on the cot. It was still warm and it smelled like her: jasmine, honey, sweat. A current ran through his body.

Emiliana washed her hands and then carefully poured water on his eye, absorbing the pink runoff with clean gauze. "She got you right in the lacrimal caruncle," she said, and Stanislavo had to smile, despite the pain, at her nurse's precision. "Close your eyes, please."

Stanislavo felt excited, almost afraid, to have her so close and yet not be able to see her.

"I don't have any ointments with me that won't just irritate your eye," she said, "but I know something that'll help. I'll be right back." She grabbed the lantern and left him in the dark.

His chest felt like an engine. The closeness to Emiliana, her smell, the conversations under the tree—all of it made him forget his guilt for surviving when Ludmil had died, and for leaving his mother to worry about her only living son. The only things he could feel now were his breath, loud, and his hands, warm. A lust awakening.

She returned a couple of minutes later and cleaned the eye again, then showed him a handful of brown seeds, round and a bit textured. "Coriander," she said, and explained that the seeds would block and absorb the blood and help prevent infection. They would just need to be switched out every few hours. She placed her hands on his shoulders. "Now look up," she said and tenderly raised his chin. Her sweet breath washed over his face as her steady hands placed several seeds at the corner of his eye and on his lower eyelid. "It'll be a little itchy," she said, her voice so soft it was almost a whisper, "but you'll get used to it. Just don't rub your eyes." She was kneeling now on the floor, between his legs, holding his hand.

She came close again, and Stanislavo thought she might want to check his eye one more time, but her hand cupped his face, and she kissed him on the cheek, lingering there. Stanislavo turned his head slowly, their noses barely touching, their mouths half-open and hungry to meet.

4

HER MOTHER liked to say that Emiliana had been working at the military hospital since before she was born, because when Mamá Rodríguez was pregnant with Emiliana, she would go by the hospital there in Puerto La Cruz to sell conservas de coco she prepared every morning. In fact, Emiliana's first memory was of being with her mother in their kitchen, before sunrise, preparing the sweets. Mamá would hand her the fragrant mixture of shredded coconut, papelón sugar, and lemon peel, still warm from the pot, and show her how to roll it into little balls, squish them, and place them on a piece of banana leaf. Even now Emiliana would sometimes still dream of the gummy coconut paste—on her hands, in her hair, smeared on her shirt—and wake up hungry, with a finger or two in her mouth.

Emiliana's mother also liked to say that it was both providence and destiny that her daughter, nearing thirty-five, was there at the hospital now, working as a nurse. Ten years ago, when Emiliana had started the job, she might have agreed. But what she lived through at the hospital had cured her of any belief in providence; God had vanished in the worst years of the Pérez Jiménez regime, when she lost count of purple fingernails, burned toes, and broken ribs. Her stubborn belief in destiny kept her at the hospital, however, and she made herself a promise that she would not stand still if the violence ever happened again. The six years since the end of that dark parade, in '58, had felt, in comparison, like a sunbath. But there had come, first President Betancourt's, and now President Leoni's, new wave of maimed men, and the patient she had treated a year and a half ago, with electrical burns to the bottom of his feet, had sent her running to the nearest Communist Party meeting in Puerto La Cruz. Her life since that first meeting had been so full of purpose, she felt, that everything other than the revolution was duller than dirt.

And now this thing she hadn't expected. Stanislavo. The night they had spent on the cot that she couldn't, hard as she tried, push away from her mind. Not like the few men she had shared her body with, all of whom had been no more permanent in her mind, or her bed, than morning dew.

Tomasa—who loved Stanis, who was seemingly the only person who could make him smile—told her it was a bad idea. "He's great. He is," she said. "But he's not one of us, Emiliana. He's a white boy with a pistol in his pants. He's here until he isn't. And then what?"

And then what? This was Emiliana's fantasy. They take down the government. They go to Dominica and bring Kalinago culture back to Venezuela. They live on the coast together. Teach farmers and fishermen. Have a bunch of babies and die fat and old after a night of dominoes with Tomasa and Tucán. She wanted to scream all of this to her friend, but said none of it, because of course Tomasa was right. Still, if Emiliana believed that fate had put her in that hospital, that fate had brought her to that Party meeting in Puerto La Cruz, that she was helping the country change through her actions at the Mochima camp—and she did believe all of this—then wasn't Stanislavo also her destiny?

Plus, she just liked him. The way he listened when they walked the forest together. The seriousness in his acquisition of knowledge (he already could name most of the plants that Mamá Rodríguez had taught her could be of use). The way his hand, covered in freckles and hair, looked as it rested on her naked belly. This excitement she felt right now, counting the two days left until she would be back in Mochima. Love was part of the revolution too, goddamn it. If not, who were all those fucking poets Tomasa hoarded in her treasured bookcase?

Emiliana heard Doctor Rengifo whistle for her before she saw him walking down the hall to the nurses' station. He had the young resident in tow, Doctor Vivas, and they looked like a wolf and his cub.

"We need you," Rengifo ordered and turned back the way he'd come.

Emiliana hurried and caught up.

"It's a girl, thirteen, in labor," Rengifo said.

Emiliana could already imagine the complications. Such a small body. She rushed to the hand-washing station.

When she saw the child, her worst fears were confirmed. The girl's skin, at some point a vibrant brown, was now the color of concrete. The doctor didn't need to say it: preeclampsia, anemia. And when Emiliana examined her, dilated ten centimeters and ready to give birth, she noticed the lumps and growths and sores. Herpes, untreated for some time. The girl was conscious, but just barely, and so scared.

The two doctors strategized. They moved around the girl, working quickly and deliberately. Rengifo was good at his craft. Emiliana disliked the man — racist, misogynist, soured by the job — but she had learned plenty from him, not least of which was how to deal with his type of man. Vivas was good as well, not a given for residents. But it was Emiliana who shone here, agile and efficient, everywhere at once, except in the doctors' way. Always ready when they barked orders but acting on her own initiative as well. Unsurprisingly, she was also the only one talking to the girl, making her feel like a human being rather than a slab of meat.

The baby didn't want to come out. The exhausted girl, already depleted by her underlying medical conditions, could pass out at any minute.

Vivas struggled with the birthing forceps, unable to get the grip he needed. "Push, goddamn it!" he screamed at the girl as he struggled to latch the two pieces of the instrument together. As if it was her fault that he couldn't make it work.

Emiliana was angry, at Vivas and Rengifo for being so horrible, at the person who had done this to the girl, and at the place that allowed all this to happen. She hated everything except this young woman and her baby. She cleared sweat from the girl's brow and spoke softly to her, so softly it could have been a secret.

"We're getting through this," she said. "You and me, okay?" Emiliana could see all the fear tangled in the girl's small body, but also a spark there in her eyes. "When I tell you to push, you're going to push with everything you've got. You're going to give me everything."

The girl nodded.

"I can't get this thing to catch!" Vivas said, working the forceps too hastily, attempting to force them.

Rengifo supervised him with no urgency. It seemed more important to him for Vivas to struggle through this, to learn under pressure, than it was to relieve the girl's suffering.

"Let me try," Emiliana said.

She put her hand on Vivas's, his veins bulging from the iron grip he had on the instrument. His hand relaxed, and he let go of the forceps and stepped aside, exasperated with his own failure, even angry at her, Emiliana thought.

"Wait until I tell you," she said to the girl, reassuring her with a kind look.

She could feel the baby's head with one of the arms of the forceps. No wonder it had been so complicated for Vivas — so much inflammation in the canal, probably more symptoms from the STD, plus bruising and swelling of the baby's head from the force Vivas had already applied with the tool.

"Wait," she repeated.

The girl was barely hanging on. Emiliana shifted the other half of the instrument ever so slightly to the right and there was a satisfactory click as the two halves clasped together, the forceps in place now at each side of the baby's head.

"Now, mi amor, push," Emiliana said, adrenaline rushing. "Push!"

The girl pushed hard, and the baby's head shifted and then breached.

"Push!" Emiliana screamed, willing the girl fully conscious.

And then the baby's shoulders came through, and then the rest of the body all at once with no more resistance. Vivas was there to catch him, the little baby boy, his face and head all bruised from the forceps, which Emiliana let clang onto the ground like a church bell. Vivas cleared the baby's mouth and struck him on the back once. The baby cried.

"Take care of him," Vivas ordered, presenting the baby to Emiliana like an unwanted thing.

But Emiliana said no, staring a hatred into Vivas so powerful that the resident took a step back. "You do it," she said. "I'm going to make sure this girl is all right."

Vivas was about to protest, but Rengifo interrupted. "Do as she says," the wolf ordered his cub.

It took a while, but eventually she and Rengifo saved the girl's life. Emiliana made sure the new mother met her baby, and after she was asleep and the infant safely swaddled, she left the room, where she caught Rengifo about to head out.

"The girl's dad is outside?" she asked.

"Yes, I've already told him they were out of danger."

"Did you call the police?"

"What do you mean?" Rengifo said.

"This girl has been abused. For years. That man is likely the abuser."

"That's not our problem. We saved the girl and her baby, that's what matters."

"But doctor. You saw her. You saw the infection!"

"I said no!" he yelled. "If you speak one word to that man, I don't care how good you are, you're fired. I can't control what the fucking savages do out there," he said, pointing out the window. "I can only control what happens in here."

She wanted to say more, but she knew Rengifo and what this would mean for her, and for her work with the Movement. This was her place. She needed to be here for when it mattered. But didn't this matter? Wasn't this what the revolution was for? To make sure girls were no longer disposable? Part of her believed she was naïve: The world would still be controlled by men after the revolution won — if the revolution ever won. But the other part had to believe things could get better. She let that part win. She swallowed her rage as Rengifo walked away.

Later, she wrote a note on a piece of paper and woke the girl up. "Listen to me," she said. "Whenever you're feeling strong, you take your baby and you go here, all right. You promise?"

The girl nodded and opened the note, which held directions to San Ignacio.

"You tell Tomasa I sent you."

5

Stanislavo, Nunzio, and Molina were scouting to make sure an ammo shipment promised by Cuba had made it to a nearby cove. It was their fourth attempt.

Strange, after nine months of grassroots organizing and living a peaceful revolution, to be reminded that war was still being waged. That arms were necessary. Stanislavo's own revolver had been nothing more than a prop. His time in Mochima had not taught him to be a guerrilla fighter. A guerrilla teacher, perhaps. A guerrilla comrade, for sure. The way Nunzio talked to the villagers about their animals, the way Molina organized marbles tournaments for the kids, the way Tomasa created the first women's farming cooperative among Arapito, San Ignacio, and Bananal. Or how Tucán had taken that group of boys and made something out of them; yes, they trained with weapons, but that wasn't all they did. Tucán had organized a book club, and he made sure that those who couldn't read came to the adult literacy program Stanislavo ran three days a week in Tomasa's library.

Above them all, in Stanislavo's eyes, was Emiliana, who *was* the revolution. If they could be even a quarter of Emiliana, they would build utopia together. The young mother she had brought to San Ignacio a couple of months ago had also been a balm to everyone.

The girl and her baby boy had lifted even Stanislavo, whose baseline, it seemed, had always been to be serious and bitter. Now he spent nights with Emiliana in his tent and met with her again after training with the men. They would play with the girl's baby, walk to their tree, join in on domino matches with Molina and Tucán, who had become skilled partners, almost impossible to beat. President Leoni had moved his forces to the west of the country, where most of the armed conflicts had begun to take place, allowing the Mochima camp the freedom to expand and gather strength. Which also meant that it was now the logical place to bring in the bulk of the armaments needed to supply other fronts.

Nunzio had a cough, the kind that lingers for weeks, sticking to the back of the throat like the burrs that clung to every piece of fabric they owned. But he knew the Cuban smuggler, whom he'd met at Universidad Central a year and a half ago, and wanted to greet him. Plus, the military had been silent. No one in the Movement's network had seen or heard any activity in the area. Their own people in the surrounding villages had confirmed it. So Nunzio came with them, coughing into his snotty sleeve.

It was afternoon and the mosquitoes were vicious, an affliction made bearable only by the view. They sat under a patch of cacao trees, fat with fruit, and from their ledge they could see down into the dark blue cove, the jungle coming right to the water like a thirsty animal, and behind it the clear cerulean sky. The peñero was there, as promised, anchored a few feet from shore. On the sand sat a crate half-covered by a green-colored tarp.

"There it is, señores," Stanislavo said.

"Where's the Cuban?" Nunzio said in a raspy voice. "Wasn't Julio supposed to be waiting with the cargo?"

"He's probably pissing in the trees or something," Molina whispered.

"No, something doesn't look right," Stanislavo said. He pulled a pair of binoculars from his knapsack. "Look," he said, passing the binoculars to Molina. "Footprints."

The sand was littered with them. Molina scanned the cove with the binoculars. He pulled out his gun and Stanislavo did so as well.

"What are you guys doing?" Nunzio said. "Put those things away, coño. We're not shooting anyone."

A rustling sounded behind them, followed by the voices of two men in conversation. As the voices got closer, Stanislavo's grip on his revolver grew slippery, and his chest tightened, as if a snake had coiled around him. The three of them found cover and let the two men pass. Boys, really, dressed in all-green uniforms, with soft hair under their noses, and rifles slung over their shoulders. Stanislavo trained his revolver on the taller of the two while Molina aimed at the other one. The boys stopped to admire the view, turning their backs on the trio, not ten feet away.

"Show me her picture again," said the taller one.

"Don't start with that shit."

"I'm serious. I think I'm in love with your sister."

Stanislavo weighed his options. Bile rose, bitter, to the back of his throat. He had tried to forget this since they arrived in Mochima, the possibility that he would have to point his gun at someone and pull the trigger. He had not known to expect the physical reaction: the way saliva pooled under his tongue as nausea set in, and the sudden pain in his left side, like a stick to the ribs. If he had been put in this position the first week of his arrival, the soldiers before him would already be dead, and he and Molina and Nunzio would be running down the jungle pathways, so familiar to them now they couldn't be caught. But something about the way the boys talked reminded him of his own men, and his finger froze on the trigger. Molina would back him with his own gun if he decided to fire. He knew that. But Nunzio lowered Stanislavo's arm and shook his head no. The two of them stared at each other. Murdering these boys would cross a border that Stanislavo did not want to be on the other side of.

Then horror passed across Nunzio's face. His eyes bulged and his whole body heaved like a dam trying to hold back monsoon waters. His three consecutive coughs were loud despite both of his hands clutching at his mouth to muffle them. Both boys turned, their rifles pointing directly at the trio. Stanislavo and Molina trained their revolvers on the boys in return, but nobody fired.

"D-don't move," the shorter boy stammered.

The other soldier put a whistle to his mouth and its piercing sound overtook them all, flying down to the cove like a missile and skimming the Caribbean waves toward the horizon.

They were surrounded in mere seconds, it seemed. Stanislavo hadn't realized how heavy his gun was until it dropped to the ground. He stretched his hands, callused, dirty, and empty, above his head and took shallow breaths, in rhythm with his pulse. His two friends likewise had their hands raised, fingers spread out and palms to the sky as if awaiting a divine gift.

6

THEY WERE BLINDFOLDED, bound, and pushed into a peñero by four men, the two boys who'd captured them and two others, older and meaner. The rest of the soldiers had stayed behind in the cove, seizing the supplies and munitions meant for the camp. Stanislavo lay next to his friends in the bottom of the wooden skiff, a plank jabbing his left side with every wave the boat chopped through.

"We're heading east," Molina whispered. "Keep track of how long we're on the boat."

Stanislavo was glad for Molina's focus, but not surprised. It's why Stanislavo had brought him to Mochima, and one of the reasons the group had thrived here. But instead of focusing on their survival, like his more practical friend, Stanislavo couldn't stop thinking about Ludmil, dead on the passenger seat. He tried, unsuccessfully, to banish him, but blindfolded, with only the dark, he could draw nothing but Ludmil's face on the black, empty canvas of his brain.

They were on the peñero for fifteen painful minutes—a short distance by sea, but with the dense coast in this part of the country it would have been impossible to traverse by land. Then Stanislavo was pushed off the skiff. Still blindfolded, his hands bound behind his back, he struggled to keep his footing as he waded onto the shore. He fell face-first into the seawater and swallowed a big gulp of it. Strong hands pulled him up and tossed him farther along, and he crawled out using only his legs and torso, like some semi-evolved creature escaping the primordial ooze. Half his face sank into wet sand as he coughed the brine out of his lungs. His blindfold had slid halfway down his face, and he saw Nunzio and Molina, still on their feet and still bound, standing on the beach. They were both soaked through, Molina's shoulders squared to the sea, his chin up, ready for whatever came. Nunzio was listing to one side, his right arm tucked against his ribs. Behind them rose a wall of green jungle.

The sand stunk of algae, and Stanislavo rolled onto his back. A squadron of pelicans flew over him—so close he could see their gray feathers fluttering.

Then one of the older soldier's faces came into view above him. "This one is getting a suntan, Pancho," the man said.

The soldier called Pancho approached. He was ugly, with a hairy double chin and a mole next to his mouth. "Vacation is over," he said, and kicked Stanislavo hard on the hip bone. "Up. We've got some walking to do."

The soldiers marched them along a path away from the beach and up a steep incline into the jungle. Their blindfolds had been removed but they were kept bound, making it difficult to maintain their balance on the muddy uphill stretches. By the time they got up the mountain, Stanislavo was bruised from slipping, with a red spot blossoming on the right knee of his fatigues.

The path connected to an old dirt road, wide enough to drive on, which they followed for an hour. Stanislavo was trying to figure out where they might be, what the name of the road was—mentally scanning the maps he thought he knew by heart—but nothing came to him. They arrived at a gate. The archway bore letters made from wire, spelling out MI ENCANTO, with the o at the end hanging like a droopy eye.

Pancho put two dirty fingers in his mouth and whistled. An armed soldier appeared and opened the gate. When Pancho asked where the comandante was, the soldier replied that he'd left that morning and hadn't yet returned.

"You know where?"

"No, vale, nobody tells me anything."

"The life of a soldier," Pancho said as he pushed Stanislavo through the archway. "Not knowing shit, except how it tastes."

"At least we're not these hijos de puta," the soldier said.

"That's right," Pancho said.

The sun was about to set as they marched to a house that had clearly once been beautiful. Now the veranda furniture was choked in place by vines. The heavy branch of a tornillo tree had collapsed on a portion of the building. The white stucco of Mi Encanto was sickly, with green splotches reaching from the ground toward the roof. Behind it the setting sun stretched its oranges, reds, and pinks like the wings of a lazy gull.

They walked past two military trucks and an old ambulance into the house. It served as a garrison. All these months of craftwork, network building, and scouting, Stanislavo thought, and they didn't know anything about a garrison of soldiers a few beaches away from their camp. It spoke to the difficulty of the terrain that they had been so close and yet missed each other completely. There were enough men here, by the looks of it, to have razed the Mochima camp if they'd wanted to.

Inside the house, it stank of men. But it was well organized. Bunk beds filled most of the ground floor—just thin mattresses wrapped in crisp green covers. Four soldiers sat at a table in an improvised mess hall in the living room, a set of dominoes between them. Pancho jabbed his rifle into Stanislavo's ribs, and the group emerged into the servants' quarters, everything tight, less generous. The stench was worse here, a waft of human waste coming from Stanislavo's left. It was one of the garrison's latrines, nothing more than a system of bucket seats made with pieces of reclaimed wood.

Stanislavo was thankful once they emerged from the house onto an ample back patio. This hadn't been just a home, it had been a farm. The back was an old drying patio for coffee and cacao beans, with moss-lined terra-cotta bricks in hues of red and orange giving off stored warmth from the day's sun. They walked a bit farther and came to a roofed but unwalled structure with large machines, including what Stanislavo recognized as an industrial roaster, a huge iron barrel that would spin while workers kept a fire going underneath, though currently it stood silent and unmoving, the huge chain that made it rotate rusting on the ground.

Grunting followed by shuffling feet and a whimper sounded from behind the machines. Stanislavo and the others were pushed around a corner, where an old man with the tanned and weathered skin of a fisherman stood tied to a metal column, one of many supporting the warehouse's roof. His head hung down and bloody saliva formed a long string that almost touched the ground. A shirtless man faced him, not very tall but big in all the other ways that mattered. Not heavy like Molina, whose weight was a softness never confused with strength. This soldier's mass rippled with power as he struck the tied pescador with two uppercuts to his ribs, one left and one right, his boxing form impeccable. What truly scared Stanislavo was the expression on the man's piglike face: He looked bored. If there was any sadism there, it was buried under a veneer of tedium.

Three other fishermen sat on the ground to the side of the column, watching the spectacle with bruised faces. Stanislavo had never seen them in any of their organizing meetings, or even in the classes they held in San Ignacio, which meant that most likely they were just men suspected of something they hadn't done. Or maybe a group of fishermen had made noise about getting organized and the military had pounced preemptively. Whatever the case, they were a demonstration of things to come for Stanislavo and his two comrades. Two more soldiers stood behind the three bound fishermen, eating green mangoes with salt, a shaker passed among them between punches and bites.

"We've got a few more for you, Javier!" yelled Pancho.

The pig-faced man turned his head. "Good," he said. "This

one stopped making noise a while ago." His words were slow, his vowels round. When he untied the old fisherman from the column, he crumpled. Javier the Pig dragged him by the leg to where the other three prisoners sat. "What do you want me to ask them?" he said to Pancho.

"The comandante isn't here, so no questions yet. Just soften them up a little."

"You've never brought me city boys before," Pig said. "Look at his freckles."

He grabbed Stanislavo by the rope that bound his wrists behind his back and yanked. Something ripped in Stanislavo's left shoulder and he yelped.

"We haven't even started, catire," Pig said. "You're not in the ring yet."

Once they got to the column the soldier untied Stanislavo's wrists. His left arm was limp and throbbing, and when Pig lifted it to tie his hands behind the column the pain transformed into a feeling so white-hot that Stanislavo was surprised he didn't see a glow. He clenched his teeth, trapping a scream inside. A sloshing at his feet, combined with the sharp tang of the scent, told him he was standing in a puddle of urine. Not his — it belonged to the man before him, most likely, or to the three others, or all the men who'd been through here. And suddenly he was more afraid of pissing himself than of getting hit.

Then a punch in the gut — like someone had dunked him in ice water. He gasped, but air refused to comply. His body wanted to bend over but the column pulled it back, applying pressure on his shoulder and tearing his muscle more. Nunzio and Molina, looking afraid and defeated, were made to kneel next to the fishermen. Stanislavo coughed, and those little in-between breaths brought in precious air. Pig approached for a follow-up and Stanislavo's body clenched. This punch, a tight uppercut, connected to the left side of his torso, on ribs already bruised from the boat ride. His bones cracked, a sound he'd never heard his body make before.

Pig was teaching him a lesson about his own anatomy, one punch at a time: This is how it feels to be out of breath, this is how it feels to break a rib, this is how it feels to lose a tooth, this is how it feels when blood comes out of your ear. Here it is. This is your body in pain. After the fifth punch Pig danced away. He threw a couple of air jabs and then a cross, ready for round two. He hopped close again, and Stanislavo shut his eyes.

"Hey! Hey! Stop!" a voice called out.

When the next punch didn't land, Stanislavo opened one eye and Pig's dumb face was frozen. A man approached from behind the machinery. A man with a certain walk. A man in charge.

Pig turned around and struck a salute, no longer dangerous, like a sheathed knife. "¡Sí, mi comandante!" he said.

Stanislavo could breathe again. But without his fear to keep him alert, he felt near collapse, as if a dam had burst and flooded him with all his exhaustion and pain at once.

The man in charge came closer. He was young, maybe a couple of years older than Stanislavo. His face was clean-shaven and pock-marked, a childhood of acne forever scarred on its surface. He took out a handkerchief and used it to inspect Stanislavo's face without touching him. The man smelled of cologne: sandalwood and citrus.

"Bienvenidos, señores," he said. His breath was clean.

Stanislavo felt a warmth in his pants. He didn't know if he'd pissed himself during Pig's punches or if it had happened after hearing the man yell for Pig to stop. Everything blurred out of shape and he slid down the column into a heap on the ground. Cold water brought him back. Pig stood over him with an empty metal bucket.

"You're Stanislavo Atanas," the commander said in a low voice. Then, a little louder, "And the tall one here is Nunzio Guelfi, and the fat one is Jaime Molina, and you've been in Mochima for seven months? Eight? Something like that. You must feel like real guerrilleros now, no?"

Stanislavo didn't say anything. Just sat in water and piss.

"My name is Alexis Méndez-Correa. Welcome to Mi Encanto.

It's going to be your home for a while, so I hope you enjoy it." He squatted down on Stanislavo's level. "I know what you're thinking, Señor Atanas. You're wondering how much more we're going to do with you, and how much it's going to hurt before you give me the information I ask for." Méndez-Correa grabbed him by the hair and lifted his face. "Not to worry. I have orders from the minister to keep you three fresh. 'We don't hurt bargaining chips,' he told me. But others are not as lucky as you three. I've been told that caserío San Ignacio is really thriving these days?"

Stanislavo thought of Alexandria, as he'd privately christened Tomasa's library, of the books in flames. He thought of Tucán and the boys. He thought of Emiliana. He felt fear then, pure and uncut, the kind he had felt only once before, in the moments between looking into Ludmil's empty eyes in the passenger seat and when his parents arrived at the scene of the accident.

Méndez-Correa stood up again. "Pancho!"

Pancho took a few steps forward and stood at attention. "¡Sí, mi comandante!"

"Take these three to the room upstairs. No more hitting."

7

THEY WERE KEPT TOGETHER, probably because there was no space in
the house to keep them apart. Whatever the reason, it was a great
relief to Stanislavo to have Molina and Nunzio close. Their cell was
one of Mi Encanto's bedrooms, with a locked door and barred windows. Remnants of furniture, old toys and books, and trash discarded
by the room's previous occupants, whoever they'd been, were strewn
about. There was one stained, thin cot to sleep on for the three of
them. Opposite the cot sat two buckets. With no running water, and
having seen the latrines downstairs, Stanislavo could imagine what
the buckets were for. Between their whispers and sleeplessness, the
first night moved slowly, with Nunzio and Molina doing their best
to help Stanislavo, whose body ached from the beating.

The next morning a guard brought him pain medication. "From
the doctor," he said. The guard had brought water as well, and having not drunk anything since their capture, they shared it in greedy
gulps.

They passed the first few nights in fear: of what might happen
to them if Méndez-Correa changed his mind about torture, of what
might already be happening to their friends in San Ignacio and at
the camp.

The house was large, and there were other prisoners, though

they could only hear them—through the bones of the old villa. Sometimes they heard unintelligible chatter, like the sound of rats shuffling in the walls, but other times what they heard was clear: Torture was always unmistakable and, as the first week went by, familiar. Trying to identify the person who'd emitted the scream was its own form of punishment. Could any of them have been Stanislavo's men? One of Tucán's boys? Tucán himself? Nobody cared if a communist indio from a village or caserío turned up with a fractured skull or burned soles. Nobody cared if a Black fisherman trying to organize turned up with lashes on his back. But white city boys had some value. White city boys like Stanislavo were worth saving for a rainy day.

The meals were scant, stale arepas with butter, eggs boiled for so long the yolks were rock-gray. Stanislavo could see the weight falling off his friends. Nunzio's face, already chiseled even before moving to the mountain, was growing sunken. Molina's, slower to change, took on a melted quality.

Boredom was a mainstay of captivity; Stanislavo felt crushed by the lack of stimulation even more than by the awful food, dirty water, and sharp stink of their bodies. But Méndez-Correa kept his promise. After that first day, there had been no more beatings. To pass the time the three friends made a chess set out of trash: pebbles for pawns, and larger objects—bottle caps, shards of glass—for the other pieces. A rusty pencil sharpener was selected as the black queen. At first, more than one argument resulted from mistaking the pieces, but as the weeks ticked by, each piece might as well have been carved by Rodin, they were so unique.

They had received no word of San Ignacio or of their camp. It had been anguish, to know they could do nothing to help their friends. Stanislavo wished more than anything else that if, or when, Méndez-Correa had decided to hit the camp, Emiliana had been away in Puerto La Cruz, at the hospital. Would she be there still?

The other thing that happened—as the panic subsided, as they grew accustomed to their circumstances, and as their anger rose—was that they started to plot. Yes, they were surrounded by a small garrison of soldiers; yes, they were being held, unspoiled, for some unknown purpose; but this wasn't a true prison. Mi Encanto had not been made for this. These men—boys, really—didn't know shit, and their commander, Méndez-Correa, was often away. Escape was possible.

8

THE GUARD OPENED THE DOOR to their cell, pushed Molina inside, and locked the three of them in. Once the guard was gone, Molina unbuttoned his trousers and reached inside. He pulled out a plastic bag filled with an inky liquid and held it up to Stanislavo and Nunzio like a prize.

"We have it," Molina said. "The guard came through."

This bag of pig's blood was the first step in their plan. The day before, from their only window, they had seen two guards leading a pig into the house with a frayed rope tied around its neck. The guards walked past the old ambulance and into the house, and the spotted animal followed them like a sad dog, oblivious he was about to meet his end.

The friends had been discussing the possibility of faking an illness, something that would get one or more of them transported to the military hospital. To Emiliana, hopefully. They had talked about it back at Mochima: If anyone was captured, they should attempt a transfer to the hospital, where security was laxer and Emiliana's access would make escape possible. Emiliana had been in agreement that it was possible. In fact, she had prepared for it, just in case.

But Mi Encanto had its own doctor who looked after the soldiers. Dr. Pastillita, who, when he felt like it, came around and tossed them quinine pills to prevent malaria. Whatever they faked wouldn't have to convince only a couple of pimpled green shirts, but the doctor as well. And it needed to be something serious, not something that could be treated here.

Nunzio, a third-year veterinary student before his decision to join Stanislavo, had been the one to make the connection to the pig. "If we could get our hands on some of the pig's blood," he said.

The plan took shape from there. Molina talked to Joselo, one of their guards, who agreed to the price. That afternoon, while the pig hollered, Stanislavo used a rock to knock out Nunzio's molar and, more important, his molar's gold filling. While Nunzio squirmed on the dirty floor of their cell, the guards drank beer and cooked the pig over an open flame. The smell of it filled the room and made them dizzy. Even Nunzio, amid waves of pain, kept saying that he would give another tooth for a bite of pork.

"Gordo, you're my hero," Stanislavo said now, as Molina held forth the bag of blood.

When he grabbed Molina's face and kissed his forehead, his orange beard swept his friend's spectacles off his face and sent them clinking to the ground. As Molina bent to retrieve them, Stanislavo noticed his thinning hair. Had he been balding before Mochima? Before their capture? He touched the crown of his own head, relieved by the feel of his thick, matted hair, surprised by his vanity in such a moment. Then Molina's eyeglasses, with dirty tape and string holding them together, the left lens cracked, were back on his face.

"Thank you, Nunzio," Stanislavo said. "We couldn't have done this without you."

Nunzio held the right side of his swollen face. His voice sounded like he had a mouthful of cotton balls as he muttered, "Anything for the Cause, brothers."

"Now it's just the matter of drinking it," Molina said.

They all sat around the bag of blood, which lay flaccid, like a sad balloon, on the ground between them. It had seemed so full when Molina held it up. Nunzio spit some of his own blood onto the ground and smiled, his mouth half-open.

Molina had done the work to get it. Nunzio had paid for it with pain and gold. Stanislavo was tasked to drink it. At first, he had refused to be the one, because this plan meant freedom for just one of them. But Molina had convinced him. It was true that because of his tight connection to Alfredo, Stanislavo knew the most of the three of them.

He wondered how President Leoni was planning to use them, what he was saving them for, but he'd stopped trying to guess, thankful that they'd been spared real torture. As the three of them agreed, however, that could all change. Tomorrow they could be strapped to a chair and connected to a battery. Stanislavo knew the names of people who had infiltrated the government, knew meeting places for the Movement's leadership. He had to be the priority for escape, whether he liked it or not.

"Give me that thing," he said, and reached for the bag. "You sure it's not going to kill me?" he asked Nunzio, as if his friend's stint in veterinary school made him an expert on swallowing day-old pig's blood.

"It shouldn't," Nunzio replied. "I mean, after you're out, make sure you get some antibiotics and check for parasites, you know?" Nunzio averted his gaze. "It'll make you sick as hell and you'll start puking it out pretty soon."

"Here goes nothing," Stanislavo said.

He unknotted the bag and started drinking. The blood was slimy and dense, with coagulated chunks that lodged briefly against his gums and cheeks before traveling down his throat. The taste was as though he'd licked a battery covered in manure.

For the first few minutes he wondered if the blood was going to do anything. His friends kept asking how he felt, but apart from the taste coating his mouth he sensed no change. Then a low rumbling started in his gut.

"I think it's starting," he said.

"Remember," Molina said, "an ulcer won't keep you in the hospital for long. A night or two at most. You have to make your escape quick. If you're back here in the next couple of days, after all of this, I'll kick your ass." He fidgeted with his eyeglasses, pointlessly cleaning the lenses with his shirt, which was as dirty as a mop.

What was left unsaid, but what they were all no doubt thinking, was the hope that Emiliana was still at the hospital, that her cover hadn't been blown, something they could not know until—and only if—Stanislavo arrived there. Her presence would be his best chance at escape.

"Tell the doctor you suffer from peptic ulcers," Nunzio said. "That you've had pain for about five days." He stumbled through the words, still hurting from the missing tooth.

"Yes," Stanislavo said, "that I think it's the dirty water. I know, okay? I'm ready."

Stanislavo had never been a dreamer. When he slept, blackness smothered him. But since the capture it was Emiliana and Ludmil, every night. Details were fuzzy, but their faces lingered each morning.

The rumbling in Stanislavo's stomach stopped and was replaced by heaviness. "It feels heavy," he said, "but it's not hurting at all."

"Do you feel like throwing up?" Nunzio said. "We need to time this right."

"No, I don't."

"You're going to have to make yourself throw up," Molina said. "We can't have done all this for nothing." He stood and walked to the door, where he listened for the noise of guards.

"How long can I wait?"

"Not much, I'd guess," Nunzio said.

"Well, you're a vet, aren't you?" Molina said.

"I did six semesters of veterinary school before you roped me into this shit, Molina. They don't really cover simulating an ulcer in Basic Animal Anatomy. I'm not a doctor, coño. What the fuck do I know?"

"Okay, that's enough," Stanislavo said, and stood between them. "You're right, Nunzio, we're doing this now. If I wait, it'll be worse."

They started the ruckus.

Molina banged on the door and clanged two metal cups together. "Guards!" he screamed repeatedly.

Stanislavo fell to the ground in the fetal position and moaned. Nunzio knelt next to him, the back of his hand on his friend's forehead. Stanislavo prepared his retching, contorting his stomach into strange shapes, imagining rotting flesh and the time as a child when Ludmil had held him down and forced him to eat a fat maggot they'd found under a log. Acidic bile crawled up from his stomach into his mouth, but the guards weren't here yet. He needed to keep the vomit down until they were. He swallowed hard. The sound of stomping sent adrenaline up his spine, his pulse rose, his veins swelled. Then one of the guards, along with Pig, burst through the door and pushed Molina aside, training their rifles on the three prisoners.

"What the hell is going on in here?" Pig said.

"We don't know what's happening to him!" Molina said.

"He's burning up!" Nunzio said, continuing to hold his hand to Stanislavo's forehead.

"He'll be fine," said Pig, who had grown a greasy mustache since their arrival.

"I don't know, Javier," the other one said. "He looks pretty bad."

Stanislavo willed the contents of his stomach to rise, to crest, to flood, but it was useless. He dry-heaved without a trace of blood coming out.

Pig knelt beside him and shook him by the collar. "Are you faking? If I take you to the doctor and he says nothing's wrong with you, you're not going to like what happens."

"He's been sick for a while," Nunzio said. "He's not faking, can't you see, he's about to pass out!"

"About to pass out, my ass," Pig said. He put a knee on the ground and delivered a solid punch to Stanislavo's gut. "Does that hurt, you liar?"

The punch didn't connect that hard, but Stanislavo let out a piercing scream anyway. Molina, adding to the theater, ran to his friend. The other guard promptly kicked him away and pointed a rifle at his face.

"It's his stomach, you bastard!" shouted Molina. "He has an ulcer!"

"I don't fucking care. You move to that wall." The guard pushed Molina hard, and he crashed against the brick wall of the room.

Stanislavo finally felt a rumbling through his body. It wasn't the crimson tide he wanted, but it was something, and he was not going to waste it. In a fit of fake coughing he spit on Pig, taking no small pleasure in his disgust. Stanislavo was relieved to see red splatter covering Pig's face.

"Coño, Javier," the other guard said, still holding his rifle up. "He's spitting up blood. I think we better take him to Pastillita."

After hearing the magic words, Stanislavo relaxed his body and closed his eyes, pretending to be unconscious. The guards went out, locked the door, and said they'd be back with a stretcher. Molina peeked out one of the barred windows.

"What the fuck, Stanis!" Nunzio said behind clenched teeth. "Why aren't you throwing up?"

"I don't know, I don't feel nausea at all, I don't feel anything except for full. If that hijo de puta hadn't punched me, I don't even think I would've thrown up what I did."

Stanislavo took his index and middle finger and pushed against the back of his throat. His fingers tasted salty and dirty, and his fingernails scratched his uvula. The thought of those fingers, which he hadn't washed in weeks, being in his mouth created more revulsion than the pressure on the back of his tongue. But still, nothing.

"What the hell, man," Nunzio said.

"You tell me, 'Dr. Guelfi,' you said I'd be painting the walls red by now."

"Must be all that borscht your mother fed you as a kid, Stanis,"

Molina said from the door. "Don't blame him, Nunzio, he's used to keeping down disgusting red soup."

Stanislavo, still on the ground, chuckled despite himself, but Nunzio didn't seem pleased.

"What?" Molina said. "If we die today, which is looking likelier all the time, at least I'll be able to laugh at our stupidity."

"It is funny," Stanislavo admitted.

"Estamos jodidos, aren't we?" Nunzio said.

"Royally," Molina said with a nervous smile.

They heard the boots coming. Stanislavo went limp, closed his eyes, and let a strand of pink slobber drip from his mouth.

"Promise you'll tell my dad I'm okay when you get out?" Nunzio whispered into Stanislavo's ear. "Tell him I love him."

Then Pig and the other soldier stormed in carrying a military stretcher.

Even after three months in captivity, Stanislavo thought of himself as heavy. He was shocked, then, at the ease with which the soldiers picked him up off the floor, at how little energy they seemed to expend as they whisked the stretcher down the long hallway and into the bedroom that doubled as a doctor's office he'd never seen before, since Pastillita, the doctor, had always come to see them and not the other way around.

Everyone, even the guards, called him Pastillita, and Stanislavo had never learned the doctor's real name. The nickname fit him, not only for the obvious connection between his profession and pills, but also because of his eyes with their tiny irises that resembled black aspirin floating in yellowed milk. Pastillita had an unsettling gaze that missed little—in that he and Stanislavo were alike—and he was a clever man who would not be fooled by a small splattering of blood. He was also a drug addict—betrayed by the subtle track marks along one arm, well taken care of, but still there. Maybe that's why he was here, in the armpit of the country, looking after illiterate soldiers and sick prisoners. Maybe this is where junkie doctors ended up. Or maybe not, maybe he was as bored as the rest of them and whatever he pushed into his veins was the antidote.

The guards transferred Stanislavo from the stretcher to a bed. The sheets were stained from the previous tenant—with what Stanislavo hoped was mostly sweat, though of course could have been from much worse. For all he knew, these sheets were the last physical markers of a person now rotting in an unmarked hole in the jungle. He felt the beginning of something in his stomach—hopefully nausea. Pastillita sat him up on the edge of the bed, his legs hanging down. Stanislavo was like a child waiting to be inoculated. His lie was naked in front of this man, who held Stanislavo's life in one slender hand.

"Open your mouth," Pastillita said.

He was thin and small with a voice to match: high-pitched and fast, like air trying to escape a balloon. Pastillita pressed Stanislavo's tongue down with a metal spatula, inspecting his airways with a military flashlight. He then pulled a thermometer—it might as well have been a cocked revolver—from the front pocket of his coat and shoved it beneath Stanislavo's tongue.

A ruptured ulcer without a fever did not exist. Stanislavo knew it. The doctor would know it. A patient vomiting half a liter of blood would be rushed to the military hospital in a heartbeat, fever or no fever. A patient without a fever, complaining of stomach pains and writhing on the ground, would be given a beating and thrown in a dark place.

"Cierra la boca," the doctor instructed and began to press on his belly.

Stanislavo winced in pretend pain as he closed his mouth around the thermometer. He uttered whiny yips, ouched and oohed through Pastillita's prodding. He was sweating, his heart rate skyrocketing, the cold glass of the thermometer clicking against his teeth.

"Hmmm," Pastillita said.

Stanislavo could practically hear the gears moving inside the doctor's head. He would be found out any moment, all that useless pig's blood sloshing in his stomach. Pastillita pushed once more, hard and deep, into his abdomen.

It came to Stanislavo then—what he had to do. On the next prod, he let out a scream that would be heard by every single person in the house and clenched on the thermometer, breaking it into pieces. He wondered if his friends would think his deception had been discovered, and that this was torture and not acting. He wondered if they were afraid they would be next.

The broken glass cut his inner lip, and mercury slid down his throat and out his mouth. It tasted like nothing, like thick air, but the idea of the poison settling inside him did what his filthy fingers had not. The bitter taste of bile gushed into his mouth, and then a steady stream of crimson poured out of him uncontrollably. It traveled in a majestic arc and landed on Pastillita's face and chest, soiling his white coat. Stanislavo fell from the bed, squeezing every last bit of theater he could from his nausea. He crawled while vomiting on Pig's boots and trousers.

He writhed and cried out, but on the inside he was laughing. He laughed at the guards' faces, contorted in disgust. He laughed at Pastillita, still paralyzed, his little eyes looking down at his red chest. He laughed at himself for thinking this stupid plan would work. He even laughed at the thought of his comrades stuck in their cell for God knew how long, shitting in buckets, forgotten by everyone except those who loved them most.

Pig delivered a boot to Stanislavo's face and then he couldn't laugh anymore. He couldn't do anything. He was floating in black.

9

STANISLAVO WOKE TO the rumbling of tires on a dirt road. His head felt full of rattling seeds, each vibration lacing pain throughout his body. A foul smell came from his ragged, swampy trousers. It was humiliating, to have soiled himself like a child, but Stanislavo took pleasure in his captors' disgust. He could also sense their fear. It confirmed his value to the regime: Méndez-Correa would be in big trouble if Stanislavo died in custody.

Slowly, Stanislavo got his bearings. He was in the old ambulance that had always been parked in front of Mi Encanto, as if a prop, in the only view they had from their cell window. It was a British car, an Austin Sheerline that must have been state-of-the-art in the '40s, when it would have been something to admire. The bright white body, boxy but charming, with a rounded roof and a circular mounted sign with a red cross at its crown; the wide windshield framed in chrome; the canine snout housing the engine; the two headlights, round and big, like eyes to a massive metal bulldog. This one was brown and gray instead of white, stained by years of rust and bird waste. One of the headlights had fallen out and the red-cross sign on its roof dangled by an electrical cable.

The inside, which he had only ever imagined, was in a similar state. Stanislavo lay on an orange leather gurney, cracked by age but still by far the most comfortable surface he'd been on since his capture. A guard sat on a bench opposite him—not Pig, but the other one, the rookie with no nickname. Cabinets for medicine and equipment, rusted and long emptied, filled the confines of the cabin. Above both the gurney and the bench were wide windows revealing rolling views of thick forest, and the occasional farmer with a mule. Pig drove the ambulance, and Méndez-Correa was his co-pilot.

Stanislavo was getting closer to Emiliana, he knew it, he was on his way to her and could feel her alive and well. It was selfish, but if he died today, it would feel good to die beside her.

"The prisoner is waking up, comandante," the soldier said. "Should I handcuff him?"

"Can't you see that man is half-dead?" Méndez-Correa said. "No cuffs."

The garrison commander was well put together. He was different from the soldiers he managed in that regard. Unlike Pastillita, it didn't seem that this posting was any sort of punishment for him, but an important rung in the military ladder. This man was killing communists, performing a sacred duty to flag and country. A season or two of jungle and mosquitoes hardened such a man, gave him perspective. Was that so different from what Stanislavo himself was doing?

The progress to the military hospital in Puerto La Cruz was slow. Stanislavo didn't know which was worse—the state of the ambulance, his stink, or the roads. They had miraculously reached the highway without breaking down or getting a flat tire, which allowed them to pick up the pace. At the Bandera roundabout Pig took the curve at such speed that the ambulance went on two wheels and Stanislavo was thrown from the gurney. He crashed into the soldier guarding him and knocked both of them into the tight space between gurney and bench, with Stanislavo atop the guard. Amid the screeching tires, the shouts of "coño" and "hijo de puta," Stanislavo found his hand squarely on the guard's sidearm, which had fallen from the boy's trousers. He felt the call of the hard steel and forgot all about his escape plan. Five shots from the guard's revolver to take out three men. The choice again was clear: to kill or not?

This gun was its own plan. No Emiliana needed, no hospital. Even if he wasn't fast enough, or sharp enough, and Méndez-Correa shot him dead on the side of the road, at least he would go out on his own terms, not those dictated by the regime. And he would spare Emiliana whatever trouble was headed her way. But then he thought about Nunzio and Molina. If he killed any of these men, his friends would pay. They would be made examples. The garrison would drown in their screams before Pastillita put them out of their misery and into the dirt.

Stanislavo removed his hand from the revolver and squinted in pretend pain, then grabbed his abdomen and rolled toward the bench and away from the guard's limp body. The guard regained his composure—and his gun.

Méndez-Correa hit Pig in the back of his head with an open palm, hard. "El coño de tu madre, you're going to kill us all, you worthless piece of shit! Get out of the fucking car, I'm driving."

It was night now. Pig and Méndez-Correa exited the ambulance and crossed paths in front of the car, their silhouettes lit by passing headlights. Puerto La Cruz shone in the distance. Stanislavo could remember bathing at its beaches as a child when he and his brother would visit his dad's sister and his cousins, floating in the moonless night as the plankton came alive in a blue glow every time his legs and arms treaded water, watching the bioluminescent trail his cousin made swimming to shore. He could remember the freedom he felt as they ate bananas there in the warm sand with the stars above and the sound of shuffling crustaceans around them. He wondered if he would ever see his cousins again, or if by letting go of that gun he'd said goodbye for good to sand, to bananas, to the neon blue of plankton.

10

THE HOSPITAL WAS an efficient, brutal building. Its windows, spaced at consistent intervals, betrayed the facility's layout. Stanislavo could imagine the rooms belonging to the windows, all the same. The sterile beds and sterile curtains and sterile floors. The sterile hallways that connected them and the sterile nurses' stations and the sterile nurses all wearing their sterile crisp white uniforms. All of them except for Emiliana, one revolutionary soul who he hoped would hand him his freedom.

The ambulance rumbled into the hospital entrance, perhaps never to start again. The grounds were empty, with no guards on patrol, not even a nurse or a custodian smoking. Pig stormed into the hospital and soon came out with two big orderlies pushing a gurney. It was close to midnight now and the night was lit by a full moon. Everyone moved as if this was life or death, both reassuring and frightening Stanislavo. His lie was working, but was it working too well? Would any semi-decent doctor be able to see through the ruse when no evidence was found of actual ulcers, no fever, no internal damage? Stanislavo feared an endoscopy more than a firing squad.

The faces of the orderlies, when they caught a glimpse of him in the guts of the ambulance, turned ghastly. These were hardened workers used to half-dead, dismembered, disemboweled guerrilleros. No doubt they treated men with electrical burns to their testicles and removed splinters from underneath bruised fingernails on hands that were ballooned and purple. Their expressions, both horrified and perplexed, made him wonder what he looked like.

They rolled him through the wide swinging doors. It was bright, with fluorescent light that judged everyone equally. Sweat slid down Méndez-Correa's pockmarked face, gathering on the collar of his uniform, and his eyes darted from side to side. If Stanislavo was soon destined for a shallow grave, he would at least go there with the satisfaction of seeing Méndez-Correa sweat it out.

The hospital lobby had a great mirrored wall, and it was here that he saw himself clearly for the first time in weeks. While imprisoned they had been using a tin cup as a mirror—on it, his reflection looked distorted and strange, as it had in the fun-house mirrors the circus would bring to Maracaibo, when he and Ludmil were kids. He was distorted and even stranger now, more nightmarish than in any circus mirror. His beard and mustache grew stringy and wild, like a forest fire. His eyes were sunken, and his skin had a grimy greenish tint, like a man growing mold. But mostly he was covered in a bloody crust from his mouth to his feet.

"Where's Dr. Rengifo?" Méndez-Correa asked the attending nurse, a middle-aged matronly woman with muscular arms and legs.

"He's in Caracas," she said. "A family emergency."

"Who the fuck's the doctor, then?"

"The only one in tonight is Dr. Vivas. He's sleeping but I'll go get him. Orderlies, take him to the fourth floor, military wing. I'll send the doctor there."

Then Stanislavo was on the move again, through hallways and nurses' stations as sterile as he had imagined them to be. What he hadn't expected was how relieved he felt by how clean everything was.

They entered a large elevator.

"I don't like lifts," Pig said, making the sign of the cross.

Méndez-Correa gave him a stare that wired his mouth shut.

When the elevator doors opened on the fourth floor, two guards were stationed there; at the sight of Méndez-Correa they immediately stood at attention. Farther down the hallway four other guards kept watch on specific rooms, and one sat by the door to the stairs leading down to the other floors. It was a gauntlet.

Stanislavo was rolled into a room at the end of the hallway, the three soldiers in tow. Both hospital beds were empty. A large window centered on the north wall let in the moonlight, creating a big spotlight in the middle of the room. A door opened into a bathroom along the right wall. Stanislavo was transferred to one of the beds. The sheets smelled so clean he was almost ashamed to dirty them. He was not pretending to be in so much pain anymore, hoping that perhaps the doctor wouldn't resort to any drastic means of exploration. He also hoped that Emiliana would walk in, and that she had a plan. Stanislavo himself was out of plans, and out of energy. It had been only a matter of hours since the charade had started, but already it felt like a lifetime on a tightrope.

Dr. Vivas burst into the room. He was a skittish man, round and hyper, his coat rumpled, his thin, wavy hair out of place. And he was young. *The devil knows more from being old than from being the devil*, Stanislavo's mom used to tell him when he was a kid, whenever he and his brother would try to pull one over on her. Young was a good thing.

"Symptoms?" Vivas asked, as if to the room itself. He seemed unsure of whom to talk to.

"Stomach pains and vomiting blood," Méndez-Correa responded. "He says he has an ulcer that ruptured. Doctor, this man is important to President Leoni. ¿Entiende usted?"

Méndez-Correa locked eyes with Vivas, and the young doctor swallowed hard, his spiny Adam's apple bobbing up and down.

"Con permiso."

Stanislavo heard her voice before he saw her. His body softened, and he was surprised by the instant and overwhelming desire to cry. She was alive. Whatever Méndez-Correa had done to the camp, to

San Ignacio, he had not touched her. She was still here, still a nurse, still Emiliana. He fought hard to keep it all in, killing the gasp in his throat. Emiliana. Beautiful Emiliana. She nudged her body between Méndez-Correa and the doctor.

"Doctor," she said, "I'm going to take his temperature to confirm a fever."

Her hair fell on him as she got close. He breathed in. He looked in her eyes and saw her terror. She couldn't know that this was fake, she couldn't know that all he had was a belly full of pig's blood.

"Just an ulcer?" Emiliana asked. And Stanislavo noticed a crack in her voice, not enough for anyone who didn't know her to notice, but piercing to him. Her hands explored his body, as if looking for something worse. "Nothing else?" she said.

"Nothing else," Méndez-Correa confirmed. "As far as I know."

Stanislavo looked into her eyes and saw relief staring back. And then something like understanding—it was clicking in for her. They had discussed this in camp, faking an illness. She knew now that this was a ruse.

Emiliana leaned in again, taking his pulse. Shielded by her curtain of hair, she risked a small smile, just for him. A black jet charm in the shape of a fist, something he'd never seen her wear before, hung from a golden chain around her neck.

He opened his mouth and felt the cool glass of a thermometer for the second time that day. Emiliana took a wet towel and started cleaning his face and neck with warm water. The scabs of dried blood and grime dissolved down his face, dripping onto the sheets. While Méndez-Correa informed Vivas of the prison doctor's diagnosis, Emiliana removed his shirt and continued cleaning his body. Every place her hand touched was a blessing. She removed the thermometer when Vivas approached them. Her hand trembled as she placed it in the front pocket of her coat, out of sight.

"He's got a fever, Doctor. With the symptoms, a ruptured ulcer seems reasonable."

"Thank you, Emiliana, let me take a look," Vivas said and started pawing Stanislavo's abdomen. "Breathe in deep, please," he said, and Stanislavo did as told, his face contorting in fake pain. "I don't feel any swelling surrounding the stomach or digestive tract," the doctor said, looking up at the ceiling, talking to himself.

"What does that mean?" Méndez-Correa asked.

"Well, it's unusual; usually you see some swelling or bruising." The doctor glanced at the commander. "But with a high fever and a history of ulcers, it has to be that."

"Is he going to live?"

"I'm concerned about infection, but it seems to be just a peptic ulcer. If it was a rupture, he'd be in much worse shape. An endoscopy will reveal more. Antibiotics and a couple of weeks of recovery and he should be fine."

Méndez-Correa sat down. It was as if he'd put down a fifty-pound pack after a long march. But for Stanislavo the word *endoscopy* was a bony finger running down his spine. One look inside him and Vivas would know the truth.

"Emiliana, please bring me the endoscope," the doctor said.

"We informed Dr. Rengifo yesterday before he left for the capital that the lens broke," she said. "He was going to send it to Caracas to repair."

"Well, okay, then. Let's treat for *Helicobacter pylori*. Also get him pain medication and monitor his fever. And please give the man a good cleaning—we don't want any other diseases spreading around." The doctor walked over to Méndez-Correa. "Your prisoner will be fine, sir. You have my word. I'll have a room made up for you and your men."

Pig and the other guard were covered in blood. They leaned their tired bodies on their rifles.

"Comandante," Emiliana said, "I will stay here with him. I'll set up a chair for one of your men outside and bring some coffee. In the meantime, you go ahead and get some rest. I will personally come get you if anything happens."

She had gathered herself, seemed perfectly confident, all except for her right hand, tucked in her pocket. For a second Stanislavo thought Méndez-Correa would agree.

"Impossible, señora. This man is to be watched at all times."

Emiliana's stoic face hid any concern.

"Javier, you stay in the room for first watch," Méndez-Correa said to Pig. "You'll be relieved in four hours. As soon as this prisoner is feeling stronger, I want a two-man contingent on him at all times. Seems like we'll be here a few days at least."

"At least," Vivas agreed.

On the way out of the room Méndez-Correa stopped and looked back at Pig. "Watch him good. Anything, you come get me."

"Sí, mi comandante," Pig said.

Everyone left the room except for Emiliana and Pig. He dragged a chair to Stanislavo's bedside and sank into it.

"How do you like your coffee, mi amor?" Emiliana asked, sugar in every word.

"Brown and sweet, like my women." He ogled her.

"Of course, coming right up," Emiliana said and walked out of the room.

"I'd fuck that." Pig laughed and pushed Stanislavo's shoulder. "In a war every hole is a trench, am I right?"

Stanislavo imagined his hands around the man's neck.

Emiliana returned with a large cup of steaming coffee. Stanislavo had forgotten the way coffee smelled. The earthiness of it. It was another form of torture.

Emiliana handed the coffee to Pig. "Here you go, mi amor," she said. "I'm going to get this man cleaned up. Doctor's orders."

"Wait, I'll go with you."

"Nonsense, mi amor," she said, her hand on Pig's shoulder. Her fingers were long and elegant, her nails cut short. "Why don't you enjoy your cafecito here in the chair? You look so tired. This man will sooner sprout a tail than give me any trouble. Look at him."

It was all Pig needed. He sniffed the steam rising from his cup and let out a long, loud sigh.

11

EMILIANA HELPED STANISLAVO out of bed. When she put her arm around his waist to help him walk, she was astonished at his size: He was half the man she remembered. And when he draped his own arm around her neck, his bony elbow hurt her shoulder. It took everything she had not to burst out crying.

By the time she had walked him to the bathroom and locked the door behind them, it was Stanislavo sobbing. Emiliana turned on the shower to mask any noise. Stanislavo fell to his knees and she embraced him. She kissed his head.

"I'm disgusting," he whispered.

He tried pushing her away, but she didn't allow it, she pulled him back against her. He melted into her. She couldn't help it, she started to cry as well.

"Shh. Tranquilo, mi amor." She held his face. "We'll get you out of this, I promise."

"I'm sorry we got caught. I'm sorry."

"Stop it," she said. "There'll be time to talk all of this out, but I need you to be strong. We have to do this now."

Stanislavo took a deep breath. She was doing everything possible to send strength his way.

"Don't worry, the guard won't last long," she said. "His coffee is half sleeping pills. Clean yourself good. There's shaving supplies in the drawers. I'll get you some clothes. Be quick and be quiet."

"What's the plan?"

She had been thinking about this since Stanislavo had been captured, the possibility of one or all of them ending up here. She was ready. "I hope you know your way around a rope," she said, "because you're going out the window tonight." She knelt in front of him and kissed his cheek. The kiss made her burn. She was going to get him free, no matter what. "You stink, comrade," she said, forcing a smile, willing it to push them both toward hope. "Shower now." She stood and wiped the tears off her face, smoothed her nurse uniform. She pulled him up. "I'm glad you're alive, Stanis," she whispered, and put her hand on the bathroom door.

Then she felt it, the sharp pain in her midsection that had hounded her for the last few weeks. The little person in her womb growing every day. Her other hand went to her stomach and she winced.

"Everything all right?" Stanislavo said.

"Oh yeah, just a little cramp," she said. She looked at her baby's father—he was in profile, by the shower curtain, his shirt off. He hunched a bit and she noticed the notches of his spine. "Get ready, I'll be back."

When she emerged from the bathroom, the guard was already asleep, but she was quiet nonetheless getting out of Stanislavo's hospital room. In the hallway she walked with confidence straight to the nurses' station, where she dialed the poet's number, hoping he wasn't on one of his benders. He was going to need to drive Stanislavo out of here.

12

STANISLAVO THOUGHT the water would never run clear. After it touched his skin, it ran black into the drain, then brown, then pink, until at last it was the color of watered-down milk.

Suddenly Emiliana was back in the bathroom. "The guard is down," she whispered through the shower curtain. "I need to gather some stuff and make sure everyone is where they're supposed to be. I'll be back as soon as I can. I've left some clothes for you here."

His rib cage stuck out. He counted the ribs, then went over his nearly concave belly, his thin legs, then his ugly feet with toenails that resembled bear claws. He washed his hair and body again with the blue soap. When he finished showering, he wiped down the mirror with his hand and, with the scissors from the shaving kit, trimmed his beard, careful not to nick his skin. The whiskers painted the sink with Van Gogh flair: reds, oranges, and browns. He looked a bit like the painter, he thought, with his green eyes, his pale complexion, his orange hair, his prison-diet sharp features. With some bad luck he could still end up without an ear—that would be the least Méndez-Correa would take from him. He finished shaving. Felt truly naked without his mustache. Then he dressed, the belt pulled to its last notch.

When he opened the bathroom door a crack and peeked into the hospital room, Pig was out cold—one shoulder slung over the back of the chair, his head back, his open mouth revealing rotten molars. His rifle lay on the linoleum floor beside him. It occurred to Stanislavo that he could take Pig hostage. But what then? How far would he make it with a whole regiment on his tail? He calculated the consequences, the variables too uncertain and complicated. Besides, Emiliana had a plan. He would wait for it.

Stanislavo stripped the bed of its soiled sheets, still stinking of his imprisonment. He did not want to leave the task for Emiliana—he could spare her that indignity at least. He hid his dirty clothes among the sheets and slid under the crisp covers of the other bed. That way, if anyone peeked into the room, all they would see is him under the covers. As it should be.

The shower drain had swallowed not only the grime but also the adrenaline that had been coursing through him. He felt lightheaded now, and so tired. He stared at Pig, asleep on his chair, looking for any sign of stirring. Just a little while ago, with Dr. Vivas talking about an endoscopy, sleep seemed impossible, but now he had to fight it, attempting to sharpen his mind by reciting García Lorca's "Ballad of the Moon" to himself. But before *the horseman came beating the drums of the plains*, Emiliana arrived.

"A new man, I see," she whispered.

"I feel like an old one," he said. "Look, in case I don't make it out, Molina and Nunzio are alive. They are being held in a villa called Mi Encanto." He did his best to give her the necessary information about the garrison as quickly as he could, so that she could pass it on to the Movement. "How is the camp?" he asked. "The caseríos?"

"We have more important things to worry about right now, Stanis."

"Tell me, Emiliana. Please."

"I'm sorry, mi amor. Tucán is dead. They brought him here and he was already gone when I saw him. They got a couple of the other boys too. The camp disbanded after that."

Stanislavo's chest started to thump. His heart beat so hard he was almost afraid someone would hear it outside the room. "It's all my fault," he said.

"It's the government's fault, and you know that. Besides, if it wasn't for all the work we did to set up our network, everyone would've been dead or captured. But we're not. We're still out there. We're regrouping."

"Tomasa?" he asked.

Emiliana stiffened, and he knew not to push further.

"No more time for talking," she said. "We've got a job to do right now. I have the rope. It should be long enough to get you down safely."

"And the men?"

"Everyone that matters is visiting the land of dreams, Stanis."

Pig snored obligingly in his chair, as if to confirm this.

"Are you ready?" Emiliana said.

"They're going to blame you after I'm gone."

"I hope you're not morally opposed to hitting a woman, in the name of the revolution."

Stanislavo looked at his hands, bony and rough.

Emiliana secured the rope to a capped steel pipe on the wall. "Okay," she said, "it's time." She hugged him. "There's a car waiting for you. A poet—his name is Carlos Domínguez—will be there. Just go through the brush and you'll hit a dirt road." She paused, as if sensing his hesitation. "Don't worry, I've been hit before."

"Thank you, Emiliana. For everything. We'll see each other again, all right? Look, the time on the mountain, it meant so much—"

Emiliana grabbed his hands and kissed them. "Stop it. We have much to talk about, but not here. Now punch me!"

Stanislavo put his right fist up. He wished his knuckles weren't so sharp. The hand just stayed there while Emiliana looked at him.

"You're not going to?" she said.

Stanislavo sensed her annoyance. She took his fist and pushed it down to his side. In one quick motion she struck her forehead against the wall, hard and violent. She bounced back and Stanislavo caught her before she fell.

"I'm sorry," he said, "I couldn't even do this for you."

She kissed him and he was flooded with all the kisses from before, from that first time, in the hut, to the many times after that, in his tent, or by the river, or under the araguaney, or leaning up against cacao trees, or the time they walked the mules, their backs bent with medical supplies, all the way to San Ignacio just because they wanted to walk for a long time alone, kissing all the way.

"Go," Emiliana said, her face already starting to bruise.

Stanislavo grasped the rope and wriggled out the window. He rappelled down, his hands burning. The first window was dark, and he was relieved that the pane held his weight easily. The next window down had a light on, but he didn't have the strength or dexterity to avoid it, so he just hoped for the best. As he went past the window, his forearms and biceps tight, his shoes on the glass, he met the eyes of a man in a patient's robe. The man glanced over his shoulder as if wanting someone else to confirm what he was seeing. Stanislavo held tight to the rope with his left hand, his feet planted squarely on the window, and brought his right index finger to his mouth in a shushing sign. The man's eyes became wide, he glanced over his shoulder once more, and then he imitated Stanislavo's shushing gesture. They both stood still, holding their fingers against their mouths, as if on opposite sides of a mirror. And then Stanislavo continued his descent.

He jumped the last few feet and Emiliana threw down the rope, the last piece of evidence of his escape. He took it with him and ran as fast as he had when he raced Ludmil down the streets of the oil fields, not wanting to lose to his brother, not wanting to lose to himself, they were so alike. Into the brush and from there to the dirt road. Into the blue VW Beetle that the poet was driving. Down that road and down many others with no lights except for that of the full moon. He rolled down his window and breathed the fresh air. He thought of Emiliana's bruise. The poet shared cold empanadas de cazón out of an oily paper bag. Freedom was a breeze to the face. Freedom was a feast.

13

IN THE CONFINES of that blue Volkswagen, Stanislavo's feelings—euphoria, guilt, worry—bounced until they settled into exhaustion. Carlos Domínguez, the poet, wore a leather jacket even in the heat of the Venezuelan summer and drummed his long fingers to the beat of the rock and roll playing on the car radio. All he told Stanislavo was that he was taking him to a safe house in Caracas. He had a wide nose and a large mouth and talked to Stanislavo not about escape but about Octavio Paz speaking at Universidad Central.

"He's completely unconcerned with meaning," Carlos was saying. "Only with language. To him language is the object of poetic activity. The meaning is inseparable from the words."

The night landscape rolled by, the moon so bright it revealed all the shades of green in the tropical forest. The scenery felt more real to Stanislavo than whatever Carlos was saying—the poet's voice was lispy and low, lulling Stanislavo into some kind of trance state. By the time Carlos started comparing Góngora to Rimbaud, Stanislavo had fallen into a deep sleep that lasted for hours.

He woke up on the highway, the Caracas Valley unfolding below them. El Ávila, the mountain, was a green sentinel watching over the buildings, the houses and the ranchos alike. Stanislavo breathed in deep. The city was opening its doors. He would soon sleep in a real bed; hear the guacharaca's song in the morning; listen to the Guaira Sharks on the radio, the cracking of wooden bats against baseballs. All while Nunzio and Molina were punished for his escape. And Emiliana—would her part in this be discovered? Would she suffer like his friends?

Maybe Molina with his silver tongue would convince Méndez-Correa and his men that they had nothing to do with it. Maybe a higher-up would stay Méndez-Correa's hand, ordering him to take it easy on them. There were so many maybes that Stanislavo wanted to believe, but it was like grasping at vapor. Molina and Nunzio would be beaten, would be prodded, would be changed forever because of this.

The blue Beetle stopped in front of a dilapidated home on Avenida Finlandia, near the skirt of El Ávila.

"This is where the Movement wants you, Stanis," the poet said, dangling a set of keys he'd pulled from his jacket. "Alfredo will be by tomorrow. Once you go through that door you can consider yourself enconchado."

Stanislavo was now a hermit crab, and this house on Finlandia would be his shell for the considerable future. Until he talked to Alfredo, all he could do was guess, but he was sure he would be in hiding for a month at least, time he hoped to use planning an escape for Nunzio and Molina.

"I'd say, 'See you soon,' but that's unlikely," the poet said, leaning out of his window as Stanislavo walked to the gate. "So I'll just say, 'Good luck, comrade.'"

Stanislavo thanked Carlos and wished him good luck in return, then took a breath and stuck the key inside the lock.

A month later, like some bully, the mountain was spewing all the humidity trapped under its trees onto the inhabitants of the valley. Thirty-odd days in Casa Finlandia had felt like its own kind of imprisonment. Stanislavo made up continents from the gashed and peeling wallpaper. He could read only a sentence or two in a book before the letters started jumping, rearranging themselves into messages from Nunzio, Molina, and, of course, Emiliana. Vronsky and Anna Karenina danced but Stanislavo heard Molina pleading for his life. Bradbury's Martian palaces grew glass-like from the red sands, yet all he could see in the words was *We're still here.* One night he went out to the overgrown backyard — among the bent palms, the fat mango tree, and the million weeds — sat in a disintegrating rattan chair, and looked at the stars. What he saw was San Ignacio on fire, Tomasa on the ground by her books. He hoped that Tucán's boys were somewhere safe, mourning their brother. At least he knew, from Alfredo, that Emiliana had escaped suspicion at the hospital long enough to be removed from her post unharmed. She was safe and working here now, in the capital, but he hadn't been able to see her. Alfredo had not allowed it yet, an injunction that made sense but frustrated him anyway.

Alfredo considered his escape a victory for the Movement. The media coverage alone was an embarrassment for the regime: The front page had run two photos of Stanislavo, one with crutches, taken by someone at the university after a soccer injury, and another a profile portrait of him, young and muscular, from his early college days organizing against Pérez Jiménez. The lede read, *Stanislavo Atanas was able to escape the Central Military Hospital of Puerto La Cruz, where he had been taken to recover from a duodenal ulcer.*

He heard knocking at the door now. Alfredo, his one connection to the outside world. He'd been able to come three times since Stanislavo had arrived at Finlandia, never with enough answers, whether about Emiliana or Molina and Nunzio, except that they were alive. Still, a friendly face, even if inscrutable, was welcome.

Alfredo lumbered in, barely fitting through the door, with the usual: a six-pack of Polar beer, five of which he would end up drinking himself; his deck of cards; a pile of newspapers; and some books. They sat at the kitchen table.

"How's Emiliana?" Stanislavo asked. Always his first question.

"She's good," Alfredo said. She was lying low, he told Stanislavo, working an office job for a law firm run by a friend of the Movement. She accepted that she would have to stop nursing for a while. Alfredo cleared his throat. "But I'm here because of Nunzio and Molina," he said. "They moved them. They're in Cuartel San Carlos now."

Stanislavo had so often been kept in the dark since his exile to the Finlandia house — for his own good, Alfredo maintained — that he felt the relief of this fact being thrown at him, even without more context. It kept his anger at the paucity of information from boiling over. Cuartel San Carlos, where the most important captured guerrilla fighters ended up, was infamous. It was no Mi Encanto, a commandeered villa in the middle of nowhere. A compound located in the center of Caracas, Cuartel San Carlos was a fortress built in the 1700s that had survived Venezuelan independence, earthquakes, the advent of oil, and too many tyrannical caudillos to name.

"Are they doing okay?"

"They're alive, Stanis. It's something."

"We have to get them out," Stanislavo said. "At least let me go talk to Nunzio's parents. I swore to him that I would."

"Let's play some cards." Alfredo pulled the deck out.

Stanislavo reached across the table and covered the cards with his hand. "Stop," he said. "We have to do something. *I* have to do something. I can't just keep staying here."

"There's too much heat right now," Alfredo said. "Look, we've been talking about the cuartel. Maybe there's something that can be done."

"There's always a fucking *maybe* with you, Alfredo. What the hell is going on with the leadership?" Stanislavo flung the deck of cards off the table, scattering them on the ground.

Alfredo's expression shifted, revealing something Stanislavo hadn't expected: disappointment. It was his father's face in Alfredo's features.

"Always someone else's responsibility, eh, Stanis? Have you

thought that maybe you have a little something to do with all this shit we're going through?"

"You think every day I don't imagine what I could have done differently? If I hadn't brought Nunzio along, if I'd picked a different cove for the shipment, if I'd waited in Mi Encanto for all of us to escape together…It's all I do in this house." Stanislavo was standing now, his fists clenched at his sides.

"If you had killed those two soldiers," Alfredo said. "If you had used your gun, like you were trained to do."

Something stuck in Stanislavo's throat. He couldn't respond. He walked to the refrigerator and opened the door. He slammed it closed. He opened it again and slammed it again. He did it again and again and again. He didn't even realize he was screaming until he'd toppled the fridge to the ground.

Alfredo walked over with his hands up. He hugged Stanislavo, enveloped him completely. But something felt off about the embrace.

"Is Emiliana really doing all right?" Stanislavo asked.

"She's doing good, Stanis. I promise. She's good."

"Can I see her, please?"

"Not yet. It's for her own protection."

14

ANOTHER MONTH PASSED. One more month of Cuartel San Carlos for Nunzio and Molina. *Tell him I love him.* Nunzio's words about his father kept haunting Stanislavo. But the Movement didn't want to risk alerting the government spooks, who surely had their eyes on Nunzio's family. So Stanislavo made friends with spiders instead. Two months in the safe house and he'd gained back a lot of the weight he'd lost during his imprisonment. His eyes retained a spectral quality, though — whether a remnant of the prison or a result of this new Finlandia cage, he wasn't sure.

He stroked his full mustache, which had returned thick and orange, as a plan percolated. Inside the cabinet drawer he found a pair of beard scissors and chopped at the whiskers, then put on a baseball cap. He looked a different man. He felt a different man. And why couldn't a different man leave the Finlandia house? Wearing the darkest clothes he owned, he grabbed his flask and his revolver and stepped out into the cool night.

Avenida Finlandia was empty, as most of the city would be nearing midnight. He started walking toward Chacao, where Nunzio's father owned a small hardware store and the apartment above it. The beginning of his walk took him through the lush streets of Alta

Florida. Stanislavo stuck his hands inside the black jacket, which hung loose on him.

The houses were larger as he approached El Country Club neighborhood, old colonial-style homes with open front yards and driveways looping toward columned fronts where Fords and Lincolns, Rolls-Royces and Cadillacs were proudly displayed. Beautiful guava and mango trees provided fruit for gardeners to pick at the prime of ripeness so the children running through the villas' halls could have their fill. And the fruit they didn't eat the cooks would make into conservas and cakes, candies and juices, which the maids would serve to ministers and oil executives who came by for a cafecito.

Stanislavo walked by the country club golf course, taking in the invigorating smell of freshly cut grass that lingered in the air from the evening trim. He picked up his pace, heading downhill and approaching the end of the neighborhood, where the houses became more modest, though still beautiful, similar to the one he'd grown up in. Three bedrooms, two bathrooms, a large dining room and living room, and a kitchen tucked away in the back, next to a small room for the maid. The Venezuelan dream. People talked about the country as if it would always be a paradise with never-ending oil. Everyone was happy. Everyone had money.

Everyone. *What a word,* he thought. He knew better. And as he moved onto Avenida Principal El Pedregal he could prove that theory wrong. Behind some middle-class apartment buildings, you could see the slums.

While the beginning of his walk had been silent, here, by the barrio, the life of the city asserted itself. The backbeat of music escaped the riverbed like smoke from a campfire. For those who lived here the Venezuelan dream was still out of reach.

He had walked El Pedregal before, as a young member of the Partido Comunista de Venezuela, seven years ago, back in '58. It had been the freest he'd ever felt. Marcos Pérez Jiménez's regime had fallen, and people finally breathed and lived their politics in the open. Plazas and bars teemed with activists. The specter of the

Secret Police and their ghouls had vanished, no longer a weight on everyone's back. People didn't have to whisper their opinions in one another's ears anymore, fearful of who might be listening.

Seven years was nothing, yet '58 felt to Stanislavo like a long-lost era. Walking through the city at night—so far removed from the daily operations of the Movement and with overwhelming guilt for his friends' imprisonment—he feared they might never get it back. How could everyone not see? The question kept unraveling Stanislavo from the inside. Complacency had taken over after '58. With Pérez Jiménez and his dictatorship gone, with "democracy" established, with money in the right pockets, who cared if poverty ran wild as long as it was out of sight in riverbeds and on hilltops? Who cared if dissidents were still subject to the same torture as before, as long as it was kept out of the papers? Who cared if the United States stole the nation from under them, oil barrel by oil barrel?

Stanislavo cared. Nunzio and Molina cared. Emiliana cared. Tucán and Tomasa had cared. Their spirit kept him company as he approached Chacao, as he saw Nunzio's father's shop, as he noticed the black Chevrolet parked on the other side of the street and the two dark shapes filling its front seats. Crocodiles in a brown river. The sight of the car prickled the hair on Stanislavo's neck. He moved his hand to his upper lip, reaching for a mustache that was no longer there.

This was a mistake. What was he accomplishing here? Would his words for Nunzio's parents be a comfort, or was he just fulfilling a promise for the sake of his own selfish peace of mind? Maybe both things could be true at the same time. *If it were my son, I would want to know*, he decided as he walked past the car, keeping his stride confident.

Two men sat in the black Chevrolet Biscayne. The driver slept, his forehead against the side window. His trimmed black mustache and pressed white shirt would have given him away as Secret Police anywhere. The other man was awake but distracted, looking at a photograph. His posture—legs crossed at the ankles atop the dash—made Stanislavo recall the boredom of captivity.

The man turned and saw him. It wasn't a glance. Stanislavo's heart clawed its way up his throat. But he kept moving and did not turn back. As he walked, he waited for the car door to open—for a "Hey, you!" to cut the night like a dog's howl.

Stanislavo finished walking the block and crossed the street, turning left on Calle Páez. He rested against the façade of a Chinese restaurant—a red peeling wall with golden symbols—and breathed. He could return home with his tail between his legs. Or he could grow a spine and figure out a way to avoid the men. It's not like he hadn't been expecting them—so why did he feel so afraid now? The answer wasn't hard to find. He didn't want to go back to prison. It felt shameful to be so protective of his newfound freedom.

The Chacao neighborhood was grid-like, with a narrow alleyway running behind every row of buildings. Stanislavo went to the alley behind Nunzio's building, out of sight of the Chevrolet. In the alley, opposing balconies talked to each other in the language of drying clothes, potted herbs, and weathered chairs. He hoped for a back door, but Nunzio's building had none. The metal fire ladder was pulled up and out of reach. The balcony—three floors above the hardware store—was betrayed by the fraying Italian flag lying lifeless in the night. Opposite the balcony, just a few feet away on the other side of the alley, was another balcony, and on it a young man sat smoking.

"Psst," Stanislavo called, but the man seemed enthralled by the shape of the smoke he was blowing out. "Psst!" he repeated.

"¡Coño! You almost gave me a heart attack," the man said, startled—way too loud for Stanislavo's liking, the echo bouncing around the alley.

"Shhh," Stanislavo said, index finger to his lips. "Sorry, but can you be quiet?" He knew how crazy the request must seem, coming from a stranger skulking through an alley.

The man extinguished his cigarette in a coffee tin. He stood from his chair and turned to retreat to his apartment.

"Wait. Wait, please!" Stanislavo hissed. "I'm sorry but I need to ask you something. I'll make it worth your while."

"What is it?" The man leaned over the balcony.

"I know this is strange, but if you'll hear me out, it's very important that I get to the balcony across from yours, and I was hoping you might let me in your house so I can jump."

The man seemed to be figuring out if what he'd heard was right, or if he'd misunderstood the request. He looked at Nunzio's balcony, then down at Stanislavo, then back at the balcony. "You're saying you need to come into my house?"

"Yes."

"To jump onto the Guelfis' balcony?"

"Exactly," Stanislavo said. "You know them?"

"Yes, I know them. Do you?"

"I'm a family friend. I promise."

"Friends usually use the front door," the man said.

"You're right. That's impossible at this time, though. But I swear the Guelfis will be okay with it. I'll knock on their balcony door, and you can wait there to confirm with your own eyes that everything is okay."

"But why?" the man asked.

It was the most reasonable question imaginable, yet the answer was so complicated. Should he lie? Or perhaps tell some simplified version of the truth? He risked the man exposing him—but he didn't look the type, with his long black hair, his lazy posture against the railing.

"I'm a friend of their son, Nunzio," Stanislavo said and waited for a sign of recognition. The man's expression softened, and Stanislavo kept going. "I have information about Nunzio, but I can't be seen entering their building. I was hoping to find a back door, but alas"—he extended his arm to the doorless back wall of the Guelfis' building—"so that's why I'm here asking to jump from your balcony. I can give you some money if you want."

"No. No money," the man said. "Back door should be open. Apartment 3B."

15

THE MAN'S NAME was Rafael Arévalo, and his apartment eased Stanislavo's mind. A substantial collection of jazz and blues records littered the floor; piles of books (mostly math and engineering texts) were stacked throughout. The apartment smelled of cigarette smoke and fried onions in a way that felt familiar and comforting. A Universidad Central de Venezuela flag hung from the wall.

"So, how do you know Nunzio?" Rafael said.

Stanislavo felt him searching for confirmation of his intentions, some assurance that he really had Nunzio's best interests at heart. "You know he hasn't been around lately?" asked Stanislavo.

"I know Mrs. Guelfi cries on the balcony most days," Rafael said. "I know Nunzio is missing." He rested a hip against his ratty couch.

"I have a message from him for his parents," Stanislavo said. "But there's a black car parked in front of the building, and they'll arrest me and maybe the Guelfis too if I use the front door."

The honesty soothed Stanislavo. And it seemed to relieve Rafael as well. A silent understanding formed in the small confines of the Chacao flat.

"Well, go for it," Rafael said, extending his arm to the balcony. "The railing is not super sturdy, so be careful."

Stanislavo opened the sliding door and stepped onto the tiled floor of the small balcony. A lonely wooden chair and a coffee can filled with cigarette butts sat in one of the corners. He looked over the railing. The fall wouldn't kill him — if he landed on his feet — but it would break things: shinbones or ankles, femurs or hips. The Guelfis' balcony had seemed closer when he was judging it from below. What had seemed like merely a long step then was now a leap. On the ground, with enough space for a good lead-up run and without a balcony railing to clear, it would have been simple enough. But that wasn't this. He sensed his nerve failing him.

"Would you happen to have a ladder?" he asked. "Something I can use as a bridge?"

"I'm afraid not," Rafael said. He joined Stanislavo at the railing and peered down into the alley. Stanislavo could see Rafael's brain making the same calculations. "But if we leave the sliding door open you could start running from the living room, get some speed."

They went back inside, moved a stained coffee table and a lounge chair that stood in the way. But the railing was going to be too high for Stanislavo to jump over and still make the gap. He moved the chair on the balcony in front of the railing, so that it would serve as a middle step between the balcony tiles and the lip of the rail, if Rafael steadied it.

Stanislavo was poised against the far wall of the apartment now, ready to kick-start his momentum by pushing off with his hands and his right foot. He had a clear path to the balcony and the chair, which Rafael held rigid with both hands. Beyond the rusted metal railing and the six-foot gap of air and fear lay the Guelfis' balcony, with its white wooden railing, cherry tomato plants, and the Italian flag, now fluttering in the night breeze. The mental image of failure was impossible to shake: gravity pulling him down, his hands grasping at air followed by the cracking thump of his body against pavement, a leg bent at an impossible angle, teeth and blood littering the dirt-covered alley. Hospital, police, prison.

Stanislavo thrust himself off the wall and let his body take over.

Rafael closed his eyes and faced away, as if exculpating himself from whatever was about to happen. Stanislavo ran. He leaped.

A wind gust blowing through the alley hit his torso with unexpected force, and it seemed, for a second, capable of carrying him away. The Guelfis' balcony drew closer, but not at sufficient speed. Although the beginning of his jump had felt like a cheat to gravity, as his momentum carried him up, physics lassoed his hips and pulled him down, his legs bicycling in an involuntary search for purchase. Stanislavo reached for the Guelfis' balcony and his left hand found the top of the railing. His body slammed against the balcony and he managed to slide his right arm through one of the openings in the railing, which he hugged with all his strength as his legs churned against nothingness. He pulled with his left hand, the railing cutting his palm, then pushed against the tile of the balcony floor with his right hand and swung his leg up, hooking the railing with his foot like a contortionist. At last he was able to climb. He fell over the railing into the safety of the enclosed balcony and let his heart settle. Across the alley Rafael whooped and hollered.

"Shh," Stanislavo admonished him from the cold tile of the balcony. "You're going to wake the whole neighborhood up!"

"Mierda, sorry," Rafael whispered.

But no one stirred. Stanislavo caught his breath. The cloudy sky hid the constellations that would remind him of Mochima. Then he stood and knocked softly on the Guelfis' sliding-glass door. He stepped back and flattened his shirt and jacket, ran his fingers through his hair and straightened his back. Hopefully the sight of a man's shape on the balcony would not give Mr. Guelfi a heart attack. When there was no response, he knocked again. His stomach felt ill. A bulb inside the apartment flicked on, illuminating the living room. Stanislavo cleared his throat.

Antonio Guelfi appeared, wearing striped pajama pants and no shirt. He was thin and tall like Nunzio, with lupine features. His face and torso were all angles: sharp nose, sharp shoulders, sharp elbows. His chest was covered with hair, mostly gray but with some youth remaining still. Round spectacles sat on the long bridge of his nose. Clutching a bat, he moved to the front door of the apartment and looked through the fisheye.

Stanislavo knocked on the glass a third time and raised his hand in what he hoped would be taken as a friendly salute. Mr. Guelfi jumped and turned to the glass door, holding the bat with both hands, like a sword. He tilted his head and took two cautious steps toward the balcony. Still holding the bat and without taking his eyes from Stanislavo, Mr. Guelfi searched the wall. Light flooded the balcony.

Could Mr. Guelfi see him now? see his face? recognize his son's friend? Mr. Guelfi adjusted his spectacles. Then the lightning of recognition struck him. He dropped the bat on the ground and rushed to open the glass door.

"Mr. Guelfi, it's me, Stanislavo. Nunzio's friend. Do you remember?" They had met many times before, and the words sounded anemic coming out of his mouth.

Stanislavo would not have blamed Mr. Guelfi for any reaction: a punch to the face, a silent closing of the door, a scream that broke the night's peace. Instead, Mr. Guelfi came closer and hugged him. At first Stanislavo froze, his arms pinned by the embrace. But Mr. Guelfi's warmth—the love that radiated from the man, so real and honest—softened him. Something inside him shifted, like a rusted gear jolted into motion. His body moved to return Mr. Guelfi's hug, and in the embrace all of his terror, his guilt, his profound sadness poured out of him in sobs, in quakes that possessed his body. He clung to Mr. Guelfi like a scared child to a good father.

"I'm sorry. I'm so sorry," Stanislavo mumbled in between sobs, while they held each other on the balcony.

"Tutto sta bene, ragazzo. Shhhhhh," Mr. Guelfi soothed, stroking Stanislavo's back.

His friend's father was also crying now, and Stanislavo feared that he thought the worst. That Nunzio was dead. Stanislavo fought to regain his composure and retreated from the embrace. He held

Mr. Guelfi's bare shoulders with his hands and looked straight at him. The lenses of Mr. Guelfi's spectacles were thick, making his red and tear-filled eyes seem larger.

"Nunzio is alive," Stanislavo said.

Mr. Guelfi collapsed to his knees and wept, convulsing himself now.

Stanislavo sat next to him and tried to return the comfort. He explained how they'd been captured together at the coast and that Nunzio had been moved to the San Carlos fortress. "He wanted me to tell you that he loves you very much," Stanislavo said. He pulled Mr. Guelfi up from his knees and helped him inside the apartment. "I'll share everything I know," he said.

They sat on the soft sofa, under a painting of Bologna's Piazza Maggiore.

"Cosa succede, Toni?" Stanislavo heard a scared voice. Nunzio's mom, Martina.

"Niente, cara. Come here," he said, trying to hide his crying. "It's Nunzio's friend, Stanis."

Mrs. Guelfi rushed into the living room, her hair rolled and pinned.

"É vivo," her husband told her. "Nunzio is alive."

Mrs. Guelfi ran into Antonio's arms. They cried together in a relief so pure that it filled every inch of the small Chacao apartment. Stanislavo was afraid that any movement or sound would break this moment between the Guelfis. He wanted it to last. It hardened something inside him, though: He would do whatever was necessary to get their son back.

"Tell us everything," Mr. Guelfi said.

Stanislavo unburdened himself. He started at the beginning and went through their experiences at the guerrilla camp, their capture, Mi Encanto, his escape, the information he had from the Movement regarding Nunzio and Molina's transfer to Cuartel San Carlos. The Guelfis listened intently. Mr. Guelfi had his arm around his wife, whose hand gripped his bony knee. In the hardest parts of the story—Stanislavo's beating by Pig, the description of their holding room, the removal of Nunzio's tooth—Mrs. Guelfi buried her face in her husband's chest.

In their faces he saw his own parents, who had never received this kind of relief. They must have seen the headlines about his escape and yet had no idea where their son was. It wasn't lost on him that he could feel all of this grief for Nunzio's mother but not for his own. His constant dreaming of Ludmil had started to reveal his own resentment toward his parents, especially his mother. She had become a shadow after Ludmil died. Disappeared so utterly from his life that it felt to Stanislavo as if he had lost two people and not one. His dad had asked him to be patient, to understand. And he had forced himself to. He was a good boy. And in a way he owed this penance—he was the one who had been at the wheel, after all. But his mother had never come back to him. He wondered sometimes if part of his getting involved with the Movement was a way to get even.

"He wanted me to tell you that he loves you." Stanislavo finished. "That he wants you to be proud of him."

Stanislavo did not see pride, however. He merely saw two bereft parents holding each other's hand so tightly they might break bones. He had expected questions, but Mr. and Mrs. Guelfi sank quietly into the couch, like exhausted animals in quicksand. Maybe they were afraid of the answers? Maybe they were too uncomfortable to ask? Stanislavo wanted to confess: *It should have been all of us or none of us.* He wanted to ask for forgiveness. But the words *I'm sorry* were only that—words—and Stanislavo was already tired of them. They stuck in his throat as he tried to swallow all the pain and disappointment.

Finally, Mrs. Guelfi spoke. "Is all of it worth it?" Her voice was low, but not weak.

A few months earlier Stanislavo would have said yes. Now he wasn't so sure. The Movement was disorganized, scattered, indecisive. And for what? The people didn't care. After their resilience and fire had taken down the brutal Pérez Jiménez regime, a contentment settled in, as American money and the comfort it provided doused the flames, and people went home with the task half-accomplished.

"I don't know," Stanislavo admitted. "Maybe it will be someday. That's my wish."

"What can we do to bring him home?" Mrs. Guelfi asked.

The truth was they could do nothing. The government was winning, had perhaps already won. It was important to make an example out of the resistance and dissuade anyone else from rising. Cuartel San Carlos was doing what it was meant to do—serving as a boogeyman for revolutionaries. The Movement's leaders were struggling to deal with the stories that came from inside the prison's walls. Only a few inmates in the Movement had been released, each one limping, swollen, and bruised in places reached only by instruments.

He couldn't help it: hearing Mrs. Guelfi say *home* made Stanislavo think about his own mother again. To keep from her the knowledge that he was safe filled him with shame. But here was Mrs. Guelfi, a mother he could talk to. A mother he could hold and soothe and give love to.

He spoke as if to his own mother, holding her hand. "I'm sorry I did this to you. I'm sorry I didn't come sooner."

And then the spell broke and Mrs. Guelfi was only Mrs. Guelfi. Nunzio's mom.

"I'll bring him back," Stanislavo said. "I don't know how yet, but I promise you I'll get Nunzio back." It felt good to hand out hope. And it surprised him that, when the words came out, he believed them.

16

THE NEXT DAY Stanislavo called Alfredo. "We need to talk," he said. A couple of hours later, Alfredo was knocking on the front door of Casa Finlandia.

Alfredo grabbed the can opener and punctured a beer can with two holes, letting out a satisfying rush of air and foam. He handed the can to Stanislavo and opened another for himself. The kitchen table was covered in newspapers from the past week.

"You shaved," Alfredo said.

"They've said nothing about me since the escape," Stanislavo said.

"That doesn't mean they're not looking, you know that," Alfredo said and drank.

"They have bigger fish to fry. I'm finished hiding. I've already told Nunzio's parents about their son, about where he is."

"Why would you do that, damn it!" Alfredo slammed the can on the table. "It only makes things worse! What if they go to the cuartel? What if they try something stupid? They could get thrown in jail themselves!"

"They won't."

"How do you know that? You can't!" Every time he raised his

105

voice, Alfredo vibrated. His double chin, his massive arms, everything trembled.

"This is the problem with the Movement," Stanislavo said. "You think that by keeping people out you're protecting them. That by lying to them you're doing good. The Guelfis needed to know about their son. If you would just bring them in, level with them…I told them I would get him out. I'm going to get both of them out, Alfredo. And I'm going to do it with or without the Movement. I'd rather have your help, but I'm not going to keep waiting for you." Stanislavo had not taken the first sip of his beer but the cold can felt good in his hand, the weight of it.

Alfredo paced. "Listen to me. This is bigger than you and your ego, and yes, this is bigger than your two little buddies stuck in San Carlos." His voice gained speed and resonance, like a train leaving the station. "They knew what they were getting into. *You* fucking knew what you were getting into!"

Stanislavo stood, leaving the still-untasted beer can atop the newspaper, the condensation dripping and making the ink illegible. He walked to Alfredo and put a hand on his broad shoulder. Heat radiated from Alfredo's coiled body.

"I love you," Stanislavo said. "But Nunzio and Molina are my brothers. You don't know what we went through. You can't. You and the others in leadership are too far removed from what's going on."

Alfredo looked away and pushed Stanislavo's arm down. "You think it's easy? Organizing all this? Keeping the fight going?"

"Maybe we shouldn't be fighting," Stanislavo said.

"Where is this coming from? A year and a half ago you couldn't wait for me to put that gun in your hand and send you to the mountains."

"I've changed my mind. This isn't Cuba, and none of you are Fidel, thank God for that small mercy. There's a political will for change—I saw that myself in Mochima—but not for warfare. Let's get back to forming a party."

"You're dreaming," Alfredo said.

"We'll convince them. But not by shooting people in the jungle. They will beat us at that, they already have. How many do we have in the cuartel right now?"

Alfredo was worn down, but even hunched and defeated he painted an intimidating figure. "Damn it, Stanis. Come talk about it at the next meeting."

Finally, Stanislavo thought. Alfredo was offering something real. Here was an opportunity to plead his case in earnest. He'd never attended a leadership meeting before, but he knew he could convince them. He had to.

Alfredo sat at the kitchen table again. "Just so you know, what I originally came here to say was that we felt okay with you leaving the safe house if you kept your face clean-shaven and took it easy for a few more months. But you can never wait for good news, can you?"

Stanislavo knew that Alfredo was caught in a tough position, trying to keep the peace, trying to keep people in the Movement, all while a palpable air of desperation was spreading. In a couple of years, the Movement had gone from this urgent, necessary machine that people agreed with and defended — that people whispered about in barrio hangouts — to a nuisance in the mountains. It was more complicated than that, of course. And the goals of the Movement — the creation of strong labor unions, real representative government, the dismantling of the oligarchs' privilege — were all still good and true. But the Movement was being obtuse; the way to those goals was no longer uprise and armed rebellion. The people didn't want that, and what was a revolution without the people?

"Thank you, Alfredo," he said, closing the door to further argument.

17

THE MEETING was in Sabana Grande, at Aitor, a small Basque restaurant that belonged to Deunoro Fermín. Stanislavo didn't know Deunoro well, except that he could cook. There were stories about him being a sharpshooter during the civil war, but most Spaniards who had come to Venezuela escaping Franco had one story or another told about them, not many of them true.

Stanislavo walked to the side alley and opened the delivery door to Aitor. It was morning, before Deunoro had to open the restaurant to his lunch customers. Stanislavo passed the small walk-in fridge, where two young men were loading boxes of mollusks onto shelves, and reached the main dining room. A short bar, with space for about six people, was adorned with a mural depicting San Sebastián — the saint, not the city — beneath which were arranged a few bottles of booze. Beyond the bar lay the kitchen: four gas burners and a plancha. A couple of big pots bubbled on the burners, the smell of thick marisco broth making Stanislavo go weak, while heat rose off the empty plancha.

Only two people had arrived, Alfredo and a young man Stanislavo had never seen. He was olive-skinned, hairy, with large hands that seemed not to belong to the otherwise average body. The fingers were thick as carrots, with dark hair on the knuckles — strong hands. He looked Middle Eastern—Lebanese, Stanislavo guessed. There had been a steady influx of Lebanese migrants to Caracas, some of them associated with the Organization of Lebanese Socialists, which the Movement had quickly tapped for easy recruits. The man appeared to be in his early twenties, and Stanislavo was surprised to see him here, given that this was a meeting for the higher minds of the Movement, the first one that Stanislavo himself had been invited to. He'd been sure that he would know every single name in the room, and that he would be by far the youngest. Suddenly he no longer knew what he was in for.

Alfredo stood and opened his arms. Stanislavo had never been effusive with his affection, but Alfredo exuded a gravitational pull to which he had always succumbed. It was hard to see Alfredo now and not remember the day he'd first met him, at the oil workers' meeting. Stanislavo's initial reluctance to his embraces was always followed by a sinking into Alfredo's frame, the scent of his piney cologne. Alfredo never ended a hug, so Stanislavo would always push away after a few seconds of anxiety.

"Thanks for coming, brother," Alfredo said, and Stanislavo could see that he meant it. "Listen, don't go getting a big head, but you made some good points the other day. I want you to know that I really listened to you. This is Nassim, by the way. Nassim, this is Stanislavo."

Although Stanislavo's own hand was not small, shaking hands with Nassim felt like the first time your father showed you what a handshake was. Stanislavo immediately liked Nassim's seriousness, the sense of purpose in his posture.

"Comrade," Nassim said with a thick accent. "Un placer."

"A pleasure," Stanislavo agreed.

"Stanis, I think you'll like Nassim," said Alfredo. "He has some interesting thoughts about Cuartel San Carlos."

"Yeah? Tell me," Stanislavo said.

"Let's not get ahead of ourselves now," Alfredo said. "This is what we're here for. We'll get to it."

More men arrived. Handshakes, hugs, smiles, and hellos were handed out generously by everyone, especially Alfredo. Aside from Nassim, Stanislavo was acquainted with all of them, but none well enough to call them friends.

Deunoro manned the plancha. He placed coarse salt on its flat surface, then pressed the salt tight with a large spatula until it created a hot bed, upon which he laid spotted prawns the size of bananas, each one sizzling and emitting tiny pops and whistles.

"You guys start it off!" Deunoro called from the burners as he cracked what seemed to Stanislavo like all the eggs in the country over a huge frying pan.

The small talk died down, and Stanislavo squirmed in his wooden chair, scratching at the armrest with a finger, envying Nassim's stillness as he wondered whether the Movement would deny his request to free Nunzio and Molina. If so, would he just do it on his own?

Alfredo dispatched the welcomes and announcements while Deunoro and the two boys Stanislavo had seen earlier went to each chair with a steaming plate of golden scrambled eggs topped with two perfectly cooked prawns covered in flakes of salt from the plancha. As everyone started to tear the heads off the langoustines, Alfredo stood up and spoke.

"Everyone here knows Stanislavo Atanas. He's been enconchado for the past two months in the Finlandia house, after escaping the military hospital in Puerto La Cruz. We've decided that it's safe for him to resume activities and he's expressed some points to me that I think we need to seriously consider and address today. Here to my left, a less-familiar face: Nassim Merabi is a faithful recruit who moved here from Beirut a few years ago, through our partnership with the OLS, and he'll play a key role if we decide to move forward with the purpose of this meeting."

"As-salaam alaikum," Nassim said.

"We're here to discuss Cuartel San Carlos. Lots of good men

are suffering, some who might divulge important information. This isn't a new conversation. I know a few of you have strong reservations. And I know a few of you"—here he looked straight at Stanislavo—"have strong feelings about the urgency of taking action. A new revelation has come to light that might change the minds of some previously in opposition to taking this action."

Stanislavo didn't know what Alfredo was talking about.

He went on to recount the military perimeter around the garrison, which was well guarded, with checkpoints on all approaches, and nonmilitary vehicles, which were allowed only with permits, subject to searches. Visitors meanwhile were allowed on foot only and with previous authorization.

"We know all this, Alfredo," interrupted Alejandro Paredes, one of the older men.

Señor Paredes, the moral center of the Movement, always advocating for peace and compromise, was wise, and he looked it, with a receding hairline and long dangling earlobes. He would be central to any future discussion of ending the armed rebellion and transitioning to a fully political apparatus. He had also been averse to risk as far back as Stanislavo had known him, which in this case put him at odds with Stanislavo's objective.

"Which is why these discussions always come to a quick halt," Señor Paredes continued. "It does no good to get a few key prisoners out of San Carlos if they can't escape the perimeter. Though I'm thankful for Deunoro's breakfast, don't tell me we've come here just to arrive at the same point as before." Señor Paredes sucked the head of one of the prawns.

"This is why our friend Nassim is here," Alfredo said. "Nassim's uncle is the owner of Abastos Beirut."

The room went silent. To Stanislavo this meant nothing, but clearly to everyone else it was big news.

For the benefit of those who weren't aware, Alfredo explained that Abastos Beirut was located across the street from Cuartel San

Carlos, inside the perimeter. Grocery shipments to the store, which were permitted in large trucks twice a week, often went without inspection. This was now their way in and out of the perimeter.

"That's good," Señor Paredes said, "but how do we get the prisoners from the cuartel to the grocery store? It's not like they let them go for refreshments once a day."

Stanislavo knew the answer immediately, even before Alfredo spoke it.

"We do what people everywhere have been doing to escape prisons since time immemorial. We dig."

18

EMILIANA GATHERED HER COURAGE. The bougainvillea that grew wild on the Casa Finlandia fence reflected its deep pink onto her white linen dress, clean and smooth except at the hem, where delicate sewn-in yellow and red flowers danced. On her chest hung her black fist necklace, like a keyhole to her heart. She held her pregnant belly with one hand, while the other rested at her hip.

It had taken her weeks to realize Alfredo would never come through with his promise. "Once things calm down," he kept saying. And then he stopped taking her calls. But she was still in the Movement. She still heard things about tunnels, and about Cuartel San Carlos. Once she decided to go around Alfredo, it wasn't that hard to find Stanislavo. She had known Carlos Domínguez, the poet, a long time, and when she pleaded, he finally divulged the location.

She hesitated now, her fist raised, then brought it against the door in three hard knocks.

Stanislavo opened the door. He had meat on his bones again, no longer the specter she'd seen at the hospital two months ago. But there was also something beneath his visage, a darkness she hadn't observed in him before. The weight of his captured friends, perhaps more than that.

He stood in the doorway, stunned.

"It would be nice to sit," Emiliana said, after waiting for a greeting that didn't come.

Her voice seemed to shake him from his paralysis and he rushed her with an embrace. At first she didn't hug him back, not wanting to be soft, at least not until she said what she had come to say. But her heart took over. They pressed close, and the heat of the life between them pulsed. She hated that fear was present, too, blocking their joy of being together for the first time since that night in the hospital, but she could not contain it.

He held her at arm's length and looked down at her belly, then back up at her. "I'm sorry," he said. "I'm sorry I didn't get in touch. I've been stuck here. I — I didn't know."

"It's all right, Stanis. I've been trying to get hold of you, to tell you, but the Movement wouldn't allow it. I should have said something at the hospital, but—"

"I get it. Probably not the best time. How..." But his question faded away.

"I'm twenty-seven weeks," she said, watching him do the math. "A bit past six months," she clarified. "Look, I have to sit, I'm sorry." She walked to the table.

"Of course, of course." Stanislavo cleared the mess of newspapers and dirty mugs.

She sat and waited. Waited for him to be happy. And with every second that passed, her dread multiplied. *Ask me about the baby*, she willed. The quiet was a lash to her back.

"I like your face without the mustache," she said. And she hated herself for being the one to break the silence.

"I don't," he said and covered his mouth.

It was harsh — like a rejection. She thought he might apologize, and it would have gone a long way.

Instead, he only said, "How have you been?"

The question was so profoundly inadequate, so downright inane, that Emiliana pushed her chair back and stood. "I shouldn't have come."

"Wait. Wait."

Emiliana rested her belly on the table. Everything felt hot. But she waited as he'd asked. And for the first time since finding out she was pregnant, just after Stanislavo's capture, she realized how much she needed him. But that wasn't quite right. Even in her vulnerability she was strong. She didn't need him. No, it was that she wanted him. *We can do this. I'm here for you*, she wanted him to say. Or not even a sentiment so grand, something as simple as: *Do you think it's a boy or a girl?* or *Are you and the baby healthy?* or maybe *I'm sorry I haven't been there for you*. Anything. Anything that said he saw her. But no.

What he said was: "I'm getting them out, Emiliana." He stood and went to her.

She was in shock. What was he saying? Something inside her crumbled.

"The Movement is finally letting me *do* something. I'm going to dig a tunnel and get Nunzio and Molina out."

He reached for her hand, but his touch felt poisonous. She recoiled.

"I should have listened to her," Emiliana said.

"What?"

"Tomasa knew it."

"What are you talking about, Emiliana? I'm telling you!"

He actually smiled at her; he was delighted. She couldn't believe this was happening.

"We're going to get them out!" he continued. "And now that you're here, we can do it together."

"So you're going to go dig a tunnel for the Movement. And I'm going to, what?"

Stanislavo quieted, his excitement extinguished.

"Tomasa knew you wouldn't stick," Emiliana said. "She knew you would turn tail on me the moment it stopped being convenient."

"I don't know what you mean. I could have left the Movement at any time after what I went through. I'm still here!"

"Yeah, it's all about you. You're here for the Movement, you're here for your friends. Doesn't that feel good? To be so *there* for everyone. You're going to save them, right? Like you were going to save Mochima. Like you were going to save Venezuela?"

"That's not fair."

"Don't you see, Stanis? You always have an option. If you want to go be a revolutionary, you go. If you want to stop being one, you stop. If you get captured by the government, you can choose to escape and leave your friends behind. You don't get tortured, because why? Have you asked yourself that question? Why did Tucán suffer when they got him, and you didn't?"

"I—I don't—"

"This is your baby. But you still get to choose whether you want to be a father. You want fair? How's that fair?"

More silence.

"Say something!" she screamed.

"I love you."

It was the first time he had said it. He'd never said it in the jungle, or even that night in the hospital. But it wasn't enough now. And even though she felt it too, she wouldn't say it back.

"Choose now, Stanis. You can try to rescue your friends. Put the Movement first, even though they haven't done shit for the people you cared about so much in Mochima. Even though Alfredo didn't tell you I was pregnant, even though I've been asking him to. They've lied to you for the past two months."

"I'm not putting them first! I promised Molina and Nunzio. They're my brothers. I'm doing this for them, not for the Movement or Alfredo."

"And this is your child," she said, looking down at her belly. "Your daughter. I can't explain, but I know she's a girl. She has a name already."

"We can do both things! I swear I'll be a good partner to you, a good dad to our child. Please, just let me get them out first."

She was so tempted to say yes. To fall back into this dream of revolution, of changing the world. But the baby kicked at that moment, reminding her of all that was at stake. Would it always be like this? She and their daughter coming second to Molina, to Nunzio, to Alfredo, to the Movement, to whatever cause Stanislavo would adopt later? Tomasa, who'd been her sister before she was murdered, had warned her it would be this way. *He's here until he isn't.* It was hard not to see the wisdom, and it was impossible to argue with a ghost.

"I can't," she said. "I can't do it."

She didn't expect what happened next. Her anger evaporated. The heat that had been all-consuming suddenly vanished. Now only disappointment remained. She walked to the door.

"Emiliana, wait," he said.

And she did. Again. She hoped the next few words would be the sound of Stanislavo changing his mind.

"What's her name?" he asked.

The tenderness of his acceptance, without questioning, of her certainty that she was carrying a girl, almost unraveled her resolve. But instead she opened the door to leave, and said, "You'll never know."

19

STANISLAVO LEANED over the bathtub, his hair held in place by the tar-like substance now covering his head and his gloved hands. At first it had been just a tingle on his scalp, like a swallow of club soda, but now it was starting to burn. He washed his hands and the black swirled away. In the mirror—clean-shaven and with black hair and eyebrows—he looked the way he felt: mean and angry. His cheekbones could cut. The dark bags under his eyes were pronounced. His green eyes, which had always played third violin to his orange mustache and hair, were now like deep pools hiding predators. He wondered if Emiliana would recognize him if she saw him. She had surely had their baby by now. Was it a girl, as she'd been convinced it would be? But looking like this, he could lie even to himself; he didn't have a baby out there. He wasn't a father.

He had tried to find Emiliana a few days after she had left Casa Finlandia, forcing Alfredo to tell him where she was. But she was gone. The apartment they set her up in, empty. The argument with Alfredo had been brutal, and if it hadn't been for his comrades, rotting away in San Carlos, he would have ended it all with the Movement, there and then. Alfredo promised him that he would find her, but he didn't trust him to. Alfredo had fallen from the pedestal Stanislavo had put him on. Their relationship was fractured, never to be repaired. Now only Molina and Nunzio tied him to the Movement, to Alfredo. He would spring them, then figure out everything else.

Stanislavo went out to the wild backyard and sat on the rattan chair, then pulled out his flask and drank Cacique rum in sips. Five months now alone in this blasted Finlandia house, the last three spent on planning. Crickets and toads buzzed in a symphonic harmony so loud it took Stanislavo a minute to let it settle into the background of his thoughts. Emiliana's face came to him first. And then he imagined what their baby girl might look like. Regret barked at him. If she came back, he'd decided, he could do it, he could leave the Movement. He could even turn his back on Nunzio and Molina. But without her, the thought of his friends' rescue was the only thing that kept him sane. He focused on them, and he was able to push Emiliana out of his mind.

Stanislavo fell asleep that night to the lullaby of insects. He dreamed of Ludmil as a boy, running in the backyard of their home in Mene Grande. Stanislavo looked out at him from inside the house, through the window, feeling the summer heat on the pane. His brother ran shirtless, in circles, so fast that Stanislavo couldn't understand how he did not fall. Then Ludmil stopped, stared straight at him, and knelt. He stuck his hand in the dirt, as if he were submerging it in a pond, fished for something at the bottom, and pulled it out. His closed fist was covered in oil—black, viscous—oozing down. Once the oil reached his elbow Ludmil opened his fist and revealed a mango, small, yellow, somehow untainted by the petroleum. Without taking his eyes off Stanislavo, Ludmil bit into the mango, skin and all, and Stanislavo woke up.

He was brewing coffee when he heard the door. Three quick knocks, a three-second pause, followed by a last knock. He let Alfredo and Nassim in. Alfredo carried a briefcase, Nassim had a dry-cleaned suit slung over his shoulder. Stanislavo poured each of them a mug as they sat at the kitchen table.

Alfredo pulled something from his pocket. "Tu licencia," he said. Stanislavo thumbed through the small rectangular booklet, bound in leather. The first page had his new name, Saúl Guerrero, his newly acquired physical description, and a space for the photo they had not yet taken.

"We'll finish it once you've taken a shower and changed," Alfredo said, an acknowledgment of the black stains still on Stanislavo's face from the hair dye. "Your cover is as a merchant who's bought half of the Merabis' shop."

Stanislavo couldn't believe he was going through this again. They had come up with it together in the last two months and gone over it ad nauseam already. While Alfredo talked about his new persona, Nassim sat as still as he had that day in the Basque restaurant. Stanislavo wondered why Nassim and his uncle were risking so much. Everything rested on their loyalty, on their determination to see this plan through.

"We also got the engineering instructions from our expert in Cuba," Alfredo said. "Everything you need to dig that hole properly."

Stanislavo glanced at the pages. Everything felt so perfunctory at this point: the details, the cover, even this man he didn't really know, Nassim, sitting across from him. None of it would hold any meaning until his hands were moist and dark with dirt.

He was glad when Alfredo was done. Even his voice had become grating since his betrayal. Stanislavo simply said, "Got it." He stood and grabbed the suit from Nassim. As he walked to the bathroom he overheard Nassim whisper, "Is he all right?"

Stanislavo turned the water as hot as it would go. His skin turned red. His scalp fizzed and was singed. Still more black ran off his head and swirled into the drain. Then Emiliana's face came, as she had looked at him when he stood in the kitchen, mute. Gone past disappointment into disbelief.

Nassim drove the brown Chevy Two-Ten down into old Caracas. Its colonial homes and ample plazas usually felt safeguarded from time's passing. Now it looked like the city existed in two times at once. The National Pantheon—with its three colonial spires, the old royal palms that surrounded it, and the Venezuelan flag blowing in the wind—seemed, still, untouched by the years. But everywhere men in uniform held rifles, as in some Jules Verne story where future soldiers had come to conquer a land stuck in the past.

The view to his right made the hairs on Stanislavo's arm rise. It was a tall, bricked wall. Each brick was gray, spotted black with humidity and mold. The clay-tiled roof, typical of colonial construction, was still present, but turned ugly by the building's purpose. The wall went on until the end of the block, interrupted every few feet by a barred opening, long and narrow, and buttressed at the corner by an ancient guard tower.

"El cuartel," Stanislavo said.

"Yes, that's it," Nassim said.

This fortress couldn't have been more different from Mi Encanto, their prison in the jungle. Just the sight of the place let Stanislavo know that he could have never attempted this without the Movement. It was one thing seeing it on a map, that straight line from the walk-in cooler at the back of Abastos Beirut to the cuartel's holding pens. On paper the red pen might as well be tracing the distance of a goalkeeper's kick to the other end of a soccer field. But once Stanislavo arrived at the store and stood at its threshold looking across Calle Nueve de Febrero and onto the twenty-foot-high wall of Cuartel San Carlos, he imagined the two hundred feet that lay on the other side of the wall: guards' quarters, latrines, torture chamber, prisoner yard, kitchen, pens. Then he hated that line on the map because it had promised something straight and easy, a point A and a point B, a beginning and, more important, an end.

The line was a lie.

Stanislavo took in his surroundings. Three soldiers talked at the corner of Nueve de Febrero and Avenida Norte Cuatro. All the way down the block to the right he could see the outline of the military checkpoint they'd passed on their way in. To the left lay another checkpoint, where three soldiers were inspecting a truck with vegetables.

Nassim's hand on his shoulder startled him. "Let me show you around," he said. "Introduce you to my uncle."

Stanislavo surveyed the grocery store. It was larger than he'd imagined, six aisles leading back forty feet. The shelves were full of things piled atop other things with little regard to logic: Pencils and notebooks shared a bowed shelf with cast-iron pans; a case lined with canned pineapples and peaches gave way to girls' dresses. At the end of the aisles were groupings of fresh, clean produce—tomatoes, heads of purple cabbage, mountains of plantain and yuca root. Spices in glass containers washed the air with cardamom, coriander, and cinnamon. They walked by bags of grain and Stanislavo had an urge to plunge his hand into the white rice, anticipating its warm, milky fragrance rising as he prospected. He was about to do so when he noticed the man walking toward them.

"Nassim! As-salaam alaikum, habibi!" The man kissed Nassim once on each cheek.

Nassim's uncle, Kashir, was a large man—broad back, broad chest, broad face, all resting on big bones. His head was square, bulldog-ish, his ears each sprouting an alfalfa patch of gray hair large enough to touch his shoulders when shrugging. He had a pencil behind one ear, and he held a clipboard with Arabic script so intricate and beautiful Stanislavo could have framed it.

"Bienvenido a Abastos Beirut, Stanislavo," Kashir said in an accent that conjured olives and dates. "Or should I call you Saúl?"

Stanislavo extended his hand but Kashir pulled him close for an embrace—enveloped him, really, like Alfredo—and gave him two kisses.

"We open in twenty minutes," Kashir said, "and I've got inventory to finish, habibi." He raised the clipboard. "Nassim, I've got the left fridge ready for you."

"Thank you, Amo," Nassim said, and guided Stanislavo to the back of the store, behind a small deli counter, and through a door that led to a space out of sight from the main floor.

Within the room were two walk-in refrigerators, side by side.

Nassim used his whole strength to pull the heavy metal door on the left fridge open. It burped frosty air. The entire inside of the walk-in, ceiling and all, was covered in tiny ice crystals and was empty, having been cleared of whatever had been there before.

Stanislavo asked if they could turn it off.

"Afraid not," Nassim said. "Both units are controlled by the same breaker, and we need the other one on."

"We'll need jackets, then."

As he walked out of the freezer, Stanislavo noticed that the inside of the door had no handle. Once shut, it could open only from the outside.

20

NASSIM AND STANISLAVO sat for dinner in an office there in the back room, opposite the empty freezer. A pickax, a shovel, and a gasoline-powered circular saw leaned against the wall. The instructions from the Cuban engineer, only half of which Stanislavo understood, were littered around them. Nassim skimmed a page that Stanislavo had already annotated in pencil. The basics of the tunnel were thus: Tall and wide enough to accommodate one man on hands and knees, it would require simple weight-bearing structures every few meters, to prevent collapse (*Or for use as refuge in case of collapse,* the engineer had written in red pen, as if an afterthought); would need to be dug at least twenty feet deep, but preferably twenty-five (to avoid city pipes and suspicious noise); and, most dread-inducing of all, would take an estimated twelve months to complete, even with two men alternating two-hour shifts for eight hours each evening, after the shop closed for the day. And that was for two men with expertise. How much longer would it take for them? Stanislavo wondered.

"Nassim, what are you doing?" he asked.

In response, Nassim turned the page around and showed him the drawings of a bracing structure.

"No, I mean what are you doing helping me? Why are you doing this?" Stanislavo waved his hand in a circle as if to encompass everything around them: not only the grocery store but also the cuartel, Caracas, the country itself. He'd swallowed this question for weeks now, too afraid to ask Alfredo, or Nassim, as if manifesting the words would somehow change their minds and make them back out of the whole thing.

Nassim shifted his weight on the chair. He looked back at the page and then set it down. "Have you ever been to Beirut?" he asked.

Stanislavo shook his head.

"It's a beautiful city. Centered around the hill of Achrafieh. It looks out past Roman ruins and the spires of mosques into the blue of the Mediterranean. Some days the water is the exact same blue as the sky, and there are no clouds, and there's no horizon. It's just God hanging down a blue sheet." A wisp of a smile appeared on Nassim's face. "I would go to Achrafieh with my uncle Kashir and my dad—and Farez, the baker, would join us sometimes. They would all bring the same book and talk about it, or just devour their newspapers. I was a kid, five or six."

Nassim ripped a piece off the warm pita bread and used it to pinch a chunk of feta cheese. A drop of oil fell on the schematic and expanded. Stanislavo imitated him. The sharpness of the cheese gave way to the rich, fatty bitterness of the raw olive oil it had swum in for days. It wasn't hard to imagine a salty Mediterranean breeze hitting young Nassim's face as he listened to his dad and his uncle.

"And soon it wouldn't just be the four of us sharing eggplant and bread," Nassim continued. "Sayid Battah came with salted sardines; Sayid Hibri with his grape juice; and Sayid Sarraf, who rarely brought anything but was so funny no one cared. Year after year, I listened to the dreams of my father and his friends: liberty, socialism, a united Arab republic. A place where we could decide our own fate."

Nassim stopped talking and remained still.

"And then one day, when I was sixteen, my dad and I found Farez dead, shot three times in the back of his shop, flour and blood everywhere. And then Sayid Battah 'drowned.' And eventually they killed my father too."

Silence again, even heavier than before.

"The Americans had invaded us. That fucker Eisenhower was trying to keep President Chamoun in power—against the law. They started killing communists left and right. Uncle Kashir talked to my mother and brought me here." Nassim leaned back on his chair and opened his arms wide. "I take the bus to the ocean every other weekend and sit on the beach, and it feels a little like home."

"Why Venezuela?" Stanislavo asked.

"It was far enough. Kashir had a good friend who was here, who sold him Abastos Beirut. And I also think he wanted to be on the true frontier of ideology. Latin America is ready for a change, more than the Middle East." Nassim looked over the plans for the tunnel. "What we're doing here could make a difference, Stanis. Who knows how far it can spread, after?"

Stanislavo thought about how beautiful it was. Nassim trying to find justice for his father, but in a different country. Same as Deunoro, the Basque—Tyrant Franco on his mind any time he held a meeting at his restaurant in Sabana Grande; or Nunzio, fighting for a country that his Italian ancestors would have found hard to locate on a map. Had history been a bit different, Stanislavo would have been born in Europe and not here. Venezuela would be just another place his finger could land on if he spun a world globe. Yet here they all were, fighting to make it better.

Kashir opened the door from the grocery and peeked in. "Nassim, I need you in the front. I'm going to my study to do some work."

"On my way, Amo," said Nassim and stood.

Kashir walked past Stanislavo. "All good, friend?"

Stanislavo nodded.

Kashir walked to the office next to theirs and fiddled with a set of keys. When he stepped inside and closed the door, the lock clicked behind him, and the light shone around the edges of the doorframe.

* * *

"We're closed, Stanis," Nassim said.

"Finally," Stanislavo said, putting on his coat.

He felt like an overstuffed puppet as he carried the circular saw into the freezer. Nassim propped open the door and joined him. Once Stanislavo had flipped the gas switch and laid the machine on the icy floor, he braced a foot against it and pulled the cord. The blade spun to life, its sharp edges disappearing in the blur, and Stanislavo thought how funny it was that a saw was at its most dangerous when you couldn't see its teeth.

He lowered the whirling instrument slowly. The layer of ice gave way to the blade and then he hit the metal. The wail was shocking, in both loudness and pitch. The sparks caught on the ice, lit it red, and the ground around Stanislavo became amber. The metal box of the freezer shook around them as Stanislavo scored the first line, about four feet long. Drops of fire touched his face and body, but also something colder, gentler. When he stopped to reposition the saw for the second of four cuts, he saw what it was. The ice crystals that had once clung to the freezer walls were swirling around him. It was snowing inside Abastos Beirut.

Halfway through the second cut the sound of something broke through the high-pitched howling of blade against metal — like life interrupting dream. Stanislavo turned his head to the sight of Nassim waving his arms and Kashir poking his head into the freezer, his brow as knotted as an old tree. Stanislavo released the trigger and set the tool down.

"Tawaqquf! It's too loud!" Kashir said. "You're going to bring the whole cuartel regiment to investigate!"

"You can hear it out there?"

"You can hear it out in the street! You can't do it anymore. Not until we figure something out."

Stanislavo studied the door of the freezer, about a foot thick. "What if we close the door?" he said.

Kashir and Nassim looked at each other, then at the door.

"It opens only from the outside," Nassim said.

"Yeah, one of you would wait for me to knock on the door to let you know I'm ready to come out."

"We can try it," Kashir said. "Let me bring you some light."

He left, and Stanislavo could hear the door to his office opening and closing, and then Kashir returned with a flashlight and a soldering mask.

"And this," he said. "So you don't go blind on us."

Stanislavo grabbed it, wondering what a grocery store owner would need a soldering mask for. "Okay," he said, "let's do it."

"I'll be right on the other side of the door," Nassim said. "Amo, you go out in the store and let us know what you hear."

Kashir nodded and left.

Nassim stood beyond the freezer's threshold, his hand on the door handle. "You ready?"

Stanislavo pinned the flashlight between his knees, lowered the mask onto his face, and grabbed the saw. "Ready."

As Nassim pushed the door closed with both hands, the light from the back room became a slice, then a line, and then nothing. The flashlight beam bounced against the icy walls in a nightmarish tinge of yellow. Stanislavo pressed the saw's trigger and pushed the blade into the metal again. The scream, now in a confined metal coffin, was profane. After finishing the second cut, he stood up, flipped his mask off, and knocked on the inside of the freezer door. The lock disengaged, and the door cracked open.

"Did you hear it?" Stanislavo asked.

Before Nassim had a chance to respond, Kashir came into the back room from the store. "Did you start the saw yet?" he said.

"I could barely hear it from outside the door, Amo," said Nassim.

"You know what this means, right?" Stanislavo said.

The two men remained silent, waiting for him to answer his own question.

"We don't have to wait for the store to close anymore to get to work."

It felt strange to smile, he hadn't done it in such a long time, but this changed everything. It wouldn't take them a year to dig the tunnel, after all. With daytime hours suddenly possible, they could shave months off.

Stanislavo took Kashir by the shoulders and pulled him close. "We're going to do this, amigo!" he said. Then he pushed him back into the hallway, pushed Nassim back as well, and lowered the mask. "Now lock me in. I'm going to finish cutting this damned hole."

As snow danced all around him he remembered Molina and Tucán playing dominoes, unbeatable as a team, setting each other up perfectly, slamming tiles on the table as if they could read each other's minds. The way their laughter reverberated through camp infected everyone around them. He remembered Nunzio, stretching tall like a giraffe, picking cacao fruit from trees, to bring to Tomasa for her to process, Titi the dog at his heels. He was overjoyed the memories came to him so pure, untainted by thoughts of torture, pain, death. What a relief it was to discover that the beauty of those months in Mochima still existed within him.

He missed his friends so much.

Stanislavo made a promise to himself. He would not think of Emiliana and their child. That was done. The only way to do this and remain sane was to focus on the tunnel. The tunnel, and Molina and Nunzio, were all that mattered now.

21

How MANY BABIES had Emiliana helped to deliver as a nurse? She had held fat ones, with scratchy, guttural screams; little ones who whimpered at first before giving way to ambulance wails; and even dead ones, not strong enough to survive the journey from womb to world, and then it was the mother who cried out as she kissed her little one's head, sticky with fluid. But this was different, hearing her own baby cry. The sound was as terrifying as it was astonishing. The way it moved through her, lighting up everything inside.

María Tomasa Rodríguez had been born two weeks earlier, and Emiliana still felt completely lost. Give her a cut, a burn, a bullet wound, and she would stitch and salve and close it up. But this baby was all riddles for which she had no answers. Yet when little María slept, bundled against her chest, and her warmth flowed into Emiliana like a river into the ocean, the world around her fell away.

When she'd left Stanislavo at Casa Finlandia that day after their argument, she had cried all the way back to the apartment, the baby quiet inside her, not moving at all. Alfredo, angry, had called, having been informed of her visit by Carlos, the poet.

"Listen, Emiliana, I just want to make sure you stick to your word. We can't have you distracting Stanislavo right now. He's got a job to do."

"Is this the Movement talking?" she asked. "Or him?"

Alfredo was silent. Then he said, "We'll continue to take care of you. We're already setting aside money for you and the baby. But you have to promise to stay away from Stanis. For now. Maybe in the future things can—"

"You and Stanis want to buy me off?"

"Emiliana, it's not—"

She hung up, in shock. A part of her couldn't believe Stanislavo would have approved this request. But the picture of him and Alfredo together, figuring out how much money it would take to get rid of her and her baby, made her wretch. No matter what she tried, that thought played in her head like a horror movie on loop.

She called a cousin who lived in Catia, who knew nothing of revolution, of camps, of Spanish poets. The cousin agreed to take her in until she found her footing. Emiliana left the Movement's apartment just as she had found it—maybe even a little bit cleaner—except for a note on the table: *Fuck you, Alfredo. Tell Stanislavo that we have nothing for him. He made his choice.* She and the baby would be fine. Emiliana knew it. She was unafraid. She held her belly—the baby inside, the only thing she would accept from Stanis from this day forward—and left the apartment and the Movement.

After leaving, the rest of her pregnancy had made time strange. Emiliana had felt warped by it. Sometimes, when the nausea wouldn't subside, an hour felt like a day. She prayed for vomit to relieve her then, but it wouldn't come, so she just sat there with her pain. In other ways time went so quickly. It could seem like yesterday that Stanislavo had come to her hut in Mochima that night. Like yesterday that she'd helped him escape the hospital.

As the due date came closer, she fantasized about returning to Casa Finlandia with the baby in her arms. She was gathering her strength. If Stanislavo would only meet them, he was sure to see in her tiny face what Emiliana saw. And he would recognize that the world they had dreamed of in Mochima could still be made, if only on a smaller scale.

As a teenager, Emiliana had never been one to swoon over boys, to be struck dumb by infatuation. Boys had seemed to her a nuisance, and as she stepped into her power as a woman, the few men she was close to were more like tools. When her lust for them frayed, so did the relationship. But Stanislavo had set something alight in her that she hadn't known existed. His intellect, his courage, and most of all his sense of optimism for what the world could become had been a force magnetic. She had no point of reference for what she'd felt on those first days in the Mochima camp, watching him take Tucán under his wing and stoke a fire for knowledge in him, rather than a thirst for violence. Or the way he and Tomasa had dreamed out the future of San Ignacio as if it were a mecca and not merely a bunch of huts and ocumo plants. She was surprised when there was no resistance in her to his pull. She was strong enough to escape his orbit at any time, but she had not wanted to.

But now María was here. And when she slept in Emiliana's arms, even the thought of Stanislavo faded. Her exhales were these little sighs that were so sweet Emiliana didn't want to go to sleep herself, lest she miss them. In the face of a joy so pure, her passion for the Movement and for change became mist. She could almost persuade herself she didn't care that Tomasa and Tucán were dead. That their lives and those of the other dead farmers and fishermen and factory workers would be forgotten. That Méndez-Correa and his ilk were out there razing villages, killing the future one man or woman at a time. Emiliana had a daughter. Her face was golden milk; she had soft, brown hair, and pale brown eyes shot through with amber. All cheeks, and fat rolls, and ten toes and ten fingers.

Yet when María woke, and when she cried, the rest of Emiliana's fucked-up life arose from the dead. Her belief in the Movement had faded. Her life as a nurse would most likely be over, she could never use anyone she had worked with as a reference, her years of experience just words. And the risk of getting found out—of what would happen to María if they arrested Emiliana—sufficed to keep her docile, underground. She knew what the government did to the children of captured revolutionaries, if they were young enough and white enough. Had heard stories of babies taken away and given to rich families who couldn't conceive. Her comrades were in their graves. And Stanislavo had chosen his friends over his own daughter.

But right now, in her cousin's apartment in Catia, María slept peacefully beside Emiliana. She would never know about the Mochima camp. About the batata harvest in San Ignacio, about Tomasa and Tucán kissing by the mounds of sweet potatoes. She would never know about the araguaney tree where Emiliana had first dreamed her; her love for Stanislavo was new then, but so real.

This was it, she thought. The start of a new world. A new her.

22

IT HAD BEEN five months since Stanislavo cut that hole in the floor of the walk-in freezer. Five months of twelve-hour days split into shifts, except every other Sunday, when Nassim took the car to La Guaira and spent the day at the beach. Stanislavo still dug on those days, not wanting to stall their progress. And what progress it was: They were cutting the engineer's estimates by half. Maybe the engineer had miscalculated the distance, maybe it was the softness of the soil, maybe it was the four extra hours a day (one extra shift apiece) they were getting in, maybe he and Nassim were born for digging. Whatever the case, Stanislavo didn't want to jinx it. As long as they could figure out what to do about the dogs, they would reach the prisoner pens in less than a month.

Stanislavo had first heard the barking three days earlier, right on top of him as he lay on his side and used the hand-sized pickax on the soft loam. Hearing street sounds in the tunnel was not uncommon. Sound operated in strange ways underground, traveling and bouncing without rhyme or reason. Sometimes he picked up conversations as though they were happening at the next table in a restaurant: He'd heard guards share stories of a daughter's birthday or of Magallanes winning the baseball championship. Other times he would close his eyes and hold his breath, and the silence would be so complete that all he heard was his own body pumping blood through him. Those were the moments when it was impossible to keep Emiliana off his mind. Every few weeks, through gritted teeth, he would ask Alfredo about her, his only communication now with his old friend and mentor, since their fight after Emiliana's visit. The answer was always the same. She's gone. Nobody can find her. At times Stanislavo feared the worst: that Méndez-Correa had tracked her down, revenge for the embarrassment of his escape. But mostly he believed that she had disappeared because of him. Because he hadn't been the man she deserved. His whole life now seemed like penance for that sin. He often focused on Nunzio and Molina as a means of driving her out. The best way he'd found was to remember the details of his friends' faces. He always started with Nunzio's Roman nose, its harsh bridge, bent like an eagle's. By the time he was exploring Molina's round head, his arms would be sore and he'd have made great progress.

At first the barking was just one dog. Stanislavo would worm himself down into the tunnel, crawl the ten minutes it took to get to the end, and as soon as he started digging, he would hear it on top of him: *bark, bark, bark*. The tunnel had already crossed beneath Calle Nueve de Febrero entirely. They were now below the sidewalk next to the cuartel wall, where guards and soldiers walked at all times of day and night, patrolling the perimeter. Aboveground, he could see the spot from the store's front door—if he walked to it and stretched out his hand he would touch the stone of the fortress's wall.

Stanislavo had seen the first dog while Nassim was working. A yellow mutt with a black snout and a tail that curved upward would stand right in the middle of the sidewalk and bark straight into the ground as he lifted his front paws and stomped. Stanislavo alerted Nassim and they stopped for the day, hoping the dog would move along and they could continue the next morning without risk of alerting a guard. But the following day, a few minutes after Nassim began to dig, the yellow dog jogged to the same spot, this time with two other curs in tow. While the yellow dog barked and stomped, a little poodle mutt, its fur so matted that it formed hardened disks, scratched at the pavement, and a wolfish gray dog howled and spun in circles chasing its own mangy tail.

"Goddamned dogs," Stanislavo muttered under his breath.

And then a tall soldier walked to the dogs—curious about the commotion. The man approached cautiously, with both hands raised. He talked to the dogs. The yellow mutt froze in place and growled, while the little one yipped and hopped a few paces away. The mangy gray one just wagged its tail submissively. Stanislavo's head went cold, his hands tingly. What if they were too close to the surface? They had started to dig their way slightly upward, according to their instructions, but had they done it too fast? What if not only the dogs but also the guard could hear Nassim's digging?

He ran to the freezer and pulled three times on the rope with the red shoelace tied to it. It was one of the systems they had devised. Whoever was digging would always be connected to this rope by the waist. Three yanks meant to stop immediately and be quiet. Then Stanislavo ran back to the front window.

Having scattered the dogs, the soldier was there alone, standing right on top of Nassim. He tapped the ground with the butt of his rifle. Stanislavo pictured clods of dirt falling on Nassim's head. The soldier knelt on the pavement and placed a hand on it. He then raised an arm and started waving. Another soldier, squat and thick, joined him. The two of them conferred and the first man pointed at the dogs. Nassim could probably hear them. The second soldier seemed bored, his arms crossed, pulling on his cigarette. He knelt as well, with difficulty, said a few words to the taller soldier, then walked back to the corner he'd come from. The taller soldier rose and followed him, but before he disappeared from view he stopped and turned his head in the direction of the grocery store, then looked back at the spot where the dogs had been and scratched his head.

* * *

The room opposite the freezer, next to Kashir's office, had become their tunnel office. It was a combination workshop, library, mad-scientist laboratory, and dining room. There was even a cot in there. Stanislavo hadn't gone back to Casa Finlandia in weeks. On one table were Nassim's latest experiments with digging tools — handles of various lengths and metal ends of changing shape and sharpness depending on whether they were dislodging rocks, or shattering them, or scooping loam. Tacked to a corkboard were schematics with designs for lighting systems and the ropes and pulleys they used to remove the sugar and flour sacks filled with dirt, which Kashir then smuggled as "inventory" to his other stores. Books were stacked on the floor, engineering tomes that Nassim devoured, and the novels that became a refuge for Stanislavo in his hours of rest.

Nassim came into the office with dinner, a plate of rice and sliced almonds, each saffron-tinted grain a tiny gem. Steam rose from the plate in circling plumes that smelled of jasmine, cream, and clean earth. As always, he'd also brought pita bread. Stanislavo had developed the habit of eating like Nassim did, pinching his food with bread instead of using utensils.

"I heard their conversation," Nassim said. "The young one is suspicious. We're lucky the lieutenant brushed him off. And the dogs are not going away."

Stanislavo nodded as he chewed. Their attempt to capture the dogs had gone so poorly that now the dogs wouldn't come near the store. If Molina had been here, he would have already figured it out, he thought. And then, as if he had prayed to his friend for an answer, the idea came. But they would need Kashir's help.

Kashir lived a divided life. In the evening, once the store closed and he came to the back room, a shadow fell over him, a shadow that had become darker the longer they worked on the tunnel. Earlier on, he had often shared dinner with Nassim and Stanislavo, and at moments Stanislavo glimpsed the man Kashir must once have been, on that hilltop in Beirut, his hair black instead of white, his midsection gathered more closely to his frame, his eyes less glassy. But he hadn't joined them for dinner recently. Tonight, after closing, Kashir had done exactly the same as yesterday, and the day before that, and the day before that: He'd handed Nassim the store's inventory and list of orders, kissed him on the cheek, and locked himself in his study. It was the only room in Abastos Beirut that Stanislavo had never entered. Nassim called it his uncle's sanctuary, a room full of memories and sadness, and while there was no doubt some honesty in those words, something was being made in that room. Stanislavo could hear the sounds of industriousness.

That was Kashir's night self. But he spent his days running the store, always at the front chatting up the customers, most of whom were soldiers. He had a talent for it. He made everyone laugh.

"I think the colonel could help us with our dog problem," Stanislavo told Nassim and his uncle.

Kashir and Colonel Ruesta, an officer from the prison, had become close in the past months. Sometimes the colonel would park himself on the front porch for hours. He would grab beer after beer from the refrigerator behind the counter, like he owned the place, until it was time to stumble back to the cuartel.

Stanislavo wanted Kashir to convince Ruesta to kill the dogs. They could invent an attack by the dogs, convince the soldiers they were a safety hazard.

"What do you mean *an attack*?" Nassim asked.

"If I got bit by one of them," Stanislavo said, holding his forearm up, "Kashir could make the case to Ruesta."

"You're going to pretend to be bitten?" Kashir asked. "Like wrap something on your arm?"

"An actual bite would be better, something to really get Ruesta going."

"Those dogs run as soon as they smell you, Stanis," said Nassim. "How the hell are you gonna get them to bite—"

"There's a guard dog," Kashir interrupted. "In the neighborhood. He always rushes the fence when I walk by. I'm sure he'd bite."

"With one change," Nassim said. "I'm the one who gets bit."

Stanislavo protested but Nassim cut him off. "Ruesta barely knows you exist," he said. "You're back here all the time. Let's keep it that way. Besides, if the dog bites his friend's nephew, that's a better story. He's more likely to do something about it."

An hour before opening time, with light just starting to seep into the store through the barred windows, Kashir came in holding on to his nephew. Nassim had folded his left side onto itself. The image of Nunzio standing on that Mochima beach, bent and blindfolded, rushed back and twisted something inside Stanislavo. He could tell how bad Nassim's injury was from his blood-soaked sleeve, which Kashir gently rolled up. The skin was raw and jagged, ripped so close to the elbow there was a flash of bone.

"I think the damn dog broke a bone," Kashir said.

"He needs a doctor," Stanislavo said.

"Not until Ruesta sees it," Nassim said.

"Let's at least clean it up, then," Stanislavo said.

While Kashir left to fetch Ruesta from the cuartel, Stanislavo grabbed a bottle of peroxide and some cotton T-shirts from the grocery shelves, led Nassim to the bathroom, and sat him on the toilet. With one hand Stanislavo held Nassim's arm and with the other he began to pour the peroxide freely onto the wound. For a second it looked like water, dislodging debris and pieces of dry blood, but then it foamed, and with the bubbling Nassim screamed.

"Qaf! Qaf! Stop pouring!" he yelled with tears in his eyes.

The foam gave way to small spurts of blood. Stanislavo grabbed the T-shirts and as Nassim sobbed he wrapped two of them tightly around his friend's arm, each one immediately absorbing the blood. Nassim's face had taken on an unnatural greenish glaze, but he was breathing and calm.

While Nassim rested on the toilet, Stanislavo washed his face in front of the bathroom mirror. His visage had become chiseled, his back muscles encroaching on a wider neck. The beginning of brown-red roots sprouted from the place where he parted his hair to the side. He was growing tired of dyeing it again and again, especially now that he rarely left the store and saw no one except Kashir and Nassim. He couldn't wait to recognize himself again, to get back to the real Stanislavo, even if he didn't quite know who he would be after all of this. He knew he was through with the Movement, with anything to do with Alfredo. He'd have to leave the country for a while, after the tunnel was discovered, which meant getting farther away from Emiliana, from their baby. Bogotá? Mexico City? But he would rescue his brothers and have them with him. He'd repair things with his mom, tell her all he had wanted to say that day when he held the hand of Nunzio's mother in place of hers. Ludmil would have wanted that. Molina would know what to do about Emiliana, and once Stanislavo came back to Caracas, they'd find her. That would be enough. That would be more than he deserved.

"Nassim, I'm sorry," he said.

He couldn't look at his friend directly, so instead he looked at him in the mirror. Nassim had risen from the toilet and now leaned on the open doorframe, his back to Stanislavo.

"I'm sorry you and your uncle are in this shit with me. Sorry I got you into this mess, all for two boys you've never even met."

Nassim turned his head, in profile, the strong nose, the dark brow turned downward, almost angry. "It's not all about you, Stanis. It's certainly not all about your friends. Wake up." Nassim stumbled out of sight and went to the front of the store to talk to Kashir and Colonel Ruesta.

Stanislavo clutched the sides of the sink, staring at himself in the mirror again, falling into the infinite green well of his own eyes. "Wake up," he repeated.

And suddenly he remembered a moment early in the tunnel work, when he and Nassim were still digging down, trying to get deep enough so they could turn toward the fortress. They worked together then, not in shifts. It was still new enough for him to feel a little fear every time he stepped into that freezer. There in the confinement of the tunnel, caked in dirt and sweat, Stanislavo had finally asked about Nassim's father. To his surprise, Nassim's story cascaded forth without filters, without pretense, with an abandon that seemed to Stanislavo like the retelling of a dream.

"You remember sixteen, Stanis? When you think you're a man but you're still just a boy? I had just seen Farez's shot-up body, and I heard the stories of crabs crawling on Sayid Battah by the docks, but I still thought my dad was invincible."

Sixteen. The same age as when Ludmil died. Of course he remembered that age—he remembered everything of what it felt like. He and his brother had also been playing at being men then.

"My dad was God to me. Sacrilege for a Muslim to say that, to even think it, but he was." Nassim squeezed dirt through his fingers, like a kid with Play-Doh.

"It was Saturday. I know because I had a fútbol match every Saturday. And after every game we would drive out to the Rock of Raouché. I was getting sick of it, walking among the tourists to look at the same thing every week. But he loved it so much, and so did Mama."

Stanislavo pictured them walking. Remembered walking with his parents and Ludmil to go get shaved ice from the company store, in the oil fields.

"This Saturday, there was a rare summer storm, so no game. Abbi insisted on going to the rocks. 'You have to see the rocks in the rain, son. The storm clouds on the horizon. It's like out of a movie!' But I just wanted to take a Saturday off, read my books. Even my mom looked at him funny. So we stayed behind. I hate that I can't remember the exact words he said on his way out. I hate it so much. And then the whole house shook and my ears were ringing and I ran outside and the car was aflame, and my dad was nothing."

Stanislavo remembered his father at Ludmil's funeral. How he'd sat next to the coffin and people had come and talked to him, and touched him, but he'd sat still, as if he were part of the décor. But if his dad was a statue, then his mother was air. No one touched her.

No one could. Stanislavo had stood next to her, hoping she would reach out, touch him. But she never did.

"President Chamoun said on the radio that dissidents had nowhere to hide," Nassim continued. "Two days later, an American jeep rolled down my street, and I ran to my father's bedroom and grabbed his gun. My mother screamed at me, grabbed at me. Her voice was just noise. Sayid Sarraf and Uncle Kashir had to pin me to the ground, wrestle the gun from my hands. It's a small miracle I didn't shoot them. One week later I was on a boat out of Beirut with my uncle. Then on a plane here. I wanted to burn everything to the ground. I still do."

Stanislavo pried his left hand free from the sink now, then his right. His eyes—still fixed on their mirror image—were harder to peel away. In a flash it all came together. Nassim changing the subject every time Stanislavo mentioned Molina or Nunzio. Kashir and the sounds coming from his office. That clotted feeling at the back of his throat every time Alfredo called to check on their progress. Nassim and Kashir weren't interested in rescuing his friends. They wanted to do exactly what Nassim had told him: to burn everything to the ground.

Stanislavo couldn't catch his breath. He stumbled out of the bathroom and leaned on the freezer door, then shuffled toward Kashir's office and tried the doorknob. He expected it to be locked but it just clicked open. With the commotion of the dogs and Nassim's injury, Kashir had been careless. The room was full of innocent detritus: a couch; a side table with a photo of a younger Kashir and a man who looked just like Nassim; stacks of books; and, on the desk, a half-written letter in Kashir's beautiful Arabic penmanship, the inky script appearing to dance like dark flames. But what drew Stanislavo's eye were the electrical wires all over the desk, and, next to it, a pile of explosives large enough to blow half of Cuartel San Carlos up into the sky.

He ran to the courtyard behind the store and vacated his stomach in heaves. Once he finished, all that remained inside him was an anger hot enough to singe. He had laid himself down at the foot of the Movement. Had renounced his beloved. His offspring. Even when doubts hounded him, he had put forth his tongue to receive Alfredo's communion wafer. How stupid could one person be? How blind?

He wiped the vomit on his hands onto his trousers, already bloody from Nassim's injury. Then he went to the tunnel office and lay down on his cot. All he could do for now was think.

Later, when Kashir came in to update him—about how they'd worked it out for Ruesta to get rid of the dogs—Stanislavo faked a smile. The next day all that was left of those dogs was a patch of blood stains on the pavement.

With Nassim unable to dig while his arm healed, the next few days it was just Stanislavo in the dark heat, pretending to make progress. For half of the day he would dig enough to fill only a bag or two. "We've hit a patch of hard dirt," he lied. "It's like digging through concrete." The other half of the day he would lie on his back and think.

He had come to love Nassim—their bond was real—and perhaps he could confront him, persuade him to stick to the original plan. Or perhaps he could sabotage the bomb in some way. But without knowing what he was doing, he might blow up Abastos Beirut and half the city block. He could go above Alfredo's head to the leadership. There had to be at least a few of them who weren't happy with the plan, if they knew about it at all. Alejandro Paredes— maybe—had enough sway to change things. But getting to him at this point, sidestepping Alfredo, would be near impossible. Plus, they were almost under the fort now. There would be little to stop Nassim and Kashir from planting the bomb while he was away.

But what he could not abide was doing nothing. Letting the prison go up in a rain of rock and limbs. Yes, some in there deserved it. An extra week of digging might result in the perfect spot to maximize government casualties and spare the prisoners in the east side of the complex. Who knew, maybe some prisoners would escape in the chaos. Maybe that was part of Alfredo's plan as well. He could go talk to Alfredo, request that they add a second part to the plan, some sort of rescue party after the bomb goes off. But even then, would Nunzio and Molina's lives be worth all that carnage? Not only of the soldiers and officers, but of the other people who worked in the cuartel, of the people who happened to be walking in the street at the time of the explosion?

He thought about the day they'd been captured in the jungles of Mochima. How long ago that seemed now. If only he'd pulled the trigger — killed those two soldiers, protected his friends. What would it be like to have blood on his hands instead of a shovel? Maybe he would be with Emiliana now, with his baby.

But he hadn't killed the two boys. And he wouldn't let that bomb go off. Maybe that meant he would never see Nunzio and Molina again. Maybe it meant that he wasn't a true revolutionary. Maybe it meant that saying goodbye to Emiliana had been for nothing. And maybe, one day, he could be at peace with that.

Stanislavo went to the office and wrote a letter to his parents. The paper was stained brown by his dirty hands. While Nassim took inventory and Kashir worked the register, Stanislavo grabbed provisions — water, dried food — and carried them to the freezer, where he placed them neatly in a corner. It would be enough to last a couple of days. Then he cleaned himself, got dressed, and waited in the office until the store closed. He wrote another letter, to Emiliana — one for which he didn't know the address.

Kashir and Nassim came to the back room with a heavy pot, a lamb stew that had been bubbling for the better part of the afternoon. The scent of coriander, cinnamon, and cloves tested Stanislavo's resolve. How he had loved these meals with the Merabis, sharing their food, sharing hard work, day after day, for nearly six months now. Nassim looked so much better. Colonel Ruesta had sent a medic to patch him up, and the antibiotics and pain medication had transformed him in just a couple of days. The two men joined him in the tunnel office.

"You finished early today," Nassim said with a smile as Kashir rested the pot on the table.

Stanislavo feared they could hear his heartbeat, he was so nervous about what he was planning to do. "We ran into a problem in the tunnel," he said. "It's bad."

"What is it?" Kashir said.

"I think it's better I show you."

Stanislavo stood from the table and walked to the freezer. He opened the door. Nassim went in first, Kashir following close behind, while Stanislavo stayed by the door, his hand resting on the handle.

Nassim walked to the hole in the ground, knelt, and looked into it. "What is it, Stanis?" His voice echoed in the room.

Kashir's eyes cut to the supplies that Stanislavo had left in the corner. But by then it was too late—even for Stanislavo to say he was sorry. He shut the freezer door and locked them in.

23

STANISLAVO COULDN'T PEEL his hand off the handle. He could make out yells from the other side of the door, but just barely. When he reached Kashir's office, the door was locked this time, but there was no need for subtlety anymore. He forced the door open. The bomb contraption wasn't connected to the explosives yet; it was just a mass of wires and electronics, a sort of half-formed fetus. He took it to the bathroom, turned on the spigot, and dropped it into the tub to drown. The explosives he carried very carefully and placed them inside old tomato boxes, which he loaded into Kashir's truck, parked in the courtyard, hiding them behind boxes of dried goods and spices. He imagined the truck exploding as he drove away from Abastos Beirut, how the streets would smell of cinnamon and anise and black tea for days.

He took all the money from the register, and from the bags the Merabis kept in the back office for their weekly bank deposit. It would be enough to get him to Mexico City. To figure out what to do after that. The tunnel office was lifeless, except for the stew, still untouched, yellow fat forming a thin layer on its surface. He scrubbed his presence from Abastos Beirut. It took him hours, but by the end every document, schematic, and letter was in a barrel in the courtyard. He lit its contents on fire.

He started Kashir's truck, and smoke from the barrel drifted into the night sky like a weak prayer. After making the tight turn from the alleyway behind Abastos Beirut onto Calle Nueve de Febrero, he drove east, the cuartel wall on his left, tall and still impenetrable. He hit a small pothole and thought for sure he'd explode. But nothing happened.

He knew it in his bones when he rolled over the tunnel, could imagine the sound making its way to Nassim and Kashir, who were now probably in the dirt, escaping the cold of the freezer.

The first stop he made was at a bank of the Guaire River. He pulled up to a vacant lot, unloaded the explosives, and tossed them into the fast-flowing water. He abandoned the truck there and walked to Avenida Libertador. At this time only drunks and prostitutes walked the street. He hailed a taxi.

"You look tired, amigo," the slight cabbie said. He was sporting a starchy guayabera and a mustache that reminded Stanislavo of his own, months ago—long, wild, and covering most of his upper lip. "Long day?"

"Long year, jefe," Stanislavo replied. "To La Castellana. I'll let you know which streets to take. Gracias."

They wound through the lush streets, the trees beautiful in this part of the city, shading wide sidewalks and boulevards from the shine of the moon. Eventually they arrived at his parents' place, a house that betrayed his dad's social standing. A company man, he could even be called an oilman now that he'd been with Caribbean Petroleum all these years. Long gone were the days of treating workers. Now he tended to the wives and kids of high-placed executives, with whom he drank cognac after he finished. His mom meanwhile had quit medicine as quickly as she could, after Ludmil's death.

"¿Me espera aquí, compa?" he asked the driver, who turned the engine off.

At the end of the driveway Stanislavo opened the mailbox. He pictured his mother waking up in the morning, 5:00 a.m., like clockwork. Stepping into the shower as the coffee bubbled. Taking one cup over to his dad's nightstand and drinking her own in the kitchen, listening to the radio—maybe turning the volume up if the guacharacas were particularly loud. Later, she would walk outside and get the mail, walk back to the kitchen and stand by the refrigerator, sorting the mail into piles: one for bills, one for Dad, one for herself. She would stop at the stained envelope, recognize Stanislavo's horrible handwriting. Would she call Dad? Or would she read it alone? Probably the latter. He wished for her to read it alone first. It was more for her than for his father anyway. He had written to her everything that had happened: in Mochima, at Mi Encanto, Casa Finlandia, and Abastos Beirut. He told her he was sorry he'd hidden from her. That he wished she could talk to him, tell him how she felt about everything, about him, about Ludmil's death, about her past in Poland. And he admitted how alone he had felt all those years without her, after Ludmil. He also left specific instructions for what to do about the Merabis, trapped in that freezer. What to tell the police and the media if she didn't hear from him. The letter was heavy in his hand. He left it in the metal box and closed the lid.

"Listo, vámonos," Stanislavo said to the cab driver, and he gave him directions to Alfredo's house. It wasn't very far. Nothing was far in Caracas at this time of night, the scenery unfolding on the window like the old black-and-white movies that had played in the Caribbean Petroleum Club theater. Like *City Lights*, the last movie Ludmil had ever seen.

Stanislavo asked the cabbie to wait again. He gave him some bolívares and told him it would be ten minutes, no more than twenty, and then he'd need a ride to the airport. "I'll pay you double what you usually make," he said.

The cabbie nodded and turned up the radio.

Stanislavo walked up to the house and knocked on the front door.

Alfredo, half-asleep, fumbled with the strap of a bathrobe. One of his eyes squinted and his massive head cocked to the side. "Stanis, you almost gave me a heart attack." And he pulled him inside with his mallet of a hand. "I almost made Julia jump out the window with the kid. Military police have been everywhere recently."

Stanislavo nearly apologized.

"What happened?" Alfredo said. "Is everything okay?"

Words still wouldn't come, but Stanislavo looked at Alfredo in a way that burned.

"Okay, not here," Alfredo said. "Let's go to my office."

They walked through the dark house to a small room dominated by a big, messy desk and books everywhere.

"Sit, please." Alfredo pulled a bottle of Dewar's White Label and two glasses from a drawer and poured. "You know about the bomb," Alfredo said.

"Yes." The single word scratched his throat coming out.

"Tell me you didn't do anything stupid," Alfredo said, closing his eyes as a sigh escaped from deep within.

"Your tunnel. Your bomb. They will never happen."

"You mean *your* tunnel," Alfredo said. "Your tunnel, Stanis. You dug it, not me." He drank the scotch in one gulp and poured another.

"How could you do that?" Stanislavo said. "Not even to me, but to Nunzio and Molina, to the others we were getting out. They've given everything for you. For the Movement!"

"Oh, please." Alfredo was angry, annoyed. "This is why I didn't tell you anything. Maybe if you'd killed those two soldiers instead of letting them capture you. Maybe then Molina would have been here." He paused, softening a bit. His voice was quieter when he finished what he was trying to say. "And Nunzio would still be alive."

"What?"

"Nunzio died three months ago, Stanis."

Alfredo pulled a stack of photos from a drawer and thumbed through them until he stopped at one and tossed it across the desk. There he was, Nunzio, his nose broken at the bridge. Even under the bruises that covered his whole body Stanislavo could recognize his old friend.

"I've got more," Alfredo said. "You want to see? Here's Espino." He handed him the photo of a boy, maybe twenty, whom Stanislavo had never met. "Aquí está Lorena. Aquí está Emeterio." Alfredo pushed the stack and the other pictures fanned out on the desk, perhaps a few dozen, toward Stanislavo, most of them spilling to the floor. "Every week I get a couple. The government sends them to old safe houses, to old party addresses. I'm sure there are more we haven't recovered. Maybe there's one of Molina too. Who the fuck knows." Alfredo sucked in his teeth.

Stanislavo got to his knees and frantically searched the photos. "Is Emiliana here?" he asked, desperate. "Is she?"

"Calm down. Emiliana is alive, as far as we know." Alfredo pulled a note from his desk. "She left this at the apartment where we'd set her up, the day she left."

Stanislavo took the note. Stared at its hard words. "One more thing you didn't share with me. Fuck you," he told Alfredo. He grabbed Nunzio's photo and placed it together with Emiliana's note in his pocket. The photo was heavy, as heavy as a broken promise. To Nunzio. To his parents. "The government will know about the tunnel tomorrow at ten p.m. Enough time for you to go get Nassim and Kashir. They're fine, just trapped in the freezer. And don't bother trying to hold me here, I've left a letter with someone I trust, someone you won't be able to get to in time. They'll give the government the information regardless of what happens to me here." Stanislavo imagined his father making the call to a well-connected friend. Having to say that his son was involved.

He walked to the office door, wondering if Alfredo would reach into his drawer and pull something else out, something that could burn a hole into his back and make his world dark.

And with that he walked out of the house and out of the Movement.

When he got into the cab, he thought about asking the man to drive to his parents' again. He imagined walking into the house. Kissing his mom. She would help him track down Emiliana, so that he could send her the letter still in his pocket. If Emiliana's prediction came true, he would meet his daughter. Hold her tiny hand, promise that they would be a family and that he would never look back, not at Nunzio and Molina, not at the Movement. He would renounce the country even, if he had to.

"So, the airport now?" the cabbie said.

Stanislavo made a sound and nodded. The car came alive.

TWO

1998

24

Emiliana watched from the bed, gathering her strength, as little Eloy ran around, bumping into things.

"¡Se ve, se siente, Chávez presidente!" he shouted. He was a ball of energy in his green fatigues and red beret. "¡Abuela!" He ran to her bedside. "You have to get ready. I'm going to vote!"

"Oh yeah?" She brought herself to a sitting position, her back to the headboard. When she coughed, the sound was like glass scraping pavement.

Eloy jumped on the bed. "¡Se ve, se siente, Chávez presidente!" he repeated.

"Eloy!" María yelled from the kitchen. "Let your abuela rest!" She walked into the room with a glass of water and a fistful of pills, kaleidoscopic in their assortment and none of them a cure.

Emiliana had to fight her daughter all the time these days. So doting, so concerned! *Go DO something,* she said, often. *I can get my own damn pills, I can make my own damn food, I can go to Portu's store myself.* How had María come out so mousy? Genetics were a scam. But even though Emiliana wanted to, she didn't fight her today. She had to be on her best behavior. She couldn't give her daughter any excuse to keep her home, not from the election.

"Thank you, mi amor," she said.

Eloy's bare feet sank into the mattress. Emiliana still had the urge to take those toes and put them into her mouth like when he was a baby.

"And who are you going to vote for?" Emiliana asked.

"¡Mi comandante, Hugo Rafael Chávez Frías!" He clicked his heels and stood at attention, right on the bed, and the mattress springs screeched.

"¡Chávez, amigo!" María said and picked a piece of lint from Eloy's shoulder.

"¡El pueblo está contigo!" Eloy and Emiliana chanted back.

"Mami," María said, "the bus will be here in about an hour. Are you strong enough? I don't want you to go if you don't feel up to it."

Emiliana was about to snap at her daughter, she almost couldn't help it, but she swallowed her pills instead, each one scratching her raw esophagus—like swallowing burrs—and said she was fine. After three attempts at getting her right arm into her sleeve she had to call her daughter. She hated this. A year ago, she would have raced María up the hill and won. Now something as simple as getting dressed left her out of breath.

"Did you shrink this?" Emiliana said, though she knew the answer was no. How angry she was at her daughter for bearing witness to her weakness, how buried under layers of shame her love for her was.

"I don't think so," María responded, so even, so calm. After she guided her mother's arm into the cursed sleeve she moved in front of her and attempted to button the blouse.

"I got it," Emiliana barked and pushed her hands away.

"All right. Okay." María retreated.

"I'm sorry, mi vida," Emiliana said and grabbed María's hands— even that hurt. "I'm just so nervous."

"About what, Mami?"

"About losing."

"We're not going to lose, Mom. You've seen the polls; you've seen the people."

"They always find a way to fuck us," Emiliana said.

María couldn't argue with that.

25

THEY HEARD THE BUS before they saw it: whistles, chants, music, the celebratory blare of its horn. María couldn't tell who was more excited, Eloy or her mom. Eloy moved more, jumping and dancing. A few months ago, her mom would have done the same. But despite her frailty, the palpable aura emanating from her was something else. She radiated pride. María hadn't seen it in so long. The cancer had dampened her mom's fire, but it hadn't doused it. Could anything do that? For weeks María had been so worried about Election Day, what it could do to her mom, what it could take from her; she hadn't thought about what it could give.

The school bus, converted to a massive poll-ride, was covered in Chávez decals. There he was walking through the streets of Petare in his slacks and shirt; there he was, his face brimming with joy and hope, his handsome brown face looking straight at you; there he was holding hands with his beautiful blonde wife, Marisabel, the only thing about him that María's mom didn't like.

Heads poked out of the windows, a whistle in nearly every mouth. The voice of Alí Primera, the people's singer, rang from the speakers, which crackled and popped with the strain.

"I can do it," her mother snapped before María could even say anything, grabbing on to the railing and taking the step up into the bus.

María stood close behind, ready to catch her if she stumbled.

"Thank you, muchacho," her mother said to the driver, a man about María's age, handsome and joyful.

Eloy darted in between them and ran into the bus, dancing to the music. "C'mon!" he said.

Her mom leaned on every seatback, pulling her way to the back of the bus, where Eloy had found empty seats. The cacophony of joy overwhelmed María, even annoyed her. She had a long day ahead of her.

"Wipe that scowl off your face, mujer," her mom told her, melting into the seat. She breathed in and closed her eyes. "I'm going to be okay. This day is going to be great."

María wasn't sure whom she was trying to convince. But by the time the bus made it to their voting location, Escuela Normal Miguel Antonio Caro, even María had joined the party. Eloy stood between the rows of seats and danced to Salserín's "De sol a sol." He knew all the moves, just like Servando and Florentino, and when the chorus hit, he circled his hips and slowly spun in a circle. María, her mother, and the rest of the bus sang the song and admired little Eloy's moves, so similar to the boys from the band.

Her mother didn't have to lean on anything on her way off the bus. Whether adrenaline or providence, María wasn't sure, but she didn't question it. Her mom's back was straight, her eyes clear. Every step she took toward that voting booth seemed more of a cure than any of the things their harried doctor had prescribed during the past year.

"Next year you'll come here for school," her mom told Eloy, who held her hand.

The school was beautiful and run-down at the same time, like some decrepit Spanish villa, with palm trees flanking its entrance and the bust of the man after whom the school was named covered in pigeon droppings. Smiling soldiers near the entrance guided the throngs of voters to the school gymnasium. Large billboards with printed lists of ID numbers instructed people which voting table they had to line up behind.

Her mom skipped the tables and headed toward the senior and disabled line. "I think we're going to win," she said.

María looked around the school turned polling place. Line after line formed, behind a dozen tables. So many people, and they were all like them, María thought. And they were all happy.

"I've never seen it like this," her mom said.

María had been coming to vote with her mother since she was a child, the same age as Eloy or earlier, and it was true. Yes, there had always been hardcore political people in the barrio. And her mom had always been an organizer, dragging more than her fair share of voters to the polls to cast their votes for candidates who had no chance of winning. Some candidates had even moved people, shaken them into action. But none like Chávez. Escuela Normal Miguel Antonio Caro was electric.

26

SHE DIDN'T FEEL IT. For the first time since that morning in the shower, when Emiliana had run into the lump, the sense of dread trailing her like a dog had gone off to sniff something else for a change. She could breathe again. She didn't know how long it would last, but she made a promise to herself that she would not call it back. It would come whenever it damn well pleased, she knew that, but the later, the better. In the meantime, she would enjoy its absence.

Her daughter seemed different these days. Her worried expression had been so permanent lately that Emiliana had forgotten how María looked without that knot between her eyebrows. She had always been so beautiful, the way her freckles created a landscape on her face, a map that Emiliana could follow to her daughter's eyes, a hazel that on sunny days would reveal veins of gold, shimmering. María hated her freckles—her *marks*, she called them. Hated that she stood out wherever she went. Kids were cruel, always, and Emiliana had tried to get María to see that her uniqueness was something to be proud of.

One evening after work, when María was eleven, Emiliana had found her in the bathroom, her eyes red and swollen. María was hiding something behind her back, and her forehand was raw, as if she'd been dragged on pavement.

"What happened?" Emiliana had said and pulled her daughter's arm out from behind her back, inspecting her wound. It was glistening red. María held something inside her balled fist. "What do you have there?" Emiliana asked.

María clenched harder, her tears really coming down now.

"María, show me." Emiliana put her daughter's fist in her hand, the knuckles white and sharp. "Please, mi vida."

María's hand relaxed and revealed a crumpled piece of sandpaper, with traces of skin and blood stuck to its rough surface. "Jazmín gave it to me. Said it would help. I just wanted to take the freckles off."

"Oh, baby," Emiliana said, and brought her daughter against her chest, her heart breaking for her little girl. "You're perfect the way you are, mi amor. Don't let anyone ever tell you different." She held her by the shoulders and looked into her eyes. "You're a warrior, a descendant of a long line of warriors going back to the kings and queens of the Kalinago Sea."

"Who's my dad?" María asked, startling her.

It wasn't the first time the question had come up. María had been curious before, had mentioned the subject or poked around the edges of it. But this was the first time she had asked the question in a real, direct way, at an age when she could start to understand the answer. Emiliana had never been able to decide what kind of answer she owed her daughter. Anger swelled inside her then, at Stanislavo. For having left her — left them — the way he did.

Emiliana knew he had left the country after what happened with Cuartel San Carlos. The story of "the bomb that didn't go off" was in all the newspapers. And she also knew that in the '70s, when President Caldera wrapped up the pacification process and made the Communist Party legal again, he had returned. She saw his bylines in *El Nacional*, reporting on the resurgence of the political left and the urgent need for true social democracy. At first, she thought he would find them, and it hurt to admit that she had hoped he would. But he hadn't. Had he at least tried?

"Your dad left us. He's not important," she told María that day.

The truth was as hard and heavy as a cinder block. Emiliana hoped at the time that its delivery could be the start of a harder María, of a warrior María. Who else could have come from her and Stanislavo? But her daughter would never become that person, no matter how much Emiliana tried to mold her. In a way, that had been María's only form of rebellion. Today, she was a gentle, kind, quiet woman. Well, there were worse things to be in the world.

"I love you," she said to María now, and held her hand as they approached the seniors' voting queue.

"Aw," María said and gifted her a small smile. "I love you too, Mami."

"I love you too!" Eloy yelled, pulling Emiliana's hand, hurrying forward into the mass of people waiting to cast their vote.

And so they moved together in a chain. Eloy pulling his grandmother, his grandmother pulling her daughter. Emiliana was no longer disappointed that María wasn't more like her. But she was afraid. Afraid that María wouldn't be strong enough to do things on her own after she died.

The seniors' line was long, and, hardly unusual, was moving more slowly. But eventually they made it through. Emiliana handed the man at the table her cédula de identidad and signed the election book.

"Your right thumb right here," the man said and presented her with the ink sponge.

Emiliana pressed down, that satisfying wetness, and made her mark next to her name. The man gave her a ballot.

"Where does mine go?" Eloy asked.

The poll worker winked at Emiliana. "We have a special book for first-time voters," he said, and pulled a small notebook from a pack by his side. He opened it to a blank page. "Write your name right here."

Eloy wrote it carefully, tongue sticking out the side of his mouth.

"And now your thumb please, sir," the man said.

Eloy was ecstatic as he left his tiny imprint in the man's notebook. "I voted!" he yelled.

"No, honey," Emiliana said. "Not yet. We're going to do that next."

Eloy looked at his mom, confused.

"Go, Eloy. Go with your abuela. Go vote." María shoved him gently and started filling out her form.

Emiliana and Eloy walked hand in hand to the booth. She showed Eloy the ballot, which depicted all the political parties, thirty-six in total, and the faces of the candidates the party supported.

"Why are there so many Chávez?" Eloy said. "Which one do we vote for?"

Emiliana explained that each square represented a political party, and each party supported one candidate for president, so they were voting not just for president but also for a political party. "Mark right here, on this one," she said, pointing to the MVR party square. "Fill the circle nice and dark, okay?"

Eloy filled the bubble.

"Now we fold it like this," she said. "You want to put it in the box?"

"Yes!"

They exited the booth and walked to the ballot box. Emiliana picked Eloy up. She hadn't done it in months and was surprised—thankful—that she still could. Eloy slipped the folded ballot in the slot on his first try. When he looked at her, Emiliana thought she would be blinded, he lit up so bright.

"Now we dip our pinkies!" she said.

Eloy was confused again. "What?"

Emiliana pointed to the poll workers making sure everyone dipped their pinky fingers in ink. "It's the last step," she said, "so everyone knows you voted, and you can't go vote again somewhere else. It keeps everything fair."

Emiliana dipped her finger, and Eloy did the same. His fingernail turned a deep blue, almost black.

"You did it!" Emiliana said and embraced him.

His little legs hugged her torso, and he nuzzled his face in her neck. She inhaled, took him in. Hugged him so tight. She hoped this wouldn't be the last time she could hold him like this, but she didn't know, so she let the moment last as long as her arms would allow.

27

MARÍA PAID FOR A TAXI on their way back, even though the driver
was charging double the usual. The day had gone well. Better than
she could have hoped. But she still felt exhausted. All her worries
weighed her down, and she sank into the soft seat of the car.

Eloy showed the driver his stained pinky, telling him all about
how he had signed his name and put his thumb on the paper. "We're
going to win," he said.

"You think so?" The driver looked at him in the rearview. "From
your lips to God's ears, son."

Back home, María brought the small TV into the bedroom and
lay down with her mom, whose eyes were half-closed. María had
to be so still, as any movement on the bed caused her mom to let
out a pained groan. *Don't fuss over it*, María kept telling herself. She
wanted to respect her mom's wishes, to stop hovering, stop worry-
ing. Eloy came and went, asking "Did we win?" every now and then.
He would hop on the mattress and worm his way in between them,
watch the news for a few minutes, get bored, go play with his toys,
then come back.

"We won't know until late tonight," her mom told him.

"So then why are you watching the news?" Eloy said, annoyed.

"He has a point," María said, mussing his hair.

"Can we play cards?" he asked.

María looked at her mom, who smiled. "Sure, go get them," María said.

Eloy skipped off.

After they played cards, everyone slept but María. Her mom snored softly, interrupted by sudden bouts of coughing. Eloy was on the couch, already tucked in for the night. María watched the news, the volume on the TV all but muted. Then Chávez's face filled the screen, above the word *President* in big bold letters.

How much longer would she have her mom with her? Months? A year? But she was here now, sleeping next to her. About to be so happy. María savored the liminal moment.

"Wake up," she whispered in her mom's ear, caressing her shoulder. "We won."

They cried in bed together. They waited for President Hugo Chávez to arrive at his rally in Ateneo de Caracas. A Venezuelan flag the size of a small building covered the balcony where he would stand and accept his victory in front of thousands of supporters reveling together. The camera showed a man holding a papier-mâché bust of Simón Bolívar—it danced to the tune of salsa music. If fate had been less cruel, her mom would be there, too, instead of watching it all on such a small screen.

And then he was there. The crowd exploded. Fireworks blasted. Chávez started to sing the national anthem and everyone joined in. When Chávez spoke, he said something about the songs of Alí Primera, and the crowd shushed, ready to listen.

But at this crowning moment, instead of staring rapt at Chávez like everyone else, her mom turned to her. "I want to tell you about your dad," she said. "I'm sorry I've never told you enough about him, even those times when you were really curious. I want to tell you now."

María's chest tightened. She had given up on knowing anything about her father years ago. Her mom had always been so impenetrable. These few words instantly brought back the thirst to know where she'd come from. She felt like the little freckled girl who would look at herself in the mirror, trying to figure out the equation of her appearance, solving for her absent father.

Her mom looked for a book on the shelf and found it—the Andrés Eloy Blanco poetry collection that had seen so much use when María was little and now came out only every New Year's Eve, when her mom recited "Las uvas del tiempo" to her and Eloy. María had grown up on Blanco, could recite "Píntame angelitos negros" from memory, and in fact did so to little Eloy often. When they had been thinking about names for the baby growing in her belly and her mom had suggested the poet's name, it had felt immediately right.

Her mom pulled a photograph from the Blanco book now and handed it to her. It showed four men surrounded by lush jungle. They were dressed in ragged clothes. A man with the biggest nose she'd ever seen stood farthest to the left, with a rifle slung over his shoulder. Next to him was her father, all freckles and mustache. She didn't need her mom to point him out, though she did anyway.

The story was so big: rebel camps, a love affair, prison camps and escapes, bombs. And in the middle, her mom. She had shriveled almost down to the bones, but still she radiated pure power. And then there was Stanislavo Atanas. Her dad. Just like Eloy's dad, there until he wasn't. But María's wasn't an epic love story. Eloy's father hadn't promised her that they would build a whole new world together. He'd merely used her until he found out about the baby, then flown out of their lives forever. María entertained no delusions of a return.

But Stanislavo Atanas was so much larger than life as to be almost otherworldly. If not for her freckles, if not for her mother's nose on her face—how had she come from the two of them at all? Here were two giants, colossal in their courage and daring. How had she always been so meek? So afraid?

Seeing her mom next to her, sick, María hated her father. For leaving his daughter alone twice: first when she hadn't yet been born, and now when her mother was about to die.

Chávez had finished his speech. Talking heads on the TV analyzed the monumental moment the country was living. In their bedroom, their own private seismic event took place. María understood why her mom had done it. Why she had never tried to go back to him. María had no compassion for anyone who could turn his back so easily on the people who loved him. On his own child.

"I should have told you earlier," her mom said. "When Eloy's dad left. I should have told you then."

"Why didn't you?"

"I feel so weak whenever I think of your dad. Of that time. I'm ashamed. I wanted to be strong for you when Eloy's dad left, and I felt like if I opened myself to my pain, I would become a burden instead of the support you needed."

They embraced.

"But I'm glad I told you now, baby. All the strength that I have I'm giving to you now." Her mom held her by the shoulders, her grip as strong as María had ever felt it. "Soon you're going to have to do this alone. I'm so sorry about that. I'm sorry that I won't be here to help. But you are an amazing woman. Capable and strong. And the way you love others, my darling girl, it's the most beautiful thing in the world. You can do it. My strength, the strength of our people, is in you—always remember that."

María wanted to tell her mom that she would get better, that they could do this together for many more years. But the words didn't come out—only tears did.

THREE

2002

28

STANISLAVO HAD CELEBRATED his sixty-third birthday just a few months past, and his orange mustache was gray now near the corners of his lips. He ran his index finger and thumb over it, wiping the sweat away.

It was April 11, and the scene at Vargas Hospital was apocalyptic. The only thing close to it had been in '89, during the Caracazo, when the bodies of protesters and looters lay raw on the city's pavement. After years of leading guerrilleros in the jungle, a prison escape, and more than thirty years of journalistic beats that included Mexico City, Bogotá, and a return to Caracas, it was nearly impossible to surprise Stanislavo. Yet here he was, stroking his sweaty upper lip. César, his photographer, had his Nikon F4 camera glued to his right eye.

Vargas Hospital was one of the oldest hospitals in the city. Founded in 1888 and built as a replica of the famed Hôpital Lariboisière in Paris, it had been constructed with no expense spared. Glimpses of that grandeur remained. The Doric columns stood, majestic, the gasp-inducing beauty of their intricate Gothic patterns near the ceiling still visible through the mold. Meanwhile the hospital crumbled around them—every year of its hundred-plus had taken a toll. A chalkboard hanging on a chipped marble wall contained a list of items the hospital was out of: *Electrocardiogram paper,*

Bilumen and Trilumen catheters, Fuses for ventilators and BiPAP, Electrodes for external pacemakers.

How many stories had Stanislavo run on the state of public hospitals in the past year? Twelve? How many stories about Vargas specifically? At least three. Public hospitals depended on federal funds, and because Vargas was part of the Caracas municipality, and because Chávez hated Caracas Mayor Alfredo Peña, federal funds had trouble making it here. The hospital survived on some charity, but mostly on the ingenuity of its staff.

"How do you treat a gunshot wound with no gauze?" Stanislavo had asked a nurse once.

"Con la ropa," she replied, and took him to a room where two nurses were cutting old scrubs into rectangles. "But we're running out of that too."

There are not enough scrubs in the country to stop this bleeding, Stanislavo had written for the paper.

Stanislavo's pen hurried today, marking his notepad with undecipherable blue scribbles—a note-taking system, fast and efficient, that frustrated any editor Stanislavo had ever worked with. Now he was the editor, but forced out of the newsroom into his old role as a reporter by this historic moment, trying and failing to organize his reporters from his phone, with the cell towers unable to handle the overload of calls.

Stanislavo missed nothing. The nurse's black nametag, JOHANNA MEDINA, clattering to the floor after a gunshot patient grabbed hold of her scrubs. The rip in the back of Dr. Ogaya's coat that someone had taken the time to mend. The blood dripping from a young man's finger onto the tiled floor—the boy was eighteen at most, never to be nineteen. "This one's Code Black," a resident told the orderly, and that was enough for him to let the gurney roll until it stopped on its own, unattended, and run to a life he could actually save. Later, two other orderlies set that same boy's lifeless body quickly but gently on the ground, and took the gurney away—one final indignity that the boy would not remember.

The triage system, as far as Stanislavo could tell, was as follows: Code Greens could wait. The hospital was full of Greens, mostly people recovering from the effects of tear gas. The hospital was full of swollen and red faces, one set of bulging eyes after another leaking tears, noses pouring snot, everyone coughing to expel the gas they'd been forced to breathe for the past couple of hours. Fractured skulls and broken arms were likewise Greens; even some bullet wounds were being labeled as Greens. Basically, if you were conscious and not bleeding out, you were a Code Green. Code Yellows were injuries that could become critical if left unattended, and it was a shrinking group. At first many people had been designated as Yellows, but no longer. Yellows had quickly become Greens, so that staff could treat the torrent of Code Reds—critical injuries—stumbling through the doors. Reds were most bullet wounds, with the occasional case of an elderly person close to asphyxiation from tear gas. Reds could still be saved if they received immediate attention.

Though Vargas was low on funds and supplies, everyone here knew their way around a gunshot wound. The facility had become a war hospital more than anything else, treating roughly one hundred gunshot patients a week—triple that when a particularly violent turf war was going on in any of the surrounding slums, from Catia to Cotiza. Seventy-five percent of the broken bones treated at the hospital were due to bullets.

Code Blacks, like the dead boy on the ground, were not worth the precious supplies available. Most had been struck by high-caliber rounds, like the ones shot from the military's Belgian-made FAL rifles. Even Vargas Hospital could do nothing for those.

Stanislavo heard the screams and the cries and the mourning and the pleas of a city in the throes of death—or was it the throes of rebirth?—all in this lone hallway of this single hospital.

Stanislavo had left the newsroom a few hours earlier, at noon, as the two organizers of the march—the Labor Union president,

Carlos Ortega, and the Chamber of Commerce president, Pedro Carmona—led the protest to the presidential palace. Ortega and Carmona had sold it as a spontaneous call from the gathered masses, and that pretense played well on TV. This was, by far, the largest organized march Stanislavo had ever seen. Some were saying more than a million people were marching against Hugo Chávez. Protestors spread like a spilled bowl of soup into the east of the city. Helicopters filmed this massive, multicolored stain on Caracas from above, and it was impossible not to feel the energy.

Chávez had precipitated the reaction by ordering, and receiving, a brand-new constitution, tailor-made for him and his party, which now controlled both the legislative branch and the Supreme Court. When even they didn't move fast enough for him, he disregarded them and ruled by executive order. The previous year, Chávez had written forty-nine laws in two days, bypassing all legislative powers. Venezolana de Televisión, the state TV channel, was now a propaganda machine, and Chávez used it deftly. In a public broadcast, he had fired the board of directors of the country's public oil company, an act that had triggered a call for a general strike. And now this: close to one million people—blue-collar, white-collar, no-collar—screaming for Chávez to leave. Screaming to keep the march going for seven miles west to his front door: "MI-RA-FLORES! MI-RA-FLORES! MI-RA-FLORES!"

Stanislavo had been hearing from credible sources that Ortega and Carmona had in fact orchestrated the protest to a T. The march to Miraflores had been the plan all along. It looked like a coup; it smelled like a coup. And though it was perhaps a well-deserved one—maybe even one truly fueled by the people—it was hard for Stanislavo to get behind a coup of any stripe.

There in Vargas his attention turned to an old man who stormed through the hospital doors holding a bleeding boy. Beside him a woman with a motorcycle helmet too big for her head screamed for help. César's shutter whirred, and Stanislavo could already see the photo on the front page of his newspaper: the crying woman mid-scream, her helmet straps dangling, her shirt bloody; the dying child melting into the old man's arms; two cops flanking them, shotguns in hand. This was the price being paid by the people of Caracas.

Dr. Ogaya hurried down the hallway, away from the shot child.

Stanislavo ran after him and pulled on his coat. "Ogaya!" he called.

"What do you want, Stanislavo?"

"You have to look at the kid."

Dr. Ogaya, appearing both exasperated and exhausted, fought against Stanislavo toward the front door.

"The kid is dying, man!"

Dr. Ogaya finally budged, and Stanislavo led him to the man still carrying the child.

"I need a gurney *now!*" Dr. Ogaya yelled at no one. Stanislavo reopened his pad and made some more notes intelligible to none but himself.

29

MARÍA RODRÍGUEZ did her best to drown out the despair coming from the injured people surrounding her. She focused on the sound made by the wheels of the gurney as it rolled down the hallway. One of the wheels was stuck, *click-clacking* on the tile, and the doctor and nurse struggled to keep the gurney moving straight. The doctor had asked María to stay behind, but one look at her let everyone know there was no way that would happen, so the doctor didn't fight her. Don Jacinto and the police officers had remained in the lobby, Jacinto promising he would wait, and even amid all this horror, María's heart had swelled with gratitude for him.

"We'll take an X-ray," the doctor said.

He was about to turn right, onto a long hallway whose windows revealed an atrium open to the sky. The spot must have been beautiful when it was first built. Now the remnants of a fountain were adorned with ornate but useless fish-head spouts that probably hadn't spit water in decades.

But the nurse pushed the gurney in the opposite direction. "I'm sorry," she said, "we're out of X-ray plates."

"Goddamn it!" the doctor screamed. "Go make sure. I'll head straight to the OR."

Two men were following them, María noticed. One was pudgy,

his skin ebony, a shaved dome speckled with sweat. He wore a brown vest and had a camera stuck to his face. The nonstop fluttering of the shutter enveloped him. The other man was tall, freckled, and covered in a mixture of orange and white hair—sprouting from his head in every direction, springing in tufts from the top of his shirt, carpeting the backs of his hands, and forming a prodigious mustache beneath his nose. She would have guessed him to be in his sixties, but he moved like a wild blaze jumping from dry limb to dry limb.

"What's your name?" the blaze asked her, a notepad in his hands.

"María," she replied.

The man wrote it down. Was this part of the admission process? Hospital procedure?

"Can you tell me what happened, María? Were you at the march?"

Chaos swirled around them. The gurney dodged other patients, other nurses and doctors running past.

"My son," she said. "He was shot by a stray bullet. We were just home."

"Where do you live?" he asked.

"Cotiza. What is this for?" she said, wondering if this was how the hospital would come back for her later, telling her what she owed.

"Stanislavo Atanas, journalist," the man said, stashed his pen behind an ear, and reached out his hand.

The world stopped. She knew she was walking because the gurney with Eloy's body on it kept rolling, and she was keeping up with it, but she also didn't feel her body at all. Her legs were not moving, or rather she wasn't moving her legs—something else was. The man continued talking, asking questions, but she couldn't hear them. She couldn't hear the wheels of the gurney anymore, the sticky one that *click-clacked* every second or so. All of it was gone. His face wasn't like she'd imagined it to be, all those nights, hundreds of them, thousands. But he was also exactly as her mother had described him. A withered version of that blurry photo in the jungle. Wild eyebrows. Deep green eyes. Fire-colored hair. All those freckles decorating his neck and hairy arms. María looked at Eloy, so much darker than this man—the melanin had been bestowed by her son's beautiful father. But Eloy's freckles, and her own, had been gifted by someone else. Stanislavo Atanas. Her father. Who escorted her and her son now, into an operating room in Vargas Hospital.

The blue-tiled operating room was illuminated by a large light hanging from the ceiling. Beneath it lay an operating table, currently occupied by the unconscious body of a man spotted with purple welts. A doctor and a nurse worked all about him like two busy bees around a flower.

"We're going to have to share, Dra. Silva," said Eloy's doctor as he pushed the gurney beneath the center light, while still giving the other doctor and her nurse room to maneuver around the operating table. "Stanislavo, that's enough with the questions," he added. "Leave the notepad and go wash your hands."

"¿Qué?"

"I have no nurse, no orderly, and your buddy won't stop taking pictures. I need your help."

The man. Stanislavo. Her father. He went to the sink. How nervous he was. He tried to place his notepad in his back pocket, but it fell to the floor.

María stood a few steps back from the gurney. Though her feet were firmly planted, she felt herself float to the ceiling, up above them all, above the purple man on the operating table next to them, above his doctor and nurse, above her father washing his hands and the photographer working his camera, above the doctor whose nimble hands cut through Eloy's blood-soaked shirt with sharp scissors. Above Eloy who was so pale that he now looked like a white child, could have been La Señora's son he was so white. But no, it was her son. It was her beautiful brown boy. Because La Señora's sons had real walls to protect them from stray bullets.

30

STANISLAVO PULLED ON rubber gloves and applied pressure with cut pieces of green scrubs to the child's abdomen, right on top of a tiny hole. The child's stomach felt soft and squishy, as if Stanislavo were pressing down on a water balloon.

"You. Photographer," Dr. Ogaya called. "Take this key. Go down the hallway three doors to the office on the left. There's a locked cabinet. Bring all the gauze you can carry."

"Coño, Ogaya. You've been holding out on us," the other doctor said. "Were you not at the 'no hoarding medical supplies' meeting?"

"And at the 'conserve anesthesia' meeting too," Dr. Ogaya said. "Neither of us is doing that, I see. Fuck those meetings, Silva, and fuck this hospital."

Stanislavo took stock of the child's body. All his clothes were cut and hung off the sides of the gurney, pinned beneath him by his prepubescent frame, fragile as a twig. An intravenous line came out of his right arm, connected to a hanging bag of plasma.

"On the count of three we're going to roll him over toward me," Dr. Ogaya said. "Gently, okay? I'm going to inspect the exit wound. If there is one. *I hope there is one*," he added in a whisper. "One. Two. *Three.*" The doctor poured Betadine on the wound, then wiped it with gauze. "Okay, clean exit wound. Thank God. Roll him back. Easy, now."

Dr. Ogaya poured the rest of the bottle over the child's torso, wiping all the way from his chest to his pubis, the brown liquid spilling onto the ground, staining Stanislavo's pants and shoes. Dr. Ogaya's movements seemed violent to Stanislavo, and for the first time, from the corner of his eye, he noticed the boy's mother — *María,* she'd said her name was — holding her mouth shut. She was looking at her son, but Stanislavo could also feel her staring at him.

César stormed back in, carrying a mountain of gauze. Dr. Ogaya thanked him and told him to leave it on the table next to Stanislavo.

"I'm going to make an incision from his sternum all the way down to his pubis," the doctor told Stanislavo. "I need you to be ready to absorb all the blood you can, okay? See that tube that's making the suction sound? You're going to suck up the blood as I make the incision so I can see what I'm doing."

Dr. Ogaya inserted the scalpel into Eloy's skin and moved down through the child's torso in the straightest line Stanislavo had ever seen. He expected blood to explode out like a volcano, but it didn't — it just pooled, like a bowl of milk being slowly replenished. He sucked the area clean of blood.

"Okay, good job," said Dr. Ogaya. "Now I'm going to pry his skin open, and you use the suction tube as you pack gauze inside his cavity. Gently, okay? Try to keep it close to the skin, and remove the gauze once it's absorbed all the blood it can. Ready?"

Dr. Ogaya opened the child's belly with a metal contraption. It all reminded Stanislavo of dissecting frogs in biology class, but here everything moved, like a pot of dark, meaty soup that bubbled with each beat of the child's heart. Stanislavo inserted the gauze — more than he thought would fit in so slender a frame — then removed the soaked, crimson fabric from the cavity, throwing the mess into the bin. With most of the liquid gone, the inner workings of the child, still moving, were revealed. The boy's organs made Stanislavo consider his own. This mess of moving meat was within him too.

"He's gone," he heard someone say. "Time of death, 3:23 p.m."

But the voice was not Dr. Ogaya's; it belonged to the woman doctor, whom Stanislavo had forgotten even existed.

"David, what can I do?" she asked.

"Gracias a Dios, Dra. Silva. I believe the bullet missed major blood vessels and organs."

The nurse, an older woman with kind eyes, guided Stanislavo away, his hands finally letting go of the boy's belly. "We can take it from here," she said as the doctors conferred on what to do next—on how to salvage the humanity dripping from the gurney onto the floor.

Stanislavo sat on the ground next to the child's mother, who was hugging her knees.

"What's your boy's name?" he said.

She looked deep into him. As if she were searching for something. But she heard him this time. "Andrés Eloy," she said.

"Like the poet?" Stanislavo asked.

"Yeah," she said. "Like the poet."

31

THE NURSE USHERED María out of the OR. With Eloy sewn up and alive, she found herself too tired to protest. So she sat with Stanislavo on a bench in the foul-smelling hallway.

"They call me Stanis," he told her.

Her father presented his large hand, but she couldn't lift her arm to meet it. It hung there for — what? — moments? hours? days? María couldn't tell. It was still covered with the white medical glove. Or, rather, María knew it was white, but its rubbery surface was streaked with red marks. She stared at it.

"I'm so sorry," her father said, and removed both gloves and let them drop. He extended his arm again, and the copious hair on the back of his hand stood up like spines on a cactus, still electrified by the plastic. "Stanis," he repeated.

María finally took his hand. She wondered why he didn't recognize her right away. Couldn't he see it? She looked like her mother. Paler skin, sure, but her same dark eyes, her same nose. The only thing she had inherited from this man, it seemed to her, was the constellations on her skin. She wanted to scream at him.

"María," she said.

"María, your son is going to be okay," he said.

He put a hand on her shoulder, and her whole body tensed. She recoiled.

"Sorry," he said and pulled his hand back.

Her world was a haze. She questioned if this man next to her really existed or was some apparition conjured by her mind. She half-wondered if her mother would appear now, raised from the dead, and sit on her other side to complete this family portrait. Questioning her sanity, she cried into her hands.

"What does Eloy like to do, María?"

"He's a good boy, such a good boy," she said in between sobs.

"I'm sure he is. But what does he like to do? Does he play baseball?"

"Yes."

"What's his favorite team?" Stanislavo asked.

"The Caracas Lions."

Stanislavo grabbed her shoulders and gave her a serious look. "That won't do at all, María. If it's the last thing I do, that kid is going to become a Sharks fan."

His mustache pulled up and revealed a smile. There, she saw her face in him, the same glint in the eye, the same tilt in the head, the way his eyes became smaller with a grin. They smiled the same.

Then Stanislavo's phone rang. His smile died away, the phone bringing him out of the fragile bubble they had managed to build. "I'm sorry," he said, "I have to take this." He stood up.

María wiped the tears from her face and stood as well. "Wait," she said.

He did, standing above her. But she couldn't say a thing. Stanislavo put the phone to his ear and walked away. She made as if to follow, but she hadn't taken two steps when the nurse grabbed hold of her arm. Eloy was still in critical condition, the nurse told her, but he had pulled through the hardest part.

María's knees buckled and she fell to the floor. She watched

Stanislavo as he disappeared into the busy waiting room and was absorbed into its madness.

"He's going to make it," the nurse said. "Did you hear me, María?"

She had. She looked at the nurse then. "Thank you," she repeated, again and again, from the floor.

32

"ARE YOU WATCHING THIS?" Sandra Peterson, one of Stanislavo's reporters, yelled from the other end of the line. The daughter of a Swedish mathematics professor and a Venezuelan sifrina from El Hatillo, she was as tenacious a journalist as Stanislavo had ever met. "Where the fuck are you? Still in Vargas?"

"Yeah, still here. This is the first call I've been able to get in an hour."

Sandra was calling from the newspaper, where she and others had returned before the Guard could confiscate their equipment and film. They had some damning stuff, she said: the military handing out guns to Chavista civilians on one side, the Metropolitan Police shooting live rounds into Chavista crowds on the other.

Her voice cracked a bit and she cleared her throat. "But are you in front of a TV?"

"Whatever you do, Sandra, don't hang up. I'm getting to one."

A group of people had gathered around the small color TV in the waiting room—a couple of nurses; an orderly; two residents who looked barely out of high school; and a handful of civilians of both sides, some wearing the garb of opposition marchers (Primero Justicia shirts, white T-shirts emblazoned with FUERA CHÁVEZ) and others in the typical red-and-green motif of Chavista supporters. César, whom Stanislavo had lost track of after Eloy's operation, was also there, shooting away at the scene. Everyone was watching Chávez speak from his presidential office in Miraflores.

Chávez spoke a lot, all the time, for hours on end. And he was good at it. It was the most powerful weapon in his arsenal. But now he was anxious and confused. He spoke of a small march, of small outbursts of violence that were either completely controlled or soon to be extinguished. Utterly out of touch with reality. As if people hadn't seen the footage for the past several hours.

Per law, all TV stations had to transmit official presidential addresses in full. Every week Chávez would eat up hours of regular programming—and therefore advertising revenue—in his addresses. He would use this unlimited time to campaign for issues he cared about, berate his opponents, gain unfair advantage in local and special elections. But today's speech was even worse. He was hiding the atrocities being committed by his armed forces against its own people by commandeering the airwaves so these acts couldn't be seen. But then something happened that Stanislavo hadn't expected. As Chávez talked about Jesus Christ on the cross, Channel 4, Venevisión, split the screen. On one side, Chávez minimized what was happening. On the other, live footage showed the full-scale war being waged just beyond Vargas Hospital, in Avenida Baralt, mere blocks from the very palace where Chávez was speaking. The media was exposing Chávez as never before: an emperor with no clothes.

The few Chavistas in the crowd looked away from the TV screen, hard for even the most hardened loyalist not to shudder at the contrast. Some of the opposition marchers screamed curses: "Liar! ¡Hijo de puta! ¡Maldito!" Then one of them yelled "Assassin!" and then dozens of people in the waiting room—those whose lungs could function despite the effects of the tear gas—started chanting "¡A-SE-SI-NO, A-SE-SI-NO, A-SE-SI-NO!"

"Sandra, you still there?" Stanislavo said into his phone.

"Aquí estoy, jefe."

"Start compiling a list of reporters and their whereabouts for me. I want you in the shop organizing all of us. It's going to be a long night."

33

María had been with Eloy for four hours, holding his hand, stroking his hair. It was nighttime now and he was still unconscious. He had his own bed in a shared room with other recovering patients, five of them total. This place of safety, away from the chaos in other parts of the hospital, was godsent. She had updated Jacinto in the waiting room, and he had returned home, promising he would be back with Magali the next day.

A nurse kept coming by to check on them. She reassured María that even amid all this awfulness, miracles would still be found. The nurse brought María black coffee and a little bag of sugar. The first sip transported her back in time, pregnant with Eloy, her mom at the stove brewing a pot, her hair straight and long, with still some strands of black in it. María had moved in with her when the symptoms started: the never-ending nausea, the lower back pain. Eloy had been a huge baby, and a kicker. It had been her mom, really, who'd raised Eloy as much as she had. And then her mom had gotten sick, and it had been María's turn to hold her mother's head as she vomited.

The cancer had moved so fast. "You're going to need so much strength," her mom said. "It's going to be just you and him." María didn't want to believe that her mother could leave them so suddenly, having been so strong—just a few months before her illness, her mom could beat her in races up the steep stairway to their place. The saddest part of these days was that Eloy no longer talked about his abuela and seemed mostly to have forgotten her, except when María prodded his memory. He was starting to ask about his dad, though. A ghost María didn't know at all, except that he could dance and he could vanish.

"Go for a little walk, María," the nurse said. "Eloy is going to be out for a while longer. Go stretch your legs."

María held the azabache fist hanging from her neck and stood up. When she walked out of the room, the nurses' station had a TV playing to the remnants of the chaos the lobby had lived through. The screen was blue, with a scrolling marquee that read THIS STATION IS OFF THE AIR. One man in a Chávez T-shirt reached over the counter and changed the channel to Venezolana de Televisión. The government station showed yellow ducklings following their mother into a pond.

"What is this?" the man said and kept clicking, but every station was blue except for the nature documentary.

María couldn't go outside, where gunshots were still popping off with regularity. And walking through the hospital was a crucible in itself, with every surface occupied by bodies, most of them in physical pain, some past it already. She went by a man on a bench next to a potted palm tree, his face half-bandaged. The man's torn yellow shirt revealed the ample gut of beers on porches, of beers at baseball games screaming from the cheap seats, of beers after church wearing Sunday bests.

He reached out his hand and grabbed her wrist. "Agua, por favor," he said. His grip was tight, of someone holding on to something important.

"Of course, mi amor," María said, kneeling so they could see each other eye to eye. "I'll be back soon."

She made a couple of turns to where she remembered a water cooler. The trash bin meant for cone-shaped paper cups was stuffed to the brim with bloody gauze. She pulled a cup from the metal cylinder and tried to dispense water, but the plastic container was empty. She lifted it out and peered into the cooler as if willing water to spring up like an aquifer. Just then a nurse pushed a cart full of machines down the hall.

María called, "Hey, there's no water!" but the nurse didn't even slow down. "Hey!" she called again.

The nurse kept going, the cables from the machines dragging on the floor like cans dangling from a JUST MARRIED car. María searched for a maintenance closet or a storage space, opening doors around her at random. One was an office with two bare desks. The second was a large room full of piles and piles of files, on racks and on shelves, in boxes and in cabinets. The third door she tried was locked.

She sat in a row of joined chairs next to a sleeping woman who didn't appear injured. Maybe another mother waiting for news on her son? Maybe a wife looking for a husband, told to wait? The woman smelled sour. Or was that her own body? Even in sleep María could trace the worry in the woman's sunken eyes, in the stiffness of her crossed arms. She looked at the water cooler, the empty plastic bottle on the ground next to it, and she cried, heaving until the row of seats shook. It was ugly crying: slimy, wet, loud. She felt a hand on her shoulder, then an embrace, and the woman next to her, now awake, joined in her weeping.

Behind her tears María saw a white-coated shape approach with a purposeful stride, nose stuck in a file. She broke her embrace with the woman and stood in the doctor's path. "Hey, stop," she said. "There's no water in the cooler." She pointed to the dismembered machine.

The doctor glanced up from the file. "You'll have to talk to someone else about that, sorry," he said, and attempted to step around María.

She blocked him. "No, there's no water," María insisted. "I can get it, but you need to tell me where it is."

The doctor, young and handsome, with dark skin and toned

muscles, stood a foot and a half above her. "Señora, I'm sorry, I'm very busy," he said, and stepped around the other side of her.

María snatched the file from his hands. "Look at me, doctor. You will help me find this water or I will not let you do your job."

The doctor huffed, pulled out a set of keys, and unlocked the door of the third room: a storage closet with cleaning supplies, brooms and mops, and, on a rack, three plastic water-cooler bottles, heavy with water. "There you go, miss. Now can I go save a man's life?"

"Yes," she replied and hugged him. "Thank you!"

He stood in front of her and reached out his hand.

"What?" María said.

"My file, señorita. I need the file you took from me."

"Oh, sorry!" she said and handed it back.

The doctor grabbed it and left.

The woman on the chairs helped María carry the water bottle. "You must have really been thirsty," she said.

"It's not for me," María said.

She filled one paper cup to the brim and then another. She trotted back to the thirsty man in the torn yellow shirt. The palm tree and the bench were still there, but he was not. She checked farther down the hallways—nothing. She ran to the nurses' station, where a nurse was helping a man who was searching for his son. "He's twenty-three, here's a picture of him, we got separated at the march, but we can't find him anywhere!" The man held the photo out to the nurse and María could feel his pain inside her own body, like falling down through the sky with the land rushing up to meet her.

She couldn't look. She didn't want to recognize in the photo the face of one of the many dying boys she'd seen since she arrived. Instead she ran back to the palm tree. She was sure this was where she had left the thirsty man. She searched the other people in the hallway, straining to find the half-bandaged face, the torn shirt, the tender belly. But the man was nowhere. When María glanced down at her own shirt, she was wet with spilled water, clutching nothing but two soppy, empty paper cups.

34

THE CLOCK ABOVE the TV in Stanislavo's office was approaching 3:00 a.m. on April 12, 2002. Channel 4 was on, the signal having come back sometime during the night. The TV repeated over and over the footage from earlier in the day: Chávez supporters firing from the Puente Llaguno overpass down into Avenida Baralt. And there was Richard Peñalver, a municipal council member for the Chavista party, unloading his handgun. This had been the drop that made the cup overflow, serving as proof that the government fired on its own civilians, that Chavista politicians were murdering their own.

The military had turned on Chávez publicly after that. One branch after another paraded in front of the cameras and apologized to the Venezuelan people. Vásquez Velasco, the head of Chávez's army, ended his address: "This is not a coup d'état. This is not insubordination. It's a position of solidarity with all the people of Venezuela. Mr. President, I was loyal until the end, but the violation of human rights that took place today cannot be tolerated."

Stanislavo had never liked Velasco, but he agreed with him now.

Sandra Peterson came into the office, looking haggard but alert. She was the only one of his reporters who went into and out of his office as she pleased. Sandra had been Stanislavo's first hire when he decided to launch the paper, a week after Chávez's election. He'd stolen her from *El Nacional,* where she'd worked under him for a couple of years.

"Sorry, boss," she said. "I needed to get out of the newsroom for a second. Mind if I join you?" She sat and adjusted her chair to face the TV.

At first he had been a mentor to her, and now they shared a beautiful friendship. In moments like this one, with Sandra slouched in the chair, her blonde hair unruly and knotted from the chaotic hours preceding them, Stanislavo thought of daughters. The one he might have out there already, Emiliana's child. The one he'd almost tried for, with Nohelia, his ex-wife—his misguided attempt at getting Emiliana out of his head after he'd failed to find her. Their relationship had been so fraught—Stanislavo always distant, his heart wishing for something else—that they never quite got around to having a child. By the time the marriage ended just a few years later, they were both thankful they hadn't.

Daughter or not, after this strangest of nights, it felt good to have Sandra close by, someone to confirm that everything happening was real.

The Puente Llaguno footage cut to a live address by Lucas Rincón, inspector general of the armed forces. The clock read 3:00 a.m.

Sandra took out a notepad, and Stanislavo turned the volume up. The address started almost pleasantly: "People of Venezuela, good morning." And then two sentences that would change the history of the country. "The members of the military high command of the National Armed Forces of the Bolivarian Republic of Venezuela deplore the regrettable events that occurred yesterday. In light of these facts they have asked the president of the republic to resign his post, which he has accepted."

"Which he has accepted?" Sandra repeated. "Did he just say Chávez resigned?"

"Where's Cabello?" Stanislavo asked. "Sandra, get on the phones, track down the vice president."

They both went out into the newsroom, which appeared to be a sculpture garden, with every single reporter rooted to the floor and staring at the TVs.

"Hey!" Stanislavo yelled, and everyone turned to him. "I know this has been a long day. But this is when our job is most important. Moments like this are the only reason we got into this line of work. Now is when it counts. So we're going to go out there and do the job and do it right. The question to answer is transition of power: Who's in charge, who's in charge, who's in charge? Answer that question first. And someone get me that resignation letter. If Chávez resigned, there's proof. Find it."

Then his cell phone rang, an unknown number.

"Stanis," a man said. "Can't talk long, listen to me carefully."

It was a voice he hadn't heard in decades, yet it was unmistakable. It belonged to Jaime Molina. Instantly Stanislavo reverted to the young man he'd once been: Jaime Molina's friend, Nunzio Guelfi's friend. He might as well have been back in the jungles of Mochima.

"Molina?" he said, seeking confirmation he didn't need.

"I'm sorry to call, Stanis. But reporters on my side have no credibility right now, and I can't trust anyone else on the opposition with the information I'm about to give you."

Though they had not spoken since the day Stanislavo left the Mi Encanto jungle prison in an ambulance, of course he knew of Molina. The year Stanislavo arrived in Mexico, after the tunnel-bomb story broke, Molina had finally been released from Cuartel San Carlos. The story brought to light some of the atrocities the government was exacting on captured prisoners, and Molina, along with a few other captives, had been freed as a show of good faith by President Leoni. By then, Stanislavo and his parents had been diligently repairing their relationship. Although they were separated by more than two thousand miles and a sea, the letter he'd delivered to their mailbox before departing had dislodged the calcified memory of Ludmil's death into something they could at last pass around and talk about. And they had. After Stanislavo returned to Venezuela,

Ludmil's ghost became a companion to the three of them rather than a wraith.

In one of those early conversations, Stanislavo's mother mentioned she had run into Molina, who was thin now. Quiet too, she said. Which, more than anything, spoke to Stanislavo of the horrors his friend had lived through. He wrote Molina many letters after that. Eventually he received one back asking him to stop. Molina wasn't interested.

After pacification in 1969, allowing for a formal return of leftist parties to government, Molina became a political strategist for the Communist Party, then played various roles as the party splintered into different factions. As a journalist, Stanislavo was always aware of him; he even saw him from time to time in election years, if the left had a particularly exciting candidate. Molina was constantly somewhere in the background, pulling levers. The two old friends never talked, but inevitably there came a moment when they looked at each other and nodded in recognition of the world they had shared.

Unsurprisingly, Molina had been part of Chávez's meteoric rise. Never in his innermost circle, but still an important man in the party. With a voice that mattered. But it was one thing to know that Molina was still a person in the world—a man existing, living his life as he saw fit—and quite another to hear his voice after so many years. Stanislavo couldn't imagine whether Molina felt the same, but when he heard Molina speak, it wasn't just the voice of another man—it was the voice of a brother.

"What is it, Molina?"

"The military has taken Chávez to Fort Tiuna. He gave himself up peacefully to avoid any bloodshed. He was ready to resign, as long as he got safe passage to Cuba for him and his family. But now some of the generals want to arrest him. That's not what he agreed to! So if he turns up dead—if *I* turn up dead—you know who had him last. He has not resigned. Lucas Rincón lied on TV. Hugo Chávez has not resigned! Do you hear me?"

"I hear you, brother. Are you safe?"

"For now. I'm going into hiding with my family before they throw me in a dungeon. We've both had enough of that for a lifetime, right?" Then Molina hung up.

This story was metastasizing. It was hard to keep it all in his head. Was it a coup? Was it not a coup? Had it started as a coup, but now, after the violence against civilians ordered by Chávez himself, had it transformed into a legitimate and constitutional transfer of power?

Less than two hours later—with the vice president and the rest of Chávez's inner circle either underground or rounded up, and those at his periphery denouncing the president and jumping ship—Pedro Carmona, the Chamber of Commerce president, came on TV and announced himself the new president of Venezuela. He was in the presidential palace. The right-wing businessman, an organizer of the April 11 anti-Chávez march, had been one of the most vocal leaders of the opposition. Carmona enjoyed the support of the country's political elite and its larger private companies—what Chávez liked to call the *oligarchy*, or *los escuálidos*. But his counterpart from the center left—the labor-union leader and fellow march organizer Carlos Ortega, whose involvement had ensured that the opposition coalition comprised more than just the discontented rich—was not part of Carmona's address. Indeed, Ortega was nowhere to be found—perhaps just one more tumor to excise now that power had been wrested from Chávez.

Stanislavo ran his fingers through his mustache. "As soon as the sun is up, I'm heading to Miraflores," he announced to the room.

35

ELOY TRIED TO TUG his right arm, but it was caught up in tubes. He was a tangled puppet. He opened his eyes to a blurry shimmer and shut them again. The lightning bugs kept dancing under his eyelids. His left arm had more give, and he touched his face, feeling his button nose and then up to his small curls.

He heard someone snoring softly. He heard beeps at regular intervals. He heard the shuffling of feet. Farther away, he heard voices on top of voices, as if they were trying to climb on one another for air. Farther still, fainter but there, he heard bangs. Not so close as to be scary, but like he heard when he was sleeping at home on the nights he didn't walk to his mother's room. The nights he was brave.

His hand traced back down his face, his sharp chin, then his neck. He kept his hand on his chest for a bit, finding comfort in the heartbeat: *I am with you, I am working, we are one.* He moved farther down, and his fingers hit gauze. It was soft but in the wrong way, with none of the warm life of skin.

His hand recoiled and he called out: "¿Mami?" But the sound was raspy and gurgling, like grinding stones underwater. *"Mami,"* he pleaded, not only for his mother to be there but also for his own voice, the one he knew to be his, to return.

Part of him wanted to open his eyes, but most of him was afraid.

Afraid of the beeping, afraid of whatever was tying him down, afraid of the wetness he could now feel in his belly, as if he had peed the bed. Afraid most of all that when he opened his eyes his mother wouldn't be there, that he would be alone, or even worse, that a stranger had replaced her.

"You have to be brave," he whispered to himself, and the whisper sounded more like him.

He forced all his fear to go to his fisted hands, the size of lemons. He opened first one eye and then the other. Initially the light washed over him like a thick blanket, but slowly it unthreaded itself, allowing him to make sense of shapes: beds, strange machines, a TV hanging from a wall, a side table with a glass of water, a window with blue curtains...

And right there, next to him, slumped in a chair, her hair going every which way, his sleeping mother.

36

BEHIND THE STINK of iodine and isopropyl alcohol María could still smell Eloy—cocoa butter and nuts. She held him tight. It was him, and he was awake. He was alive. He was still her son. But while he appeared to recognize her, he wasn't speaking at all.

The nurse walked in and put a hand on María's shoulder. "Well, look who's up!" she said, rubbing María's back with healing circles.

María looked at her, eyes wet. "Can he speak? He's not saying anything!"

"Maybe don't hold him so tightly, mi vida," the nurse said, and put her hands on María's hands, guiding Eloy's head back to the pillow. The woman stroked Eloy's hair and whispered, "Say hello to your mami, baby."

Eloy's mouth opened. "Hola, Mami," he said, soft and a bit raspy, gritty dust on a breeze.

Life came into María's body. A breath of life unlike any she had taken since the day she'd pushed her son out, since she had first seen his little body—slippery, stained, a bit bruised—held up by his tiny ankles, like a skinned rabbit, and spanked by a doctor. María thought of how her mother might have felt when she herself was born. And it came to her then that maybe she had only really breathed—truly breathed—three times. The time she was born. The time Eloy was born. And now, the time Eloy survived.

"Hola, mi vida," she said. "It's all going to be okay, mi amor. You're going to be okay."

Wanting to believe it, she looked at the nurse to confirm it—in her eyes, in her body language—but the woman had already turned around.

"I'm getting the doctor," she said.

"What happened?" Eloy asked.

María struggled to find the words. "You got hurt, bebé." She placed her hand on his belly. "Right here in your panza," she said. "This little thing flew and—*pop*—made a little hole here," she said, pointing her finger at his belly, "and then—*pop*—came out the other side. But you're okay now, mi amorcito. You're awake and you're with me."

"I had strange dreams, Mami. Motorcycles, little angels."

Already he was getting winded, still so weak that he was like a stick-figure drawing of her son.

Dr. Ogaya came in with the nurse. His face had grown stubble since the last time she'd seen him: hours ago, days ago, hard to know. His coat was so stained it frightened her. She had the urge to protect her son from the sight of him, this harried monster. María expected him to soften at the sight of Eloy, this little, broken thing in the bed, but Dr. Ogaya did not.

"Vitals," he said, pushing aside María, who relinquished her grip on Eloy's hand.

The nurse read out the chart and María grew angry that her son was being reduced to a piece of paper. *Look at him*, she wanted to say. *Eloy's right there, awake, living, breathing.*

Dr. Ogaya folded down the sheet covering her son's bony body. The gauze wrapped his torso, starting at his hollow chest down to his fading blue underwear. A thin line of blood stained the wrap from where his belly button would be all the way up to his sternum.

How could a child survive this? María wondered. To be opened up like this? How do you put something so fragile back together?

Dr. Ogaya and the nurse lifted Eloy to a sitting position, carefully, and started unwrapping the gauze. They took turns, handing the end of the wrap to each other as they revealed Eloy's poky ribs, the half-moon-shaped birthmark on his lower back, and the scar dividing her son in two. If he was alive, then that scar was alive too. Although he was calm, and sleepy, and did not seem to be in great pain, his scar was an angry thing—meaty, purple-red, hungry for something. It seemed as though it would be able to breathe on its own.

"This might hurt a little," Dr. Ogaya said, his eyes avoiding María, avoiding the boy in front of him.

He palpated the soft flesh to the sides of the scar, and every gentle push of a finger felt like a hatchet lodging in María's back. Eloy's frame squirmed at each prod.

María put a hand over his eyes. "Shh, mi amor," she said, "it's almost done." Eloy's tears made her hand wet. "Almost done, right?" she asked Dr. Ogaya.

He removed his hands from Eloy's belly as if it were too hot to touch. "Señora, if you want to do my job, then be my guest."

María's body became stone, except for her eyes, which welled up.

"Unless you've got a medical degree, then I would appreciate it if you focused on calming your child and not interfering with my work. Thank you."

María's jaw locked down so hard she thought it would never open again. She wiped her tears with her forearm and looked at Dr. Ogaya's face, his knotted brow. She counted the stains on his sleeve. She looked at his hands, his long, dexterous fingers always prodding, feeling, searching like a dog's snout. She wanted to cut those hands off. And then she thought about the stains again. How hard it must be to live your day by the passing tick-tock of wounds, of gashes, of holes. If all she saw was angry scars, like Eloy's, wouldn't she be angry back? At the wounds, sure, but also at the people who carried them?

"Nurse, come talk to me," Dr. Ogaya said.

He turned and started walking away without even a glance back at María. He huddled with the nurse out of earshot, at the edge of the room, and María could see the nurse trying to make a point. Dr. Ogaya's back straightened, his shoulders tensed.

María glanced at the TV, the reruns of President Chávez's address, before he had been taken away to God knows where. Then the brand-new president, Pedro Carmona Estanga, appeared on the TV. He seemed to think that everyone was excited, that the whole country had asked — no, demanded — that he shepherd them into a new future, with no crime, no poverty, and, above all, no Chávez. María knew that in her part of the world that wasn't true. That Chávez, even with his faults, was one of them. No one there behind Carmona looked like Eloy. No one there would protect her and her son from more bullets. All Carmona said was more of the same. Nonsense spoken by people without sons in the hospital.

Then she heard Dr. Ogaya shout: "I need that bed, goddamn it!" And he stormed out of the room.

The nurse stood there for a second. She tugged down on her blue scrubs and took a breath before walking back to María. "The doctor says Eloy will be ready to go soon," she said with a small, forced smile.

"He's not ready, though, is he?" María said.

"No, he's not. But we need the bed. I'll work on getting him as much time as I can."

The nurse was as disheveled as she was, María noticed. Maybe as sad. Her name tag read MARISOL. Such a beautiful name: *sea* and *sun*. How María wished that name could become a true refuge.

"Tell me he's going to be okay, Marisol; just tell me that."

Marisol struggled to say anything. "Look, here's the doctor's prescription," she said. "I'm going to tell you right now, you won't be able to find this pain medication in any pharmacy that I know. If you have someone with connections, anyone at all, see if they can find it for you."

"Is he going to be okay?" María broke down in sobs now, grabbing at Marisol.

The nurse pushed her away, gently. She pulled a key from her pocket and moved to a small cabinet by Eloy's bed. Looking around to make sure nobody was watching, she unlocked the top drawer, then plucked out a glass bottle full of white pills. "Put this in your purse," she whispered. "Twice a day, morning and night, until the pills are finished, all right? He's going to be okay, María. Your boy is going to be okay."

María believed it. She had to.

37

THE NURSE BOUGHT Eloy one more night in the hospital bed. He slept through to the morning, and María had to wake him when her friend Magali arrived to take them home.

"¡Vamos, María! Let's go!" Magali said now, pushing Eloy in a wheelchair down a hospital hallway. The rubber wheels screeched as she bumped indiscriminately into gurneys, nurses, waiting-room furniture, and patients. "This taxista is a friend of mine, but he's not going to wait forever. I already had to cash in a favor for him to even bring me to this mess!"

María loved her friend, but she wished it was Don Jacinto pushing the wheelchair. Magali always beat a war drum, and the chaos of the past three days had only riled her more than ever. She was railing against the coup, against the betrayal of Chávez, the only decent man in the whole country.

Then she moved on to Don Jacinto. "Do you know that old fool is okay with all of it?" she said. "It's because of people like him that we lost the commander. They'll all pay, mark my words."

A man opened the door for Magali and Eloy, his tan shirt hanging crooked, its buttons attached in the wrong holes.

"Gracias, compadre," Maga said.

The heat and the stink of old smoke slapped María in the face.

The taxi driver had half his body out the window of his beat-up red Fiat. He hit the roof of the car three times, rattling the little plastic taxi cap, which was strapped to the roof by elastic cords. "Finally, mujer," he said. "I was about to leave!" He slid back into the driver's seat and turned on the machine, an old hag coughing herself awake.

"Sit in front," Magali said. "The back doesn't have seat belts. I'll put Eloy on your lap."

She lifted Eloy from the wheelchair as if handing out a leaflet, and María was terrified by the ease of it. On her lap Eloy seemed to weigh less than a blanket—but he was warm, and awake, and hugged her tight. She strapped herself and Eloy in while Magali, as if she'd been a nurse her whole life, lifted the wheelchair and collapsed it on itself.

"What are you doing?" María asked through the open window.

"Giving my godson an early birthday present," she said, and tossed the wheelchair into the back seat, clambering in after it. "And don't start with your shit, María. You're going to need the chair, so I'm giving you the chair."

María kept quiet and kissed Eloy on the top of his head.

"Punch it, Fredi," Magali told the driver. "I hope I never set foot in this place again."

María closed her eyes and wished for the same thing.

"Fuck all of you!" Magali screamed out the back-seat window, a middle finger piercing the air.

An orderly ran out of the hospital, shouting, "Hey! You can't take that chair!"

But Fredi was already on his way, sticking a hand out the window too, middle finger up. "Fuck you!" he yelled in laughter.

María started to laugh too, little Eloy rattling on top of her. And before her mind could tell her it was wrong, her own middle finger was in the air, her nail jagged from biting, its red polish cracked and down to the cuticle. "Fuck yoooouuuuu!" she howled, as Magali, sharing the back seat with the wheelchair, slapped her shoulders.

* * *

The barrio looked like a man after a weekend bender. María leaned her head back as the taxi weaved slowly around broken barricades, debris, and patches of broken glass. A few people passed them walking down the hill, carrying signs and marching clothes. Chávez supporters. María wondered what they were doing. Wasn't this over?

Eloy slept, his head resting on her chest. Her heart nearly jumped out of her body when she saw a severed arm in the middle of the road, until she realized it had been attached to a mannequin and not a person, a remnant from a clothing store whose front window had been smashed open.

"Nobody looted in the city," Fredi said, "but the barrio is another story. You should be glad you weren't home, María."

Fredi turned the radio dial, the frequency whirring in and out. For a country where the president had just been thrown out, there wasn't a lot of news. Fredi finally landed on the trombone intro to Roberto Roena's "Mi desengaño," and before they knew it the three of them were singing along, Fredi banging the clave on the steering wheel with his fingers, María and Magali singing that "la vida ha de continuar" while the little red Fiat sputtered up and up and up the hills of Cotiza.

The car stopped in front of María's house—her small shack with the red brick wall in front and the corrugated zinc roof, brown from rust. Her two plastic chairs sat to the side of the front door, coated in a layer of grime. María left Fredi and Magali flirting in the car and exited the taxi, carrying Eloy, who still slept, the pain medication doing its work. She found herself trying to match his calm breathing, as for a moment it made her worries vanish: about the medicine eventually running out; about leaving a sick child at home while she went to work; about the next time bullets started flying; about her father. Her father, suddenly existing. He had saved her son's life, and then was as gone as he'd ever been. But breathing in sync with Eloy made her at one with the world, even thankful for it, in all its utter strangeness.

"Well, look who decided to come back," Don Jacinto said. He stood in the middle of his patio, surrounded by his ferns, next to his motorcycle. Light bounced off the fuel tank. He held a wet towel, dripping water and foam onto the ground. He was shirtless, his ribs visible, white hair tangled on his chest. He dropped the towel inside a plastic bucket and walked to her. "How's the boy doing?" He placed a hand on Eloy's head. "How are you doing?"

His tenderness made María want to cry. "He's doing good, Don Jacinto." She thanked him again and apologized for getting him involved in all of her and Eloy's drama.

"Stop it, mujer," he said. "That's what neighbors are for, right? That's what friends are for."

"¡Viejo!" Magali yelled at Don Jacinto from outside the Fiat. "There's a wheelchair in here. Make yourself useful."

Jacinto's eyes lingered on María for a split second, and then he walked to the car. Magali leaned on Fredi's window, laughing with him, their faces close, and María knew she'd be seeing Fredi around more often. Jacinto rolled the wheelchair to María.

"No, gracias, I've got him," she said, not wanting to relinquish Eloy. She carried him into the house, put him in bed, and pulled the sheet up to his thin neck. He was so beautiful that she could hardly bear it. She turned around and left her son to his dreams.

Everything in the rancho was as she had left it: her birthday card at the kitchen table; two old arepas, as hard as rocks, on a plate. On the ground she could make out the profiles of her body and Eloy's, dust halos where they had taken shelter from the bullets. She looked at the wall the bullet had pierced. Maybe if she'd saved enough money to put brick there, as she had done to the front. Maybe then Eloy would have been spared. She walked to the metal pane, but the bullet hole wasn't there. In its place was a plaster patch.

"I figured you wouldn't want to see it," Jacinto said, his hands in his pockets, standing in the doorway next to the folded wheelchair.

María wrapped her arms around his waist, resting her head under his chin. She felt his bony frame against her, sharp but warm.

She could smell the sweetness of his sweat and the lemony aroma of the grease soap. It was a good smell.

Still in his arms, she kissed him on the cheek. "Thank you," she whispered, and she thought about kissing him for real. Letting herself go soft, letting herself be held, no longer worried about anything except the taste of the sugary coffee on Jacinto's lips.

"María!" yelled Magali from the outside. "Just got a call from my organizing group. They need my Círculo down at Fuerte Tiuna. Looks like this shit ain't over!"

María composed herself, straightening her blouse, the brief moment with Jacinto over. She was thankful that Magali hadn't seen them from where she was.

"We're going down! ¡Uh, ah, Chávez no se va! ¡Uh, ah, Chávez no se va!" Magali chanted with fervor.

The Fiat's engine revved, then the car sped off down the hill.

38

Ávila Mountain shone emerald, morning light hitting its green skirt and taunting Stanislavo with a mirage of normalcy. He and César drove west to the Miraflores neighborhood and into a deserted battleground. The place still smoldered, the streets empty of people, of police, of soldiers, but full of the remnants of war: half-destroyed barricades, spent tear-gas canisters, rags, crushed water bottles. A lonely tennis shoe lay in the middle of the road, its laces still tied.

Vehicles were parked all around the presidential palace. Some were the vans of TV stations; others he recognized from their decals as print media. But most were bulletproof SUVs or sparkling new BMWs or Mercedes. Chauffeurs chatted in small groups.

Getting into the palace was much easier than Stanislavo had expected it to be after—or was this still during?—a transfer of power. Someone had set up a sign-in desk by the main door, but no one was manning it; the desk just sat there empty under the line of tall royal palms standing guard around the colonial building. Stanislavo and César walked right in. Massive columns welcomed them into a lush inner courtyard. A morning breeze traveled its corridors, caring nothing for who its inhabitants were.

It felt like arriving late to a wedding reception at El Country Club. Smiling men in suits mingled and talked to one another. Bank executives, lawyers, heads of foreign companies, titans of industry, real estate moguls, foreign diplomats—all of them were dispensing congratulatory hugs. The ice in glasses of scotch clinked as birds chirped in the inner garden. Thinking back to Vargas Hospital, Stanislavo couldn't reconcile the disconnect. Had less than two days truly separated this bizarre scene from the chaos of April 11? From that boy he'd helped? From his poor mother? He'd had trouble getting the woman out of his head and made a mental note to call the hospital and check on how they were doing.

During the long night hours at the paper, Stanislavo had come to a private understanding with himself. Chávez had committed an unforgivable crime. All evidence seemed to suggest that he had ordered the military to violently quell peaceful demonstrators. When they refused, Chávez had ordered armed civilians to do it. In Stanislavo's mind—and, he imagined, in the mind of any rational person—Chávez had violated the most important mandate of his own Constitution. It meant that deposing him was inside the margins of the law. Even knowing that opposition leaders might have manipulated the massive crowd to force Chávez into a corner didn't exonerate him.

Among the rich and powerful, ranking military men in uniform also mingled, forming small cliques. They seemed more somber, concerned, engaging in conversation with civilians at times but mostly keeping to themselves.

"César," he told his photographer, "make sure you cover lots of faces. I want to know everyone who's here."

Many things bothered Stanislavo about this scene, but especially the absence of anyone from Chavismo. There was no one. Not even those considered Chavistas-Lite. If this transition was going to work, there had to be Chavistas in the mix.

Not only was there no one from the Chávez party here, but he also saw no one from Labor. If Interim President Carmona had been the right ventricle of the beating heart of the opposition, then Ortega had been the left. Business and labor working together had been the most powerful argument the opposition had presented against the authoritarian bent of Chávez's term: *We're both angry, we're both tired, we're both concerned.* But where the fuck was Labor now?

A few minutes later, when Sandra called him to say that Ortega had left the city, Stanislavo was not the least bit surprised.

Molina, meanwhile, was unreachable. Whether he'd gone underground or been captured was impossible to determine, but Stanislavo hoped he was safe.

Now Carmona walked in his direction, surrounded by his advisers: an insular group of the über-wealthy, a couple of long-term right-wing political operatives whom Stanislavo liked to call *the old wolves*, and Father Muñoz, a prominent religious figure from the most conservative branch of the Venezuelan Catholic Church.

"Dr. Carmona," Stanislavo called.

The man stopped and looked at him. Recognized him. Smiled. "Stanislavo Atanas," he said and extended his hand. "Nice to see you here."

"Can I ask you a couple of questions?"

"Always working, huh?" Carmona chuckled.

Stanislavo asked where Ortega was, and Carmona assured him they were working closely, with Ortega busy organizing the union, preparing to rebuild the country together with him.

"He's not on a plane heading out of the city right now?"

Carmona opened his mouth to say something, but no words came out.

"Dr. Carmona, is Chávez's letter of resignation in your possession?"

One of the old wolves intervened, ushering Carmona out of Stanislavo's earshot.

"Where's the letter, Dr. Carmona?" asked Stanislavo, loud enough for people around him to notice.

Carmona hurried away, smiling, shaking hands with others on his way across the palace. Stanislavo turned his attention to a nervous palace guard standing by a hallway. This wasn't an officer vying for position, mingling with the upper crust of Venezuelan society, scheming for a role in this new Venezuela taking shape; this was un soldado de a pie, a year or two out of the academy, probably from a poor part of the country. He reminded Stanislavo of the government soldiers in Mochima all those years ago, the soldiers he'd almost killed more than once, and it seemed so ridiculous to him now. How could he have thought that was even an option? But then he realized something that had escaped him the whole time he'd been here at the palace: This young man was part of the Presidential Honor Guard, one of the soldiers specifically tasked with protecting Chávez and his home at all costs. These were the soldiers the high command had individually picked for the job. And now that Stanislavo was looking, he saw the others quietly standing guard as well, and they were the few sour, sad faces inside a room full of grins. No one had dismissed them, no one had ordered them to leave. In the day's confusion, no one had noticed that Chávez's most trusted men were still watching over Miraflores.

Stanislavo's phone rang again.

"Boss, Chávez is on a plane," Sandra said.

"To Cuba?"

Everyone assumed the island was the place Chávez would choose for exile. In fact, Stanislavo was surprised he wasn't already there.

Nobody knew, Sandra said. There was a lot of talk about having Chávez face trial for yesterday's deaths. Exile was no longer enough.

Stanislavo hung up and Carmona came out to address the crowd. Like some sort of God-appointed emperor, he dissolved everything: Constitution, National Assembly, Supreme Court. Besides being unconstitutional, it was supremely stupid. The military wouldn't put up with it, Stanislavo knew, and Carmona couldn't preside without the military. Getting Chávez out of power wasn't the coup; *this* was the coup. Carmona had stolen the country.

Stanislavo could only imagine what was happening in the ranchos of Petare and Catia, in the small towns of Apure and Barinas. In apartment buildings in Los Valles del Tuy. More than half the country would be raging over this grand larceny, while the rest would be lulled to sleep by a false sense of victory. There was no way this was the end of anything. It could only be the beginning.

Back at the newspaper, Stanislavo reflected on the head-spinning swiftness of events. He felt as though he had just left the boy, Andrés Eloy, in the operating room and his worried mother outside. He had been able to reach Dr. Ogaya at Vargas Hospital; the kid had recovered, and the woman, María, had taken him home. He had a strange urge to talk to her, to make sure they would be all right. But his reverie was interrupted by his phone. An unknown number again.

"Hermano." Molina's voice was on the other end.

"Hermano, are you okay?"

"Lala and the girls are fine. I sent them to Puerto La Cruz with my aunt."

"I'm so glad."

"Thank you, Stanis. Look, Chávez is still alive. I trust you to report on this fairly."

"And you want it coming from someone who doesn't like Chávez."

"Sure, that too. But there must be proof in case someone kills him." They had just gotten their hands on a note written by Chávez himself, Molina said. From Turiamo, a naval base on the coast. It was dated today and clearly stated that Chávez had not resigned.

"Can you send me a copy?" Stanislavo asked.

"I'm faxing it to you now."

Staying on the line with Molina, Stanislavo ran to the fax machine. When he got there it was already screeching out a grainy copy of the note, torturously slow.

Turiamo, April 13, 2002
at 14:45

To the people of Venezuela...
(and whoever it concerns).

I, Hugo Chávez Frías, Venezuelan,
President of the Bolivarian Republic
of Venezuela, do declare:

I have not resigned the
legitimate power that the
people gave me.

Forever!!
Hugo Chávez F.

The handwritten note was a rallying cry: to the international media, to Carmona's coupsters, to Chavista politicians, to the military, but most of all to Chávez supporters.

Just before Molina's call, Sandra had let Stanislavo know of reports that real danger for Carmona and his government was already building in Maracay, a city a couple of hours west of Caracas. The seat of the military, Maracay's base had remained shut. General Baduel, who was very tight with Chávez, controlled the best-trained men in the country—as well as the small fleet of F-16s that Venezuela owned.

Stanislavo had a hunch that Baduel was getting ready to strike back as soon as he deemed it prudent. Standing there at the fax machine, holding Chávez's note in his hands, he told Molina there was something going on in Maracay, that General Baduel might be planning an attack on Caracas. "I'm worried, Molina. Things could get really bloody if Baduel comes into the city with fighter planes. Tell me nothing crazy like that will happen."

"It's not an attack, Stanis."

"Are you sure? There's no going back from that."

"It's a rescue," Molina said. "He's going to get Chávez back."

39

María couldn't have cared less about what was going on outside her rancho. It didn't matter that it was after midnight and the night was dark and smoke-filled. It didn't matter that all she could hear was people walking by, going down the mountain, shouting and calling for the president's return. She didn't care about Chávez, didn't care about the country or the city or the barrio. It didn't matter that Magali wasn't answering her phone. It didn't matter that the only thing coming up the mountain was the sound of fireworks and gunshots and chaos. It didn't matter that her father was out there, that he suddenly had a voice and a face and a body.

All that mattered was that Eloy slept through it all. His warm breath on her neck mattered. The way his heartbeat shook her palm mattered. His tight curls, just beneath her nose, mattered—the scent of almonds and dirt. Every few minutes he stretched his legs and curled back up—that mattered. She counted his breaths. She counted the brown freckles on his face. She counted his long lashes. She counted everything she could, and it all added up to her one son.

40

STANISLAVO GOT AS CLOSE as he could to the palace, but three blocks away it was already impossible to keep going. He parked the car in front of a wedding-dress shop, its metal security gate rolled down. The gate looked as if it had been beaten without mercy, but it remained clipped to the sidewalk by its lock. Graffiti on it read CHÁVEZ, ASSASSIN!

Surrounding his car was a caravan of people walking up toward the palace. They wore red berets. They wore red shirts. They held up signs. They held up copies of the Chávez Constitution. They held up small crosses and rosaries. They chanted "¡Chávez, amigo, el pueblo está contigo!" over and over again.

Stanislavo hoped no one would recognize him. He was hardly a household name, but he'd been vocal in his opposition to the president. He'd been on TV before. Chávez had mentioned him by name in many a Sunday broadcast, whenever he particularly hated one of Stanislavo's editorials. Chávez did not like being hit from the left; he loathed the fact that Stanislavo's arguments could not be swept under the easy classification of *capitalist*, *oligarch*, or *escuálido*.

Still, those three blocks up to the palace felt like a high-wire act. The people clumped tighter together and Stanislavo had to push his way through. Men and women cried in anger and desperation, they wanted their president back and screamed for it. Along the ground lay printed copies of Chávez's note, the same one that Molina had faxed him. He kept pushing forward, a salmon going upstream. Overhead, the Caracas night sky, clear and starry, glinted at the thousands gathered there.

Finally, he made it to the entrance and onto the grounds. His best bet was to pose as international press. They'd done the work of getting the government's message out to the world. Without them, this unlikely comeback would have perished on the vine.

"International press!" he shouted to the two Presidential Honor Guards at the gate. "I'm a reporter with ABC in Madrid!"

The guards looked at each other. "Credentials," said the one on the left.

"Hermano," Stanislavo said, "somebody pulled it off my neck on the way here. It's been impossible to reach the gate. I'm sorry."

"Wait a second, I know you," said the guard on the right.

Stanislavo recognized the young man: the same Honor Guard he'd locked eyes with inside the palace that morning.

"He's not international press," the guard said. "He's probably with *El Nacional* or something."

From behind, a hand grabbed his shoulder, and he looked back at a round-faced woman yelling, "¡Escuálido! Liar! This one is from *El Nacional*!"

Then more hands assaulted him and he could no longer tell what the people were screaming. Someone pulled him out. The young guard stood above him, but on the other side of the crowd. He called for calm and kept the angry mob away.

"Are you fucking crazy coming back here?" the soldier said.

"It's my job," Stanislavo said. "And for the record, I don't work for *El Nacional*."

Then he heard a familiar voice.

"Stanislavo?"

Molina's face looked down at him. Still the same puffed cheeks, still the same round glasses stuck atop his small nose. His hair was grayer than the last time Stanislavo had seen him—at some rally in Fuerte Tiuna a couple of years back—and gone on top, but he still bounced energetically with every step.

"What the fuck are you doing here?" Molina said.

"My job," Stanislavo repeated.

Molina and the soldier both helped him up and Molina took him inside. The palace was full of members of Chávez's party now. They gathered in small groups that emanated nervous chatter. The Presidential Guard stood proud at their posts.

Molina led Stanislavo to an empty office and closed the door behind them. Stanislavo was breathing hard, adrenaline still coursing through him from his encounter with the mob.

Molina pulled out a chair. "Sit," he said. "Breathe."

Stanislavo obeyed.

Molina knelt in front of him. "Damn," Molina said. "You still haven't lost your fucking hair." He slid his hand over his own bald head. "Motherfucker," he said, smiling.

Stanislavo couldn't help it. He chuckled. He hugged his friend. They held on to each other for a while, and it felt to Stanislavo like recovering a long-lost heirloom.

Molina pulled out another chair and sat opposite him. "You shouldn't have come, Stanis. If the wrong people had recognized you…"

"Well, you know me."

"I do. You never quit," Molina said. But the words, which he had started with a smile and a glint, seemed to sour in his mouth. Molina adjusted his glasses. "Except us," he added. "Except the Movement."

And suddenly the noise from outside, the chanting, faded, as if Molina's indictment had created a bubble around them.

"I didn't quit the Movement," Stanislavo said. "It pushed me away. You know what Alfredo did, how he kept Emiliana's pregnancy from me, how he lied about the bomb. I explained it all to you in my letters."

"Sorry, I thought I was over all of this," Molina said. "But I see you and it comes back. I couldn't respond to those letters, Stanis. You have to know that. It was all too fresh. Nunzio…"

It was as if Molina had reached inside him. Stanislavo had found some closure for Nunzio's death. Antonio and Martina Guelfi, Nunzio's parents, had responded to his letters. When he returned to Caracas, they had welcomed him into their apartment—through the front door this time. Somehow, they didn't blame him. It was the first time he had felt exonerated since leaving Abastos Beirut, and their grace allowed him to start the process of moving on. But here was Molina. His old friend. Opening the wound as if it had been made yesterday, not almost forty years ago.

"You were our brother," Molina said. "We gave you your freedom. We saved you from Mi Encanto. Do you have any idea what we went through in there? What they *did* to us after you escaped?"

Stanislavo remembered how he had felt digging that tunnel. What it had meant for him to reach his friends.

"What they did to Nunzio? He wasn't strong like we were, Stanis. We both knew that. He wanted to be strong. But he wasn't."

"I tried," Stanislavo finally said.

"You should have blown it up," Molina said. "You should have finished the damned tunnel and carried that bomb in. Lit the fuse yourself."

"But you and Nunzio—"

"Nunzio was already dead! And I wanted to be by then! I wouldn't have cared. I would have welcomed it. It would have served them right."

Molina was hunched on the chair, his gaze cast down, his hands hanging low. Stanislavo reached for them, found no resistance in his friend.

"I did the best I could," he said. "I really did."

Molina sighed. "I believe you, brother. It's just—I see you and still feel all this…resentment." Molina stood up. "How could you have left us? Left *me*? We could have built something better if you'd stuck with it."

Stanislavo shook his head. "This thing is off the rails," he said. "It's been off the rails for decades. I couldn't have done anything to make it any different. Even you can't, and you're the most convincing person I've ever met. Are you going to honestly tell me that you've been able to change Chávez's mind once? One single time?"

"He's my president," Molina said. "He's tired, like all of us, of this shit. Of the boot of oppressors on our throats."

"Oh, please. Don't come to me with that. You don't believe that! He's the same! The same as all the others before! Remember when we stewed about Betancourt's men buying land in Spain and France? Building hotels on Margarita Island? Driving Cadillacs from American factories? All while Venezuelans starved? Look around you! It's the same."

Molina cleaned his glasses with his shirt, and it reminded Stanislavo of their first day in the jungle, arguing about how to reach the camp.

"How many bank accounts does Cabello have?" Stanislavo asked. "How many did he have before Chávez became president? Mark my words, in a few years this will be known as Venezuela's most corrupt government. Nothing will compare to it. Not what we fought against in the sixties, not who came after, who were even worse. Nothing." Stanislavo had to catch his breath. "How can I have left? How can *you* have stayed!"

Stanislavo waited for Molina to stand up for himself, to argue. But he didn't.

Then they heard it. The sound of helicopters. Molina tore off his glasses and wiped his face. He exited the room and Stanislavo followed him out of the palace. Five black stains speckled the cloudy night sky. The black mechanical insects blocked clouds and stars as they approached.

"Baduel did it," Molina whispered. "Baduel did it!" he said. "¡Llegó Chávez!" he screamed at the top of his lungs. "He's here!"

"LLEGÓ, LLEGÓLLEGÓLLEGÓ, LLEGÓ, LLEGÓ." The chant started by the entrance and echoed out into the thousands gathered by the palace. It was the same rhythm the opposition marchers had screamed as they approached the palace three days ago, but with the opposite meaning now.

Molina looked up to the sky in wonder and amazement, and he wept. Stanislavo knew that they would never talk about Nunzio again, about the tunnel, about those days. The helicopters came closer and closer until one by one they landed on the palace roof. There would be the wrath that followed Chávez's return. The revenge. It was a matter of time. Stanislavo hoped that the country would survive it.

41

MARÍA HAD MISSED a week of work. La Señora had called her a couple of times, had said the right words—how horrified, how concerned, how sorry she was about Eloy—but then had always ended with the same question, undergirded by a current of frustration: "So, when do you think you'll be back?" María was sure that the only reason she still had a job was that most maids like her were still trapped in the barrio. Alicia, the nanny who likewise worked for the Romeros, hadn't been able to make it to work either. Life hadn't resumed yet in Caracas after the protests, after Chávez's comeback. Public transportation was still pretty much paralyzed.

"¡Mami!" Eloy cried from the bedroom.

She jumped in place, just like every other time she heard a noise coming from him. "¿Qué pasó, mi amor?" She knelt by the bed. "Does it hurt?"

"I just wanted to show you this." Eloy lifted a piece of paper: a drawing of two figures with a ball flying between them, sun and clouds and three birds gliding above them. "I wanted to make the grass green, but I only had a pencil."

"It's so good, Eloy!" She took the paper from him. "Is this one you?"

"Yes. And that's Wili, from school."

"That's so nice, mi vida. Maybe Wili can come visit. Would you like that?"

"Yes!" Eloy perked up but immediately winced in pain, his hand jumping to his belly.

"Okay, okay," María said, and held him. "Don't get excited. I'll see if I can get him to come."

"Promise?"

"Promise. Now let's change your bandages."

"No, Mami, no."

"We have to, mi amor. It'll feel better later, I promise."

"But it hurts!" He started to sob.

She handled him carefully, leaning him on his left side and undoing the metal clasps, then rocking him from side to side as she unwrapped. His quiet cries broke what remained of her heart. The final layer of bandage always stuck to his wound.

"Okay, deep breath, mi amor."

Eloy held it in. He scrunched his eyes closed so hard that all María could see were wrinkles around his button nose. María peeled off the gauze, and bits of the creamy wound came off with it. Eloy's little hands held on to the sheets.

"Done, baby. Done."

Eloy let out his breath all at once, and as he relaxed his face, María saw how wet it was. The scar seemed to be catching its own breath with him. María wanted to erase that scar from the world.

Getting to Casa Verde took twice as long now. Very few buses were operating, and you had to fight your way onto those that were. The carritos that usually carried her the last leg were not operating, so she joined the servant pilgrimage, dozens of them walking through lush green streets in maid dresses, gardener overalls, security-guard uniforms, waiter livery. They strolled by houses with beautiful names such as *Menena, El Palmar,* and *Marbella,* whose tall fortress walls kept out even their gazes—until a pilgrim would ring a bell and disappear inside. By the time María reached the cream-colored walls of Casa Verde and the metal gate that led to the front yard, only one maid remained walking, the rest of them having already been swallowed up.

She rang the bell and the buzz-in was instant, as if the Romeros had been waiting by the intercom on the other side. It was through this doorway that the house's name became obvious. On either side of a terra-cotta path twisting to the off-white house grew walls of tropical green in the form of palm trees and mango trees; guava trees and limoneros; plants with leaves the size of elephant ears, thick enough for children to slide down; orchids and bromeliads clinging to the bark of a rubber tree; verdant vines connected to all the trees. Grasshoppers and cicadas and flying ants and the birds that ate them assaulted the senses. Five green parrots nested on a giant chaguaramo, the royal palm tree to which all other plants in the garden paid reverence. The birds conversed with one another as María walked under the palm tree on her way to the front door.

The door opened before she knocked. María had never seen La Señora like this: her hair was a mess, she wore one of Señor Romero's old T-shirts, she had no makeup on. Even then she was still beautiful. She held little Gustavo Antonio, his pudgy three-year-old body spilling out of her arms—María couldn't remember the last time she'd seen Señora Romero carry him. Behind her, Jorge Luis rolled on a skateboard through the living room, about to crash into Señor Romero's favorite sculpture. He avoided it at the last second, crashing instead against the coffee table. The sight of him, of his untroubled boy-ness, made her heart squeeze. He was the same age as Eloy, almost to the month. How freeing it must feel to live somewhere where boys didn't have to think about bullets.

"Jorge Luis!" La Señora screamed, and Gustavito covered his ears. "Thank God you're here, María."

La Señora pressed Gustavo on her, and María dropped her bag to catch him in time.

"Alicia hasn't been able to look after the kids, and Señor Antonio has been working nonstop at the bank. Did you know some animals tried to break into the bank during the whole thing? It was so horrible! Antonio could have easily been there! They should shoot every single one of them in the streets."

La Señora didn't wait for María to respond; she just walked to Jorge, snatched the skateboard from his hands, and walked upstairs. Gustavo's chubby index finger looped through María's hair, gently.

"¿Cómo estás tú, Gustavito?" she asked him and pressed her nose against his cheek. He smelled a little rancid, but under that scent he retained the sweet, milky aroma of toddlers. "Are you gonna help me clean today?" she asked, and Gustavo nodded.

The living room was a graveyard of toys. María stepped around hills of building blocks, armies of soldiers, balls of all shapes and sizes — some for sports the rules to which María couldn't have imagined. But not even that prepared her for the state of the kitchen. Not one dish had been washed since she'd last been here. The Romeros had gone through two sets of clean china and were now working on their third: the magnificent Royal Copenhagen set that La Señora had inherited from her grandmother, Madame Armand. Rarely had María seen it. She recalled the first Christmas dinner she'd worked at Casa Verde, as Madame Armand stood looking over her shoulder as she scrubbed the china clean of the roasted pork and gravy, of the wild rice, of the sweet-potato purée. It had been both terrifying and thrilling to hold them. How delicate they were, how light. They were shaped like a wide-open flower, the edges of each petal carved and gilded with tiny gold leaves. The plate itself was smooth white porcelain, while in the middle yellow flowers bloomed on green stalks. On every plate the plants were a little different; some had five bulbs, some three, the leaves angled in various ways. Even the backs of the plates were beautiful, with something written in cursive in a language María didn't understand but could read: *Pedicularis sceptrum-carolinum,* read one. That same plate now sat atop a pile in the sink, a red crust of spaghetti sauce dried over its sublime flowers.

María set Gustavito down on the floor and handed him a rag. "Okay, Gustavito, go help."

He trotted away and started play-cleaning.

"Jorge Luis!" she yelled, and a few seconds later Jorge stumbled into the kitchen holding a toy truck. "¿Quieres un pan con canela?"

"¡Sí!" Jorge Luis squealed.

"¡Sí!" Gustavito imitated his brother.

María locked both kitchen doors so she could keep the boys within sight, then grabbed two slices of bread. She smothered them with butter and sprinkled white sugar over them, then she did the same with cinnamon and put them in the oven. "Okay, you boys let me know when they're ready."

Jorge looked through the glass oven door. Gustavito had to hop to catch a glimpse. While the boys waited, María scrubbed. She began with the Copenhagen plates, slow and gentle, dipping them in the warm water and carefully dislodging the bits of dried food. How sad it would be if part of the gilding came off with the crusty sauce! María didn't think she could stand something this beautiful getting ruined.

"¡María, ya está!" Jorge Luis said.

"¡María, ya está!" Gustavo parroted.

She finished drying the last of the fancy plates. When she opened the oven, the smell of butter and sweet cinnamon filled the kitchen, and she wished she had made a third slice. "Cuidado, it's hot," she told them.

The two boys sat obediently and ate while María continued working on her pile.

One hour passed, then two, then five. She tackled the house room by room, in each one locking the children in with her, inventing games. The two boys made the work harder—especially Jorge Luis, who was starting to rebel at her instruction—but she was also thankful for them. They were beautiful, La Señora's boys, with their blond curls and red cheeks. Jorge Luis was sweet with Gustavo (so long as he followed his older brother's orders), and Gustavito was eager to please him.

Occasionally, she heard La Señora's bell. She remembered the day La Señora, still pregnant with little Gustavito, had introduced it to her. "It'll be great!" she'd told María as she presented the small silver bell. "I saw Karla had it in her house. I won't have to yell anymore. The sound of a bell is so much more pleasant, don't you think?" Framing it as a question gave the false impression that María had a choice in the matter, or perhaps showed that La Señora was trying to convince herself there wasn't something doglike and humiliating about the whole thing. And at first the beautiful young woman did seem to have an inner struggle with using it. But three years in, La Señora had clearly made her peace with it, any reluctance long ago shed through the repetition of bell rings, each one striking María as though she were being tugged by a leash. Today there was a bottle of Chardonnay in La Señora's room, and with every ring of the bell the bottle had less wine in it.

By the time the sun set, María had cleaned the house, bathed the children, and fed them. She left the kids playing their video games and went to the only room she hadn't touched. She gently knocked on the door to the master bedroom, but La Señora didn't answer. María pushed the door open and peeked in. It took her eyes a few seconds to adjust to the darkness. The heavy curtains were drawn, and the AC was loud. La Señora was asleep on the bed. The bed's four wooden posts reached toward the ceiling, each one intricately carved in an upward spiral and topped with a finely detailed pineapple whose every scale, every spike, had been hewn by someone's tools.

"Senõra," María whispered from the door.

She walked in. La Señora's mascara had run down her face, and the white sheets were stained black by her crying. Three pill bottles were open on the nightstand.

"Señora, ¿está bien?" María placed a hand on her shoulder.

La Señora murmured gibberish and turned her body away. María started picking up the mess: clothes, half-empty glasses of water, and three that still stank of alcohol. She went to the master closet and collected the dirty clothes she found there. She filled La Señora's hamper to the brim but noticed that Señor Romero's was empty, and that none of his clothes were on the floor—it appeared he'd not been home in a few days. María then scrubbed the master bathroom from top to bottom. On her way out, carrying the mountain of clothes to put in the laundry, she heard La Señora's voice rising from the deep, wobbly and weak.

"Amor, is that you? Antonio?"

María put the clothes down. "No, Señora, es María," she said.

"¿María?"

"The house is nice and clean, and the boys are in their rooms playing."

"Come here, María. Don't go yet." La Señora reached out her hand.

María approached and gave La Señora her hand, unsure. Had they touched before? María didn't remember shaking her hand when they'd first met, four years back, but maybe she had. La Señora's hand was soft, like a child's. She pulled María toward her, compelling María to sit on the bed. The lady cried into María's hand—great, big, wet sobs. She shuffled her body closer to María's and let it all out, whatever it was.

She embraced María's waist now, crying into her back, and María felt La Señora's pain rattling through her own spine. And she remembered Eloy's father, the pain she sometimes felt when, in Eloy's face, she detected traces of him. His short curls, his thick eyebrows, his dark skin. She remembered her mother the night Chávez had won, their talk, her mother telling her the way she'd felt when Stanislavo let her go: alone, abandoned, betrayed.

María freed her arm and placed it on La Señora's beautiful hair. "Shhhh," she cooed. "Shhhh, ya está."

La Señora heaved a few more times. "I think he's having an affair," she said. "I know it. He says he's busy with work, but—can you stay tonight, María?" she pleaded.

"I can't, Señora, Eloy's at home."

La Señora froze, her breath steadied, her crying quieted. She cleared her throat and let go of María's waist. A wet spot on her maid's dress stuck to the small of her back. La Señora shuffled on the mattress and leaned back on the ornately carved headboard.

"Of course. Eloy." La Señora grabbed a hairband from her nightstand and gathered her hair. "How's he doing?"

"Better," María said, looking over her shoulder at La Señora's face, a complete mess of caked eyeliner. "But he's so little, you know? I'm scared." She felt her own tears gathering now, warm behind her eyes.

"I can't imagine. I don't know what I would do if that happened to Gustavo or Jorge."

It was the kindest thing La Señora had ever said to her.

"Thank you. It's hard," María confided.

But La Señora's face had shifted. Without the tears, it was cold again. She didn't say anything else, just stared ahead into the darkness of the room.

María was no longer welcome. She stood and picked up the clothes. "I'll just put these in the washer and head home, okay?"

La Señora nodded, sniffled once more. María walked out of the room feeling dizzy and with something inside she could only describe as emptiness.

42

IT WAS EIGHT when she got off her last bus and started walking up the hill. The night was clear, the sound of frogs enveloping Cotiza in evening lullabies. People were out, still picking up pieces of the barrio from the ground.

She saw him, Eloy's friend, on her third set of vertiginous stairs—Wili's small body leaning against the red brick wall of El Portu's store. He wore his school shirt and pants, tattered, never mind that schools had been closed for the past week. He clumsily attempted to roll a coin over his knuckles but it was too big for his fingers.

"Wili? What are you doing out at this hour, mi vida?"

The boy palmed the coin and put it in his pocket. When she approached him, he stank. Not of body odor—Wili was too young for that, just Eloy's age. He smelled of garbage. The stench at first kept María away, then made her feel guilty, and she drew closer.

"Hola, Señora María, ¿cómo está?" Wili said, staring at the concrete.

"Why are you not home? Where's your uncle?" She looked around, as if to conjure Wili's caretaker, knowing she would fail. "When's the last time you had some food?"

Wili's eyes went large, and he didn't have to say anything to let María know that everything inside this little boy screamed hunger.

She led him up the steps, her arm around him. "Let's go get something to eat, okay? What do you like in your arepas?"

"Margarine," he said.

"We've got that. Do you like anything else?"

"Ham?" he said.

"We've got some ham."

Wili looked up at her and smiled; he was missing one of his teeth.

They went up the serpentine steps and finally arrived at María's hill. She walked fast, in a hurry to see Eloy and make sure he was all right. Wili kept up as best he could. She burst into her rancho and Don Jacinto was sitting there at the plastic table, holding a newspaper.

Jacinto put a finger to his mouth. "Shhhh, he just fell asleep."

María dropped her bag and peeked in the bedroom. Eloy's belly went up and down under the gauze. A thin strand of saliva hung from his mouth. She wanted to touch him, kiss him, but didn't. Instead, she went to Don Jacinto.

That embrace after she'd returned from the hospital had surprised her. How it had triggered a desire for this man, much older than her. He was a widower. Had a couple of children, long since moved out. His daughter worked in some fancy hotel on Margarita Island and sent him tchotchkes—ceramic palm trees, shot glasses, figurines—that he kept on his windowsill. María had no idea where to put this sudden crush, how to feel about it. She just knew she didn't want to face it and was thankful that Wili was here, something to distract her from the little fire that started every time she saw Jacinto.

"Where's Maga?" María asked as she sat.

"She went to a Bolivarian Circle meeting," Jacinto said.

Magali had become even more radical in the last few days, and now she lived in meetings. The Circles were in full recruiting mode, using the coup to scoop up acolytes. These civilian militant groups did anything the government asked of them: showing up at countermarches and rallies, intimidating opposition leaders, blocking access to government buildings. If not for Eloy's condition, Magali would have dragged María to the meetings with her.

"I swear that woman is something else," Jacinto complained. "She calls me *viejo* one more time—"

"Thanks for taking over, Jacinto. I don't know what I would do without you two."

"Who's the boy?" Jacinto pointed his chin toward the bedroom, where Wili leaned against the doorframe watching Eloy.

"It's Wili, Eloy's friend from school. I think he's been living in the street. For a few days, at least." She walked to Wili and put a hand on his greasy hair.

"¿Qué le pasó?" Wili asked.

"He had an accident."

"Did he get shot?" The words came out of Wili so dry, so adult.

"Don't worry, he's going to be fine. He just needs to rest and have some medicine."

"Good." Wili moved from under María's hand.

Don Jacinto gathered the few things he'd brought: the newspaper, the small radio he always carried. He stuck a blue pen behind his ear. "Bueno, llegó mi hora," he said. "I can do this again tomorrow. The garage hasn't reopened yet. The whole street was looted."

María went to give him a kiss on the cheek, like she had done a million times, but she hesitated and made the whole thing stilted and awkward, then blushed. "Gracias, Jacinto. Por todo."

"None of that. You and Eloy are family." He walked out the door.

"Okay, Wili," María said. "The bathroom is right there, go clean yourself up. I'll put some of Eloy's clothes in there for you. When you come out, you'll eat the best arepa you've ever had—margarine and ham, right?"

"And cheese?" he asked.

"Of course!"

Wili walked to the bathroom door and peeled off his polo shirt. On his back his brown skin was taut against his bones, all his ribs there to be counted. Three dark welts formed an inverted Z.

"Hey, wait," María said. She joined Wili and explored his torso, finding more scars. Badly healed marks pocked his body: lines, points, gouged shapes that curved around his arm. None of them were fresh. "Wili, what happened?"

But he stayed silent.

"Okay, go ahead, mi vida," she said. María pulled a smile from somewhere inside and gave Wili a kiss on the forehead. "Make sure to get that soap everywhere, okay? Even behind your ears!"

"Si, Señora María." He trotted into the bathroom.

María pulled the almost empty bag of Harina P.A.N. from the cabinet and poured the flour into her red plastic bowl, peeling at the rim. She added a pinch of salt, then water straight from the faucet, and as she worked the dough she cried again. How many times had she cried in the past week? For Eloy, for Magali and Jacinto, for herself, even though she was ashamed about those times the most, and now for Wili. Then Stanislavo, her all-of-a-sudden-real father, popped into her head. She hadn't had the space to process that. Here was Eloy without a dad, Wili without a dad, and even the boys at Casa Verde, if their mother was to be believed, might end up without one. Was Venezuela the land of missing fathers? If not for Jacinto and his little Margarita Island souvenirs, she might have thought so.

By the time the shower stopped running, the arepas were on the skillet and her face was dry. There was only one slice of ham left, and she packed it into Wili's arepa with the care typically reserved for more important things.

That night, after she'd tucked Wili in on the couch and cuddled next to Eloy in bed, María was flooded with the image of Wili taking small, deliberate bites of the arepa; with the sounds he made after swallowing; with the way he licked his fingers, glistening with melted margarine. All of that together lulled her into a deep sleep, filled with lucid dreams. The next morning she remembered just one: She was Eloy's age, wearing a yellow dress and walking through a forest, the sun sparkling through the canopy. A monkey, this little mono tití with blond fur forming a mask around his eyes, jumped down onto her shoulder. He whispered something in her ear that made her laugh. She fought to remember what he'd said, but it was gone.

María liked to wear a little bit of makeup every day. Nothing like the other maids on her bus, who might as well have been heading to the disco. She just used some foundation, trying to minimize her freckles, and worked on her eyelashes, to frame her hazel eyes. She liked her eyes, how big they were, how much they said, the gold veins running through them. The only man she'd ever dated apart from Eloy's father had said how beautiful they were, those sprigs of wheat. She had spent so much of her life hating everything else about the face in the mirror. Now her reflection couldn't help making her think of Stanislavo, and it drained away some of her self-loathing. She had someone to compare herself to. Someone to blame.

She heard laughter coming from the bedroom and went to spy on the boys.

"Draw Professor Julián next!" Wili squealed, next to Eloy on the bed.

Eloy wore that heart-melting look of concentration he'd had since he was a toddler. He held a pencil and made confident marks in a notebook. He cocked his head every few seconds, inspecting his work before going at it again. Wili, propped up on a pillow, supervised Eloy's progress. And then all of a sudden he let out a sharp, high-pitched laugh that threatened to shatter the lightbulb. Eloy joined in, casting the notebook onto the sheets.

"Look at his mustache!" Wili hollered. He curled a finger over his upper lip, jerked his head left and right, and made his voice deeper: "Today we are going to talk about Mesapopapa."

Eloy's laugh came in waves, and the waves lapped at María's feet. It was a balm, this laughter—for all three of them.

Then Wili noticed her, and the boys' laughter subsided.

"Perdón, Señora María," Wili said, and quickly stood up from the bed.

"No, mijo, está bien," she said.

"Mami," Eloy said. "Can Wili stay for a few days?"

"Is it all right with your uncle?" María asked. But she regretted the words the moment they came out. What a question to ask this boy! His uncle had let him roam the streets for who knew how many days, and María expected him to—what?—suddenly care? Did she expect Wili to go and ask him? "Never mind that," she said. "Of course you can stay for a few days." She would have to stop by the abasto to get some food. The pantry and the fridge were empty, and so was her bank account.

Wili jumped back on the bed, and Eloy winced a bit from the commotion.

"Okay, okay—remember to take it easy! Eloy also needs to rest, and his belly is still sick."

"Sí," they said together in their school voices.

María smiled. "Wili, Don Jacinto is going to come look after you boys in a little bit. I'm heading to work. Eloy, don't fight Don Jacinto when he changes your bandages, okay?"

Eloy nodded, serious now.

"Cool!" Wili said. "Can I look when he changes them?"

"Sure," Eloy said, shrugging.

"Okay, boys. Be good!"

"Sí," they repeated.

Eloy picked up the notebook. "Who should we do next?"

"Principal Benavente! But you might need two pages for him!" Wili puffed his cheeks out as big as they could go.

43

ON HER RIDE into Casa Verde, María turned her thoughts back to La Señora and the moment they had shared the night before. She'd never really thought that she and La Señora could share something other than space, but there it was: the pain of living at the whim of men. Their womanhood had grazed each other's. María was glad she didn't have to deal with Eloy's father anymore. It was true that raising Eloy on her own was hard, near impossible sometimes, but he wouldn't have been much help anyway. She missed him sometimes, in her weaker moments—the way he'd seen her in the early days, running his finger along her collarbone, dancing to Los Adolescentes—but overall, she was glad he'd left. And then there was Stanislavo Atanas, who had never even looked for her. True, her mother, by her own admission, had made it hard. But still. Another man who had left. So yes, she saw herself in La Señora, crying in bed. How could she not? She had been her. Twice over. And she wanted to tell La Señora that she would come out of this stronger. She regretted that she hadn't said it last night. But maybe it wasn't too late. She also felt Don Jacinto lurking in her thoughts. What would she invite if she gave in to this bubbling thing she felt for him? Jacinto could be a column to lean on. But Jacinto was also a man, perhaps no different from the others.

La Señora didn't open the door disheveled and struggling to

keep the boys in check. Instead it was Señor Romero, tall and hand-some, well-built, with that perfectly trimmed brown beard and his coiffed hair swooped to the right.

"Hola, María," he said. His teeth were also perfect. "Come on in."

"Gracias, Señor." María bowed her head and walked to the kitchen.

Alicia was back. She carried Gustavo.

"María!" Gustavito yelled and stretched out his arms, but Alicia turned around so that his head faced the other way.

She didn't say hello, just continued mixing some oatmeal for the boy with her free hand. Alicia was nineteen, big and pretty, with wide hips, strong arms, and long, curly hair. She'd grown up in Cotiza, not too far away from María's own rancho. María remem-bered how early she'd begun developing, how quickly the men had started looking at Alicia with hunger. Eventually, María stopped seeing Alicia and her family around.

The next time she saw her was the day the Romeros hired her, a few months ago, but Alicia never acknowledged their shared history. Maybe she truly didn't remember María, but María doubted it. "You know people and then you *know* people," Magali had told her. "She just doesn't want to be seen as coming from Cotiza, you know?"

"She used to work for los Gutiérrez," La Señora had said. "Comes highly recommended." María remembered feeling excited about having someone else in the house, someone she could connect with. But Alicia didn't like to be near María, as if there was a risk the two of them might be mistaken for each other. She avoided the kitchen entirely. Once, when María asked Alicia to hand her a rag, Alicia had snapped at her: "I don't get paid to clean. I've got my own job."

They shared space only once a day, at 2:30 p.m., after María cleared the lunch table and Alicia put Gustavito down for a nap and Jorge Luis was busy with his video game. They turned on the TV and watched the telenovela *Betty, la fea*. María saw glimpses of who Alicia was then. The girl laughed with her whole body, her pupils dilated. Whenever leading man Armando went in for the kiss,

Alicia's own mouth puckered the tiniest bit. Alicia argued with the TV and reprimanded the characters on the screen. While María also loved Betty and her adventures, she wouldn't have enjoyed the show nearly as much had Alicia not been there, so enchanted by the whole thing. It was one hour of freedom in that house, and it was nice to have a companion for it, even a reluctant one.

La Señora walked into the kitchen. She was back to standard form: pleated yellow slacks ending at the calf, yellow high heels, an exquisite silk blouse with a green leaf print, pearl necklace, and matching pearl earrings framing her porcelain face. There was something in the way their eyes met—some flickering recognition of their intimate moment yesterday, a seeming nervousness that made La Señora disconnect. María wondered if she should go to her, ask her if she was all right. Ask her about Señor Romero. But then he came into the kitchen and grabbed her from behind and hoisted her up, and she smiled like a little girl being tossed into the air by her father.

"Put me down!" La Señora said through giggles. "You're going to wrinkle my blouse!"

"You look too good!" he thundered. "Too beautiful to be out there without a chaperone."

It was as though La Señora were a lighthouse, with joyous beams flashing out of her ears and mouth and eyes. "Oh, stop it," she said. "I'm going to get my hair done."

"But it's perfect already," he said.

La Señora stuck her tongue out at him as she blushed. "Well, it's going to be even more perfect tonight." Then she turned her attention to María. "The boys' playroom was left a mess last night, María. You can't just leave the room looking like that and head home." She walked to the kitchen counter, grabbed a checkbook, and placed it in her purse.

María knew then that whatever she and La Señora had shared would never be spoken out loud again. It would be as if it had never happened.

44

ELOY WOKE, as always, with an itch he couldn't scratch—not only because his mom wouldn't let him, but also because even his thin fingers couldn't fit through the tightly wrapped gauze. It started with tingling and then itching and then pain in a line from his chest to his belly button. The pain was warm and wet, moving a little, as if choosing where to pop up according to its mood, like a mouse with many holes to choose from. Depending on when Eloy woke up, he would see his mom or Magali, sometimes Don Jacinto. But mostly his mom. And she would bring him a glass of water, prop his head up, and place one chalky pill on his tongue. The pill was too big for his mouth and hurt going down. He understood now that there were different kinds of pain: there was the hot, wet pain, sometimes like a stab right into his chest bone that sliced him in two; there was scratchy, choky pain; there was dizzy pain, as if someone was inflating a balloon in his head; and then there was the pain that didn't live in his body. It came when he heard kids walking by his house on the way to school. When he woke up and his mom was at work, and Magali wasn't there, and he could hear Don Jacinto revving hija de puta's engine but couldn't find the strength to move. It came at night, with sweating, when he saw his mom's eyes—baggy, dark, tired—as she placed a cool towel on his forehead.

But not this morning. Because this morning Wili was here. Still, the scar felt like something rotten today. Eloy didn't want to cry in front of Wili. What if he wouldn't want to be his friend anymore after that? He tried his best to keep it in.

Today Wili wanted him to draw Nevado, who was as dumb as he was tall, just a dumb old tree. Eloy had started to draw branches on his dumb head when the scar burped. He yipped and bent over. The tears came out, but he closed his mouth tight.

"Are you okay?" Wili asked.

Eloy kept his mouth glued shut and shook his head no, his eyes closed.

"It's okay, Eloy, it's all right."

He felt his friend's hand going up and down his back. He couldn't hold it anymore. He leaned into Wili, rested his head on his bony shoulder and cried. Wili didn't laugh, didn't make fun. He just stayed there, holding him. A while later, when Don Jacinto walked in the door, most of the pain had gone away. What remained was the fear of the bandage change.

He would contain his tears this time. Wili would see that he wasn't afraid of that angry line, of the monster mouth that was now a part of him. No matter how ugly it looked, no matter what it sounded like from the inside when the gauze was peeled away, Eloy would not cry.

45

CHÁVEZ'S FIRST SPEECH back as president was as conciliatory as Stanislavo had ever heard him. He was still afraid, it seemed. And how could he not be? To have walked that ledge. But all hopes of a changed man had vanished in just a couple of weeks. Revenge was now Plan A, Plan B, and Plan C. The government was targeting the media like never before, investigating its involvement during the days of the abortive coup. The architects of *El Carmonazo*—that was what the Chávez propaganda machine had started calling the attempted right-wing insurrection—quickly went into hiding or left the country. But perhaps no Venezuelan institution had been shaken to its core more than the military. That betrayal had been the knife between Chávez's shoulder blades. The president had expected the Chamber of Commerce, the media, organized labor to turn. But the military? His own men? The milieu that had made him? Chávez was combing through the military ranks like a mother scrutinizing her child's lice-ridden scalp. Meritocracy, seniority, talent—it was all going out the window. In their stead was prized just one quality above all: loyalty.

The new lie being peddled by the government was that most of the dead were Chávez supporters, felled by opposition-bought mercenaries and snipers. Stanislavo had seen firsthand evidence to the contrary in Vargas Hospital. His newspaper had compiled lists of the dead and was interviewing the families of victims, as well as survivors and eyewitnesses. No investigations had been launched into the highly credible allegations that Chávez and his closest allies had granted armed civilian militias a license to kill. Richard Peñalver—the selfsame councilman that cameras had captured shooting down from the Llaguno overpass—was now being lauded as a "hero of the revolution."

Victims on the Chavismo side had been paraded before the cameras. Stanislavo's deputy, Sandra Peterson, had interviewed some of them; a few had even landed jobs in the presidential palace. On the other side, one opposition woman, recovering from a bullet that had shattered her jaw, instead was visited by military police who threatened her not to contact the press. She and her two sons talked to Sandra anyway.

Stanislavo was on Avenida Baralt now, on the same block where fire had rained down on marchers and journalists. Everything was still closed; death clung heavily to the business awnings, the graffiti not yet washed from the metal security gates.

The only thing that had changed in the past two weeks was that dozens of government workers had come by and filled in every bullet hole they could find. They had retrieved every shell casing. They had erased every shred of evidence that could in any way bring light and clarity and truth to the events of April 11. But even if Stanislavo Atanas could feel the country under his feet again, he and everyone else who had lived through the coup knew how monumental the earthquake that shook it had been.

Almost forty years ago now, he had been in the jungles of Mochima, waiting with Nunzio and Tucán for the coffee to brew, Titi the dog napping at his feet. Molina had gone to get supplies at San Ignacio the day before. Stanislavo remembered it all so clearly. He was warmed by the campfire, smelled the bubbling coffee, heard the cracking of Nunzio's joints as he stretched his ridiculously long arms toward the sky and yawned.

And then Molina had emerged from the banana plants, carrying a backpack heavy with batatas and yuca. "I found a couple of strays on the road," he said.

Emiliana and Tomasa followed him out. They were giggling, holding hands like schoolgirls. Titi ran to them, tail wagging, her excited yelps and hops making everyone smile. Tomasa crouched, letting the pup lick her face.

Stanislavo stood and Emiliana walked to him and put her arms around his neck. Kissed him so deeply he fell into himself and thought he would never come back up.

Oh, how he wanted his friends back! How he wanted that life back! The future had seemed so full of light it was hard to look at it directly. Now, in Avenida Baralt, the future was a precipice. Nunzio, Tucán, and Tomasa lived only in his memory. Molina was part of a machine intent on ruining what was left of the country. His parents had died, leaving him the only person in the world who cared about Ludmil. Emiliana had disappeared, by all accounts hated him. He had never met their child.

All he had was a newspaper. What a pittance.

As he walked the avenue back to his car, back to his job, he thought again about the woman from the hospital: María Rodríguez and her son, Andrés Eloy. That experience with them—the intensity of the operating room—had marked him in a way that felt different.

But the country was smoldering, still, and then his phone rang. Sandra. He forced the mother and son out of his mind and answered the call.

46

AT ONE POINT the bottle felt so full that María thought it would never run out. One pain pill in the morning, before the bandage change, one pill at night before bed. Maybe one administered by Don Jacinto or Magali when María was at work, depending on how the scar behaved.

Wili wasn't at the house every day, but most days. He was medicine too. When Eloy laughed, when he drew, when they told stories, he forgot about the scar splitting him in two. María didn't know where Wili went when he left, in and out like a friendly street cat. He wasn't there today, and María looked forward to a Sunday with just her and Eloy. The scar had mostly dried up; Eloy was moving now, going to the bathroom, going to Jacinto's to listen to ball games. His skin was no longer grayish but back to a lively brown, shiny and smooth.

María shook the bottle and heard the emptiness between the lonely clicks. Two pills? Three? She sprinkled them into her hand. Two. She had replenished the antibiotics, but the pain medication had been impossible to get.

She listened to her son's soft snoring and buried her nose in his curls, then whispered, "Buenos días, mi amor."

Eloy turned his body away from her. He had started to move as he slept, like he'd done before the bullet.

"Vamos, flojo," she said. "It's almost ten! Don't you want to go out with me?"

He opened one eye. "Are we going out?"

"Yes! I'm taking you out."

Both eyes were open now, but sleep's gravity still held him to his pillow.

"Vámonos, pues."

María cracked one of the pills in two, as she'd been doing for a week. She didn't need to change the bandages, which were dry. She helped Eloy with his favorite shirt, showing Baseballsaurus, a spiky-backed dinosaur clutching a baseball bat, ready to swing at the next pitch. With her thumb she wiped the crust from his eye.

"¿Cómo te sientes?" she asked. "Does it hurt?"

Eloy shook his head.

"Okay, if it starts hurting, you tell me. We'll come right back."

Eloy nodded and María attempted to help him off the bed.

"No, I can do it on my own," he said.

María's mother came back to her so clearly then that she almost started crying.

"Everything okay, Mami?"

"You reminded me so much of your grandma, just now. Do you remember her, Eloy?"

"A little," he said.

"She loved you so much."

"I know," he said as he lifted his foot and threaded it into his shorts. Gingerly, so as not to disturb his belly.

It was a beautiful Sunday morning, with small white clouds so evenly spaced that God could have been a mathematician. As María stared up, Eloy let go of her hand and walked to Don Jacinto, who sat beneath his ferns, applying pressure to the narrow end of a pool cue with his knee and then holding it up before his eyes, like an impossibly long Pinocchio nose, to examine its straightness.

Eloy asked what it was, and Jacinto explained that the humidity lately was making the wood act all funny and he had to get his pool cue straight. He examined its tip now.

"But what is it?" Eloy asked.

"The shaft of my pool cue. For billiards? I'll take you sometime, if you want."

"Really?" Eloy glanced back at his mom. "Mom! Can I go with Jacinto to play billy-ards?"

Jacinto laughed. "Not now, little one. When you're better."

"I'm much better, though! My mom and I are going out!"

"Oh yeah? Where are you going?"

Don Jacinto looked at María, and she promised herself she would talk to him soon, about whatever it was she was feeling. "To the pharmacy," she said. "And if this little one has the energy," she added, tussling his curls, "to the park."

"I feel great!" Eloy said and put his arms up like a muscle man.

"That's good, little man. Take care of your mom while you're out, all right?"

"Yes, I will," Eloy said.

He hugged Jacinto, and María had to turn her head away, it was so sweet.

They walked down the hill, and then down the stairs that weaved along the mountain like sets of crooked teeth. María let Eloy set the pace. Once in a while he would stop. "Are you okay?" she would say. "¿Te duele?" And he would shake his head.

El Portu was sweeping the floor of his bodega. He was a stout man, with more hair in his ears than on his head, but he still combed the few strands he had left. It looked like a cow had licked them into place. His black eye had been healing for the past few weeks, since the looting, when three kids, just a few years older than Eloy, had beaten him up and cleared out his liquor inventory.

"Buenos días, Señora María," he said with his thick Portuguese accent. "How's little Eloy doing?"

"I'm doing good, Portu! We're going to the park!"

"He's been doing so much better," María agreed, putting a hand on Eloy's head.

"Well, come choose something for the park, then." Portu set the broom against the wall and lumbered behind his counter. The store was still half-empty, but the candy display was full.

María patted Eloy's back twice. "Go, mi vida."

He knelt on the floor, his head level with the rows of goodies. His finger pressed against the glass and scrolled over his options— Chiclets, chocolate, gummies—and he landed on one, a tube of Ovo-maltina, and tapped on the glass three times, looking up at Portu.

"Here you go, Eloy, que la pases bien en el parque."

Eloy held the orange tube of malted chocolate cream like a tro-phy. María mouthed a slow *Thank you* to Portu, who nodded and went back to his broom.

It was Eloy's first day back in the world, and it seemed fitting that the sky was blue and the people were good. When Eloy smiled, showing his teeth through chocolate-covered lips, María felt some-thing leave her body, something heavy and black that had made her feet feel like bricks these past weeks. When they reached the bus stop, she lifted his shirt to check the bandages. They were dry.

Downtown was alive again. In recent weeks it had been a militarized zone. Chávez had come back terrified, the fear had been in his voice and in his body when he spoke on TV, and the way it manifested was in the presence of the army everywhere, but especially here, where so many government buildings stood. But life had snuck in between mil-itary barricades and control points. Men and women peddled pirated DVDs, knockoff purses, salsa music compilations. They haggled with shoppers. Food vendors grilled meat patties, squirted bottles of gua-sacaca, and steamed perros calientes. María pulled Eloy close, pro-tecting him from the bumps of Sunday pedestrians. They walked for a block and made it to El Buen Vecino, where the pharmacy window glowed with greenish light coming from a neon cross.

The pharmacist, a grandfatherly man with a long saggy neck, was collecting money from a woman, not much younger than María. "Muchas gracias, señorita," he said and flashed his nicotine-stained teeth.

In the second their eyes met, María knew he didn't have the medicine.

"Hola, señora, nice to see you again," he said. "We haven't gotten the medicine in yet, I'm afraid." He dinged the register drawer closed. "Is this the boy?"

"Yes," María said and approached the counter. "Do you know when they're coming?"

"So you're the one that got into this mess, huh, young man?" The pharmacist looked down at Eloy. "You've got your mother running all around town hunting down pills."

María knew the man was just trying to be nice, but she wanted to grab him by his lab coat, yellow on the sleeves and reeking of cigarettes, and demand an explanation. This was the third week of having promised the pills.

The pharmacist apologized. His shipment should arrive on Thursday, he said, but with everything going on he didn't know if that would happen. With the coup and all the craziness, nothing was moving.

"I only have enough for another couple of days at most," María said. "Is there anything else I can give him?"

The man pulled out a small plastic bottle from under the counter. "Only acetaminophen," he said. "Not quite the potency you need, I'm afraid, but it's better than nothing."

María stared at the pills and thought about Eloy's greedy scar, how it demanded so much. It fed on Eloy, of course, but on her too—on her anxiety, her helplessness, her frustration. She pulled the cash from her pocket and put it on the counter.

"I've heard that some of the pharmacies on the East have been better supplied," he said, pulling on his turkey neck. "Maybe check there when you're at work?"

"Gracias," she said and walked back to the door.

Eloy was distracted by children's toothbrushes, their packages colorfully adorned with giraffes and elephants and tigers. Just as she was about to yank him away, her instincts turning mean, María caught herself. She was here for him—they were partners, not adversaries.

Outside the door, Eloy slipped. His right knee hit the sidewalk, but he bounced back up like a rubber ball. "I'm good!" he said.

He wiped the dirt from his knee, revealing underneath a few thin, reddish scrapes. Such a common sight on her son before all of this. His knees and elbows, the heels of his palms, the outside of his calves had always been striped like a tiger. How he loved to play baseball with the barrio boys in the sandlot next to the old cemetery, to slide into the bases, dive for grounders, pick up dirt before stepping to home plate and rubbing it hard into his hands. Her dirty tiger boy was always bruised and scratched, but back then it had meant happiness.

As Eloy straightened himself he whimpered, then bent back down and clutched his belly.

"Are you all right, mi amor?" María lifted his shirt and peeked at the gauze. The left side of the bandage had drawn a thin, red smile.

"Oh no," she whispered and looked in his eyes.

"Ouch—it's hurting a little, Mami."

"Yeah, honey, I can tell. Let's go home again, okay?"

"What about the park?"

And for the hundredth time since her son had been shot, María's heart broke. "We won't be able to go to the park today, mi vida," she said, even as she imagined the laughter of it, the smell of the wood chips, the way Eloy's butt would screech on his way down the slide. Another Sunday they would see it and hear it and smell it, but not today. Today the scar had other plans, and the park was another offering surrendered to it. "I promise we'll go soon, okay? When you're better."

"But I feel better, I swear!" he said, still unable to stand upright.

"You're not ready yet, Eloy. But you will be soon, and then we'll go play and get ice cream, and we'll bring Wili with us. Would you like that?"

He nodded and María began to usher him down the street. A man in a red beret held above his head a pole hung with T-shirts shining crimson against the midday sun. "¡Uh, ah, Chávez no se va!" he chanted before announcing the price of his wares. A bearded man shoved CDs in María's face. "Complete discography of Fania All-Stars right here, beautiful," he said. "With hips like that, I know you like to dance. Four thousand bolos." María sheltered Eloy along. "All right, bella, don't be mad, two thousand bolos and you take it all." She kept moving.

The bus depot was crowded, every bus like an hallaca with too much filling. The drivers' assistants hung from bus doors, yelling out destinations and collecting fares. The other side of the city: Los Ruices, La Urbina, Petare. María's side: El Retiro, Catia, Propatria. She pushed through the hordes, hoping that Eloy would be okay—that his tender belly wouldn't be struck by wayward knees.

When she got to the bus door, she handed the money to the assistant, telling him that her son was sick. "Do you think you could help us find a seat for him?" she said. "I can stand, it's just for the boy."

"What do you want me to do, lady?" he barked and glanced into the bus. "Just go on inside." He immediately went back to grabbing money from other people's hands.

They pressed in between an older woman carrying a Don Regalón plastic bag and a set of identical twin brothers, both wearing Magallanes baseball jerseys. She heard the man collecting fares yell: "¡Estamos full!" And then the disappointed harrumphs of those left behind.

For the next twenty minutes, María held Eloy as his little body tilted and swerved to the rhythm of the people on the bus. Finally, they made it to the set of stairs that led home.

"Me duele, Mami."

They both looked up the jagged hill.

María knelt in front of him. "You want a piggyback ride?"

He'd lost so much weight since his surgery that she hoisted him up easily. But with each step she felt that dark weight return, the tar lodging in her toes first and then crawling to her heels, and then up to her ankles and her calves—like oil oozing in reverse. By the time they got home it dripped out of her ears, her eyes burned from it, and her teeth were stained black.

Magali hadn't come through with the pills either. The Barrio Adentro free clinics, which Chávez had talked about all the time before the coup, had been shuttered since his return. "I've got people on it," Magali said, "but it's hard out there, comadre, I'm not going to lie."

It had been five days since the last half-pill had touched Eloy's outstretched tongue. Not even Wili was a balm now. The scar was not infected, the antibiotics still doing their job, but Eloy pawed at it obsessively—while awake, no matter how much María reprimanded him, and while asleep, much more savagely, and harder to prevent. Two days ago María had awakened to gauze all over the bed; the edges of Eloy's scar all pus; scabby stains on the bedsheets. Eloy was deeply asleep, his fingertips covered in brownish rust. When he told her about his dreams, Eloy described giant clawed hands lifting him up by the waist and one long finger prodding him inside.

María had attempted to talk to Dr. Ogaya at the hospital a few times. The nurse, the one who'd given her the medicine, couldn't do anything else. "Keep the wound clean and administer over-the-counter pain medication," she said. But the acetaminophen had no effect on the pain.

She had asked La Señora for help, of course. Almost two weeks ago, María had humbled herself and mentioned it in the kitchen.

"I'll ask Jimmy for them tomorrow at the club," La Señora had said.

Jimmy—Dr. Taylor, to María—was a friend of the Romeros whom María saw often. Tall and fit, as if chiseled out of marble, he spoke with a thick gringo accent and frequently switched to English. He was married to Gabriela Taylor-Macías, another friend of the Romeros whom María recognized from TV. She was a former Miss Venezuela who had placed third in the 1998 Miss Universe Pageant, and since then she had been trying to make it as an actress and TV personality. She was at once gorgeous and unreal, her face always trapped beneath a thick layer of concealer through which María could discern traces of acne. Gabriela's perfect measurements had been helped along by two or three surgeries. She was also devoid of talent and about as interesting as a wet piece of bread, which is why she had never really broken into Venezuelan TV, even though every other actress in the country boasted her same pedigree: from swim-suit model to Miss Venezuela to soap-opera star.

The idea that Jimmy and Gabriela would come through with the pills was a pipe dream. María meekly reminded La Señora every few days, nervous every time that she would bark at María to stop bothering her. But of course nothing had come of it. Neither Jimmy nor Gabriela had been at the house for weeks, not since sometime back before the coup attempt.

Magali told her: "You should get in touch with your father. He's the owner of that paper, the one Chávez talks about sometimes," she added angrily. "He owes you. He can get you those damn pills."

But María had resisted so far. It felt almost repulsive to her, the idea of looking into his face again. It felt like a betrayal of her mother. He did owe her, though. He owed *them*. She let that possibility float there. What it would be like to show up at the newspaper and say "Hello—remember Emiliana Rodríguez?"

47

THE NEXT MORNING María left Eloy squirming in pain, in the care
of a frightened Jacinto. She couldn't take another day off work, but
mercifully, the auto shop where Jacinto worked had had a power out-
age and he was home.

When she arrived at Casa Verde neither La Señora nor her husband was home. Alicia was there, staring at a *Sábado gigante* rerun
on the small kitchen TV while the little one tried to figure out how
many marbles he could fit in his mouth and the big one threw a
tennis ball against the living-room wall, every thud a stain María
would have to wipe off later.

"Mahhuuuiiiiaaa," Gustavito said as a dozen glistening marbles
plunked onto the wood floor and rolled toward her like glass slugs.
"María!" he screamed again and ran to her and hugged her knees.

She swooped him up and spun.

"Again!" he said, and she did it, but promptly put him down so it
wouldn't become the game of infinite spins.

The *thunk thunk thunk* of the tennis ball against the wall continued as María poured herself a cup of coffee.

"Buenos días, Alicia."

Alicia mumbled something back, a spoonful of cereal in her

mouth. She stared at Don Francisco interviewing some starlet, his eyes mostly on the woman's cleavage.

"Los señores, where are they?"

"They went to the club."

Thunk thunk thunk.

"Why didn't you go with them and take the kids?"

Alicia lifted her shoulders to her ears. "You a cop now or something? I don't know. Something about a tennis tournament, didn't want to deal with figuring out lunch plans. You know how they are."

María started washing the stack of plates in the sink, yogurt already encrusting the rims of the bowls.

Thunk thunk thunk.

"Could you get Jorge Luis to stop that, please? He's going to get that wall filthy."

Alicia didn't say anything. But the way she looked at María stung. María turned away and focused on the plates. She heard the clanking of the spoon in Alicia's bowl and her chair pushing back from the kitchen table.

Thunk thunk thunk.

"Here's another plate for you," Alicia said, leaving the bowl on the table. "Okay, babies!" she sang.

And then Gustavo ran behind his nanny, and the thunking of the ball finally stopped. The spoon had bounced out of Alica's bowl and landed on the wooden table, dripping milk, and María had to breathe deep.

She began in the kitchen, as always. She had her system, starting with filling up the dishwasher, and then, as it ran, working up to down, dusting and wiping upper cabinets, dusting and wiping countertops, dusting and wiping lower cabinets. Today she also had to deep-clean the oven. She wouldn't worry about the floors until the end. She lingered on a glint on the chrome of the refrigerator handle. The work was a familiar and comforting routine that let her fall into her own breath and listen to her heartbeat. Alicia and La Señora, Jacinto and Magali, Stanislavo, even Eloy and Wili and the scar and the pills would dissipate behind the scent of lemon verbena. The light from the wide window above the sink made the whole kitchen shine. She slung the moist rag over her shoulder and wiped her hands dry on the white apron tied around her waist. Everything in its place. Except Alicia's bowl, in the exact place she'd left it, the spoon still sitting atop a puddle of souring milk.

Then she moved room by room, each one an opportunity to get into a rhythm. When Alicia turned on the music and danced with the children, María let her hips help. Some days, time flew. This was one of them. She would pause cleaning at eleven to get food ready. For lunch she kept it simple, thankful that los señores were away. She had a small pot going with white rice; three butterflied chicken breasts that she'd marinated in a garlic-and-onion mojo, one of them cut into strips so the kids could dunk them in ketchup; and ripe plantains that smelled almost rotten as she peeled them but filled the kitchen with their sweetness as soon as she placed them in the hot skillet.

The smell called the children and Alicia downstairs. María looked right at Alicia, savoring her face as she looked at the cereal bowl, still on the table, and gathered herself. María waited for her to say something. Anything. But she did not. When Alicia grabbed the bowl and spoon and took them to the sink, María just stepped to the side and walked to the stove. She turned the browning chicken, feeling warm as Alicia scrubbed her own dish.

"Who wants some chicken fingers?" María said.

"Me!" Jorge Luis said.

"No, me!" Gustavito yelped behind his brother.

María fixed their plates and squeezed a farting dollop of ketchup for each boy. Then she went back and fixed her own and Alicia's.

"Buen provecho," she said as she placed Alicia's plate in front of her, the steam from the white rice framing the young woman's beautiful face.

"Buen provecho," Alicia said and started eating.

The kids played with the ketchup-covered chicken strips,

holding them up like matches in the dark. Anything Jorge Luis did Gustavito imitated, which was both adorable and frustrating. Gustavo was such a gentle soul, and Jorge Luis had already started to turn mean. María hoped that the younger child could retain some of that sweetness, despite his brother's influence. Even Alicia, in her sourness, softened as she ate, her eyes closed as she took a bite of the plantain tajada.

Later, when Alicia took the kids back up for some play and a nap, María rested. She tuned into *Betty, la fea* and let it sweep her away to Bogotá and the offices of Ecomoda, where Betty had already made her transformation from ugly secretary to beautiful fashion mogul. Then she resumed cleaning, and by three in the afternoon the house felt new. It was amazing how quickly she could move when La Señora wasn't around. She went to the service room, where she and Alicia kept their things. She stretched her legs and spread her toes. She massaged her right foot, drawing circles on her ankle. The small pangs morphed as they traveled up her body and came out of her mouth as sighs of relief.

She went into the tiny service restroom, big enough to fit the smallest toilet in the world, half a sink, and a corner shower with flimsy plastic frosted panes that threatened to snap if you leaned your palm on them. Still, it was a sanctuary. She turned the water as hot as it would go, and the room filled with steam. She breathed the humid, hot air in deep gulps, tasting the sweet nothingness of water. She thought of Eloy and how good it would feel to get back home early, spend an evening with him—sit down and watch *Radio Rochela* together and laugh for a change.

Maybe she would ask Jacinto to join them. If Eloy fell asleep, maybe she would finally have that talk with Jacinto. Tell him how she'd thought about him often since the hospital. How his arms held her so firmly that she was fine to just go limp. How she'd forgotten that feeling—the freedom to let herself go. His left hand spread wide across the small of her back, his long fingers leaving indentations on her skin. How she had wanted to kiss him then.

Drops of water speckled her body, and she placed a hand over her heart. When she removed it, it left a mark behind, like war paint. She took her other hand and placed it over her belly. It felt good to see herself, distorted, in the foggy mirror, surrounded by mist. Some sort of Kalinago warrior resurrected. Without the detail—without the freckles—she looked like her mother. María traced a line up from her belly button to her face, dividing her body in two. The palm of her hand brushed against her nipple. She did it again, this time deliberately. And then again, eyes closed. And then again. Then one breast begged her hand to stay, while the other hand moved down, past the tender hill of her belly, where she stopped to rest as if gathering strength for what lay before her: an ocean so vast and furious it would drown those unprepared. It felt like a miracle to visit this place again, to rediscover it after so much time away.

The shower felt like a baptism. As she moisturized the tips of her hair with coconut lotion, head down, she decided. Jacinto would be a part of their lives. Afterward, as she dressed, it felt like putting armor on a new body.

From the kitchen came a commotion. When she arrived there, toys and comic books littered the once-sparkling floor tiles, and Play-Doh balls were stuck to the once-shining chrome of the fridge door. Jorge Luis sat on her no-longer-pristine countertop, covered almost head to toe in flour. Gustavito, his hands stuck inside a mixing bowl, with flour on his nose, sneezed.

Alicia grinned. "Maybe you should have washed my bowl," she said.

"Maybe you should have washed my bowl," Gustavito parroted, then licked butter from his finger.

María's heart threatened to tear out of her chest. That ocean inside her had the power to swell and crash and pull under and drown. She walked to Alicia, very close. "Nos vemos mañana," she said and turned around.

On her way to the front door she saw a ripped comic book on the ground, one of the hundreds Jorge Luis carelessly threw around, colored on top of, ripped and mistreated. *Los Hombres X*. It showed a hairy man in a yellow-and-blue costume jumping off the page, ready to claw his enemies. Next to the comic book lay a small metal case with crayons. She picked it all up and put it inside her purse for Eloy. He deserved something nice today.

She walked out of the house at the same moment Señor Romero and La Señora returned. They were sweaty and red-faced, holding tennis rackets. They laughed as they walked up the front-yard path toward María and the door.

"Did you finish already?" La Señora asked, glancing at her watch.

"Sí, señora. I finished a bit early today. But Alicia let the kids make a mess of things, so I'm letting her clean up after them." She swore to herself that if La Señora said anything back about it, even suggested she stay and clean, she would say no. If it meant losing her job, so be it. She would let this fire carry her to the offices of Stanislavo Atanas, Eloy's grandfather, and she would demand that he step up, just this once in his life, for her and her son. He would find those pills for her and then she would never have to see his face again.

"María," La Señora said.

María waited for her to say it. To demand something of her that she would not give.

"I saw Jimmy at the club today. He said he was so sorry it took him so long. He was in Miami with Gabriela. You know she's taking some acting lessons up there?" La Señora held out a small white bag. It rattled as it hung under her outstretched hand, ready for María to grab. "Whenever you need any more, you can just call him directly. The number is in the prescription he wrote for you," she said. "I'll tell Alicia to clean up after the boys. See you tomorrow?"

María accepted the bag and stood still, surrounded by the lush green of Casa Verde. La Señora leaned into her husband, his arm around her waist as they walked to the door. María feverishly opened the bag and removed the bottle: solid, heavy, full.

FOUR

2012

48

ELOY WAS in his third semester of a marketing degree at La Universidad Bolivariana. After a few years working as a motorcycle messenger for a courier company in Cotiza, he had recently found a job as a chauffeur for a group of small businesses that shared offices in a building in posh La Castellana. There was a four-person investment firm, a small group of accountants, and the owners of Fresh Fish, a couple of guys who brought in catch from the coast, flash-froze it, and sold it for exorbitant prices to Caracas sifrinos learning how to make sushi. From Monday to Friday, Eloy drove everyone, ran errands, and did whatever they needed for seven hours a day. In the evenings he kept the well-worn Chevrolet Blazer, making it easy to get to his night classes and go home afterward.

And then, one night, Wili said he needed the car, and a friend.

Until that moment, Wili had never—not once—tried to involve Eloy in his affairs. Had never asked for help or tried to rope him into a scam. He kept that life separate, and still found time for their friendship. They would buy cheap-seat tickets for the Tiburones baseball games—Wili rooted for their rival, Magallanes—and would mostly talk for three hours straight, drinking beer after beer after beer purchased by Wili, who was somehow forever flush with a fat wad of cash. And though Wili kept his bad deeds separate, Eloy, if he was honest, had to confess that he'd always wanted Wili to bring him in on the action, and had even thought to himself that he would say yes if Wili ever asked him to help with a job.

Wili promised him it would be easy—it was something he'd done several times already—and Eloy would get a payday too. The plan was to drive around, find someone waiting outside a house on a quiet street, then force that person into their house at gunpoint and rob them. Nothing had ever gone wrong, and it had never lasted more than fifteen minutes.

Eloy and Wili had been brothers since the bullet days. The fever-through-the-night days. When nine-year-old Eloy woke up with dreams of a sharp red claw cutting him in two, it was often Wili who was there, holding his hand. When Wili was fourteen and his uncle died, the only family he had left, Eloy was the one person who knew how Wili really felt. "I'm glad he's dead," Wili whispered to him after the funeral. The Venezuelan foster-care system tried to get hold of Wili then, but María intervened. Wili's case manager, a burned-out woman with too much gray in her hair for her age and a backpack stuffed with folders, each one another child like Wili, was only too happy to cross a name off her list.

But Wili at fourteen was already a force, stubborn and slippery. There was no holding him except when he allowed it. Jacinto was just another man to ignore. María, whom he adored, was too easy to deceive. Eloy alone could settle him, but even then only for a little while.

By fifteen, Wili no longer went to school. María gave up on the dream of molding him into someone more similar to Eloy. Their home was a place for Wili to come lick his wounds: after fights, after stints in God knows where doing God knows what, after benders. But Eloy, who was always excited to see his friend come back to him, was a refuge.

By seventeen, Wili had his gun tucked into the back of his pants. And Eloy had never held one. María had succeeded in keeping him away from that life, but she failed to keep him away from Wili. It didn't matter that by then Wili was no longer welcome in their home, even though María asked after him all the time. Their friendship still thrived in the lazy afternoons on Cotiza's basketball courts or in the seats at El Estadio Universitario, watching the Tiburones play.

For the last two years, Wili had kept Eloy separate from his gun life. Eloy thought it had something to do with the respect, the love, that Wili had for María. But lately a shadow had grown over Wili that not even their friendship could dispel. And though Eloy had sworn — to his mom, to Jacinto, to himself — that he would never do what Wili did, when his friend asked for help, the *yes* was so immediate, and so divorced from any sense of morality, that Eloy wondered if it was really himself who was answering. His best friend needed him. What more was there to say?

Wili gave him a gun now. "It's loaded," he said, "so keep the safety on, right here." He showed Eloy. "You won't need to use it, I promise," he said, and told him to drive to La Florida.

Only in the car, on the way, did the question of right and wrong climb his spine. But before Eloy could back out, Wili spotted two young men standing by a metal door framed in bougainvillea.

"Park it right there," he said, "and follow my lead, coño."

And suddenly the gun was heavy in Eloy's hand, and the eyes of the kid on the other end of the barrel were wide in panic. The voice that came out of him wasn't his own. It belonged to an underground Eloy, a shadow Eloy, one who repeated Wili's words like a script: "Go in the house. Go in the house now, or I'll kill you."

Out of the corner of his eye, Eloy saw the pizza-delivery motorcycle rounding the corner. Its tires screeched once the rider saw them, guns drawn, pushing the men inside their house.

Three hours later, Eloy sat on the floor against the wall of the two men's living room, a massive painting of a horse framed in gold behind him. He sobbed openly, wondering what jail would be like, what his mother would think. Wili had gone upstairs, cell phone to his ear, still arguing with the police negotiator. The window up there had the best view of the street, where the lights of police cars flashed and a herd of armed men had gathered. Someone put a hand on Eloy's shoulder. It was one of the guys they'd robbed: Arturo, the smart one, the one who'd calmed everyone down after the police surrounded the house. He sat on the ground next to Eloy. The other guy, Quique, remained frozen on the couch, his eyes closed.

"Look, chamo," Arturo said, "you're doing the right thing, trying to convince your friend. If the cops come inside, they'll kill us all."

It had surprised Eloy that Arturo had remained serene throughout the whole ordeal—even at first, when Wili was liberal with the butt of his pistol. Eloy had been avoiding looking directly at anyone, even Wili, but he appraised Arturo carefully now and their eyes met. Arturo was tall and wide, his hand heavy on Eloy's shoulder. His five-o'clock shadow, shaggy hair, and pastel-colored polo shirt was the uniform of rich kids in Caracas.

"I shouldn't be here," Eloy said. "This is not my thing. I don't do this." His right hand, under his shirt, searched out his scar, the bump that still divided his torso in two. A nervous tic.

But he *was* here. He *had* done it. Eloy had held the gun Wili offered. He had driven the car when Wili told him where to go. He had turned into someone else—someone who wielded a gun and threatened people, who took their belongings and made them his. But finally this new person was melting away, and the Eloy he'd been for nineteen years—hardworking native of Cotiza, son of María Rodríguez—was waking up, ashamed.

"We're both here," Arturo said. "It's all about how we get out."

"I'm sorry for all of this," Eloy said. "We didn't mean for this to—I didn't want to—"

Wili's heavy steps down the stairs shook Eloy. His friend had always moved with purpose, ever since he was a kid. His intentions were mercurial, his moral sense blurry, his temper unpredictable, but his focus was undeniable. It was the opposite of most people Eloy had grown up with in the barrio, kids he'd gone to school with, who had an easygoing attitude and strove for a comfortable path.

Wili walked straight to Arturo and put the pistol to his head. Every tendon in his friend's outstretched arm was taut, but his face remained devoid of expression. The tattoo along his forearm rippled. It was the same one that Eloy himself was supposed to have. They'd gone together to get them a few years back. Hugo Chávez tattoos, totally free at Plaza Bolívar—either his eyes, or his signature. Five tattoo artists had been churning them out, ten minutes a pop. The two friends had stood in line for three hours that sweltering afternoon, but Eloy had chickened out after seeing Wili go first and struggle with the pain. They were sixteen then. Wili had chosen the president's signature in red ink.

Arturo raised his hands slowly and stood up. Eloy joined him.

"Tranquilo, Wili," Eloy said. He dusted off his pants, out of habit, though this house was so clean that the Spanish tile glimmered. "We were just talking."

"I fucking told him, pana," Wili said. His voice was high-pitched, and he talked fast without quite finishing his words. "I told him to stay on the couch."

"I'm sorry, bro," Arturo said and moved back to the couch.

Wili hit him in the head with the gun, again. Arturo fell to one knee and held his skull, making no sound, not even a whimper. Then he sat on the couch next to his friend, who was still comatose. On top of the coffee table, just across from the two rich kids, was the scattered loot that Eloy and Wili would never get to enjoy: a short stack with 237 dollars, a taller one with 56,000 bolívares, a pile of jewelry, a bottle of Buchanan's 18, a PlayStation 3, and two candlesticks that Wili claimed were silver.

"We're surrounded, Wili," Eloy said. "The kid has a point. If they come in here, they'll do it shooting. We're all going to die, chamo."

"We use them as shields and we fight our way through," Wili said.

"Wili, you're my brother, man. You know that, right?"

Wili stayed silent.

"What you're saying is crazy. Do you want to die? Because that's the only thing that can happen if we don't give up." Eloy's pocket buzzed. He pulled out his phone. "Wili, it's my *mom*. What should I do? Fuck, fuck. Do you think she knows?"

"I don't fucking know," Wili said. "The police know our names so maybe they found her? Just pick up the phone and act normal. Put it on speaker." He turned to their two hostages. "Either of you breathes a word and you've got plomo coming, understood?"

"Hi, Mom, I can't talk right now, okay?"

"Tell me the truth, Eloy, where are you?" His mom was crying into the phone.

"Tranquila, Mami, I'm here with Wili, we're just getting a beer." Eloy's voice didn't belong to him. Shame had its bony fingers around his throat.

"Don't lie to me, hijo. Just please, please tell me where you are." Her voice was like a prayer, attempting to conjure a miracle. "I'm right outside. Some cops called me and said you were here—that you kidnapped some kids? Eloy, tell me."

Eloy couldn't talk. His face shook. He felt the first tear on his cheek, then another, and then more.

Wili opened the bottle of whiskey and took a swig. But his calm veneer dissolved and he snatched the phone from Eloy's hand. "Tranquila, María, easy, don't cry. Everything's going to be okay."

"Wili, is that you? Please give up, okay? They're going to kill you if you don't. Please, Wili, I'm begging you."

"Easy, María."

"Why, Wili? Why did you do it?"

Wili didn't cry, but he swallowed hard, his bony Adam's apple pushing something down inside him.

"Wili, you've got to promise me. I know you love us. I know you love Eloy. You've got to promise you'll turn yourselves in."

"I've got to go," Wili said, shaking his head. One hand held the phone to his mouth, the other held the gun up high, by his temple. Then he folded up the phone and tossed it onto the couch.

"Mierda, chamo," Eloy said. "We have to turn ourselves in. Do you want my mom to see us in coffins? They're gonna kill us—and these two kids too."

"Fuck these fuckers."

Arturo gripped Quique's hand. His friend was crying now, but so quietly it could have been the chirping of a baby bird.

"Okay, sure, fuck them. But if they die, we go with them. And then my mom comes with us too. You know she couldn't handle something like this. You know that, Wili!"

"I just need to think, goddamn it."

But Wili lowered the gun, placing it carefully on the table beside the items they would have stolen, had things turned out differently. And Eloy knew his friend had already thought, had already cracked, had already decided. They would live.

49

ELOY AND WILI boarded the gray bus with more than a dozen other prisoners. The inside was only metal edges, as if the bus had skipped the last part of the assembly line. No cushions on the seats—except on two rows up front, and for the driver. No operable windows, no seat belts. It appeared to be held together by rusted welding marks. Each bench held two people, and in between each seat an armrest served as an anchor for securing handcuffs. Eloy and Wili assumed one of the benches, with Eloy at the window.

"Coño, pana, these seats are uncomfortable," Eloy whispered.

But Wili just stared ahead. Eloy could almost hear the fire in Wili's belly crackling, expanding through the dry brush, the brown grass, the dead trees inside him—his anger all-consuming. If Wili's skin were cut open and pulled away, ash would pour out instead of blood, revealing a smaller version of Wili made of charred wood.

Before boarding this bus, it had been four months of stale, bland meals; of overcrowded holding cells; of brief meetings with the public defender; of shameful visits from his mom, who could hardly talk she was crying so much. Four months of replaying Wili's invitation in his head and of answering *no* rather than *yes*.

After securing everyone's handcuffs, the three guards sat on one of the cushioned rows. Each prisoner was young. Some of them looked underage, even. But there were no children on this bus. Like Wili, these men had grown up fast and hard. They might have come from the same place as Eloy, but their lives had been different.

Eloy had always noticed the difference between himself and those outside the slums—the line dividing Cotiza from the rest of Caracas could have been a moat, it was so obvious. But the barrio itself produced its own hierarchy. These lines were blurrier but no less present. Having a mother like María—who worked, made a living, was able to put three meals a day on the table—placed Eloy above some of those lines. Wili's scarred back, and his drunk uncle, broom handle in hand, landed him squarely at the bottom.

With his friend staring at nothing, Eloy realized for the first time how different this moment was for the two of them. The rage that burned inside Wili was fear inside Eloy. But why should Wili be afraid? He had nothing to lose. Eloy had his mom, and his job, and a life that, before this mistake, could have been decent. Wili had a gun and his anger. He'd find another gun in prison soon enough. And his anger? No one could ever take that away.

One prisoner, with the girth of an eighteen-wheeler tire, sat behind the guards in the only other cushioned row. Special deference seemed to be paid to his comfort and well-being. He was asked if the cuffs were too tight, if he wanted a bottle of water. He swung his large head *no*.

The bus started. The low rumble rattled the seat and the handrails, and the cold, tight cuffs dug into Eloy's wrists. He gripped the armrest to keep the cuffs from doing more damage. It was already too hot inside the bus, and they hadn't even started their ten-plus-hour ride southwest, to Cárcel Patria y Próceres, in the middle of nowhere. The biggest penitentiary in the country, according to his lawyer. The man had said it like it was something to be proud of, like Eloy should be happy he was going there. It was so far away that to his mother it might as well have been the sun, although by all accounts the sun wasn't as hot.

The last time Eloy had seen his mother, a month ago, she had tried to rush him. To hold him before he was taken away from her. He could hardly face her. He was almost thankful for the guard who came between them to prevent an embrace. It would have been too painful to feel his mother's arms around him.

The hours spent on the road felt like a funeral procession, minus the ceremony. No cars followed their massive hearse, no emergency blinkers, no grieving mothers or flower arrangements. No old women who made the sign of the cross and mouthed short prayers for Eloy's soul as the bus passed. It was an individual procession, with each prisoner saying his own private goodbyes.

Sleep came in small bursts cut short by pain—his lower back screaming to change position, his head banging the hard glass when the bus smacked into one of the million potholes, his wrist bone grinding against the steel of the cuff, his scar pulsing like it did when he was stressed. Plus, he was so hungry. The highway held rows of shops selling pork rinds and beer, arepas and cachapas filled with glistening white cheese and melted butter, cold Pepsis with white frost on the clear bottles. Earlier, a prisoner with a few thin hairs on his upper lip had asked if they could stop for food and the guards hadn't even turned around. Eloy's stomach complained with wet gurgles.

Eventually, darkness met them on the highway and wore a cool breeze, bringing some relief. The guards had been progressively shedding their heavy green uniforms. By now they wore only their pants and white undershirts. The highways and roads were in awful disrepair; every time the bus hit a pothole, Eloy was surprised the whole machine didn't just fall apart. Whenever the bus tackled a hill, it slowed so much that people walking beside the two-lane road could keep pace, and an infinite line of angry cars formed behind them.

Then the special prisoner whispered into a guard's ear, and the guard stood to announce that they were making a pit stop. "Nobody get any bright ideas," he said. "Everyone stay quiet and calm, and we'll get moving shortly."

The prisoners all glanced at one another. Eloy wanted to ask whether they could go to the bathroom and get something to eat. He hoped someone else would ask. Wili was as expressive as an empty vase. Eloy wanted to shake him. What right did Wili have to be angry with him? *He* was the one who'd gotten them here. If not for him, Eloy would be driving back home from school right now, ready to sit down to a warm meal with his mom.

"Can we go to the bathroom?" Eloy asked.

Everyone looked at him, then at the guards. A guard walked to the back of the bus and pressed the butt of his rifle on Eloy's groin. He pushed, slowly but firmly, pinning Eloy between the rifle and the seat. Eloy closed his eyes and tried to breathe. The pain was dull and crushing.

"How you gonna go to the bathroom without a dick?" the guard said loud enough for everyone to hear. He then removed the rifle as calmly as he'd placed it there and returned to his seat.

The bus pulled into a gas station, clean and well lit. Suddenly the bus was flooded with the smells coming from the chicken restaurant next to the station, the gasoline fumes mixing with the intoxicating aroma of rotisserie chicken. The meat spun over an open flame, folks sat at plastic tables eating with their hands and chasing their bites with gulps of sodas of all colors. Eloy imagined himself at a table with Wili, looking from the outside at the shiny metal bus, wondering who was inside, where they were going. "Poor devils," Wili would have said to him with his mouth full of juicy chicken. "Van pa' las tumbas." And it was true: graves for living men awaited them.

Two of the guards went into the restaurant. The prisoners whispered among themselves, speculating on the possibility of a meal. But the guards came back with just two paper bags of food, already forming grease spots from the warm chicken inside. The prisoners would arrive to prison hungry and thirsty, and—for those who couldn't hold it—with their pants wet.

After all the guards and the special prisoner had a chance to relieve themselves in the restroom, the bus rolled again. The guards opened their bags of chicken, pulling out legs and thighs, the skin perfectly blistered and shiny. They produced steaming bowls of white rice and slices of sweet plantain and downed everything with almost frozen orange sodas. Every time they opened a bottle, the *pop* felt like a slap to the face. The special prisoner—one of the guards called him Topo—was no longer cuffed. He laughed with his mouth full of chicken; trails of fat slid down his chin.

Eloy closed his eyes and breathed through his mouth, the only way he could think of to cheat his hunger. He couldn't wait for the paper bags and wrappers to fly out the window and join the rest of the trash by the side of the road. After the men had finished eating, Topo looked back at Eloy. He took the last satisfying gulp of his Naranjita and tossed the bottle at Eloy in a perfect arc over the heads of the other prisoners. Eloy reached out and caught it with his free hand, thankful that he wouldn't have to deal with broken glass on top of everything else.

"Now you can pee," Topo said, and the guards laughed.

50

THE BUS SQUEAKED to a stop and silence rushed in to fill the gaps left by the old engine and the metal chassis.

"Bueno, we're here," Topo said, standing up.

He stretched his huge brown body like a bear. His hands pressed against the bus's metal ceiling, his fat fingers spread wide, and if the bus hadn't survived the million bumps on the hellish journey here, Eloy might have thought that Topo, with his massive shoulders and back, could break it open. Everyone else remained cuffed, and Eloy envied Topo the cracking of articulation, the stretching of muscle. The guards made their way to the back, unlocking cuffs and lining the prisoners up.

Eloy stepped off the bus at the end of the line, right behind Wili. His friend's muscles had a twitchiness that betrayed his blank face. Wili was thin but also strong, a fibrous, streamlined man made dangerous by his anger. Eloy wanted to share his fear in a less telepathic way—even a hand on the shoulder would have been a balm—but he knew Wili better than that. It would be taken as an affront. So he just walked behind his friend, hoping Wili was not as alone as he felt.

The guards led them through a gate into an outdoor lobby, where they encountered other guards, their weapons old and worn.

One sat behind a plastic table with a sign-in book, its pages brown and wavy. Behind him loomed a massive metal door painted a blue that Eloy had only ever seen in institutions: hospitals and government offices. The door was peppered with bullet holes that broke up the blue with speckles of rust. Some were new and some were old, the width of rust around the circumference telling their age. Jagged teeth, also rusted, protruded from each small mouth. Every hole, and there were many, had been made by a bullet traveling from inside the prison.

Above the door hung two government signs in their usual white-and-red color schemes, with images of ministry sigils and flags. The first one read:

BOLIVARIAN REPUBLIC OF VENEZUELA
MINISTRY OF POPULAR POWER FOR PENITENTIARY SERVICE
CÁRCEL PATRIA Y PRÓCERES

The second:

OPERATION "CAMBOTE"
REPAIRS AND IMPROVEMENTS TO CÁRCEL PATRIA Y PRÓCERES

The heavy door screeched as a guard pushed it open, not all the way, just enough for the prisoners to enter one by one. Each prisoner lined up by the door, ready to sign his name and leave an ink imprint of his thumb. The line moved fast, and as dread and uncertainty bubbled up inside Eloy, bile rose to the back of his throat. He signed his name, and the guard guided his thumb onto the paper, rolling it carefully from left to right. Eloy glimpsed a memory then. He rarely thought about his grandmother anymore, couldn't really recall her face, even. But he remembered her hand, veiny and soft, and how it had helped his inked thumb onto a piece of paper the day she took him voting.

Eloy peered inside the door. He stood paralyzed, unable to cross into this other world. He had constructed this prison in his mind, brick by brick; he had populated it with people; he had placed himself in the middle of it all, playing out scenarios. But faced with the real place, he froze. Until a swift kick to the ass pushed him in.

"I said *move it*, coño!" The guard slammed the door shut behind him with a clang as final as rigor mortis.

All the guards remained outside. Inside it was just Eloy and Wili and the unfortunate thousands who called Patria y Próceres home. Eloy nearly collided with a short man holding a brand-new AK-47. At first Eloy took him for a jailer—he had the posture of someone standing guard—but he wore no uniform. He was another prisoner, and he and a few others like him guarded the entrance to the government-controlled intake lobby. More than merely a new place, the prison was a new country, one with borders and armies that protected it. But here Eloy had no rights and no knowledge of the laws, if any existed. He was utterly foreign.

They landed in the prison's main courtyard, a large open space flanked on three sides by a rectangular three-story building. The ground level of the building was open, with wide columns that supported the two stories above it, creating a covered walkway all around the cement courtyard. The walkway was littered with vendors. Eloy couldn't quite tell what they sold, but the scene was filled with the usual sights and sounds of a market: haggling and conversation, the exchange of jokes, a couple of bony dogs skittering around. From all sides of the courtyard different songs played at the same time, all at maximum volume, mixing like a bad stew. If it weren't for the absence of women and children, it could have been another Sunday at one of Cotiza's outdoor fairs.

Hundreds of men, maybe even a thousand, stood in the yard and along the walkway. The space was large enough to accommodate them, but not comfortably. Everyone carried menace on his chest—most of them bare because of the heat of the dry season. (Not that it ever cooled off here much, no matter the time of year.) The two floors above the walkway were constructed of hollow cement block that allowed air to circulate through the bowels of the prison. Arms poked out of the concrete openings and half-hidden faces stared into the yard, resigned, like pigs in trucks on their way to the slaughterhouse.

A small shack on one side had a handwritten sign that read LA TASCA DE ROBIN HOOD, and the smell of food was a rope around Eloy's neck, pulling him toward the restaurant. But he had no money, and nothing to trade. An opening off the courtyard led to the rest of the prison grounds, which lay behind the massive building. From here Eloy could just make out a dirt field, a covered basketball court with stands, and in the distance an old church and bell tower, the church roof gone and the tower appearing ready to topple beneath a moderate breeze.

To the side of the courtyard, visible through the crowd of inmates going about their day, was another government sign announcing enhancements to the prison under Operation Cambote's "Vital Improvements to Prisoners' Well-Being." But the only thing under construction was a swimming pool. Two men—Eloy's fellow prisoners, by the looks of them—stood inside the empty tank, spray-painting a Playboy bunny on the blue tile.

Topo walked the pool's perimeter. He met up with another man, smaller, a bit pudgy, who was supervising the construction. They hugged, and even with Topo towering over him Eloy could tell that the smaller man was in charge. There was a deference to Topo that would have been inconceivable just an hour earlier, in the bus. The shorter man pointed to one of the workers, and Topo lifted him from the pool in a second. The man in charge berated the worker, periodically poking him in the chest. With every finger stab, the worker brought to mind a mangy dog kicked in the ribs.

Wili started walking toward the pool now with purpose, the way he did when there was something he wanted—no, needed—to do.

The first time Eloy had seen that walk they were twelve years old, playing chapita in one of the barren fields by Wili's uncle's place. Wili and Eloy had spent the whole day scavenging bottle caps, begging the daytime drunks slamming dominoes on the tables, scrounging the trash can by Portu's store, straightening out the caps that were too bent to toss properly with a pair of pliers that Wili filched from his uncle's toolbox — risking a savage beating if the man noticed. They filled an empty paint bucket with their treasure, hundreds of bottle caps: the blue yin-yang of Pepsis, the beautiful cursive of Coca-Colas, the red dots of 7Ups, and — Eloy's favorite — the sitting bears of Polar beer.

Then they ran to the sandlot, the handle of the bucket digging into Eloy's hand, Wili swinging a long broom handle as if it were a sword, fending off imaginary hounds. Wili drew home plate in the dirt with the broom handle and counted ten long strides to the pitcher's mound, where he marked a line and Eloy deposited the bucket and took up residence. Eloy pulled out the first cap, a 7Up, and stared at Wili, back at home plate and brandishing the broom handle like a baseball bat. Wili's favorite player was "El Come Dulce" Bob Abreu, and now he mimicked his power stance at home plate, the broomstick swiveling behind his head, his right elbow held high, perpendicular to his body. Eloy started his windup, exaggerating his movements, his whole torso bending backward, then flung the bottle cap sidearm. It cut the air like a tiny buzz saw. Wili swung so hard he spun in place like a trompo.

As Eloy dug into the bucket for another cap, they heard voices. Three kids approached. They were thirteen or fourteen, bigger than Wili and Eloy, their pimpled faces and lanky arms stinking of puberty. They wore their caps backward and their shorts low, and they moved with the exaggerated swagger of the older barrio boys.

"Coño, Fede," the biggest one said. "Look at what the menores got us! How many chapitas do you think there are here?"

"A hundred?" the one called Fede said.

"No, chamo, more like two hundred!" said the short and fat one, his belly and breasts stretching the fabric on a counterfeit Nike shirt.

"We'll find out soon," the leader said.

He grabbed the handle of the paint bucket and with his other hand pushed Eloy, who lost his balance and landed on his behind, raising a cloud of dirt and reaching in pain for his lower back.

"Hey, that's ours!" Eloy heard.

And then he saw it for the first time. The walk. Wili moved toward the group at a steady pace, holding the broomstick all the while. His expression was vacant, as if his features had fled his face.

After the boys ran away, their backs and arms and heads bruised and welted and bloody from Wili's savage swings; after Wili apologized to Eloy for breaking their bat; after Wili said he had to go find another broom before his uncle discovered it was missing, Eloy spent some time alone in the dirt, staring at the chaotic mess of footprints and body impressions where the kids had writhed on the ground as Wili thrashed them. He wondered where the violence in his friend had come from: *Was it simply something inside Wili, or something he'd learned?* The line he had walked toward the three kids was the straightest thing Eloy could remember seeing—straighter even than his surgery scar.

So Wili's walk *meant* something. And it had ever since that day in the sandlot.

At this moment his walk was taking him to the pool: to Topo, to the self-important boss, and to the worker. Eloy tried to catch up, but he had a hard time navigating the crowd. His shoulders brushed against other men, bigger men, who stared at him with hard eyes. But Eloy just apologized and kept moving, inching closer to Wili. By the time Eloy reached the pool's edge, Wili was already talking to the boss next to Topo. They must have known each other, or known someone in common, because the man embraced Wili and said something in his ear. Eloy was close to them now, about to say something, when Wili grabbed the pool worker by his ratty T-shirt, knocked him to the ground, and started pummeling him. Wili's face was blank again. Every time his fist came up, after each punch, it was bloodier—from the man's broken face, from his own busted knuckles. Frightened, Eloy turned his face away. His cowardly reaction startled him at first, then filled him with shame, and his shame made him look again. The worker lay limp by the pool. Wili knelt over him, wiping his hands on the man's white T-shirt, smearing it red. He rose and extended a bloody but perfectly steady hand to the boss, who nodded in approval.

"My name's Luis Suárez," the man said. "But everyone calls me Tortuga." He spoke slowly, each word like tree sap.

Tortuga had square shoulders and a beer belly. His face was round, with a wispy mustache and a slight gap between his front teeth that was more mariachi than prison boss when he smiled. He wore a Tommy Hilfiger polo shirt, Bermudas that reached just below his knees, and flip-flops. Tucked into his shorts was the butt of a revolver. Topo seemed a giant next to him.

"Topo, take this young man and introduce him around. Show him what's what. And tell him the rules." Tortuga snapped his fingers and a couple of guys materialized from the crowd. He pointed at the beat-up pool worker, moaning in pain, and the two men carried him away.

"He's with me," Wili said, pointing in Eloy's direction.

"The pee guy?" Topo said.

Wili nodded. He was still breathing heavily from the beating, but his eyes were cold and steady.

"Let's go," Topo said. "We have plenty to cover."

Topo walked to the building with the arms protruding from its windows. Wili and Eloy followed. At least Eloy's body did. His spirit remained behind in the yard, floating just above the ground, staring at the bloody stain by the pool. It then floated higher until he could see the entire prison. The courtyard, the building housing the inmates, the half-tiled swimming pool, the beautiful basketball court, and the crumbling church, the massive walls containing everything, everyone except him. He tried to fly home: to his mother, to another Wili who had never tried to kidnap anyone, to another Cotiza where there were more trees and fewer guns. But he could travel only up or down, not forward or back. He floated as high as he could go, until the prison was just a speck.

Eloy's body still walked behind Wili, however, and as soon as the stench of the prison interior hit him, the longest rubber band in the world snapped his spirit back. Eloy heard a crack, as if the whiplash had broken something inside him, but it was only the thick metal door to the yard slamming shut behind him.

"There are only two important rules." Topo's deep voice traveled through the narrow hallway, the echo bouncing ahead of them like a half-filled basketball. "They're very simple. One: You do what the boss says. Two: Everyone contributes to the Cause."

"¿La Causa?" Eloy asked.

"It's the way things run. At the end of every week, you owe Tortuga. If you bring anything in, if your family comes to visit, if they send anything, you owe Tortuga twenty-five percent. Make sure you deliver. You'll pay in cash, work, or pain, but you'll pay. Tortuga prefers cash, and that means you'll prefer cash too."

Topo led them through labyrinthine networks of hallways, rank with mold and sweat. Every few feet they passed an identical doorless square room filled with a combination of foam rectangles, blankets, and mattresses, at least twenty per room. If not for the smell of rancid humanity, the rooms would have seemed abandoned, like forgotten refugee camps. The heat was overwhelming, the air burning Eloy's throat as it went down into his lungs. He had to breathe through his mouth — anything to avoid the smell.

"Everyone in this wing is out in the yard right now," Topo explained. "It gets too hot inside after three."

"What about the people on the other side of the yard?" Eloy asked. "The ones looking out from the holes in the wall."

"Undesirables," Topo said. "They get their time. Tortuga allows them to come out from eleven to one every day, and on Sunday we all share the yard."

They reached a half-crumbling staircase. A young kid was asleep on the lower steps, his head resting against the wall. He had black curls down to his shoulders and wore what seemed to be the uniform for prisoners: basketball shorts, flip-flops patched up with tape, and a bare chest blanketed with shaky tattoos — there was a Virgin Mary cradling a baby Jesus, a pair of dangling boxing gloves with the word *Campeón*, a hand holding a knife, and Hugo Chávez's signature in red ink tattooed right over his heart. The same tattoo that Wili had on his forearm. A revolver lay on his lap, the chrome no longer polished but stained with sickly yellow spots.

Topo shushed Eloy and Wili. He moved toward the boy with a silence that belied someone of his size and deftly lifted the gun from his lap. A thick string of saliva hung from the kid's mouth. Topo pointed the gun at the boy's peaceful face. He offered Eloy and Wili a wide, impish smile that glittered like a knife in moonlight. When he cocked the revolver, the metallic *click* straightened Eloy's spine. Topo never took his eyes off Eloy and Wili. The boy remained asleep the entire time.

Topo didn't fire. Instead he chuckled and held the revolver out to Wili. "This will be better in your hands than in that lazy bum's, as long as you understand the rules."

"What the boss says, when he says," Wili told him.

"With a smile," Topo said, his face all fangs.

Wili's mouth cracked into a smile, his crooked, rabbity front teeth painting a wicked picture, eyes as empty and dark as a grave awaiting a coffin. He uncocked the revolver and secured it in the small of his back.

"That's my man!" Topo's voice boomed. "Let's go upstairs. You haven't seen the best part."

As Topo walked past the guard, he hit him hard on the back of his head with his massive hand. The boy flew to the ground and looked up, wiping the slobber from his mouth.

"You fall asleep again during guard duty and I'm taking your trigger finger."

The boy didn't reply, just started frenetically searching for his lost weapon.

Topo laughed as they climbed the steps. "Gun privileges have been revoked!" he yelled.

The upstairs was different. It smelled different, too, a milder bouquet than downstairs, with hints of car freshener and Axe cologne. Mirroring wooden doors ran the considerable length of the hallway. They might have once opened into offices, Eloy thought, in a time long forgotten, when the system still had room for non-prisoner bodies. Who would have worked here? Eloy could imagine men and women walking from door to door, carrying paperwork to be signed, release orders to review, health charts or activity schedules. Some of the doors still bore placards (JORGE CAMEJO — OPERATIONS MANAGER; ANDRÉS VIANA — HUMAN RELATIONS; STAFF MEETING ROOM), relics of a time before someone had locked the place up and thrown away the key.

"Here we are," Topo said. "My home away from home."

He opened a door to the left — its cracked sign read OFFICE OF PRISONER RECREATION — and revealed a spacious room. It was luxury compared to the conditions downstairs, and for a second Eloy wanted it. Above the headboard of a queen-size bed in disarray hung a poster of Taz, the Tasmanian Devil, his mouth fanged, his tongue hanging out, his lower body a whirling tornado. Hearts fluttered around him and big block letters read: TE AMO, DIABLO. Around the poster were plastered various images of women, some of them photographs but mostly cutouts. A desk held a flat-screen TV and a leaning tower of pirated DVDs. And on the far wall of the room a wide window faced south, not toward the cement prison yard where they'd entered but behind the prison building.

From this vantage point Eloy could see the full scope of the complex. The roofed basketball court was new, still fresh, with stands all around it, prettier than the ones in Cotiza. The wide-open dirt lot was painted with a baseball diamond. There were even what appeared to be some haphazardly constructed stables, made from zinc paneling and wire fencing, and to the southeast a half-crumbling warehouse with blue tarp tents pitched on its roof — occupied, Eloy noticed. Just south of this shantytown on the warehouse roof rose the tall bell tower, riddled with bullet holes but overseeing the whole complex. The rest of the church sat in ruins next to it, the roof caved in, rubble and debris strewn at its base. Beside the church, a field with a few cows. Every remaining space had been claimed by temporary structures: tents, shelters, small ranchos made of wood, metal, and cardboard, anything people could find to house them- selves. Beyond and behind everything—past the tall barbed walls that kept everyone inside and the guard towers that looked down on them and the guards in their green uniforms patrolling the tops of those towers—loomed the imposing rock formations and outcrops that sprouted from the arid ground like bursting fists.

"This is what you can get, if you're good," Topo said. "If you do what Tortuga tells you, if you contribute to the Cause without fail, with loyalty and courage, you can be a prince."

Eloy imagined the things Topo had done to get this room with a view. He imagined what Wili might do for his own piece of this kingdom.

"You know Torrealba?" Topo said.

"Sí, vale," Wili said. "He sold me my first hierro, ever. Some Chi- nese piece of shit that jammed all the time. He charged me full price for it too."

"Ha! That slimy motherfucker."

"He got his a few months ago," Wili said.

"No way!"

"Three bullets in the back, outside DiscoCoco."

Topo made the sign of the cross and looked up to the ceiling. "I'm going to be really nice to you," he said. His gold tooth sparkled between his full lips. "To get you started," Topo said, and handed Wili and Eloy each a wad of cash. "Ten percent interest every Sun- day, starting the day after tomorrow."

Taking the money felt to Eloy like tightening his own noose. But what was he going to do, say no to Topo? And it resolved some of his immediate needs, food the first of them. He was so hungry.

Topo led them to another door in the hallway. This one was metal with three locks on it. Topo dug into a fanny pack he wore around his waist, under his white tee—Eloy hadn't noticed it earlier, since Topo's massive stomach sat on top of it. He pulled out a long, straight-edged key and started unlocking the deadbolts. After three loud *clacks*, the door swung open.

"I wouldn't normally do this," Topo said. "But since you're Torrealba's guy…"

The room was part armory, part electronics store, part licorería, part grocery. There were kilos of pasta, bags of rice, a selection of whiskeys and other liquors, lots of guarapitas and aguardientes and other bottom-shelf stuff, but also bottles of Black Label and Buchanan's 18 and Old Parr. One whole wall was weapons—long and short, new and old. If it fired and could kill, there was space for it.

"Stay out there," Topo said.

A roll of toilet paper flew out and Eloy caught it with soft hands as a second one arced toward Wili. Then Topo came out with a plastic bag.

"Toiletries. Two of each," he said, and gave the bag to Wili. "I think there's a couple of open mattresses in Cell Five. If anyone gives you trouble, just tell them it's Topo's orders."

Topo grabbed a flask of aguardiente and a pack of cigarettes, then locked each of the deadbolts. He cracked the aguardiente open, took a swig, and handed the bottle to Eloy. Topo's expression was hard to decipher. He was always smiling but there was something fickle about it, as if the meaning could change from joy to sadism at the twitch of a lip or the glint of a tooth. Everything about the man said *caution*. Eloy hoped Wili saw that too. The flask went around a few times, and they each smoked a cigarette. Eloy felt dizzy—the aguardiente had lit a fire in his belly—but he also started to relax, and he noticed Wili do the same.

Topo poured a bit of aguardiente on the ground. "To Torrealba, then."

And the three of them took a swig.

"That's why I like to live in the country, man. You centrales have way too much shit going on, too many sides to protect. On the coast, where I'm from, you know who your enemies are. You can see them coming."

Eloy now had to pretend that these stories belonged to him too, even though he hated them, and hated that Wili had them.

"Tour's over, pups. Now pay me for the supplies and the liquor." Topo took half the money he had given them not fifteen minutes earlier, then walked them downstairs. "I'll count this as your first contribution to La Causa," he said.

An hour in prison and already they were in debt. But Wili was no longer angry, so there was that. The booze, along with getting his bearings, had shaken something loose; Eloy was starting to re-emerge. And having a true friend in here, he figured, was worth more than just about anything else.

51

MARÍA BUZZED back and forth inside Jacinto's rancho like a fly stuck between a window and a screen. Out of habit of mind, she still thought of the place as Jacinto's, despite all the years the two of them had shared here together, despite his having left it to her after he passed. The last four months, since the day her son had lost his mind, had been spent on lawyers and court dates and trying not to get fired from her job at Casa Verde. She'd had no contact with Eloy since their tear-filled goodbye at the Caracas holding cell, almost a month ago now. Just remembering it made her angry. She had thought the female guard would understand. That somehow, through their common womanhood, compassion would flower, and a short-lived embrace would be allowed. But when María had sought refuge in her son's frame the woman had blocked her, cruelly placing her mass between them with all the urgency of a bodyguard stepping in front of a bullet. Eloy was bent in sorrow. He held his handcuffed hands to his chest. His curly hair was dirty, making his body look frailer than it really was, like a dandelion with a broken stem.

"No contact," the guard said.

María hadn't touched Eloy since the morning of the kidnapping, when he'd left for work. She remembered cupping her hand to his cheek, telling him to have a good day. She tried to push past the guard, her arms stretched out to her son, hoping to go through the woman, to become a ghost. When that didn't happen, she turned the guard into her son, imagining the guard's warmth as his, her perfume as his aftershave. And her hatred for the woman became love for her son, just for a second, and she hoped more than anything else that Eloy could feel it. When the guard shoved her away and she collapsed, the hatred rushed back in, all at once. And now it was not only for the woman but also for Eloy—because he had done this. Really she hated Wili, because Eloy had followed him, and because she knew he would have followed Wili anywhere. Most of all, though, she hated herself—for believing that Eloy had made it out, that getting into college had somehow immunized him against this pox of Cotiza men, that her love for him had served as vaccine.

She did not remember, now, what she'd said to him, but she hoped Eloy did. The clang of the metal door closing behind her son had felt like a brass-knuckled punch. There had been no word of Eloy—not a single piece of news regarding his whereabouts—since their goodbye. The only thing she knew was that they would hold him for an indefinite time, with no access to visitors or phone calls, until his transport to the Patria y Próceres prison. The court-appointed lawyer, whom she'd seen from afar at tribunales, who had met with Eloy only once and with her never—and from whom she had only a dirty business card—was nothing but a hoarse voice on a recorded message. Mist in an ill-fitting brown suit. It had all been so overwhelming that she'd gone to the cemetery to visit her mother's grave. She hadn't been there in such a while that it had taken her a long time to find her. Kneeling by the plaque, the name Emiliana Rodríguez obscured by weeds, María had cried until she couldn't anymore, knowing that her mother, if she were alive, would know exactly what to do.

The night sky was pitch-black with rare summer rain clouds, pregnant with water. Everyone in the country was on edge, even those without sons in prison. No one knew how much longer President Chávez would be alive. In his rare TV appearances recently, he had looked bloated and green from chemo. Elections were looming, and for the first time in a decade, the opposition seemed the strongest of the factions. The one time María had spoken to Magali in months, all Magali could talk about was how divided the party was. "They're like vultures over a dead dog," she had said. "Trying to see who'll get the bigger piece."

María had been calling her all week, but it always went to her voicemail. The two of them had drifted apart, sure. Magali was a big deal in Cotiza now. After the coup she'd become leader of the local Bolivarian Circle, which received significant funds from the government to operate. In a matter of weeks Magali bought a nice house on the lower hill, painted red in honor of the revolution. Within a year she had a new car, a new wardrobe, a young boyfriend. She talked to María less, coming to see Eloy only sporadically and after a while not at all.

Now Magali had big, blonde hair, and her face adorned Cotiza billboards. She had run for a seat in the National Assembly and won. María had helped her campaign, more out of duty to her old friend than anything else. But Magali had barely shown up to campaign events, much less to the small headquarters she'd set up. The place was just a front: boxes of campaign material, a couple of phones, and a bored teenager to answer a phone that never rang. What Magali really spent her funds on was getting her face splattered on Cotiza walls and paying voters directly for their vote. "It's the way campaigns are run nowadays," she'd told María. "It's the way things are." After she got elected, they talked only a few times, ran into each a couple more. But María thought Magali would at least answer her phone call in an emergency. It hurt her that she'd been so wrong.

She looked at Eloy's photo now, framed and standing on the side table by the couch. It was from his high school graduation, an unposed shot. He'd been walking through the crowd and for a second had turned and seen her holding the disposable camera and given her a quick pass-by grin, one of those pictures that is at once in focus and out of focus. He'd already removed his robe and mortarboard, and wore a brown polo shirt—the public school uniform—covered with his friends' signatures. María loved that tradition, all the kids signing one another's shirts: heartfelt goodbyes, inside jokes, and the few brave confessions of long-suffering crushes, all in thick, hard-to-read marker. When they came back home that night and celebrated, Jacinto already half-eaten by throat cancer, Eloy asked them all to sign his shirt: María and Jacinto, but also Wili (who hadn't been at the graduation ceremony, of course—hadn't so much as stepped inside that school for more than two years and hated everything about it). Eloy had saved space for the three of them on the shirt's chest. Unsure what to write, María had asked Jacinto to go first. When he finished, she still couldn't come up with anything. Wili took the marker from her and scribbled his initials, the same ones that littered the walls of the barrio. She ended up writing *I'm proud of you*, which was true, but also so insufficient that it made her feel stupid.

There was one other photo: Jacinto, before the ball in his neck had started to grow. He posed with fourteen-year-old Eloy in front of Hija de su gran puta, the motorcycle that had saved Eloy's life and María's with it. They each held a pool cue. Jacinto had his wiry arm around Eloy. They were both smiling wide, their shirts similarly stained by motor oil. Deciding to accept her feelings for Jacinto had been the best decision of María's life. And even though they'd never gotten married, despite Jacinto's proposals, they had become a family.

María didn't know where to go, but she knew if she stayed in her house one more second, she would start screaming and never stop. She thought of Eloy locked up somewhere, in some room, or cell, and the walls around her suddenly moved closer. Or maybe it was that her sadness was bloating her into some kind of grieving giant, making her rancho seem smaller. She burst out the front door, gasping for air.

She was surrounded by Jacinto's ferns. Well, her ferns now—since Jacinto had left it all to her. Across the street her old home still displayed the same zinc paneling that couldn't stop bullets. The man who lived there now, a security guard at a residential building in Colinas de Bello Monte, sat in a plastic chair outside, drinking a beer, listening to the baseball game. Another thing that reminded her of Jacinto.

"Neighbor," he said, then stood and walked a few steps toward María. "Have you heard from the boy?"

"Nada," she replied. "I don't know anything. I just need some air. I need to walk."

"It's pretty dark," he said. "Smells like rain too. Why don't you lie down, take it easy. You'll know soon, I'm sure of it."

She hated that — people saying it would be okay. María knew he meant well, but she couldn't stand it. She smiled at the man, trying to be polite, though she could feel the strain of it.

When had she last been out of her house after nine? In Cotiza after a certain hour, the air turned noxious with ill intent. A sort of poisonous mist rolled through the Caracas valley and climbed the hills of Cotiza and parked itself, licking the walls of the ranchos that made up the barrio. People like María found shelter, hoping that the mist would remain outside, and mostly it did. Others fed on that venom; they filled their lungs with it in big, greedy gulps. It made them drunk, violent, and loud. It made their muscles bulge and their souls shrivel. It was their barrio at night. They had bought it with lead and blood long ago.

She walked past locked houses, the lights inside still on but the doors barred until morning. As she descended the hill, young men stood smoking outside the bars and whorehouses of Calle Carabobo. Women — girls, really — clung to them wrapped in tight red leather and yellow sequins. The familiar bass rhythms of reggaeton and the crooning of cumbias fought in the streets like packs of mangy dogs. María loved music like this. She couldn't help remembering when she'd danced with Eloy's father, clinging to him tightly enough that maybe he would stay. At her age, she danced now only while cleaning the beautiful rooms of Casa Verde, when La Señora had gone for errands. But it was still a joy to feel the rhythm invade her hips, her dance partner the broom in her hands.

She stared at these venomous people, looking for something inside them that she could recognize in herself—some set of small dignities that said *We are the same, you and I*—but with the darkness, and the clouds starting to spit on them, and the light of the bars creating only silhouettes, she could not find anything. Would Eloy be inside one of these establishments had he not been taken? Wili would. In fact, María saw Wili's face in every man. The one leaning on the bar's peeling wall. The one drinking from a flask and winking at her as she passed. The one holding tight to the plump, naked waist of the teenager in the yellow skirt. She hated all of them. But then she remembered the nine-year-old Wili who had sat by Eloy's bed while his wound healed. Wili would stare at the long red scar, the tight black string knitting the flesh together, and say: "That's so cool, Eloy!"

María sat down on the curb. Tears and rain became indistinguishable. The people smoking outside flung their cigarettes—or stepped on them, or gently extinguished them and stuck them in their pockets—and made for shelter. María stood and went up the mountain. Back home. Whatever she was looking for was not here.

Two men followed her, one heavyset and one smaller. In the darkness and the rain María could tell nothing about them except their intentions. She crossed the street and picked up her pace. They stayed on their side but kept up with her, hands in their pockets, baseball caps shielding their eyes from the rain. She held on to her azabache necklace, fingering the bumps of the small black fist. A few streetlights vomited pale yellow light that barely illuminated the old political posters high on their poles, Magali so caked with makeup that María couldn't remember her friend's real face as it had been when Eloy was young.

She paused and pretended to tie her shoe, her eyes on the two men on the opposite sidewalk, hoping they would walk on and she would see their shapes disappear, but as soon as she stopped, they did as well. They found refuge under a small awning and pulled out a pack of cigarettes. Could she outrun them up the mountain? Turn into a side street and lose them, perhaps? Every alley was a hungry mouth, and the street was so steep, her house still far away. And she was so angry.

She went right up to the men. She stared at the bigger one, the ember of whose cigarette cast a shadow on his wide nose—broken many times—and on his dirty face and sunken eyes. She slapped the cigarette out of his mouth.

"You do anything—even blink at me funny—and I will end you, ¿entiendes?" Then she faced the smaller man, with his face full of acne. "¿Me entiendes?" she yelled.

She made herself stand tall as she climbed the steep hill back home, waiting for hands to grab her. But she only heard the men laughing.

"Chamo, we better not mess with that loca," one of them said.

Once she arrived at the top of the hill she turned around. The clouds had parted, and a thin shaft of moonlight cast a spotlight on the two men, who walked away, beckoned by the throbbing music.

María woke the next morning with a cough. She had nothing to eat and no room in her head for anything but Eloy anyway. She put coffee in the percolator and turned it on, bracing herself for a hungry morning. After seeing Eloy for the last time, she had tried to stay steady at Casa Verde. She had admitted to La Señora what had happened long before, the very day after the kidnapping. The shame María had to swallow when she told her, the judgment in the other woman's eyes. The fear. She imagined La Señora telling all her friends: *Her son is a criminal, chica; you know he played with my kids when he was little?*

Though María had been alone in the house for months now and could use any type of company, it had grown increasingly impossible to be at work. When she wasn't crying, she was angry. At Eloy and

Wili, for being so stupid; at the Romeros, for their quiet contempt; at herself, for her helplessness.

A few days ago she had finally asked for two weeks off from Casa Verde, time to make a game plan with the lawyer and to run any legal errands needed. But also simply to catch her breath. To be home instead of there. La Señora had agreed, reluctantly.

Almost fifteen years working for them—knowing them, really, she thought, for you don't truly know someone until you clean up after them. La Señora's husband masturbated every Tuesday evening, when La Señora had her weekly walk at the country club. María always found the small white towel, crusty with a yellowy stain, in his personal hamper on Wednesdays. La Señora broke her perpetual diet often, with packs of guava cookies showing up in the trash, but she replaced them in the pantry so her husband would see the same unvarying supply of packs on the third shelf next to his dark chocolate.

But María knew the most about Jorge Luis, whom she had witnessed grow up into the man-child he was today. The dirty movies he watched on his laptop. The three pairs of panties he had stolen and hid in the back of his junk drawer. She knew everything about his moods. With his being the same age as Eloy, she'd known him from the sweetness of infancy, when he cooed and babbled and laughed; to the cruelty of childhood, when he'd teased Eloy for his curly hair, the few times she'd brought her son to work with her; to the meanness of adolescence, when he'd slapped her ass in front of his friends while getting drunk on his father's liquor; to, finally, the indifference of young adulthood, when if not for his hollering for a juice here or a beer there it would be as if María did not exist.

Gustavito, on the other hand, who had managed to escape the influence of his older brother, was still good to her. But he had been in Paris for almost a year now, studying French and staying with La Señora's extended family.

María called Casa Verde now, just to check in with La Señora.

An unfamiliar woman picked up. "The Romero family, how may I serve you?"

Eight words and she knew that she'd been replaced. It was the same phrase that María had delivered every time she picked up the phone at Casa Verde. It sounded just the way La Señora liked it: "Always with a smile," La Señora had told María the day she first started working. "People can tell when you're smiling on the phone." And it was true. María could hear now that whoever had picked up the handset had a grin on her face. The voice on the other end sounded young—maybe even younger than María had been when she started at Casa Verde.

"¿Aló? This is the Romero family. Can I be of service?" the voice repeated.

María hung up. She took a shower, so angry she feared the water would evaporate as soon as it touched her.

52

WILI AND ELOY walked together to La Tasca de Robin Hood. Eloy staggered, really—his head a bad carnival ride. But the smell of food pulled him along. La Tasca was a shack made from corrugated zinc, but inside the matching appliances were all brand-new, including a pristine white fridge. On the equally white range sat two deep black cauldrons with oil bubbling inside; the pots seemed ancient, something passed down through generations. The blackboard on the back carried a menu in chalk, and above it a quote in messy handwriting: *The Cause is progress: Donated by Luis Bernardo "Tortuga" Suárez.*

"Your taxes at work," Eloy mumbled.

"Tortuga is the pran, the goat that pisses the most," Wili told Eloy. "Topo is one of his luceros. I'm sure there are at least two or three more lieutenants. They're the carro in here—they make the rules and enforce them. We stay on their good side, and we'll be good."

Eloy wondered how long the prison had been run by prisoners. By which set of incremental processes the guards had been exiled from inside of the hive. How one man, this pran, could lay claim to it, and control it.

"How do we get money in? To pay them, I mean."

"We work, for one. And whenever we can we get your mom to send us some money. Tortuga will have a bank account she can deposit it into. A few people owe me some money, so I'll also pull my weight."

The idea of talking to his mother—of asking her for anything—turned Eloy inside out. He had forced himself, since the kidnapping, to keep her out of his thoughts. If he didn't think of her, then the guilt could be ignored. But it was impossible to keep that monster at bay for long. Like telling oneself not to think about an elephant.

"Let's eat," Wili said and put his arm around Eloy. The first human touch since boarding that bus.

Behind the counter a soft, round man in his mid-forties looked for something at the bottom of the fridge. He took out a plastic container and pulled off the plastic wrap that served as a lid. Long strands of shredded beef sat in the thick sauce with pieces of red and yellow ají dulce. Eloy could smell the simmering onions and garlic of his own mother's carne mechada. How the air became spicy when she added the chopped ají. How she always asked for his help, ever since he was a little boy, with shredding the long pieces of skirt steak. He would grab two forks, one to hold the carne in place, the other to pull apart the meat, so soft that each strand would fall off with the gentlest of tugs. His grandmother came to his mind again, second time in the same day. He remembered her long black hair, so different from his, how it fell on him from above as he shredded the beef. He tried to remember her face, but it escaped him still.

"¿Qué pasó, my friends? Welcome to el penal," the round man said in a rush, as though each word was stuck together. The only letter he took his time with was the *S*, the telltale lisp of someone from Margarita Island. "Bienvenidos a La Tasca. You hungry or what?"

Wili was about to order but Eloy interrupted. "Four shredded beef empanadas, por favor."

"Y dos Coca-Colas," Wili said.

"We only have Pepsi," the man said. He reached into his back pocket for a bottle opener, pulled two bottles out of the fridge, and in what looked like a single swoosh of arm and metal flipped both caps off the bottles in a perfect arc into the trash bin, where the caps made little clinks. "Me llamo Roberto, but everyone calls me Robin. Four empanadas de carne mechada coming up."

Eloy was mesmerized by Robin's fluidity, every move practiced a million times. The dough was already separated into palm-sized yellow balls, and these he placed on a circular metal press lined with plastic wrap. The press came down gently, flattening the dough into thin disks. Then Robin removed each disk, wrap and all, from the press and held it in his hand like something fragile, like something loved, and spooned a generous serving of the carne mechada into the middle of the disk. Quickly and precisely, he folded the plastic wrap and the disk became a plump half-moon. He pinched the dough together with nimble fingers, securing the meat filling, and with the tip of a fork marked the top of the raw dough, signaling it was beef (not to be confused with a small hole for cheese, or the smooth surface for chicken). From there he slid the empanada out of the plastic and into the cauldron, bathing it in the boiling oil. The sound made Eloy forget where he was. He couldn't see the empanada, but he pictured the dough becoming darker, small bubbles forming on its hardening surface, ready to fracture under that first glorious bite that would taste the same in prison as it did on the beach, the same in squalor as under his mother's care. There it was—the elephant again.

The empanadas were so hot that Eloy and Wili had to ask for more napkins to protect their fingers. They bit into them at the same time, not caring about the burning of tongues or the blistering of cheeks. The roofs of their mouths would surely swell and peel later, but for now they would delight in this taste and warmth.

The rest of the day was a parade of introductions: Wili knew some people, through other people on the outside, none of them anyone Eloy had ever met or even heard of. Here every word had a double meaning, every person had an agenda, every edge could cut. Saying the wrong thing was dangerous, of course. That was obvious. But being silent also carried risk. "Why doesn't your boy talk?" they asked Wili, and Eloy was forced to take part in conversations for which he was unprepared.

The only way he got through it was by drinking as much as he could as quick as he could. Nobody asked the drunk guy any questions. Nobody put him to the test. They joked and poked fun until Wili parked him in a plastic chair, like a child at a grown-up party. Eloy observed and tried to make sense of what he had to do — or perhaps what he needed to become — in order to belong.

Wili spoke the language here. In Eloy's world, Wili couldn't make it. The way he talked. The way he moved. The way he dressed. People would cross to the opposite sidewalk when he walked down the street. But here, Wili fit.

And Wili was his brother. They'd shared a classroom from the day they started school in their red polo shirts at six years old. Back then, Wili had been constructed out of twigs. Always on the move, as though he could be in two places at the same time. His hands always in something: the toy box, his nose, other kids' lunch boxes. They were so different. But it also made sense: What Wili put out, all that kinetic energy, Eloy had room for. Eloy craved the chaotic freedom that fizzed inside Wili and sometimes burst out like shaken cola. And Wili must have longed for peace, for someone to lean on after all the energy was spent. Eloy was happy to be that sanctuary.

For a few years after the gunshot, Wili had slept at Eloy's house most nights. Those stints would be interrupted by a tornado of yelling and flying sandals that spit Wili out the front door whenever Eloy's mom had her patience sucked dry by his antics. But a few days would pass, and Wili would walk by the house, a new hole in his shirt, a black eye, and Eloy's mom would call to Wili from the open doorway, "The arepas are almost ready — you want a bite, mi amor?" And Wili would trot in smelling like a wet dog, and the cycle started all over again.

When they were thirteen, one night as Eloy lay on the couch and Wili lay on the floor beside him, he had finally asked his friend the question that made them brothers. "Wili," he said, "did your mom die?"

"She's around," Wili said, leaning on an elbow, and his face changed.

"Where? How come I haven't met her?"

"She's here—but not really, okay? I don't want to talk about it."

But his answer made no sense to Eloy, who pressed him. "Does she work in Caracas all the time? Is that why?"

"She's here, okay! I see her every day. You see her every day, you know who she is. Just stop it."

"Who is it?"

Wili sat up then and looked at Eloy. He was crying, but it wasn't sad crying. He was angry. Eloy didn't know if Wili was mad at him for prying, or just mad at the whole big mess of both having and not having a mom, or if he was mad at something even bigger, at Cotiza, at how they lived.

"She calls me hijo," Wili said. "You've heard her."

And it all came to Eloy like a mudslide down the hill. The crazy lady. Loca Juana, with her pencil-thin legs; her red-sequin dress disintegrating on her body, every week a new bony part revealed; her mouth with more holes than teeth; the boils and warts; the smell of sour milk as she chased after them on the days that she wasn't passed out in an alleyway; the things she said that Eloy had always thought were just the words of a crazy lady who'd lost her son seeing his face in every other child: *Hijo, te quiero, come here, let me give you a hug, te quiero, te quiero.* La Loca Juana following them up the mountain with arms outstretched until Wili picked up rocks and hurled them at her, and Eloy joined in too, until one or two connected with her hollow chest or her matted hair. Wili's aim always suffered, his rocks missing her, striking the ground by her feet—never mind that he was the best pitcher at the sandlot.

Then Eloy understood.

Wili lay back down and rolled himself in the blanket on the ground. He shook and trembled inside the wrap, his sobs muffled by fabric. Eloy got down from the couch and held his friend. Wili let him into the blanket roll, and the two boys slept together, protected by the shell of their shared blanket and the warmth of their bodies.

Eloy wondered now, as a young man, if Wili had ever been given a chance to emerge from that cocoon. If there was something Eloy could have done then, or later, to make that happen. Here in prison, it was apparent that Wili had emerged. Somehow he was home. But his wings weren't orange and yellow, reflecting the sun. They were gray and black, fuzzy, dusty even as he beat his wings. Cotiza, and now prison, had never been places for butterflies. But moths? They thrived.

Eloy tried to sleep, but the cell room was so crowded that every time he closed his eyes, it seemed, his thin mattress was pulled off the ground, as if by ropes, and tilted. His swollen tongue was glued to the roof of his mouth. His breath—rancid-sweet and heavy from last night's rum—was alive, almost corporeal. He wanted to douse it with water. Drown it. Kill it. But it was the middle of the night and he didn't know where to get water. He'd noticed spigots out in the main yard, but that seemed so far. Maybe he'd seen some on a hallway inside the prison? Where was it those men had been filling gallon jugs ahead of lights-out, before being led back into the pens? In the haze of the rum, water hadn't mattered then, and he hadn't paid attention.

Eloy lay in the center of an archipelago of mattresses, mats, and blankets. Each island had one inhabitant: sweaty and dirty, drunk or high. They snored and snorted. They shifted their weight from one side to the other. They held on to things—stained pillows if they had them, a backpack looped into a scarred arm. One man he could see in the dimness held a knife. Some talked in their sleep, or to one another. Eloy could tell the difference by volume; real conversations came in whispers, whereas sleep-talkers didn't care how loud they were. The cacophony of dreams was amplified by the stone walls of the room they all shared. Sound bounced and distorted, became ghostly and strange. A cell that once could have housed six bunk beds, at most, now slept at least thirty men. None of them but one whom Eloy even knew, much less could trust.

Wili slept on the mattress next to him. He lay on his back, with his legs crossed. His right arm, extending perpendicular to his body, rested on Eloy's mattress. Wili had never been restless in bed, not even when he got in trouble as a kid, or when he was high out of his mind as a teen. Some plug disconnected when his body hit a soft place, and he would just go away. Eloy wondered if it was the only time Wili felt truly at peace.

Eloy stood and his head immediately punished him. He spun and fell, knees first, onto his mattress, thankful he hadn't fallen on anyone else, knowing what that would mean. He tried again, this time anticipating the swoon, and managed a precarious balance. Surrounded by prone bodies, he seemed to be at the center of a clump of maggots. Although each individual writhed alone, taken together they seemed to form a single organism, alive in its symbiosis. The smell hit him — the acridness of each mouth, of each armpit, of each crotch, each ear and foot, each pore and orifice merging into a symphonic stink. He stepped over the first body, then another, and another. He avoided them like a dancer in the dark, the adrenaline pushing him out into the hallway.

The hallway stretched long, with more doors, just like his, opening into other rooms just like his. The men in these other rooms also snored, and stank, and made noises. Smaller rooms with shut doors held secrets Eloy wasn't ready to explore. A scream with a hand over it escaped one of them, and the muzzled violence squeezed Eloy's bones.

In the dimness he spotted a water faucet a few yards away, sticking out from the wall, and ran for it. He knelt before it as if in prayer and turned the peeling handle. The faucet farted and growled but gave him nothing else.

He remembered there was a bathroom. It was best not to go there, he'd been warned, and to stick to one of the restrooms in the courtyard, which were maintained by the evangelicals—the young prisoners in white dress shirts and pants who did the servant labor: cleaning, running errands, washing laundry. *Worker ants*, Wili had called them. But they did not sleep here. Nor did they clean this bathroom. No one did. It hadn't been cleaned in months. In years, maybe. Eloy smelled it before he could see it. By comparison, the cell he slept in was a chapel filled with incense. Hearing the *drip, drip, drip* of a leaky sink, Eloy held his breath and went inside. Ten bare toilets lined a back wall, the stalls that had once housed them having collapsed, and in between stretched a sea of human waste that had been festering since the last time someone sat on the broken porcelain. Every cell in his body screamed *Get out!*, but there along the far wall stood the lone pedestal sink.

He took a step and then another, thankful he'd left his shoes on when he'd collapsed, drunk, in bed earlier that night. As he walked, he imagined the lawn at Universidad Bolivariana—the green grass that lay between the Simón Rodríguez Building and the cafeteria. It was still wet from the morning dew. Flowers grew in manicured patches. Bromeliads clung to the tall caoba trees. The straps of his backpack dug into his strong shoulders, and he could feel the weight of the marketing textbook in his hand, its cover smooth and glossy. The shiny water fountain called to him, and he drank his fill of clean, cold water.

53

It had been a full week since María heard her replacement on the other end of the line. In between her depression, and her attempts to figure out what was happening with Eloy, she had let her feelings for the Romeros stew in the background. But today her anger had boiled over.

María had made the journey to Casa Verde thousands of times. Blindfolded she would have been able to accurately pinpoint any location on any stretch of the trip: the potholes in front of the Don Regalón store; the stink of the trash heaps by Las Torres del Silencio; the bululú of voices chaotically getting on the bus at Avenida Libertador; the sharp turns the bus made in the labyrinthine streets of the Country Club neighborhood.

Besides Casa Verde and her rancho, these buses were where María spent most of her time. She knew people on the bus by sight, a lot of them by name, and a few by friendships forged in tight quarters—their skin forced to touch in the cramp of rush hour; their breath sweet or sour depending on the time of day and what they'd eaten; their clothes, or their odor, betraying their line of work. Today it all went by in a blur. Her mind was stuck in a loop of what she would say to La Señora.

Atop the eight-foot stucco wall that surrounded the perimeter of the Romeros' property ran two tight electrified wires. Affixed to the wall, in beautiful cursive gold cutouts, were the letters spelling *Casa Verde*. The only way in, apart from the electric garage door, was the black iron gate to the left of the house's name, and the only way for it to open was the small gray intercom with the small gray button.

María hesitated. But then something inside, barely noticeable, pushed her. Enough for her finger to depress the small gray button. Enough for the electrical components of the intercom to spark to life and travel through the wires leading into the bones of the house, there to be transformed into a screech that burst from a small gray speaker on a small gray intercom just like the one on the outside of the wall. Enough for that screech to alert La Señora, or El Señor, or Jorge Luis, or the woman who was her replacement. Enough for them to stop what they were doing and listen: María was here. María wanted to talk to La Señora. María would not leave until she did.

An electronic shriek was followed by a click as the gate's lock released. María put pressure on the metal door, and it swung open. She walked the terra-cotta path that twisted to the house. She went past the palm trees and mango trees, the guava trees and limoneros; she smelled the ripeness of the fruit. She noticed the orchids and bromeliads clawing at the bark of the rubber tree, fighting for light, and heard the insects and birds as loud as ever, the chorus led by the family of green parrots that still lived in the royal palm tree, that still reigned over this wild garden and would do so for generations to come—decades after María reached the front door, knocked on it, and talked to La Señora.

La Señora opened the door herself. She wore her workout clothes, a T-shirt with some words in English that María didn't understand but must have meant something uplifting and strong, such as YOU CAN DO IT or THERE ARE NO LIMITS. The shirt was ripped, but in all the right places, as if someone had been paid to decide where to rip it and by how much. Black tights hugged her toned legs down to her ankles, with a single stripe that included all the colors of the rainbow. La Señora was barefoot and her toenails were painted bright red, not one blemish on the varnish, like ten perfect cinnamon candies. The image of her perfect feet on the Spanish tile was a lance through María's ribs. The floors were so clean. Cleaned by someone else. Not La Señora, clearly, whom María had never seen hold a mop.

And then there was her face. Her ponytail was so tight that her light auburn hair could have been painted on. She was perfectly made-up: subtle concealer, lip gloss that caught the morning light and sparkled, the thinnest strand of eyeliner shaping her green eyes. Feline and dangerous. No smile on the Botoxed lips. Her face a blank page. Despite the makeup and cosmetology, age had started to show. Not a lot, not even close to what María had aged in all the years these two women had shared. There was something ugly in La Señora, but it wasn't age. It came from inside. The way her nose would curl up at anything that wasn't to her liking—most things, most people, most actions held an odor that irritated her. And suddenly everything that made La Señora beautiful seemed to María nothing more than a mask.

La Señora walked to the kitchen, a silent command for María to follow. María's fear subsided as they walked past the sitting room, with the large abstract painting she had dusted a million times, a cream-colored canvas with cubic reds and cylindrical blues crashing against one another in furious geometrical battles. When she cleaned it for the first time, she had been afraid she would fall into it and turn into hard edges. Instead of avoiding people, as on the bus, here María had avoided objects: sofas and side tables, a lamp with a stained-glass shade that recounted some old Roman story, a rolling bar containing Señor Romero's bottles of scotch. She touched things now as she walked past, and the power they'd once held over her melted away at the brush of a finger.

La Señora opened one of the drawers under the granite kitchen island and pulled out a check. "I knew you'd be back," she said. "For your money." She held her arm out to María, stiffly, creating as much distance as possible between them.

The check in La Señora's hand was a rotten, limp, soiled thing. It could have been a bar of gold and María would not have touched it. Without moving an inch closer, she felt as though she towered above La Señora.

Has this woman ever been happy? María wondered. *Has she ever been joyful?* She must have at some point. She had been a girl once, had surely enjoyed the sun on her young face, as María had. Had smiled at a dog on the street, or at a pretty dress. Had felt her mother's hand on her cheek, surely, had listened to her sing a lullaby at her bedside, as her mom had done for María most nights until that rash day when she was eleven and had told her mother she was too big for lullabies now.

"Carmen," said María. The first time in her life she had called La Señora by her given name. The word floated out of her mouth, so light, and severed the cord that had tied them together. "I can hardly believe you would fire me after almost fifteen years. But to be honest, I don't care. Do you remember when Eloy was shot?"

Carmen no longer looked María in the eyes.

"I cried for my son in this kitchen. I cried for him while I cooked for you and your husband. While I cleaned your toilets and watered your plants. While he lay in bed with a scar cutting him in two, I was here. I read to Gustavito, I helped Jorge Luis get ready for his tennis lessons. I almost lost Eloy again. I might lose him still."

"He shouldn't have done what he did," Carmen said. "You should have raised him better."

The words chilled María so much that it was hard to breathe. "I couldn't," she whispered. "I was here." She took a few steps toward Carmen. Beautiful Carmen in her yoga outfit. "Remember that night, when your husband had gone for a few days, probably fucking one of his girlfriends? I felt so sad for you. You were so unhappy. I prayed for you that day. Prayed that your husband would never come back. That you would find it within yourself to be your own person. Eloy was still hurt. Every hour I spent here was an hour away from my baby." María didn't allow herself to bend under the sadness of these memories. Instead she stood taller. Stretched her spine to the ceiling. Held her head up high. "That evening, after you held me. After you asked me to comfort you in bed. After you asked me to stay the night. I cried in the shower. I didn't cry for Eloy. I cried for you." María moved closer still, standing so close before Carmen that she could smell the milky lotion keeping her skin flawless and shining. "I will not cry one more time in this house. I couldn't work here one more day, even if you'd shown me kindness, if you'd had an ounce of compassion for me and Eloy, a boy you saw grow up. I didn't come here for the check, and don't want it. You gave me a job for all these years. You always paid me on time. You got Eloy those pills—you probably don't even remember. Thank you for that." La Señora stared at the Spanish tile. María did not wait for her to look up, to see if she showed remorse, sadness, shame. It didn't really matter.

María walked to the small bathroom behind the kitchen and collected her few items (a half-used bottle of shampoo, her toothbrush, a couple of shirts hanging from the shower rod, an almost-full bottle of Tylenol), placing each one in a bag. She would never be the same person after Casa Verde. She would never again allow anyone to make her feel less than she knew herself to be. It had taken only fifteen years for that to sink in. When she returned to the kitchen, Carmen was gone. The maid, a young woman wearing a pink dress, stood there holding a rag and staring at her. María said hello in a kind voice.

She was about to walk out of the kitchen when she saw the silver bell resting next to the liquor cabinet. Even silent it was oppressive. She could hear it ring in her mind. She turned it over to reveal the tear-shaped clapper. Pinching it between her index finger and thumb, she yanked and in one quick twist rendered the bell mute, then slipped the clapper into her pocket. Every step she took away from that kitchen made her feel larger—so much so that by the time she opened the front door she could barely fit through its frame.

* * *

On the bus ride back, the city looked different, passed more quickly. María had rarely made this trip outside rush hour. She smelled the restaurants busy for lunch instead of the ripe bodies of workers at the end of their shifts. Never again would she take this bus route, she realized, and touched the false leather of the empty seat next to her. As if she had a connection with the bus and not the journey. As if the bus was what she was saying goodbye to.

She looked for the lawyer's number on her phone, his name in black pixels on the orange screen, ready to leave another message. She had left so many. At first apologetic: *I understand you must be so busy. If you have a spare moment.* Then more urgent: *I really need to speak. Call me back as soon as possible.* Now they were stripped of dignity. A piece of her crumbled away with each one she left. She waited for the two rings before voicemail but was caught by surprise when, in the middle of the first ring, noise came through. She heard laughter and conversation on the other end, the clinking of silverware on plates, maybe.

"¿Aló?" the lawyer said.

María imagined him at a long wooden table inside a dark steakhouse, surrounded by the smoke of grilling meat. A whiskey and soda in front of him. Plates of steamed yuca, fried plantains, white rice. Wooden cutting boards piled with cuts of meat: solomo, lomito, churrasco, a few links of chorizo and blood sausage.

"¿Aló, who is it?" he repeated, filling the space left by her silence.

"It's María."

"María? María who?"

It stung that he didn't know. She had thought about him so much in the past few weeks, had clung to the hope that he would know something she didn't. Learning that she was so small in his mind wasn't surprising, but it hurt all the same.

"María Rodríguez, la mamá de Eloy," she said. Silence followed, and María thought he might hang up.

"Señora Rodríguez," the lawyer cleared his throat with her name. "How are you?"

María heard shuffling and the restaurant noise subsided, presumably as the lawyer found a quieter spot. The question made her want to scream. *How am I?* If she could have reached through the phone and strangled the man, she would have.

"Do you know anything about Eloy?" she asked. "I haven't received a call from him, or anyone, about his well-being."

"He's been processed and is in prison," the lawyer said, and it would have been no different if he had said nothing. "He hasn't been sentenced yet. We won't know that anytime soon, I'm afraid."

"What? He's in Patria y Próceres already?"

"Sí, señora. I think they transferred him over a week ago."

"Why didn't you tell me anything?" María's skin started to itch. "I've been trying to reach you. I've left messages."

"I've been busy with other cases," the lawyer bristled. "And I'm not Mr. Rodríguez's babysitter. They have access to phones there, Señora María. If Eloy wants to call you, he will. Maybe he doesn't want to talk?"

It hurt, that possibility. It hung there like a noose for her to slide into. But it had to be true, or he would have called—unless something had happened to him, which remained her greatest fear.

"Otherwise, you will just have to go there and visit him yourself," the lawyer said, as if it were that easy for someone with no car, no money, and now no job. "You know what, scratch that, Patria y Próceres isn't accepting visitors right now. Probably soon, though."

"Could you get hold of him, please?" She hated herself for pleading again.

"It's not as easy as making a call, señora." He was clearly ready to hang up. "Look, you have to stop calling me, there's nothing I can do until they sentence him. I'll give you a call then."

"And how long until that happens?"

The lawyer actually chuckled on the other end. "About two years, probably, maybe more. But I'll get them to count that time as part of his sentence, don't worry."

María couldn't speak.

"Maybe someone at the Ministry of Prisons could reach him," the lawyer said. "I could put you in touch with someone there..."

María knew what that meant: She could pay to talk to her son. "How much?" she asked.

"I'd have to check with my guy in there."

But it didn't matter. Even if the lawyer quoted a number, which he never did, the answer would be the same. It cost too much, and María couldn't afford it.

"Do you have some cash?" he said. "I can meet you today and we can get it started."

María's jaw throbbed from clenching so hard. She'd been grinding her teeth. Tears rolled down her cheeks. She would not give the man one more bit of her pain — or her money. "You're a piece of shit," she said.

"Excuse me?"

"Rot in hell, maldito hijo de puta."

He started laughing. "Esta mujer está loca," she heard him say, probably to his friends, wherever they were.

María hung up.

A man sat down next to her. He was reading a newspaper. She almost asked him to find another seat so that she could be alone with her desperation. And there, on the front page, was the name under the paper's editorial: Stanislavo Atanas. Every time she saw a copy of the newspaper anywhere, she would pick it up and look for his name. Stanislavo Atanas. It shamed her to do it; she felt stupid, like a little girl. But any chance she got, she read his essays and articles. She learned about him — his sarcastic sense of humor, his deep passion for justice and fairness — through his editorials.

At the same time, the hypocrisy of it all bit deep. How fair, how *just* was it that he had left her and her mother to fend for themselves all these years? That her mom had been forced to wait six months to see a specialist, the disease eating her kidneys all the while? The same man who had left her mother alone had never cared to look for his daughter. The same man who'd held together Eloy's body in that operating room hadn't known that the blood he'd kept from spilling was his own. She was tired of seeing him in print only. And maybe the time had come to present him with a bill. He had helped his grandson once, had saved his life. He could do it again. He would do it. He had to.

"Can I see that for a second?" María asked the man.

The newspaper's phone number was right there on the back page.

54

Stanislavo entered the newspaper office as he always did: grumbling to himself, hands in the pockets of his ill-fitting khakis, his steps long and hurried, uneven because of his bum knee. He moved around the cubicles like a lab rat forced to run the same maze. The buzzing of phones, the chatter of journalists, the tapping of keyboards, the busy ecosystem of his newspaper was alive. It had changed since its first days over thirteen years ago. There was still urgency, but it was mixed now with the tempered expectation of a boxing contender who knew he could never win. The opponent was too strong, too fast, and didn't play fair.

Four years earlier, Chávez had choked their supply of raw paper. For a few years they had survived on inventory—thanks to a high-placed friend who'd foreseen this exact method of repression and had urged Stanislavo to stockpile rolls of material. Recently, however, with the rolls almost gone, they had been forced from a daily paper to a weekly publication. Thinner, yes, but still required reading; everyone from taxi drivers to businessmen walked with it under an arm. Stanislavo knew the government read it as well, if only because of the bile thrown at him on most official radio and television programs. He was still getting under the regime's skin, especially now.

Hugo Chávez had cancer. A year earlier they'd found a mass in his pelvic region, and since then Stanislavo and his reporters had doggedly pressured the party to be transparent about his illness, particularly with it being an election year. In October, Hugo Chávez would try to win a presidential election for the fourth time. He had been in power for fourteen years already; cancer permitting, he was hoping for six more.

"Here you go, Stanis."

"Gracias, Graciela." They were the first words he spoke most mornings. At first the alliteration of those two almost identical words annoyed him, but now they had become a respite. He began his day thanking the woman named Thanks, wrapping his hands around the hot cup of coffee she gave him, and following her into his messy office.

At sixty-eight, Graciela was just five years younger than Stanis. Always punta en blanco: her pants perfectly pressed, her shirts — men's button-down shirts, every day — crisp. It was her uniform. Her shoes were the only part of her outfit that allowed for self-expression, and Stanislavo felt a need to divine a pattern or link them to a mood (today's ocher heels gave him no clues). Her stoicism, her reserved and cold nature, linked them together in a very meaningful way. Both of them pressure cookers of opinion and passionate belief. Both of them perceived, by those who did not know them well enough, as out of reach. As his right-hand woman, secretary, assistant, first reader, gatekeeper, and confidante, Graciela was revered. If Stanislavo was the heart of the paper, Graciela was its cardiovascular system. She had been since she arrived eight years earlier.

"Mirella called a few minutes ago," Graciela said. "She has the last few boxes with your stuff ready to go."

Mirella: lawyer, activist, his second ex-wife. He had become a cliché, marrying someone hardly more than half his age. And if Mirella had been anything other than what she was — the smartest person in any room she ever stepped in — he might have felt strange about it. Their relationship had been waged in intellectual battles that electrified them both, and made Stanislavo feel twenty years younger. The first three years of his marriage he'd spent denying her a child, a wish that had been a surprise to him. The last two were all resentment, from both sides. Now all that was left of that relationship was boxes of books.

"Do you want me to have them dropped off at your apartment?"

"Sure," Stanislavo said. "Thank you."

"I'll leave you to your thing, Stanis," Graciela said and walked to her desk, just outside his office, bare of anything except her computer monitor, her planner, and a potted orchid that never shed its purple-dotted flowers.

Per usual, a stack of four newspapers rested on Stanislavo's desk, in the only empty space, a clean square in the middle of leaning towers of papers and books. *El Nacional, El Universal*, the *New York Times*, and *Le Monde*. He read them in that order, always, jumping from headline to headline, letting the layout of the newspaper dictate where he would go next. He did not discriminate, was not swayed by fancy writing. He was methodical in his consumption of the news, but also efficient, dispassionate. He *hmm*'d and *huh*'d through the stack and every once in a while wrote chicken scratch on his notepad, or stroked his mustache, mostly white now but with hints of his old color, like orange zest on rice pudding.

Sandra knocked on the glass panel of his office, even though his door was always open. She was still here. His heir apparent. Stanislavo had no desire to retire, but when he did, and he knew it had to be sooner than later, Sandra would keep all of this going. Maybe better than he ever had.

"Jefe," she said, "Chávez is in Cuba again."

"Another round of treatment?" he asked.

It had been uncanny to witness, Chávez battling both cancer and Henrique Capriles Radonski, the young and energetic governor running against him. Chávez would disappear for weeks at a time, and then come back, swollen, green, but standing. Still delivering rousing speeches, hours long, still mesmerizing and captivating. If his body was failing, his mind was as strong as ever.

"Looks that way," Sandra said. She was heading to the campaign rally in Petare, where the Chávez surrogate Diosdado Cabello, now president of the National Assembly, was set to headline in his absence.

Stanislavo tilted his head down so he could look at her over his reading glasses. "Está bien. Take César with you for photos. Se me cuidan." Stanislavo always ended conversations with his reporters the same way. A benediction, wishing no harm to befall them in a land where harm was doled out generously and randomly.

He folded *Le Monde* and looked for his keyboard, finding it half-buried under vendor invoices. The cord snagged in the stack and papers tumbled down, fanning and falling in every direction.

"Coño de la madre," he said and knelt on the ground gathering receipts, half-written articles, a menu from the Chinese place around the corner.

"Stanis," Graciela said, peeking into the open doorway.

Her voice startled him, and he hit his head hard against the edge of the table. "¡El coño de su madre!" Stanislavo rubbed his balding head as he stood. "What?" he asked.

"A lady for you on the phone. María Rodríguez. Something about her son, in prison."

"María Rodríguez? I don't know any María Rodríguez. Just tell her I'm busy, okay?"

"Of course."

He massaged the top of his head and looked at his fingers, which came away with blood on the tips. *María Rodríguez.* He rubbed the blood between his finger and thumb, and his brain surfaced an image of a boy, years ago, bleeding to death on an operating table. What was his name? That boy whose organs he'd seen writhing. Whose eyes he'd seen come back to life like flowers unfurling their petals. *Eloy, Eloy like the poet. Andrés Eloy Rodríguez. María Rodríguez.* The woman had vaguely reminded him of

Emiliana, all those years ago. He remembered that the doctor at Vargas Hospital had later confirmed the boy's survival. He'd gone home with his mother.

Stanislavo ran to Graciela's office. "Wait. María Rodríguez. I know her."

Graciela's hand was on the phone, which she'd just placed back on its cradle. "Lo siento, Stanis, I've hung up already." She looked back at her computer monitor and adjusted her glasses.

"Did you take a message? Did she leave a number?"

Her finger pointed at the monitor, to a sentence that Stanislavo had written yesterday in his piece tying Cabello to the drug-trafficking ring known as the Cartel of the Suns. "Did you mean to say *associate* here? Or *underling*?" she asked. "Because it should be *underling*." She deleted the word and typed in its better alternative.

"Sure," Stanislavo said. "No number?"

"No. Sorry."

Stanislavo walked back to his office. *María Rodríguez. Andrés Eloy, like the poet.* He sat on his desk and turned on the monitor. "Graciela!" he yelled. "Try to find her for me, would you? María Rodríguez."

"Claro que sí, Stanis," she replied.

"And get me a copy of our paper for April 12th, 2002."

When Graciela brought back the paper, there, below the fold, he saw César's photo. María's face was mid-grimace under an ill-fitting motorcycle helmet, its straps swinging wildly. A man, older and thin, carried Andrés Eloy's limp body. They were flanked by two Metropolitan Police officers in anti-riot gear. CHAOS AT VARGAS HOSPITAL, read the headline. He scanned the story, looking for any detail on María, but the only thing there was "resident of Cotiza."

It had been a decade, but his body still held the weight of those days. Less a memory and more something he could choose to relive if he wanted to. His conversation with Molina came first. His face, so ecstatic as the helicopters brought Chávez back to the palace. Three years later, in one of Chávez's great purges, he would fire Molina in a televised address for speaking out against the decline of the national oil-company infrastructure. Molina was pushed into exile, after an accusation of corruption from his former allies. He died a few years after that, from a heart attack, in Miami. The last of Stanislavo's connections to that other life he'd lived so long ago.

Ten years on from the coup and his fears that day in Avenida Baralt had all come to pass. Nothing any longer could mask the toxicity of Chávez's regime, now going on fourteen years. The period of the oil boom had come and gone, and how many billions of dollars had been wasted and stolen, saddling the country with its worst economic and humanitarian crisis since the Venezuelan civil war.

And here Stanislavo was, still toiling away in the same office, in front of the same brick of a computer, trying to write the same story, it seemed, that he had written since Chávez came to power. The past always seemed to knock on his door. Mirella and her boxes. Molina in Miami. And now María Rodríguez. He probably hadn't thought about her since that day he called Vargas Hospital to check on them. The increasing violence, the stolen elections, the chicanery of the constitutional amendments, the wanton expropriation of property, the exploding hyperinflation, the militarization of institutions, the interminable lawsuits against his newspaper — this fucking country had chiseled María Rodríguez out of his mind.

Yet now she was there again. She felt important in a way he didn't understand, and Stanislavo hated that feeling, when someone asks you a question and the answer is right there, on the tip of your tongue, unwilling to tumble out.

55

Days had passed in a fog of hangovers. Alcohol had been Eloy's coping mechanism these first two weeks of prison life, a reliable way to calm his nervous system. But it was shot now. Numbness was the new normal.

He stumbled out into the yard, head throbbing, but rejoiced in the clean air, in the early sun. He found Wili by La Tasca de Robin Hood and ordered an empanada. Robin wrote in a warped notebook that seemed to be some sort of ledger of sales, or debt, or both. Eloy asked him for a piece of paper and something to write with and Robin looked at him like he'd asked for one of his knives.

He ripped two pages from the middle of the notebook and reached behind his ear for the yellow pencil. "I want that back when you're done."

"Yes, sir," Eloy said and took a seat in a chair next to Wili.

The callus on the inside of his middle finger was still rough, and he loved the feel of the pencil in his hand. If he looked at the page and nothing else, it was almost like being home. He started to sketch, making small, fast marks near the top of the page to conserve space. He warmed up by quickly capturing bodies. The old, wiry man doing push-ups. Three young guys rolling dice in a huddle. One of Topo's men with a rifle strapped to his back, standing guard near the prison entrance. The drawings were little more than scribbles, with no detail to them, but they captured movement and meaning: strength, danger, boredom. Eloy felt the old pride at being able to say something about a person with lines on paper.

Wili was asleep in his plastic chair, soaking up the rays, a half-eaten empanada marooned on a paper plate on his stomach. First, Eloy focused on the shape of his friend's head. It hung from the back of the chair, forcing his chin up, his neck long and veiny. Wili's face in profile was sharp. His nose, aquiline. His mouth resting in a thin line. His naked torso covered with tattoos. His long legs splayed out, with his beat-up white sneakers pointing slightly away from each other. He was serene, and Eloy's sketch showed it. Something had started to happen whenever he had time to look at Wili as he did now—in a rare moment of rest. A voice that maybe had been there for a long time but hadn't had a chance to be heard. It was at once terrifying and beautiful. Impossible to filter out. He added a few details to the drawing: the shadow that Wili's nose made on his face, the shading on his chest, two fingers bent on his left hand. The voice was more akin to a song now, tuned to Wili's long, resting body, to his toned, ropey arms.

Eloy was so focused he didn't hear the men approach him from behind. Someone snatched the paper from his hand. Three men stood there, all teeth and danger.

"Ay, menor, let's see what you got here," one said. "Are you in love with him or what?"

Eloy rose and squared off against the men, all of them larger than he was. He'd met them the previous night, but in the middle of his hangover now he could barely remember anything about them, much less their names.

The commotion woke up Wili, who was confused and out of sorts. He wiped the slobber from his mouth.

"Do you let him paint you naked, too, Wili?"

The man who'd grabbed the drawing showed it to Wili from afar. Together the three of them laughed. Eloy's insides shriveled, forming a little ball in the pit of his stomach.

"After he paints, do you suck his yensi, or does he suck yours?"

The other two bent over in laughter, while the guy holding the drawing stood tall and wide in front of Wili, who balled his hands into fists. The guy's smile grew on his face, revealing a few missing teeth. Eloy took a small step back, deciding who to go after first. The men didn't carry weapons on them that he could see, but shanks were easy to hide and could be pulled out so quickly.

Wili stepped forward. He was a good fighter, but so were most of the men here. And this was three against two, if Eloy counted at all.

"Ey!" The deep rumbling of Topo's baritone rolled over them.

It froze Eloy and the other three guys, but not Wili, who landed a fat hook on the lead guy's jaw and knocked him down to a knee.

"Ey, ey, ey!" Topo said, and ran past Eloy to grab Wili from behind just as he was about to pounce on the man.

Wili kept squirming—murder in his eyes—even as his feet left the ground.

"Stop, motherfucker!" Topo screamed in Wili's ear. "¡Cálmate!" He squeezed harder, like a monster squid wrapping its tentacles around a ship hard enough to crack the hull and mast. "Are you going to behave?" he said as Wili quieted.

Wili's muscles relaxed, and Topo's arms softened in response. The man, still on one knee, wiped his mouth with his forearm and spit blood onto the ground. Topo let Wili go, and though he was still, he didn't take his eyes off the enemy.

"Are we going to have to chain you, pit bull?" Topo said. "We can't have you tearing throats every single day you're here, you know? It's not good for morale."

Wili remained silent, not even glancing at Topo.

"What the fuck happened here, anyway? Gregorio?"

Topo looked at the guy with the bloody lip, who was up now and brushing dirt from his pants.

"These maricones were drawing each other and shit," the man named Gregorio said. "And that was a fucking cheap shot, and you know it. You're gonna regret it next time, hijo de puta." He glared at

Wili. "We don't allow that kind of shit around here. They should be sent to AIDS Town, Topo."

Topo raised an eyebrow. "Enough, coño! Show me the damn drawing."

"It's only a sketch," Eloy said, raising his voice.

Topo reached out for the paper.

"I like to draw, that's all," Eloy said.

Wili looked away, his hands, still in fists, tightening.

Topo inspected the drawing, then folded it. "I'll show this to Tortuga," he said. "In the meantime, either of you putos put a hand on each other and you'll pay."

Eloy and Wili walked toward the basketball court, drawn by the traveling echoes of bouncing balls. Fellow prisoners had gathered on the shiny bleachers in small cliques. Eloy was still shaky from their encounter with the men at La Tasca, and Wili hadn't spoken a word. But was he upset by the fight that had almost broken out, or by Eloy's drawing? Ever since those days of Eloy doodling in bed, when he was laid up after the bullet, Wili had always been supportive of his talents, leaving him alone to his sketches, sneaking peeks over his shoulder. Here, though, every action, no matter how small, had a consequence.

But there was something else at play. Wili's neck strained up, as if his head wanted to float into the sky. In his stride, every step crushed something underfoot. He kept so much inside his sinewy frame that it often seemed his body was inflamed—with hurt, with guilt, with anger, with who knew what else. And Eloy, as had been his role since they were children, only wanted to soothe. But this was no place for it—anything soft was something to eat. Resisting the urge to reach out or process what had happened in the yard, Eloy just followed Wili to an empty row on the bleachers.

More than a basketball court, this was a sports complex. It was nothing like Cotiza, with its gashed concrete and rusted chain nets. Even at La Universidad Bolivariana he hadn't seen anything resembling it. The complex sat under a tall ceiling supported by metal columns and black trusses. The court itself was painted in a combination of neon green and deep blue, the court lines a bright white. The court's center circle bore the prison team's logo—a basketball with eyes and a bandana covering what would have been its mouth—and its name, the "Malandros." Each man on the court, whether shooting or passing the ball around, was tall, with long fingers that caressed the ball goodbye. From the bleachers their movements looked like a choreographed dance.

Behind the court, still under shade, was a gymnasium with weights and barbells. Eloy recognized some of the men working out there, not by name but by association, as everyone both on the court and in the gym was someone he'd seen in the company of Topo or Tortuga. A couple of evangélicos, young men in trousers and button-down shirts, patrolled the court, making sure it was clean and handing towels to the men exercising. Around him, in the bleachers, sat other prisoners like him who paid their taxes to Tortuga and were therefore allowed to roam free. Wili, with the gun he'd been given by Topo, was somewhere in between. A social order was beginning to emerge for Eloy, and while it didn't make prison any less frightening, it gave him a structure to fit within. He just hoped that wherever he ended up wasn't far from his friend.

"Don't go around with any more mariqueras, all right?" Wili whispered. "No more drawings, no more being weird. And you need to start making other friends. It looks bad that we're always together."

But they had always been together—even once Wili started getting into more serious trouble and no longer just playing at being bad. Back then Eloy was finishing high school while driving his motorcycle as a messenger, working for a guy in the neighborhood who managed a whole fleet of bikes. He loved everything about it: the weaving between cars; the camaraderie between motorizados; the high stakes of carrying something important, and perhaps illegal, though he rarely knew what it was. That was life in the barrio, and no one, not even in church, would have ever called it dishonest labor.

And until the night of the botched robbery, Eloy had never been dishonest. Not in any way that really mattered. One question from Wili was all that had been needed to change that. Will you help me? The answer would always have been *yes*.

Tortuga walked onto the court now and bodies stopped moving, balls stopped bouncing, even the conversations at the top of the bleachers died down. Topo followed him like a circus bear on a chain. It was always a strange sight, because Topo could easily overpower Tortuga, but there was something in Tortuga's swagger that revealed a knotted and dangerous interior.

The basketball players lined up. Tortuga took his time, pacing like he spoke, with no rush at all. He went to each player and shook his hand, and when he reached the end of the line he hugged the last player the way you hug someone you know from way back. The man was even taller and more muscular than the others; word was that he'd played professional ball for Panteras de Miranda.

"That's another lucero," Wili said. "Coquito. Same standing as Topo."

"How many are there?" Eloy asked.

"Tortuga, and three luceros. We actually got in at the right time." Just two months ago, Wili explained, Tortuga and another guy, El Charly, had been in a fight for control. It was all-out war for a while. That was why no visitors were allowed these days. The government was waiting to make sure things had settled down.

Tortuga placidly chatted with Topo and Coquito. From up here in the bleachers, Eloy thought, things looked as settled as a paid debt.

Wili was thumbing his left knee, bruised and a bit swollen. "I don't know what I did to my knee, man. It hurts."

Eloy remembered Wili pounding the pool worker some days ago, his knees bare on the concrete. Then he heard a whistle. Topo stood on the sideline, finger and thumb in his mouth, staring right at them. Eloy froze, as did Wili, his legs spread wide there in the bleachers, his hand stone-like on his knee.

Topo whistled again, a heat-seeking missile. "Epa!" he yelled, then clicked his tongue twice and yanked his head, summoning them.

"Don't be weird," Wili whispered and stood up.

Descending the bleacher steps felt like a stroll to the gallows.

"Wili! Eloy! El jefe wants a word," Topo said from behind a daggery grin. He met them at the bottom of the bleachers and embraced each with a heavy arm, then guided them toward Tortuga.

The symphony of bouncing balls and screeching sneakers was overwhelming, spiking Eloy's anxiety.

"You guys are stiff!" Topo said. He pinched Eloy's shoulder with his massive hand, pinning a nerve between his fingers and twisting. "Don't be scared, it's all good." He deposited them in front of Tortuga.

"Topo told me about the little disruption in the yard today," Tortuga said, his vowels round, consonants sharp, every word enunciated perfectly.

"It was just a mis—" Eloy started to say.

"Shh. You're new here, so you don't know how this goes yet. When I speak, you listen. You talk when I ask a question."

Topo towered behind Eloy and Wili, not touching them but close enough that Eloy could feel his heat and smell his body spray.

"I saw the little drawings you made, Eloy," said Tortuga. "You want to tell me about them?"

Eloy's words lodged in his throat. Topo put a hand on his shoulder and leaned in to whisper: "Your turn to talk."

"It settles me down," Eloy said. "I just draw what's around me, you know? That's why I was drawing Wili."

"An artist!" Tortuga said. He smiled for the first time, a row of perfect teeth under the whisper of a mustache. "I told you, Topo, we've got an artist in our midst! Topo doesn't understand the arts, Eloy; he has no use for impractical things. And you"—he looked at Wili now — "you like to fight, don't you? I try my best to keep things calm. It's better for everyone that way. People are happier, and happy people means calm people: Calm people do their work and buy the things I sell, and business is good. "But don't get me wrong, violence has its place — right, Topo?"

"Yes, jefe, yes it does."

"And who am I to get in the way of someone protecting himself or his reputation?" He moved closer to Wili. "I wouldn't do that. Someone calls me a marico and you know we'll get into it, that's just the way it is." His voice changed now — angry, guttural. "So, no hard feelings, okay?" He gave Wili a couple of light slaps on the cheek. "You look like the type of chamo that needs an outlet for all that rage, and what type of person — no, what type of *leader* — would I be if I didn't recognize that, if I didn't harness that? Topo?"

"Not a good one, Tortuga."

"That's right. So don't you worry, Wili. We'll put you to good use. Everyone has a role to play here in El Penal. Ballplayers," he said, looking at the guys shooting baskets. "Fighters," he added, and grabbed Wili's wrist so tight that the skin changed color. "And artists too." Tortuga removed Eloy's drawing from his back pocket and unfolded it. "This is good — you draw well, menor. Been doing it a long time?"

"Most of my life," Eloy said, and traced the bottom part of his scar with a finger. He could still remember the box of Prismacolor pencils his mother had bought him when he was pinned to the bed by that hole in his stomach. How it had seemed as if the whole world could be rendered by twenty colors with names like rojo ladrillo, amarillo mostaza, and verde bosque. Red was blood now; yellow, the glint of Topo's tooth; green was gone, but back then there had been the ferns hanging from Don Jacinto's rancho.

"Well, I've had this idea to liven up the place a bit," Tortuga said. "We've got the court, sure. And the swimming pool is coming along. But it's not art. A revolutionary is a warrior, yes. But he's also a poet, no? An artist?" Tortuga put a hand on Eloy's shoulder.

Wili had warned Eloy how ruthless Tortuga was. On the outside he had controlled one of the most bloodthirsty gangs in La Guaira, bringing in contraband drugs through the port. As soon as he got inside, he'd eliminated El Charly. He smiled and talked about art and revolution, but it struck Eloy as a sort of posturing. He fashioned himself a prison Chávez, but under all of that Eloy sensed the rot of violence.

"Have you seen the big wall by La Tasca?" Tortuga asked.

"Yes," Eloy said.

"That's your wall, son. Well, it's *my* wall, but you know what I mean. With my vision and your talent, we'll bring some art to El Penal! I have some ideas and can't wait to get started." Tortuga smiled and walked over to put an arm around Eloy's shoulder. "What do you say we head over there and start talking?"

Eloy nodded. His body, still reeling from the hangover, from the near-fight, from the threat of punishment, felt foreign to him, like some sort of numb puppet. He was still in control of it, but only from the outside. There was a time delay. He knew he was supposed to be thankful to Tortuga, so he ordered his face to be thankful. He knew to follow Tortuga to the restaurant, so his feet took a step.

"Topo, finish making the collections. And take Puños with you," Tortuga said, referring to Wili. "Show him the ropes. Put his talents to use if you must."

Wili was getting what he wanted, Eloy reflected—some distance from him. But was that a good thing? For either of them?

56

AFTER BEING REBUFFED by Stanislavo's secretary on the phone, it took María all weekend to gather her courage, but she got to the newspaper at ten on Monday morning, sweaty from nerves or the heat, she wasn't sure. The trip had taken her a bit longer than she'd thought it would, and then she'd overshot her bus stop, forcing her to walk a good fifteen minutes back in the other direction. The newspaper was headquartered in a plain warehouse out in Los Ruices, next to a small, three-story office building. She might have missed it if not for the delivery truck with the newspaper's logo. She went past the sleepy security guard without a hassle and took the elevator to the third floor. When she stepped into the office she was greeted by disorder: voices lobbed from cubicle to cubicle, the ringing of telephones cutting the air like a chorus of cicadas, and the constant racing clack of computer keyboards, blanketing the entire space with an essence of busyness. She felt like an intruder in a hive.

But no one noticed her. There was no reception area, and everyone had a place to be and something to do. María was the only static object in the room.

"Excuse me," she said to a passing woman whose head was obscured by a stack of paper.

"Sorry, one minute," the woman said back, but kept moving until she disappeared.

María walked to the nearest cubicle, where a man in a cheap shirt, his chest hair peeking out between buttons, furiously typed before a blocky computer monitor. "Excuse me," she said.

"Don't scare me like that!" the man said, looking up at her, then again at his screen. "What?" he said and resumed typing.

"I'm looking for Stanislavo Atanas," María said, expecting to be met with questions about the purpose of her visit and who she was.

But the man only yelled, "Graciela!"

From the direction in which he'd pointed his voice, a woman, stern and beautiful, impeccably dressed, moved toward them like a cat, gliding above the chaos of the newspaper. She leaned on the wall of the cubicle. "Yes?" she said calmly, not acknowledging María.

"Someone for Stanis," the man said, jerking his head toward María without taking his eyes off the computer screen.

María extended her hand. "María Rodríguez," she said, steeling herself.

"Ah, I've been looking for you, Mrs. Rodríguez," Graciela said. "I'm sorry I didn't get your information the other day on the phone. It's been crazy here, with all the Chávez stuff going on."

María didn't know how to respond. She hadn't had a minute to think about the president, sick with cancer, sometimes here giving speeches about the future of Venezuela, sometimes gone, dealing with his own uncertain future. Not with Eloy's situation. She felt as if every organ in her body was a heart, her whole body a drum.

"Come. I'll take you to Stanis. He's a bit all over the place today, but he has some time to talk." She led María through the maze of reporters to an office in the back. "Stanis," she said, leaning into the doorway. "María Rodríguez."

"You found her? Great! Put her through." He placed a freckled hand on the phone receiver.

"No. She's here."

At that, Graciela departed and María took a step forward, into the office. There was paper everywhere. The room looked like a bookstore after an explosion. Stanislavo stood from behind what María assumed was a desk, even though she could see none of its surface. He smoothed out his shirt and ran a hand through his hair. María remembered him as fiery, everything orange, but he was gray now, with just traces of embers remaining, like a dying campfire. He was bent at the waist and appeared weaker than she'd expected, but when he spoke, that impression changed.

"María! We've been looking for you," he said in a voice powerful and deep. It transformed him, as if instantly shaving years off. "Please sit." He motioned to a chair across from the desk, but it had been colonized by a stack of books. "I'm so sorry," he said. "It's a mess in here. Just put them anywhere."

María picked up the books and placed them on the ground. She took a seat. Everything inside her thumped. How to start? What to say? It was different from her conversation with La Señora. Yes, there was anger in her now, similar to the river running through her at Casa Verde, but here the landscape was different; the waters ran somewhere she couldn't predict. And even if she never would have admitted it—not to Stanislavo, not to anyone else—she wanted more than anything for him to see her and know her. Couldn't he see her mother in her? Her long dark hair, her sharp features, her bronze skin? Couldn't he see *himself*? His freckles; his wide, strong back; his big teeth? But he didn't.

"I remember you," he said. "From Vargas Hospital, the day of the coup. You and your boy."

The river crested and then dropped over rocks. She felt the churn of it, the splash of whitewater.

"Graciela told me you called. Said your boy might need some help. What's going on?"

He seemed sincere but also removed. María diminished in that chair, surrounded by the mess of the office, the mess of the newspaper, the mess of the country, and in the center of it all this conversation.

She had the urge to escape the whirlpool, to leave without a word. But she spoke, and in her voice she found some strength.

"Eloy." She sounded strange, as if her words were coming from behind a closed door. "He's been sent to Patria y Próceres. But I don't know anything else. He hasn't contacted me and there's no number I can call. And his lawyer ignores me, doesn't tell me anything. He hasn't even been sentenced yet—"

His reaction—a shift of his weight in the chair, a slight eye roll—surprised her, bringing her up short.

"What?" she asked him. "What did I say?"

"Nothing. I'm sorry. It's just that the courts aren't really sentencing anyone. It could take years for Eloy to receive one. I know of a man who's been waiting four years for the judge to tell him how long he's supposed to be in prison for."

The way he said it, like he was thinking about his next article. The way her story was just another distraction in his day. His eyes darted beyond his office and into the hallway as one of his reporters hurried past. The river inside her flowed faster now, the stones on the riverbed clacking together.

"What did he do?" Stanislavo asked.

She couldn't get the words out. His stare was too cold.

"Did he do it? Whatever he was accused of?"

She could only nod.

"I'm sorry, María."

Stanislavo stood and looked back into the hallway, where the reporter was talking to Graciela, the elegant woman who'd led her to the office. María could feel the dismissal coming at any moment. He was searching for a polite way to get her out of here.

"The prison system in this country is horrible," he said. "I can't imagine what you're going through." He took a step toward the office doorway, his attention now firmly on whatever was happening between the reporter and his secretary. "But look, María, I'm not sure why you came here. There's nothing I can really do to help that much. Maybe I can put you in touch with one of my crime-beat reporters? They might know someone at tribunales who can help expedite the case. Graciela! Can you get Páez in here for a minute?"

The river approached a great waterfall. Two massive boulders framed the opening, with whitewater carving up the pool at the base of the drop.

"I'll tell you right now, though," Stanislavo continued, still looking beyond his office door. "Whoever Páez puts you in touch with will want some money for whatever they do. It's just how things work over there. I wish I could be of more help, I really do."

The fall now, the crash and the swirl and the chaos of white and wet was all around her.

"He's your grandson," María said, and it was louder than she'd expected it to be. An accusation.

57

STANISLAVO HAD HEARD the words clearly. Nonetheless, he was confused. He had no idea where to file them in his head. "Sorry, what did you say?"

"Eloy. My son who's in prison. Who hasn't been sentenced. He's your grandson."

The implication was clear, but perhaps these words were easier for María to say than *I'm your daughter*. She clutched something to her chest—a chain, a necklace. Stanislavo hadn't noticed it until then. He felt dizzy. He glanced back at Graciela, who was spiritedly talking to Sandra, and overheard bits of their conversation: Chávez and a Cuban nurse; a hospital in Havana; something that had gone wrong with his treatment.

"Wait, what?" he said.

He hadn't misunderstood her, but nothing else would come out. It was as if he were trapped in his own head. He was trying to remember Eloy. Then he saw him—the gray, dying boy, his long lashes, his tight curls, his freckles all over. He remembered the boy's insides, the wet, slurping movement of them. But what had María looked like then, that morning in Vargas Hospital? A mother in pain. A mother crying. How many of those had he seen in all his years as a journalist? A journalist in Venezuela, no less, the land of grieving mothers: their sons dead in shootouts, in bar fights, in the street over a pair of shoes, in hospitals because "we ran out of plasma." He remembered María as the doctor sewed up little Eloy's body with string. Her sharp, freckled face, her big eyes, her strong shoulders. Back then there had been a familiarity he couldn't quite place, but in the middle of the chaos it had been so easy to move on. Had it really been a decade since the coup? Had time passed that fast? Ten years since that boy had almost died?

"Are you going to say something?" María asked.

She stood up and was crying now, though clearly it was not from grief or sadness but anger. She unclasped the necklace, and Stanislavo finally noticed it fully: Emiliana's black fist, its luster dulled by the years since he'd last seen it. That was another life, it seemed. Another person who had gone up to the mountains and fallen in love with that nurse. But he had no doubts that the woman standing here, in front of him, was his daughter.

He fell back into his chair, feeling the weight of all his years, heavy with shame, crushing him. How could he not have seen it? There she was, Emiliana in María's nose, and there she was in that dark hair, and in María's voice! Stanislavo was transported back to Mochima under the araguaney tree, its yellow flowers littering the ground as they spoke. That itch he had needed to scratch, that answer on the tip of his tongue—it was María Rodríguez.

Sandra burst into the office, Graciela on her heels. "I'm sorry, Stanis, I know you're busy now, but we've got big news. I'm getting reports that Chávez is in bad shape. Some bad reaction to medication."

Stanislavo looked at Sandra, this woman he'd been working with for more than fifteen years now, who had grown to be the best reporter he'd ever known. "Like father, like daughter," the other reporters would joke sometimes, when Sandra scooped a particularly good story. But she wasn't his daughter. María was.

Then Páez stuck his head in. "You called, Stanis? What's up?"

"I don't know what I was thinking," Stanislavo heard María say.

"I'm so stupid." She hurried out the door, parting Sandra, Graciela, and Páez on her way.

Stanislavo stood and hurried after her. "María, wait!" he called, his voice carrying over the busy sounds of his newspaper.

He pushed Páez aside but tripped and landed on his bad knee. The pain was electric. Graciela and Sandra helped him up, but by the time he regained his balance María had rushed into the elevator.

"Are you okay?" Sandra said.

"I'm fine." He stared at the elevator's closed doors, willing María to come back.

"So," Sandra said, "Chávez?"

"Put me in touch with that nurse. The one you've been talking to. And try to reach someone on Cabello's staff. They'll know more."

Sandra nodded and rushed off.

"What happened, Stanis?" asked Graciela, still holding his arm. "Who is that woman?"

"My daughter," Stanislavo said, and it was at once a question and an answer, a prayer and a confirmation. "Get me in touch with Adriana Vila over at the Ministry of Prisons. Tell her it's urgent."

"Right away, Stanis," Graciela said.

He opened the bottom drawer of his filing cabinet, furiously searching through the folders there. He hadn't laid his eyes on these papers for decades. The folder wasn't labeled, but his hands remembered just where it was. When he opened it, Nunzio greeted him. His friend's dead body—the photo he'd taken from Alfredo's office the night he'd discarded the bomb. His stomach twisted, and he became dizzy again. Other things were there: old correspondence from Alfredo; his fake ID from Abastos Beirut, his photo unrecognizable to him, another person. But the thing he was looking for—the letter he'd written to Emiliana the night he left the Movement—wasn't there.

58

ELOY AND TORTUGA walked together, straight across the basketball court and through a percussion of bouncing balls that stopped as they passed. It was the same way everywhere they moved around the prison: everything slowed down around them, everything quieted. Crowds opened to let them through, everything a sea and Tortuga some malandro Moses.

"Do you play sports, Eloy?" Tortuga asked as they stepped off the concrete slab of the court and onto the dirt diamond next to it.

A couple of evangélicos in sweat-stained white button-down shirts pulled weeds from the infield under the punishing sun.

"A bit here and there. Baseball was my thing growing up. But most of the kids on my Cotiza team just stopped playing when it got disbanded. I haven't played much since I was thirteen."

"It's hard to keep a kid's attention when they're that age," Tortuga said. "My sons are the same way." He looked off toward the mountains beyond the compound. "I've got nine, all boys. My thing was boxing. Man, I was a good boxer. Low center of gravity. Fast." He shadowboxed in place for a few seconds, letting go of five lightning-quick punches, though maybe they just seemed that way because everything else he did was so slow. "That was before all this, you know." Tortuga waved his hand. "What about family? You have any kids?" he asked.

"It's just me and my mom. And Wili."

"Wili's your brother?" Tortuga's eyebrow rose as if on a hook.

"Not by blood, but we grew up together."

"Then he's not family, kid. The only family you've got is blood. I learned that the hard way. Is your mom going to come visit?"

"She's too far away. Caracas. Doesn't have a car."

Tortuga's face shifted to concern. At first Eloy thought maybe there was a recognition of what it meant to miss the people you love. But it wasn't that.

"That's no good, Eloy," he said. "La visita is the lifeblood of this whole operation. I don't want you to fall behind on your Causa. I've seen it happen too many times to good kids like you, centrales with family far away. They don't come visit, they don't bring in money, don't pay the fees. They *forget*"—and here he looked straight in Eloy's eyes—"that you're here. That you need things to survive, things to keep you in the light."

Eloy didn't know what he meant by *light*. But he was starting to see that Tortuga enjoyed getting him to sweat it, that Tortuga made himself bigger through others becoming smaller.

"Here there are two kinds of men," he continued. "Men in the light and men who eat light. The ones in the light are the men who pay their dues, who add to this community I've built. The ones who eat the light are the men who break my rules, who take things away. Those men I don't like, chamo. And when families forget, and when families don't visit, that's usually when chamos like you start to eat the light. I don't want to see it, okay?" Tortuga put an arm around Eloy and kept moving across the baseball diamond. "We had a little something happen with another prisoner, El Charly. He thought he could lead us better. He was wrong, of course. We took care of him." Tortuga turned his fingers into a gun and fired an imaginary shot at Eloy. "But now Los Verdes," he said, pointing at the wall that kept them in, where men in green uniforms held long rifles, "won't let visitors in. They'll be back soon, though."

They walked by two warehouses. Inside the first, machines were visible behind broken panes of glass and accumulated trash. Years ago, when the government controlled the facilities, the building must have contained workshops of some kind.

"There's a bank account," Tortuga said, offhandedly. "Ask Topo about it. Your mom can send you money there. We get our cut, but we're fair."

As they approached the second warehouse, Eloy smelled the rancid metal of blood mixed with a sweet and putrid aroma, an unfamiliar musk.

"I need to talk to the butcher," Tortuga said.

Eloy's scar pulsed. Past the door the stench was powerful—overwhelming—but he was relieved to recognize it as unmistakably animal. The building was Tortuga's menagerie, housing all sorts of beasts, both domesticated and wild. Eight piglets suckled a sow's swollen teats in a small pen, their snouts rummaging for their mother's milk. In another pen three goats munched on hay. A cage, not large enough to fit a man on his knees, was home to three capuchin monkeys; one of them stretched his thin arm through the wire and opened his hand repeatedly, reaching for something but catching only air. Vivariums held snakes, lizards, tortoises, and one chameleon who perched on a branch and moved its alien eye in spastic bursts. Tortuga's zoo hollered in a multispecies concerto: grunts, squeaks, screams, chirps, and, from the back, a roar that froze Eloy in place, the reptilian part of his brain casting him as prey.

Tortuga laughed. "Don't be scared of Azúcar," he said, pointing his chin to a cage. "She's a sweetheart. Let me introduce you."

A feline paced around a six-by-six-foot pen made of wire and roofed with aluminum panels. The cat was small and light, its long spine curved slightly, its blond fur interrupted by dark spots, some of which were just her natural markings and others of which were patches of mud that made her look sickly and sad. Tortuga squatted and put his face very close to the wire.

"Buenos días, mi vida," he cooed to the cat, who approached and rubbed her body on the cage. "Someone's in a good mood!" Tortuga grinned back at him, so innocent that Eloy could imagine him as a child reading about animals in a picture book.

"Is it a jaguar?" Eloy asked.

"No jaguars around these parts. This is a cunaguaro. Much smaller but still a fearsome predator." Tortuga stood and yelled farther back into the warehouse, "Pecueca!"

The cat, startled by the yell, glued her ears to her skull and showed her fangs. The sound she made was a mixture of a roar and a whine, both deep and high-pitched, at once scary and pitiful.

"¿Qué pasó?" someone yelled back, and an older man came out from an enclosed room, covered from head to toe in blood. He had a bulbous, warty nose, gray hair cropped tight by his ears, and a smooth dome up top. "Oh, jefe, it's you," the man named Pecueca said, and wiped his hands on his filthy trousers.

"How's the butchering coming along?" Tortuga asked.

"Good, boss. We put Nacho down just an hour ago so we're still in the thick of it. I might need another of the boys to come help. The hide has been tougher than I thought. Want to come see?"

They walked to the room. Eloy slipped as soon as his sneakers stepped on the tile—stained with streaks of varying hues of red. The carcass of a half-butchered cow lay at the center of the room. Two men hacked at its hindquarters with machetes, yanking the white-furred hide while cutting away at the connective tissue.

"Here you go, boss—puro lomito," Pecueca said, and offered Tortuga the tenderloin, already cut into thick medallions.

Tortuga took the bag and nodded, a silent thank-you. Then he and Eloy went out the same way they'd come.

They passed two more buildings, one next to the other, on the way back to the yard. Eloy couldn't see inside them, but their roofs were covered with tents made of sheets and plastic tarps, hung from rigged wire and string. Across the gap between the two roofs stretched a wooden ladder that served as a bridge. Eloy realized that this was the shantytown he'd seen from Topo's room. It must have housed twenty or thirty people. A woman walked along the roof, approaching the edge closest to where Tortuga and Eloy themselves were walking. She was tall, with long, slender legs and a wide, muscular back.

"Who lives up there?" Eloy asked.

"AIDS Town? People with life problems—you know, something off with their heads." Tortuga pointed at his skull. "Maricones, transfors, men in dresses. Look, Eloy, part of my job here—my responsibility—is to keep order. I have nothing against that stuff personally, I don't judge. A man's dick, a man's ass, it's theirs to do with as they please." He mimicked washing his hands and held them up. "But some people here—most, I would say—are not as civilized. Gays bring trouble wherever they go. Nastiness, fights, disease. I'd rather keep them separate. For the good of everyone."

Tortuga pulled Eloy's drawing out of his pocket. He studied it. Eloy could see it, too, the care of each stroke, the deliberate way he'd captured the bump on Wili's nose, the light lines that produced his eyelashes—delicate, even feminine. The sun above them felt like the obliterating lamp in the police room the night they'd gotten caught, when it was impossible for Eloy to see the faces of the cops asking him questions. A light was being shone in a place so secret that not even Eloy himself wanted to look. Tortuga handed Eloy the drawing. Eloy looked back at AIDS Town and then back at the page. They had returned to the courtyard now, surrounded by prisoners and the noise of them, gathered in the heat of the afternoon.

"It's good, Eloy. You've got talent."

"Thank you, sir."

Tortuga's eyes were big, unmoving, with a lifeless quality that scared Eloy. The Cro-Magnon shape of his skull cast dark shadows over them. And what had been, so far, a stroll through this man's kingdom was now turning into something else.

"But you're not a fag, are you? You and Wili, you're not maricones?"

"What? No!" Eloy said, the answer issued so fast it was almost as if he'd vomited it out. His whole body burned, or froze, he wasn't quite sure. He clutched the drawing now the same way he'd fingered his scar as a boy, for comfort. Seconds passed. Or months. And in that space Wili—brother and friend—floated in his mind. If he was something else, something more, Eloy wasn't ready to face that.

Tortuga stared at him. Then the king of Patria y Próceres smiled. "Good!" he said.

"Here it is, chamo!" Tortuga opened his arms wide. They were back in the courtyard, close to Robin's restaurant, in front of a big white wall. "Your canvas! I'm thinking my face here on the left, and some sort of inspirational quote, something really good. Gandhi? Churchill? Fidel? I don't know yet, but it'll come to me. How does that sound?"

Eloy was nervous, and not only because of Tortuga. He couldn't shake his unease over the conversation about the drawing. "Sounds good, boss. Yeah. We can do that."

"Great, Eloy. That's just super. We're going to be friends, you and I. I'm so tired of all these brutes here all the time. It's nice to meet another artist. You know I'm a musician, right?"

"No, sir, I didn't know that."

"Oh yeah. Wait till you see me play. There's a connection with something deeper, don't you agree? When your pencil hits paper? Same as when my hands beat the timbales." He searched for something in Eloy's face. "Yeah, you know what I'm talking about, I can tell." Tortuga looked at La Tasca, where Robin was in the process of taking a man's order. "Robin!" he yelled. "Here's some lomito for my freezer." He tossed the bag Robin's way. "Cook a couple, would you? Freeze the rest."

"Yes, jefe," Robin yelled back and immediately got to work.

The man at the counter seemed to understand that he wouldn't be getting his lunch anytime soon.

"You hungry, Eloy? Let's talk more about this wall, no?" They sat at a table and prisoners came by to pay tribute to Tortuga. He chatted amiably with them, even introduced Eloy to a couple. "He's an artist," he said, proudly. "Eloy's going to paint us a mural."

Eventually Robin brought them two plates — the grilled steaks they'd just gotten from Pecueca, along with white rice and sweet plantains. The food marked a pause to the parade of subjects coming by to kiss Tortuga's ring, and he focused on Eloy again.

"Killing is easy," Tortuga said as he chewed a piece of tenderloin. Each sentence was carefully considered, time ticking as the fork went into his mouth, as the molars tore the meat, as he swallowed. "There's no talent in it. I can put a gun in anyone's hands here. Anyone. I mean, it's a prison, right? There's nothing unique here about violence."

Eloy had his own plate in front of him. He almost hesitated to dig in, the presentation was so good. The perfectly crosshatched grill marks on the tenderloin medallion were topped with a half-melted pat of butter. A neat pile of white rice nestled beside it. Three slices of plátanos maduros, caramelized and glistening, promised sweetness unimaginable just a few minutes earlier.

"Your friend, Wili, for example," Tortuga said. "He can be useful. He, like everyone else in this place, has a role to play."

Eloy made a first cut into the lomito. The knife went through easily, the butter sliding down into the cut.

"But there's nothing exceptional about Wili. What he can do, anyone can do. Robin can do it, I can do it. You. You can kill, Eloy. I know you haven't, I can tell. But you could."

Eloy took the first bite. He closed his eyes. The meat was tender, tasted like flame and grass and blood.

"But then there are people like you, Eloy. Like Pecueca, the butcher. Like some of the really good athletes locked up here. We've got at least six professional athletes in El Penal right now. Two basketball players, a boxer, three peloteros — even a Margariteño who's a kite-surfing champion. This took me a while to understand,"

Tortuga continued. "Maybe because for a time I thought a criminal was all I was. Like your friend Wili. I was just like him. A hammer and all I could see was nails." Tortuga mimicked bringing down a hammer on three nails around his plate. "But I liked other things too, like really figuring out music, analyzing rhythms and beats. I liked the fluidity of bodies when they fought—not the punch, which is what most of my friends looked for in the ring. I noticed the fighters' feet, how fast they slid, how dance-like it all was. How their heads bobbed out of the way, gloved fists whizzing by. But I hid all those thoughts, all that knowledge. Because I worried that liking things that weren't as hard and cold as the revolver I put in my pants, or as warm and wet as the pussy I fucked, made me weak. You get me?"

"I do," Eloy said. He was tired of Tortuga's aristocratic posturing, how he droned on and on, so self-aggrandizing, but he had to admit there was something to relate to as well. He remembered, in high school, hiding his love for drawing. "It was the same for me in Cotiza," he said. "Always trying to be tough, but still wanting to be me. I had a backpack full of colored pencils, but if anyone stepped up to me, I'd have to be ready."

"Exactly. But you kept the pencils in the pack, right? That took me a long time to figure out, chamo. That I could do both. You're lucky, in a sense."

"No one here is lucky," Eloy said. And it surprised him how quickly the words had come, how unfiltered. They were perhaps the first ones he'd spoken freely in this place.

"Well ain't that the truth, menor!" Tortuga chewed through the last piece of his steak as he chuckled.

"I'll fill you in on a little secret, though," he said, serious now. "Some of us are luckier than others." Tortuga tossed a soiled napkin on top of his plate. "Go to the phone stall and call your mom. Let her know you're all right. Let her know how things work in here. Then come find me."

59

BACK AT JACINTO'S RANCHO, María fumed and cried in turns, anger and grief spurring each other on, an awful cycle. Stanislavo was still the same man her mom had told her about the night of Chávez's election, almost fifteen years ago. A coward. A hypocrite. And María was weak. Would never be what her mother had been. With no job, her savings had quickly dwindled from the expenses of Eloy's case. At least she had the rancho Jacinto had left them. And so the cycle went, until one in the morning, when she put a stop to it. If no one else was going to do anything—not the system, not the lawyer, and not Stanislavo—then María would do it herself.

She spent the next days at the courts. She felt like a leaf in the wind: from one bureaucrat to another, to another, to another. Enough to carry her through the day and out into the street at four in the afternoon, when the tribunales doors closed in her face and the only thing she could see was a procession of government functionaries gathering their personal items in time to be out of the building the second the clock struck five.

María finally broke down on Friday, weeping in front of a young, stone-faced receptionist, who surprised her by sliding her a piece of paper with a name, an office number, and a time. She spent the next two hours practicing what she would say, but it all came down to two questions:

How could she reach her son?

When would his sentencing hearing be scheduled?

At 1:30 p.m. she approached the elevators on the ground floor of tribunales, where a large man wearing a red polo shirt prevented her from pushing the call button.

"Can I help you, ma'am?"

"I have a meeting on the third floor, with Mrs. Ulloa?"

"Your appointment slip, please," he said, and extended a meaty hand.

All she had was the hand-scribbled paper.

"What's this?" he asked.

"It's what the lady gave me."

"I can't let you in with this. You need an appointment slip." He stared above her head, as if she were already invisible.

"But this is what I have. That lady over there gave it to me." María looked back to where the receptionist had been sitting, but the woman was no longer there, having been replaced by a different woman, this one with wet curls that bounced as she argued with someone.

The man grabbed the paper again. "Who gave you this?"

"A young receptionist, with straight black hair? She was there just a few minutes ago."

"Well, I'm sorry, señora, but only people with an appointment slip can come in."

A man interrupted their argument and presented a small red ticket to the elevator guard. "Excuse me, señora," he said as he gently pushed her aside. He entered the elevator and the doors closed.

"Go talk to her and see if she can give you a slip," the elevator guard said, gesturing toward the receptionist.

There was a line of at least thirty people waiting to talk to the woman. The red numbers on the digital clock above the elevators read *1:36*, and María's meeting with Mrs. Ulloa was at 2 p.m.

"Look, I have an appointment. I don't know why she didn't give me a red slip, but I have the name and the time. The lady gave it to me!"

"Lower your voice, ma'am. I'm just doing my job."

María felt like a balloon person. Skin and air. She found an empty seat in the large waiting room. People waiting in lines, people waiting in seats, people waiting leaning against tiled, institutional walls. People waiting for documents, for appointments, for sentences. People waiting for an answer. For a son.

The elevator guard went to the entrance, called over by the security guard there, just another watchman paid to enforce little nothings. The two men chatted, laughing at a joke as more people entered the building. Lawyers and bureaucrats, yes, but mostly the people they supposedly served. Whomever the legal system swept into its belly. Less a system and more a void. A huge, black maw that vacuumed people up.

María gathered her courage and moved calmly toward the elevator doors. She pressed the cracked plastic of the hexagonal button, and it shone amber, like a honeycomb. The numbers on the gold plaque above the machine flickered in and out, the 6 dying and giving life to the 5, then the 4 and then the 3. The elevator guard stared at a young woman walking by in the street. The number 2 perished on the gold plaque, and the man's silver tooth glittered as he said something to the security guard. The paper in María's pocket, with Mrs. Ulloa's name, was so crumpled now, so small, that it could have fit inside a straw. And then the elevator doors opened and air from the other floors, cooler, smelling less of cramped humanity, greeted her. María stepped into the elevator. And pressed another button. And all of a sudden she was alone. And the ground beneath her feet shook. And she was lifted.

She was deposited on the third floor at the end of a long hallway. The same off-white tile oppressively lined the walls. But there was no bustle on this floor. Polite conversation escaped from behind the closed doors that mirrored one another down the hall, offices with paper labels taped to them: *3-1*, *3-2*, *3-3*, and so on. María stopped before the door marked *3-4*, notated on a paper attached by a push-pin. Air from an AC vent right above the paper made it undulate and snap.

Inside Office *3-4* a young woman sat at a metal desk older than she was by a decade or two. Behind her hung a framed photograph of Hugo Chávez wearing his full presidential regalia and beaming a warm smile. The young woman tried her best to match Chávez's warmth but didn't quite manage—it was Friday, and perhaps the week had taken a toll.

"Señora, how can I help you?" she said.

"Yes, señorita, I have an appointment with Dra. Ulloa at two?"

"Your name?"

"María Rodríguez. I'm here about my son, Andrés Eloy Rodríguez."

The young woman typed a few things into her computer. "I don't see you in our system, Señora Rodríguez. Are you sure it was today?"

María took the crumpled piece of paper from her pocket. It was embarrassing to unfurl it, to present the meaningless scribbles from the receptionist. It wasn't even the right color. What María wouldn't give to transform it into a formal red slip, to turn the receptionist's rushed script into beautiful block letters! Like Eloy's own beautiful penmanship, neat, crisp, small.

"The receptionist gave it to me," she said, handing the paper to the woman. "I know it's not an official red slip, but—"

"It's okay. Susana does this all the time."

And the smile that accompanied the woman's words felt like when María opened the curtains in the Casa Verde living room, first thing in the morning before she started to clean.

"But it's Friday, mi amor," the woman said, and after all María had endured, that *But* felt cruel. "La Señora Ulloa is at lunch."

"No problem, I can wait."

"Sure. Feel free to sit." The woman pointed at three chairs against the opposite wall. "But—"

And there it was again. Nothing could ever stand on its own in this place. A building made of *Buts*, of *Nos*, of *Laters*.

"It's Friday, mi amor," the woman repeated.

She didn't have to explain further. Friday lunches—for some people, for government workers who could take lunches away from their desks, like Señora Ulloa—were prolonged affairs. More often than not they connected to the weekend with stitching so tight it was invisible. Certain Friday lunches were *Goodbye, see you on Monday.*

"Did she say she was coming back?" María asked.

The woman just shook her head and looked at María with a pity reserved for lost causes. "No, I'm sorry. And she doesn't take new appointments until next Wednesday."

By 3:30 p.m. María had seen the young woman, Fanny (two *n*s and a *y*, she pointed out when she introduced herself), reapply makeup, sing along to Chino y Nacho's "Bebé bonita," transcribe a couple of folders, drink two cafés con leche, and flirt with a handsome young man from the office next door. Each time they heard heels clatter down the hallway, they would both perk up. María was grateful for Fanny's kindness, for her companionship, even if the sense of urgency was lost on her.

"I'll try her one more time for you, María. But I don't think she's coming back."

Fanny dialed on her office phone. María could hear the faraway sound of the tone escaping the beige handset, once, twice, three times, four, and then the forbidding voice of the lawyer's recorded message.

60

WHETHER THEY WANTED Chávez to win or lose, to live or die, or hadn't made up their minds yet, it didn't matter. His illness hung over all of them. Like the mist now rolling down the Ávila mountain, blanketing the city with a sticky humidity that smelled of mangoes rotting on the pavement.

Stanislavo had dreamed a parade of faces. They shifted, changed shape. Chávez, pumped up with so much chemo poison he glowed green; Molina and Nunzio, first healthy and strong, as they'd been in Mochima, then withering to skin hanging on bone; Emiliana next to him in bed, staring; Ludmil, his twin, still as present in his dreams as ever, the only reason Stanislavo still recalled how he'd looked when he was a teenager; Nassim holding up his large, callused hands, opening and closing them, revealing different things: a ladybug, a tooth, a black bean. No María, no Eloy, who were somehow more present by not being there, since they were all he could think about after María's visit, at the beginning of the week.

They would not leave his mind as he warmed pita bread, poured honey on it.

Three cardboard boxes sat, unopened, in his living room. All that was left from his latest failure at a relationship. Mirella the lawyer, Mirella the activist, Mirella the lover of old Westerns. He hadn't thought she wanted kids. She was forty, more than twenty-five years his junior, when they got married. Why was he such a lousy partner? He didn't talk enough, that was part of it. He assumed too much. His two failed marriages had been the only sphere of his life where he avoided confrontation.

He had always felt that, if he and Emiliana could have made it work, it would have been different. But now he wasn't sure. What if he had turned out to be just as disappointing to her as he had been to the other women who came into his life? If he got the chance, would he be any different with his daughter? Could he?

He opened the first box. His books. And then he remembered something.

He took the books out fast, looking for one in particular. He tossed *Rayuela* to one side, *La fiesta del chivo* to the other. Isabel Allende's *Paula* landed on the rug. Octavio Paz, Dostoyevsky, Flannery O'Connor, Alexandre Dumas, Nabokov, all discarded. At the bottom of the box he started to run into Gabo's books. His dear friend. The most famous person he had known. They had met in 1958, a few months after García Márquez moved to Caracas to write for *Momento* magazine. For a short period after the fall of Marcos Pérez Jiménez, in January of '58, Venezuela had been the freest country in the world. Stanislavo still remembered it as the most joyous time in his life. He had even briefly been able to banish the pain of Ludmil. Life was lived then in the way only people who have been horribly oppressed can live it: completely, fully, and with the certainty that it would not last. In the midst of that euphoria was Gabo, skinny, mustachioed, more Venezuelan than Colombian in the way he smiled and joked and drank. He always had a cigarette in his mouth. He buzzed around Movement meetings and haunts. Gabo was thirty then and recently married, like an elder statesman to Stanislavo. In the handful of times they hung out together, they bonded over writing and the Cuban revolution. But they didn't become close until after *One Hundred Years of Solitude* was released, with Gabo already in the stratosphere. Stanislavo wrote a book criticizing the USSR's invasion of Czechoslovakia, and it made waves, eventually putting his name in the mouth of Brezhnev. It also prompted Gabo to send Stanislavo a personalized copy of *Cien años de soledad,* and within it a note inviting him to come visit Barcelona, where he lived at the time. *I'd love it very much if we could talk about so many things in your book that are evident,* Gabo wrote. *The only people who can't see them are the blind.*

There it was, his copy of *Solitude.* There it was, Gabo's note on the title page alongside his signature, as well as the flower he liked to draw on most of his correspondence. Stanislavo shook the book, unconcerned with damaging the treasure in his hand. And there it was: three folded notebook pages, yellowed with age. The letter he had written to Emiliana and María (unknown and unnamed to him at the time). He had stuffed it in Gabo's novel on the day in 1972 when he had decided to return to Venezuela and get Emiliana back.

Opening the letter felt like entering a wormhole back in time. To his year of searching for Emiliana and his daughter. Every hospital and clinic in Caracas and Puerto La Cruz, every nursing home and rehabilitation center. Anywhere a nurse would be needed, Stanislavo visited. He knocked on the doors of people he still knew from his Movement days—the ones who would talk to him, that is, since Alfredo had poisoned that well. By then it had been seven years, of course. While he had been in Mexico City, writing about the state of socialism in Latin America, going to the kiosk for the Venezuelan paper every morning to read about the Movement's latest blunder or the most recent outburst of violence in one city or another, María was somewhere uttering her first words. While he went to the market, the acrid smell of peppers assaulting his senses, Emiliana was building a life. Back then he wondered if another man was there with her, being a father to his child. When the Soviet Union invaded Czechoslovakia in '68 and Stanislavo dived into writing about the seams of the Communist Party unraveling, his daughter was a little person, had likes and dislikes, had a personality, already had a face full of freckles, just as he had when he was a kid. As Ludmil had too. Who needed a mirror when a twin brother was there?

When Rafael Caldera was elected in Venezuela and the pacification process started between the government and the guerrillas, Stanislavo moved to Colombia. It wasn't only that Gabo had put him in touch with the editor of *El Tiempo*, for which he would be heading the Venezuela desk, but also that he would be closer. To the country, to Emiliana, to his child. And as soon as the blanket pardons were given to members of the Movement, Stanislavo went back.

Reading the letter returned him in his mind to those last moments at Abastos Beirut, where he had written it as Kashir and Nassim shouted and banged on the freezer door, barely audible:

> *I'm going to find you, Emiliana. I promise. And all I'll*
> *be able to do is ask you to take me back. To allow me the*
> *immense privilege of making all of this up to you. To let me*
> *be the father I know I can be to our child. Is she a girl, as*
> *you thought? What is her name? Does she look like you?*

What a promise to break!

His cell phone rang. Graciela. "Anything with our search for María Rodríguez and her son?" he asked.

"Nada, Stanis. Haven't been able to track down an address or a phone number yet." Graciela had reached Adriana Vila at the Ministry, she said, but Doctora Vila could access the prisoner files only from tribunales, and with everything going on, the system was collapsing.

Everyone was waiting to see what happened with Chávez. Getting an institution to do anything was impossible. All of the government's resources were being funneled into Hugo Chávez's presidential campaign and the fallout from his worsening illness. This time the Chavistas were fighting against an organized and mobilized opposition, and Henrique Capriles Radonski was looking better and stronger every day. The Chavista party, by contrast, was a wounded sea monster, chaotically flailing its powerful tentacles.

Plus, as Graciela reminded Stanislavo, it was Friday.

He didn't know Adriana Vila well. She had served as a source, off the record, for a couple of pieces the paper had run about the penal system within the last year. There was certainly a rift in high-level Chavismo about what was happening to prisons across the country. Slowly but surely, control of the facilities had been ceded to the prisoners themselves, who were usually led by a single strongman called a *pran*, who orchestrated life inside the walls. In most large prisons in the country, guards now served as little more than sheepdogs, keeping prisoners in but not interfering with the inner workings of the place.

Adriana Vila led the government contingent seeking to regain control of the prisons and to do the actual job of reforming prisoners. This, of course, was a pipe dream. Throughout its history the Venezuelan penal system had never worked as anything more than a soul-crushing institution. Stanislavo knew it better than most. But he related to impossible dreamers. It's why he liked Adriana. One more Quixote in a country full of windmills.

Stanislavo asked if there was anything new from Sandra on Chávez. Graciela told him that Sandra had talked to the nurse in Cuba who was claiming to have treated him yesterday, and that the woman said he'd pulled through the crisis and was doing much better. But Sandra wasn't sure it was legit. Castro had everything locked tight, and it was more dangerous than ever for anyone there to speak out.

"Sandra says she might need you on this one," Graciela said. "The nurse is clamming up. She has a call with her scheduled at ten. Should I tell her you'll be there?"

"Yes! I'm moving a bit slowly this morning, but I'll be in the office for the call."

"Oh, Stanis, wait. I've got a call coming into my cell from the Ministry."

"Adriana?"

"One second," Graciela said.

He waited on the phone as Graciela muttered some *Yes*es, some *Okay*s, a couple of *Sure*s. She came back on the line to tell him it was Adriana's secretary. Their phones were down and things were crazy, but Adriana would be at her office for a few hours this morning if Stanislavo wanted to stop by. She didn't know if she would be able to talk any other time.

"What should I tell Sandra about the call?" Graciela asked.

"She's on her own on this one," Stanislavo said. "Tell her I'm sorry."

61

THE SOUND OF FOOTSTEPS in the hallway had increased tenfold since four o'clock. Every minute another person walked by, but in the opposite direction María was hoping for. The weekend exodus had begun. The door to 3-4 opened, but it was just the handsome man again. His tight polo shirt showed off his strong chest.

"¿Lista, Fanny?" he said. "A few of us are going down for beers at El León if you want to come with us. I'll give you a ride."

Fanny looked at him, then at María.

María started gathering her things. She stood up from her chair and was about to hand back the fashion magazine that Fanny had lent her almost two hours earlier.

"I'm sorry," Fanny said, "I'm going to stay here until five with this lady. I'll meet up with you there, though. I'll take the metro."

"You sure?"

"Yeah, I'm sure. I'll see you in a little bit, okay?"

María melted at this kindness. Her eyes watered as she sat back down. Tight Shirt walked away and María wiped her eyes with her sleeve.

"My cousin is in jail," Fanny said. "In Maracaibo. My aunt hasn't been able to speak to him in two months."

"And Mrs. Ulloa can't help?"

"She was able to get his sentencing hearing moved forward, which was huge. He'd been there for a year already without a sentence. Now at least he knows how much time he's got."

"We're waiting for the same thing. One year? Really?"

"That's nothing. I know people who've been in penales for five or six years without knowing how long their sentence will be."

María's stomach tightened.

"María, how about you just come back next Wednesday? I'm going to personally put you in Mrs. Ulloa's book." Fanny pulled out a red-slip booklet and started writing on it. "Come in first thing, at eight. I'll make sure she knows you're coming, and I'll prep her on your son's file."

Then the door opened again. It was a woman this time. She was slight and freckled and wore a man's suit. She looked young but carried herself with authority.

Fanny immediately put away the red slips, ran a hand through her hair, and sat up straight.

"Doctora Vila," she said. "How can I help, ma'am?"

"Is Señora Ulloa here?"

"No, I'm sorry, doctora. She's already left for the day."

"She's not answering her phone," the woman said, annoyed.

"Let me text her," Fanny said. "I'm sure she'll call right back." Fanny double-thumbed her personal cell phone.

"Could you help me pull up a file?" the authoritative woman asked. "I'm trying to track down a prisoner for a colleague."

"Just one sec," Fanny said. She finished typing on her cell phone, then turned to her desktop computer. "What's the prisoner's name?"

"Andrés Eloy Rodríguez."

Fanny froze, her fingers glued to the keyboard.

María wasn't sure if she had heard her son's name coming out of the woman's mouth. *It's just my mind playing tricks*, she thought. But she still wished for a miracle.

"Andrés Eloy Rodríguez," repeated Dra. Vila and pointed at Fanny's keyboard. "Are you all right?"

"Yes, sorry, doctora," said Fanny. "It's just—this is Mr. Rodríguez's mother. María Rodríguez." Fanny extended her arm, palm up, toward María.

Dra. Vila turned around, taking in María for the first time. "Huh," she said, and introduced herself to María as Adriana Vila.

She hoped this woman could help, but prepared herself for disappointment. This place seemed to be built on that, after all.

"How do you know Stanislavo?" Adriana asked.

She and María were now sitting in Señora Ulloa's office. Poor Fanny was stuck at her desk until they finished—probably wishing she had accepted Tight Shirt's offer of a ride. The office was strange. Of course the photo of the president hung behind the desk, but everything else—from the framed Universidad Bolivariana law degree to the pot where a lush spider plant thrived to the edging around the keyboard—was decked out in pink, silver, and rhinestones. All the highlighters Señora Ulloa owned appeared to be pink, and María imagined all those prisoners' files touched by Disney-princess hues. It was comical to see the reserved Adriana in this setting, surrounded by these childish obsessions. María imagined Adriana's office as the exact opposite: concrete, metal, wool.

"We met during the protests on the day of the coup," María said. "He…he helped me and my son."

"Helped how?"

"My son, Eloy, was shot that day. He was nine years old."

Adriana's stone face betrayed the tiniest sign of life. A slight tilt.

"Mr. Atanas was there working on a story," María said. "I thought Eloy was going to die in my arms. But Stanislavo corralled a doctor, and then he was there in the OR, helping. He saved my son's life."

"Well, this must be important to him. He's been calling me for three days straight, and he showed up at my office this morning. And with everything going on with the president…" Adriana coughed into the sleeve of her tailored suit. "So, Eloy is in Patria y Próceres? What happened?"

"A mistake. I know you probably hear this all the time, but Eloy is a good person."

"You're saying he's innocent?"

It was as if María's bones had been rung like a bell. It hurt to think about it so plainly. And it hurt more still to have the certainty that, no, he wasn't innocent. "He did what he's accused of. He was just trying to help his best friend."

Adriana looked through the file open in front of her. "Wilmer Torres, alias El Wili," she said.

And even though it sounded like something out of a police TV show, all María could picture was little Wili, dirty and hungry, standing on the Cotiza steps by Portu's store. "Yes," she said.

"Assault, robbery, kidnapping. These are serious offenses, María."

"Yes, I know." And she felt the condescension behind Adriana's reproach. Even though María was older, had lived through so much more than this woman, she felt like a little girl in the principal's office.

"Who's your lawyer?"

María pulled out his card from her purse and handed it to Adriana.

"Well, the first thing we're going to do is find you someone else," Adriana said and handed the card back. It would be a public defender, she added, so it wouldn't cost María much—just administrative fees and such—but the woman was good, and Adriana promised she would personally make sure the lawyer took the necessary time with Eloy's case.

María thanked her.

Adriana said she would also correspond with Judge Delgado about a sentencing hearing. It would take months—it wouldn't be a quick thing, she warned, even with her help—but at least María would be able to know that the process was moving along. "We can't really do anything else until Eloy has a sentence," Adriana said. "Then your lawyer can start to work on options of early release."

Release. Such a simple word. It meant so little to Adriana to throw it around. It meant the world to María.

"How can I get in touch with him?" María asked. "I haven't been able to talk to him since before his transfer to Patria y Próceres."

"That's going to be hard. El Penal has been on lockdown for six months now. No visitors. But there are plenty of phones inside the compound. You haven't heard from him?"

"My lawyer said there are no official phone lines there."

"Not anymore, that's true. But prisoners have cell phones, and if they don't, they can rent phones from other inmates. I hate to say this, but if he hasn't called, it's probably because he doesn't want to."

Her bluntness stunned María. But it was true. Eloy hadn't called. Unless he was unable to: He might have gotten hurt, or worse. She couldn't say that out loud, though, couldn't let her mind go there. So she remained quiet.

"I'll give you the number of one of the pastors at Patria y Próceres," Adriana said. She peeled off a pink Post-it note and wrote something on it. "He might be able to track down Eloy and get him on the phone for you."

"Thank you. Thank you so much, doctora. You don't know how much this means to me."

"Don't thank me. Thank Stanislavo."

The silence hung between them, as heavy as wet laundry on a clothesline.

"María," said Adriana. "I hope this all works out with your son. But he won't be the same" — she paused — "when he gets out."

María wondered if she had meant to say *if* rather than *when* and had simply chosen to be kind.

Outside, Fanny was filing her nails. But as soon as they came out, her eyes met María's and she winked at her once, smiling.

62

WITH NO CHANCE of his mom coming to visit, it had been easy for Eloy not to think about her in here. In fact, without a single prisoner mentioning a mother, it had been easy to pretend mothers didn't exist at all. Maybe nobody mentioned a mother because the pain in that word was so overwhelming, so universal, so large that if you let it out amid the unflinching oppression of El Penal, you'd never get it back inside you.

Eloy dialed the eleven numbers that added up to his mother's voice. It had been days since Tortuga had commanded him to make the call. He was wishing his mother would ignore the unknown number, would let the phone ring once, twice, and then forever. It would be better to listen to the monotonous tone of the phone line—get lost in the space between each electronic note—than to hear one second of his mother's voice: that dark, soothing tree sap of a voice that contained everything. He didn't want to hear her so much as take in a breath before speaking, because even that would manifest as a lance to stab him at the spot where his scar began.

But she didn't even wait for the first ring to finish. She picked up so fast that it caught Eloy flat-footed—as if he could ever have been ready for this anyway.

"Aló," she said.

Sure enough, the lance stabbed, its sharp tip catching him at his sternum.

"Aló? Who's this?"

The tip forced it way through, scraping bone as it pushed into him.

"¿Quién es?" she repeated. She went quiet. She breathed.

The lance pierced his flesh and organs now: a lung, a heart. He could sense a new word forming on his mother's tongue, the word that would impale him to this call.

"¿Eloy?" she finally asked.

"Sí, Mami, soy yo," he said. And it was as though they were the first words he had ever spoken in his life.

63

MARÍA COULDN'T QUITE REMEMBER the details of what they had said to each other, even a few seconds after they had bid goodbye and hung up. Something about a mural. Something about Wili helping Eloy get settled. Something about a zoo? It had all seemed like waking from a dream. It had made sense when they were talking, but now it dissolved into jabber.

She had told Eloy about the possibility of expedited sentencing, she remembered that, and he had seemed happy. He had asked her about Wili's sentencing hearing. She told him she would ask Adriana Vila the next time they spoke—or the new lawyer she'd suggested. It was the weekend. Monday, just around the corner, would bring with it the promise of steps being taken.

Right now nothing else mattered than the fact that she had just spoken to her son. Not the lawyer, not Vila, not the news on TV, forever droning on about Chávez, elections, cancer, operations, Cuba. *Venezuela could be on the brink of monumental change*, some bald head on the TV square had said, and it sounded to María like he was leagues under the sea. Stanislavo Atanas, her father, didn't matter. Even her resentment toward her son, his callousness at not calling her until now, almost a month and a half since they'd last seen each other, had vanished.

In gratitude for his help with Adriana, she had been making a quesillo for Stanislavo—a peace offering—when Eloy called. The mixture of eggs, milk, condensed milk, vanilla, and rum rested in the blender, waiting for the blades to spin. María walked to the bathroom, the phone still warm in her pocket. She looked into her own eyes in the mirror. Those two gold-speckled planets that lived in her head.

"I miss you," she said.

And she meant sweet Jacinto. And she meant Eloy. She meant her mother. She meant Eloy's father, who had given her Eloy, after all. She meant Magali, who was not really her friend anymore but would always be her friend, because of those days when Eloy was in the hospital. She meant Casa Verde, and sweet Gustavito, and troublesome Jorge Luis, and even La Señora. Wili, too, she had to admit.

"I miss you so much," she said.

The quesillo mixture was still there, waiting for her to press the button on the blender. She would prepare the caramel that would coat the bottom of the quesillo tin. Pour the mixture over the caramel. Close the lid and place the tin in a deep tray with water, then everything into the oven, to firm up the flan in the bain-marie. Wait patiently as the smell of sweet milk and toasty caramel made her dizzy with hunger and anticipation. Open the quesillo lid and glimpse the transformation, how something wet and sticky and raw had come out the other side as something done. Something to behold. Something to revere. Something to savor.

64

"It's María," Graciela said, peeking through the office doorway.

Stanislavo stood up. His pulse rose noticeably and he felt his face flush. María carried a tin. She shifted her weight, standing on the threshold to his office, looking for somewhere to place it, he realized.

"I'm so sorry," he said. "My office—"

"Is a mess," she said. "I know."

He moved the books from the chair opposite him, then cleared space on his desk, and María placed the tin there and opened the lid. The quesillo inside was immediately the most beautiful thing in the room, smelling of hot milk and brown sugar.

"As a thank-you, Mr. Atanas. For everything."

"I appreciate that, María, and please call me Stanis, but I'm not sure how I've helped." He invited her to sit. "I've been trying to track you down since you called," he said, "and haven't had any luck."

"La Doctora Vila," she said. "I was able to meet her at tribunales. She told me you'd reached out to her about helping Eloy." And María explained how Adriana had helped her secure a new lawyer, who'd already spoken to her this morning about some steps that could get Eloy a sentence.

"Ah," Stanislavo said. He didn't know. Adriana hadn't gotten back to him since he'd stopped by her office the previous week. Chávez was back in Venezuela, hitting the campaign trail. Rumors were that he was getting a cocktail of steroids and medication before every appearance, a necessary jolt to keep himself strong. The newspaper had been crazy for days. "But I'm glad that she's been helpful," he added.

There was silence then. Stanislavo's nervous mind tried to conjure something to fill the space. He could sense María doing the same.

"Look, I'm sorry I didn't say anything last time," he told her. "I was...in shock, to be honest. I never thought—"

"I don't want anything else from you, Stanis, if you're worried about that."

"No, it's not that. I'm ashamed—ashamed I didn't recognize you when we first met, or when you were here last time. I see you here now and it's like I'm seeing your mom." Something he hadn't felt in ages—perhaps not since that night in Alfredo's house, when he saw Nunzio's photo—was forming in him like a crack. Some awareness of irrevocable loss that would splinter him if he let it. "Your mom," he said. "Where is she? Where does she live?"

"She doesn't," María said.

Her head was tipped down, toward her hands, and when she looked up Stanislavo felt the crack inside him spread.

"She died fourteen years ago this March. Breast cancer."

"I'm sorry for your loss," Stanislavo said.

"It was hard," María said. "She was an amazing mother. But I got to live with her, got to know her. You were the one who really lost."

The words pinned Stanislavo to his chair.

"Maybe I misspoke," María said. "There is one other thing I want. I want to know why you let her leave."

"I didn't *let* her," Stanislavo protested. "She left. I had to do something important, and she wouldn't have it." But hearing himself say it aloud filled him with more shame. He was doing the same thing all over again. His pride was getting in the way of whatever was forming here between him and María, or could form if he didn't smother it.

"She told me about the tunnel," María said. "About your friends. A few weeks before she died." She paused, as if to collect herself, but only momentarily. "Were they more important than my mom? Than me?"

"That's not what I mean."

"What *do* you mean, then?"

He searched for something to say, but there was no justification for what he had done. For what his actions had caused, what they had taken away from Emiliana, then from María, and now from Eloy. If Eloy was in prison, ultimately there was only one person responsible for it.

"You're right," he said finally. "There was nothing more important than your mother. Than you."

"I really didn't come for an apology," she said.

"I believe you. But you're here now, and maybe I'll never see you again, and I would understand if that's the case. So I want you to know I am sorry for what I did. For leaving you. For not getting to see you grow up. For not giving you anything. No home, no love, nothing."

It was María who was silent now. If she had been moved by his words, he couldn't tell. In a way it was worse for her not to be angry. But he would deserve whatever he got from her.

"I found this," Stanislavo said, and produced the letter, holding it out to her. "I wrote it the night I decided to leave the Movement. You must have been just a few weeks old then."

María reached out and took the pages.

"I tried to find you when I got back here. Spent a whole year searching. Every hospital, every nursing home. I hounded the few people I still talked to who knew your mom. I went to Puerto La Cruz and looked there as well. But I never found a trace."

"She never went back to nursing," María said.

"I should have tried harder, María. I'm so sorry." His shame burned him. His eyes were hot, his belly even hotter.

Something changed in María, though. He witnessed her softening. She didn't read the letter—which he understood, since he too would have protected himself from showing whatever emotions might emerge—but she held it to her chest. "Here," she said, and pulled some paper plates from her bag. "Do you have a knife somewhere in this mess?"

It took him a few seconds to process her request, after which he opened one of his drawers, pulled out a butter knife, and handed it to her. She opened the tin and cut two pieces of the quesillo, then placed them on the plates.

"Have you ever had to carry a quesillo through two bus rides, Stanis?"

He shook his head and passed her a couple of plastic spoons he'd found in the same drawer.

"I didn't think so," María said. "You work up an appetite." She took a bite.

Stanislavo spooned a piece into his mouth as María stared at him. The caramel hit first, the gentle heat of it, like sunlight on his neck. He blushed and closed his eyes. Then the texture of the flan, its gentle give, like a warm bath. It wasn't overly sweet. Then the caramel came back, with its slight bitterness and crunch. It was wonderful.

"So? Do you like it?"

Like would be too small a compliment. "I'm trying to find the words."

"But you like it?"

"Yes," he said, still reveling in the taste. "It's delicious, María. I love it."

"Good."

"I want to keep helping Eloy, if you'll allow it," he said. "Will you give me your phone number? Can we stay in touch?"

She ripped the corner of the piece of paper closest to her, grabbed one of the orphaned pens on the desk. "I'd like that," she said, and handed him the scrap of paper, a precious thing.

65

Emiliana,

This is the hardest letter I've ever had to write. The months
since I last saw you have been a shadow. The more I've dug this
hole, the more I've become it. I don't think I believe in anything
anymore.

Alfredo has been lying to me. This tunnel was never for getting
Nunzio and Molina out. The Merabis have been building a bomb
to blow Cuartel San Carlos to the sky, and here I've been, a fool. But
I've put a stop to it.

I don't think I'll ever see my friends again. All of it for nothing.
I turned my back on you, for nothing. Our baby, for nothing. I was
trying to be everything: a good friend, a good partner. But I failed
so miserably, I can only laugh at myself.

The only thing I feel right now is shame, Emiliana. I'm
ashamed I let you go that afternoon at Casa Finlandia. How stupid
I am! To turn my back on you and what we made. I think back on
that day, replay it over and over and over. I want to travel back
to that time and push that stupid version of myself aside and take

365

his place. Of course you're the most important thing. Of course our baby is the most important thing. Of course. Of course. Of course. If I could do it again, I would leave Casa Finlandia with you and never see Alfredo again. I would wait for Nunzio and Molina and their fate, and tell them I'm sorry. Maybe, with a child in my arms, they would understand. They would forgive. Or maybe not. But I would be with you, and that would be enough. It would be more than I deserve.

I'm going to find you, Emiliana. I promise. And all I'll be able to do is ask you to take me back. To allow me the immense privilege of making all of this up to you. To let me be the father I know I can be to our child. Is she a girl, as you thought? What is her name? Does she look like you?

Maybe we can move to Mochima, live in one of those small villages by the sea. We don't have to change the country, or change the world. It'll be enough just to live our lives in a good way, in an honest way.

I love you. Do you love me, still? Will you forgive me?

Stanislavo

66

IT WAS ASTOUNDING to Eloy, the way that what once had seemed inconceivable now felt quotidian. In almost four months, life in Patria y Próceres had settled into just that: life. He had been lucky. He owed a lot to Wili, who fit so well in this place and had made sure Eloy fit with him. It was true that their day-to-day existence in prison didn't overlap that much anymore—Wili was Topo's right hand now, though *bloody hand* was probably a more apt description—but Wili was still on Eloy's mind, no matter what he did. The knowledge in his throat that had formed that morning as he drew Wili lying by La Tasca hadn't untangled itself. The sensation deep in his gut—the fear of what that feeling meant, when Tortuga had asked him if Wili was something other than a friend—still sat within him, boiling in his stomach, resistant to dissolving.

Wili had secured his own private room, not as big as Topo's, and with a less majestic view, but far better than the common areas. Tortuga had even set Eloy up in his own space, more like a large closet, but with a door that closed and a bed that wasn't hemmed in by a dozen others.

Eloy had only recently started on the mural. Tortuga had wanted him to paint some stuff in his room first, and then Topo had wanted something made for his, and then the rest of the luceros. He'd drawn Michael Jordan, Batman, too many Playboy bunnies, and, surprisingly, lots of Disney characters. Eloy had suggested some ideas for the mural, even sketched them—grandiose Diego Rivera concepts of prisoners working together to break chains of oppression—but Tortuga just wanted what he'd said from the beginning, which was to have his face up there, as big as possible.

"But we'll add a quote to it," Tortuga reminded him. "It'll be inspirational."

Eloy worked on the contours of Tortuga's crooked nose, which on the wall was the size of a child from bridge to tip. The likeness was finally coming together as he added shading and tones. He'd been afraid Tortuga would see these early stages and declare that Eloy was terrible and exact some sort of punishment. But he'd been understanding, and Eloy had talked him through the process.

Working closely with the pran had its perks. Eloy was safe, that was the biggest one—no longer worried about being targeted by other prisoners or about being robbed. He had the protection of Tortuga, whose blessing was law. He had his little room and received a stipend, enough to pay La Causa. That, plus a little cash that his mother deposited into Topo's account, gave him some spending money. He was saving for a small TV with a built-in DVD player. The prisoner selling it had promised to wait three weeks, until Eloy came up with the money. He talked to his mother twice a week now, fighting through the shame that made his voice weak and scratchy. Apparently he had a grandfather, though his mother had never called him that.

But even with his path smoothed, fear persisted. By now he well knew Tortuga's moodiness. How fickle he could be. Although the pran considered himself benevolent, he was unforgiving and ruthless if he perceived even the barest slight. Committing violence without hesitation was the only way to hold on to power in a place like this. Eloy always felt one mistake away from being thrown into el hueco, a dirt pit behind the church ruins that was covered with a metal pan and pummeled by full sun from dawn to dusk. He'd seen men emerge from it with actual blisters. On particularly hot days, which were most of them here, you could smell burning skin when someone was in el hueco.

The Verdes had finally been letting visitors back in. Only Wednesdays and Sundays, although Topo said that soon it would be every day. Eloy's mother had argued with him about coming. She didn't care that it would mean almost two days by bus, there being no straight bus line from Caracas; she would need to spend a night somewhere in the middle and change buses a couple of times. He had told her it was too long and difficult, and that there was no way she should come. But the truth was that he didn't want her to come. He was afraid of what she might see.

The previous Sunday, after the church service where prisoners in good standing gathered with visiting family members, there had been a commotion. Apparently, a junkie—achicharraos, they called them here, men with no family, no one who cared for them, and no money to pay La Causa—had flirted with the visiting teenage daughter of another man, and then, when she didn't respond favorably, had grabbed her ass and called her a puta. The prison came down on him hard. Eloy hadn't been there, but Wili said that in a matter of minutes Coquito and one of his main enforcers had grabbed the kid and locked him away in a cell somewhere.

The next day, after visitors had left, the entire prison was invited to the trial. Justice would be meted out by Tortuga, Topo, Coquito, and one more lucero, Ternera. He was older, with a pockmarked face, a large nose, and dangling earlobes, like a giant dwarf, but in a basketball jersey and with a diamond stud in his ear. He controlled the drug business in the prison. The achicharrao, who had already been beaten badly and was barely conscious, was tied to a chair. Tortuga talked about the light, about those who ate it, and about the sacredness of La Visita. The luceros discussed forms of punishment. Ternera suggested the hole. Coquito suggested lashings. Topo argued for a manero. He believed that because he had put his hands on the girl, his hands should therefore bear the scar. Everyone seemed to agree that Topo's suggestion was both the most sensible and the most righteous.

They made the man kneel. Not a man, Eloy saw, but a boy. Topo tied his hands together in prayer position: palm against palm. When the boy tried to fight it, Topo hit him so hard that Eloy was sure he would collapse, but he didn't. "You stay like that, or the bullet goes in your head," Topo said, loud enough for everyone to hear. Hundreds of prisoners stood in the yard witnessing the trial. All of them were silent as the boy, like some devout saint kneeling on the rough concrete, lifted his hands to the sky.

Topo pulled out his gun and held it up. Then Wili stepped out from the crowd and walked to Topo — his expression blank, his walk steady. A man of ice. Wili grabbed the gun, aimed it at the boy's hands, and pulled the trigger. The bullet went in one hand and exited the other, lodging in the thick wall of the building right behind them.

The boy didn't scream at first. He just looked at his hands. He angled them to his face. Then he registered his pain and let out a howl.

Eloy hadn't seen much of Wili the past week, since the trial. When he did, Wili was always with Topo. They made an odd pair: Topo large and boisterous, his threats hidden in between jokes; Wili twiglike by comparison, twitchy, a smile foreign to his face. Yet Wili was at home in Patria y Próceres. He had bloomed here, nourished by the fertile environment. He was capable of anything, as long as it wasn't good.

"Hermano."

Eloy heard Wili's voice as he layered more brown paint on Tortuga's giant left nostril. He stepped down from his ladder and placed the brush on a pan, then wiped his hands on his stained work clothes, as if that made any difference when he was already covered from head to toe in paint. He could feel the stickiness even on his curls, which had grown longer now than he ever would have allowed in the outside world. His hands, meanwhile, looked like something conceived by abstract expressionists.

Still, he opened his arms and welcomed Wili in for a hug. "Nice to see you," he said. It felt good to hold him. A warmth expanded inside him, from his chest to his fingertips.

But Wili was off. He had a glassy stare, his eyes like camera lenses failing to find focus. He was high on something. "Hey, brother," said Wili. "How's it coming along?"

He stepped to the wall, and Eloy turned to face the mural as well.

"It's coming," Eloy said. "I'm saving the eyes for last. They're always the hardest for me."

"*Pfft*, he's an ugly motherfucker, isn't he?"

Wili said this much louder than Eloy was comfortable with, but he chuckled all the same.

"Yeah, he's no Winston Vallenilla," Eloy agreed, almost in a whisper.

"Ha!" Wili exploded. "No Winston Vallenilla!" He laughed, bent over his own belly.

"Shhhh." Eloy put his finger to his lips. "Take it easy, man. Are you okay?" His hand was on Wili's back.

"What do you mean?" Wili said, coming out of his laughing fit.

"I don't know, you seem weird."

"Weird how?" Wili said, and in just a couple of seconds the laughter seemed like a distant memory.

"Never mind, it's nothing, don't worry about it."

"No, no," Wili said. "You said I seem weird. Weird how?"

"What are you on, man?"

"Oh shit, chamo, I didn't know you'd turned into María all of a sudden. Wait. Is she here?" He mockingly looked around. "Oh no, Mommy is going to catch us doing druuuuugs." Wili blew a raspberry at him. "C'mon, Eloy, no me vengas con esa mierda."

"All right," Eloy said, raising his hands in surrender. "Whatever, chamo, whatever."

"Hey, did you talk to your mom?"

"About what?" Eloy asked, even as he well knew what was coming.

"About our case, man. That fancy new lawyer she's got? Did you ask her about me?"

Eloy had, in fact, asked his mother about Wili's case, but she still had trouble anytime Eloy brought Wili into their talks. Though Eloy had not yet banished his own guilt about the kidnapping, his mother had forgiven him immediately for what he'd done. But no matter how many times he told her that Wili hadn't tricked him into anything, that he had participated willingly, his mother wouldn't hear it. She ignored the hard parts of her son's confession. And she was punishing Wili in the only way she could: by leaving him out of any conversation with Eloy's new lawyer.

"It's complicated. But Mom says there's no word on your case yet," Eloy lied.

"Okay, 'tá bien," Wili said, fidgeting with his hands. His fingernails were chewed down to the cuticles. "Did she"—he paused and stared at the ground—"ask how I was doing?"

In that moment Eloy didn't see Wili the malandro. He saw his best friend as a boy, thirteen years old, standing on the threshold of his rancho. It was raining outside. Eloy, his mother, and Jacinto sat at the table, a basket of arepas steaming in front of them. Had he felt the same way about Wili then as he did now? It was complicated, all of it blurring together—Wili his brother, Wili his friend, whatever Wili was now, someone who made him feel queasy, but not because of what Wili had become in prison. The nausea came from inside Eloy himself; his love for Wili was no longer simple.

Jacinto was telling a story about his younger days, when he was a teller at the Hipódromo Racetrack.

"This fat guy comes to my window," Jacinto said. "Cigar hanging from his mouth. And he starts screaming at me that he's been cheated, that he really picked a different horse but we gave him the wrong ticket. And then the cigar drops from his mouth into his shirt pocket and as his shirt starts smoking, he screams like a little girl, 'My nipple, my nipple!'"

Jacinto laughed hysterically, and Eloy laughed too, and his mother smiled at both of them. Jacinto had become his father by then. Had erased Eloy's need to keep asking his mother about his real dad. She'd already told him everything she knew about him anyway, which amounted to not much of anything at all. But then his mother had turned to the front door and stopped smiling. And there was Wili, soaking wet, his face half-punched into oblivion. And Eloy's mother had walked to him and hugged him.

That was the Wili in front of him now. Hoping he still had a mom, even a pretend one.

"Yeah," Eloy lied again. "She told me to say hi."

"Do you think I should call her?"

"I don't think she's ready for that just yet, hermano. But give her some time. She'll come around."

"Yeah, I'll give her some time," Wili said. He looked at the mural again, more sober now, as if the memory of Eloy's mother had brought him down to earth. "It's coming along great. You're good at this, you always have been."

Eloy thanked him, though he could see in the mural only what he would like to do over — the eyebrows too thick, the upper lip too full. Wili put an arm around his shoulder, and for a second it felt like they were kids again.

"Hey, I actually came here to tell you something," Wili said. "There's a party at Topo's place this afternoon, and this guy" — he pointed at the mural — "wants you there. Don't miss it."

67

ELOY'S ROOM had been a storage closet once. If he spread his arms sideways, he couldn't quite touch both walls, but almost. Still, it was so much better than anything he could have hoped for when he'd first walked into the prison. He had a metal door that locked. He had a place to keep his things protected. He could sleep, alone.

Screwed to the floor in his room was a metal cabinet that still smelled like the cleaning chemicals it had held for decades. It now contained Eloy's small stock of supplies: toiletries, sundries, and some clothes. For the party he looked for his cleanest shirt, a brown polo he'd bought from one of the stands in the prison yard, and got dressed.

Tortuga had taken over the top floor of what had once been the prison's administrative building. Eloy had been up there before — to chat with Tortuga about the mural, or to draw the large Playboy bunny on his bedroom wall — but he had never been invited to one of his parties. Down the hallway spilled the relentless beat of reggaeton, Don Omar's "Hasta que salga el sol." Eloy remembered dancing to that song with his friends from university at Playa Pantaleta, his feet in the sand, rum and Coke in a plastic cup, speakers shaking from the back of a friend's Toyota Machito, rusted almost to oblivion but still providing the party with its lifeblood.

"Go on up," said one of Tortuga's men, standing watch and staring at him from behind his grumpy face, obviously annoyed that Eloy had been invited and he had to work.

Eloy thanked him and took the stairs.

Tortuga had knocked down most of the walls on this floor, leaving it an open space except for one enclosed room that he used as his bedroom. A flat-screen TV surrounded by mismatched couches occupied more than a quarter of the space. The TV played *Scarface* on mute, still in the opening scenes, with Tony Montana arriving in Miami. On the other side of the big room lay a pool table, an eight-footer with dirty felt. Topo, Wili, and Coquito—long-legged and dome-headed—drank beers and shot pool. Coquito was the captain of the prison basketball team—there had been an inter-prison league at some point, but it hadn't been active since before Eloy's arrival. Coquito had played for the Panteras for three years before being convicted of killing a teammate. Like so many other men here, and like Eloy and Wili, he awaited sentencing. He'd been in El Penal for a year and a half and still didn't know how much time he had left to serve. The sound of billiard balls clacking against one another broke through the music and beckoned Eloy. He didn't see Tortuga or anyone else; this seemed to be an intimate affair.

"Look who's here!" Topo announced at the top of his lungs. "¡El Pintor!"

Topo had been calling him that since he'd started painting for Tortuga and the luceros. That or *El Artista*. He always said it with an undertone of jealousy. Eloy couldn't escape the thought that if he ever got on Tortuga's bad side, it would be Topo who'd insist on inflicting the punishment.

"¿Qué pasó, Topo?" said Eloy. He shook hands with Coquito, hugged Wili, and then was enveloped by Topo's monster chest, squeezing enough to cause some pain.

"Damn, menor, we have to get you some new threads," Topo said. "Those shoes are embarrassing."

Topo showed off his own, massive feet, decked out in Air Jordans with black tips, a white body, and a big circle on the side that changed from black to red depending on how the light hit them. Eloy's sneakers were off-brand, flaking bits of their faux leather, speckled in paint.

"We can't all be rich like you," Eloy said.

"That's right," Topo said. "So you play this game or what?" He hefted the pool cue.

Wili handed Eloy a beer and said, "Topo, you don't want to play against this guy. Believe me."

"I only play for stakes," Topo said with one of his patented grins, every tooth a fang. "Not worth it otherwise."

Eloy's heart jumped, not out of fear but out of excitement. "Next month's Causa?" he said, knowing that to Topo that meant nothing. He could just mark Eloy's prison taxes down as *Paid* and not put any of his own money down.

"Easy," Topo said. "Rack 'em up, then, menor."

Topo had a powerful break — not surprising, given his size. The cue stick seemed a toy in his hands. The balls spread nicely, except for a small cluster of two striped balls and the eight ball. Topo's break had sunk both a solid and a stripe, leaving him two easy options from where the cue ball had stopped: a down-the-rail shot on the three ball, and then the nine ball, its yellow stripe teetering on the edge of a corner pocket, a whisper away from falling. Topo went for the nine ball, immediately telling Eloy everything he needed to know about Topo as a pool player, which also aligned with his opinion of Topo as a person. He just wanted to sink balls and had no mind for strategy. He made his second shot, missed the next.

Against a tougher opponent, Eloy could have attempted to run the table. He could see the pattern. He'd have a couple of tough shots, especially on the one ball, problematic on a long rail and blocked on one side by a stripe. But he wanted Topo in the game; he needed him to hold out hope for two, three, four games. Eloy might even lose one of them just to keep him on the line.

Holding the cue reminded him of Jacinto. Of the Sunday after-noons spent at Centro Hípico Los Morochos from the time he was eleven. On slower days at the racetrack, when Jacinto was out of the cinco y seis early, they spent their time at the three pool tables that the betting place furnished for its patrons. Jacinto ran those tables, prob-ably made more money there than on the ponies. Eloy learned to play first by helping Jacinto's old buddies rack the balls, then by joining in on their practice. It was the place where Jacinto had become his dad.

When his mother had told him they would be moving in with Jacinto, when Eloy was eleven, he hadn't quite understood. At first, despite how much he liked Jacinto, he'd even felt jealous of this man monopolizing his mother's time and attention. But she was so happy around Jacinto that it was infectious. And Jacinto himself loved hav-ing Eloy close.

By the time he was fourteen, hanging at Los Morochos, Eloy could pick winners on the Gaceta Hípica just from reading a few lines, then smoke the old-timers on the felt. He could alternate between being a sharpshooter—aggressively sinking ball after ball—and, when needed against a crafty opponent like Jacinto, playing *smart pool*. Sinking sets in batches and leaving the cue ball in a difficult position for his opponent. Jacinto was always proud, making fun of his friends. "You got beat by the kid!" he would tease. "You know I taught him everything he knows, right?"

Eloy efficiently sank two balls, and on his third shot left the four ball covering a corner pocket, blocking one of Topo's remaining stripes, with the cue ball on a short rail. It would be another difficult shot for Topo, especially given his need to hit everything hard. To Eloy's surprise, Topo made it. He was a brute but had played enough to develop some accuracy. Now Topo had only three balls left: the eleven ball, resting on the rail, which he couldn't do anything with, and the two balls in the cluster. He broke up the cluster, but not stra-tegically, just hitting it as hard as he could, creating mayhem on the table and not sinking any of his balls. The eight ball struck three banks and then glided softly toward the side pocket.

"No, no," Topo said, trying to persuade it away from the dark hole and the inevitable scratch. But the ball didn't listen. It tumbled inside, clacking against the other ball in the nest.

"Oh man, tough luck," Eloy said.

"Another," Topo said.

Eloy thought about what to ask for. "That TV/DVD that El Mocho is selling?"

"Sure, let's do it," Topo said.

Wili smiled knowingly at Eloy, a rare glimpse of his friend's teeth.

"Rack 'em up," Eloy said.

Whenever Topo was about to lose his cool, Eloy would spot him a game. He'd miss a couple of shots or leave the cue ball someplace where Topo could go on an easy run, only to win it right back with interest in the next few games. An hour and a half later Eloy was set for Causa payments for the next six months; he'd secured both the TV he'd been after and some of Topo's DVD collection. He would've had the Jordans off his feet if they fit him.

Wili and Coquito had stuck around the table for a bit but were now watching *Scarface* and passing a crack pipe back and forth. It made the whole room smell of burnt plastic. Wili leaned his head back on a couch cushion, his long neck arcing back, making his Adam's apple poke out as he exhaled the piedra smoke in gorgeous plumes. His eyes were closed, his mind flying somewhere other than here.

"Okay, that's it, I'm done," Topo said, and threw his stick on the table.

"You almost had me there," Eloy lied, hoping that in the coming weeks they could do this again, already pondering what to get next.

"Yeah, yeah. You're good at this, Pintor."

"Where is Tortuga, anyway?" Eloy asked. "Is he still coming?"

"He's out getting some stuff for the party."

"Out?"

"Yeah, getting some stuff."

"Outside the prison, you mean?"

"He goes out occasionally, Pintor. He's got an arrangement with Los Verdes."

As if on cue, laughter bounced up the stairs. Tortuga stepped in followed by two women, prostitutes, both a head taller than he was—helped, no doubt, by their otherworldly wedge shoes, neon plastic that lifted them off the ground as if they were on pedestals. Their exposed legs went up and up until they met the thinnest fabric—one black dress, one white—so tight it seemed to be just an extra layer of skin.

"¡Señores!" Tortuga announced. "Meet Melody"—he held his hand up, palm out, to the woman in the white dress, whose platinum-blonde hair, ironed into submission, clashed with her dark skin—"and Azabache." He turned to the woman in the black mesh dress, whose red underwear was visible beneath it, and whose acne bumped through thick concealer. "These ladies will be our company for tonight," Tortuga said. "But before we get started, a little prayer." He pulled a short stack of bills from his pocket and moved to a corner of his apartment.

Eloy hadn't noticed it before, but now he saw a small shrine. On it were three wood-carved figurines, all of them wearing sunglasses and backward caps. Nubs on their wooden lips portrayed half-smoked cigars, while pistols protruded from their pants. Los Santos Malandros.

Tortuga placed the bills at their feet and called the women over. "Girls, give them a little sugar, would you?"

The women had clearly done this before. If not here, then somewhere else. They kissed each idol and pulled out their breasts and jiggled them.

Tortuga walked to the TV. "Hey, cut that off," he said, pointing at the movie. It was nearing its climax, with *Say hello to my little friend* just around the corner. "Don't you know Chávez is on right now?" He snatched the remote and turned to Venezolana de Televisión, the government station.

There he was, Chávez in the rain, addressing thousands in a green slicker. The wide boulevard was packed with supporters, who formed a red river winding back as far as the camera could show. Chávez was swollen, but other than that he showed no weakness. His voice thundered as it always had. The stage was large, but Chávez seemed larger.

"That's my president, coño," Tortuga said.

Chávez was talking about how important it was to wake up early next Sunday, Election Day.

Azabache cozied up to Tortuga, trailing a cloud of perfume—sweet, like melon candy—that cut through the chemical whiff of Wili's crack pipe. "Do you think he's going to win?" she asked, placing her head on his shoulder.

"Chávez is like me, bella. We never lose."

"¡Chávez, corazón del pueblo!" Azabache yelled.

Eloy traveled back in time to a bus he hardly remembered, with his mom and grandma, when he had yelled slogans too, and danced to Salserín.

Tortuga grabbed Azabache's ass and repeated the campaign slogan.

Eloy imagined what it would be like to be a woman here. How terrifying. But there was no fear in either of these women. Maybe their lives had pulled the fear from them, one event after another, until they were empty of it.

"Okay, that's enough," Tortuga said, shutting the TV off. "Hit the music," he told Coquito, and the room became all sound.

"I love this song," Melody said.

"Me too!" Azabache said.

She pulled Melody by the hand into the middle of the room and danced with her there, looking only at Melody and nobody else. Their waists snapped to the beats of Daddy Yankee, and they sang along to the verse: "Súbela, bájala, y por debajo pásala…"

Wili was the first to shake himself from the spell they had cast. He jumped in and finished: "Suelta la cadera y mueve lo que tienes ahí." There was finally somewhere to put all the energy he'd inhaled in the past hour, and his hands were up.

The women laughed and brought him into their dance. Coquito and Topo joined in too, but Eloy stood outside it all, nursing his beer.

Tortuga approached him. "You don't like to dance?"

"It's not that."

"Then what the fuck is it? You don't like my gift?"

The words sounded like a gun to his head. "Of course that's not it, jefe!"

"Ha! Chill, chamo, just joking with you." Tortuga slapped him on the back. "I wanted to invite you today to thank you for the mural. It's coming out great." He paused. "Hey, Melody!" he yelled.

Melody trotted over to them, not one full song in and already beads of sweat forming on her forehead. "Sí, mi Tortu," she said, and put a hand on Tortuga's cheek.

"My friend Eloy here is shy. Will you dance with him a bit?"

"Of course," she said. Melody grabbed Eloy's hands and placed them on her hips. His palms hit the hard bone; his fingers rested on soft flesh. She pressed her head against his chest, her scent cloying now, scratching the back of his throat. She moved his hips to the rhythm and in seconds they were grinding to the end of "Limbo." Could she tell that under his pants nothing hardened? In his horror, the only blood in him pooled in his gut.

"You're a sweet one," she whispered in his ear when the song stopped, and kissed him on the cheek. Then she trotted back to her friend.

Eloy went to grab another drink, creating some distance from the dance floor.

"Shut off the music!" Tortuga yelled excitedly. "Off! Off!" He shook his arms.

Drunk, Eloy staggered toward the stereo, where plastic sleeves of pirated CDs littered the ground. He stepped on one, a salsa vieja compilation with Héctor Lavoe's pixelated face on it, and almost fell. He managed to pause the cumbia blaring from the speakers.

"Okay, I don't do this for many people," Tortuga slurred, "but for you, my friends, I will."

Now shirtless, his taut belly protruding above his jeans, he ducked into his bedroom and came out carrying a set of timbales. He set the two cumbersome drums before him and tested the skins. *Tap tap tap*. The sound was tight and somewhat metallic, higher than Eloy had expected. Tortuga then started a simple clave rhythm: *taptaptap taptap, taptaptap taptap*. As he warmed up he added different sounds, shifting from deep to acute, depending on whether he struck the drums closer to the edge or on the metal cáscara. Then he complicated the beat, his eyes closed.

Eloy hadn't felt a connection to Tortuga the entire time he'd been at Patria y Próceres. The only thing that bound them was the need for Eloy to follow the pran's every command, since his life depended on it. But here was something to which he could truly relate. Eloy didn't have a musical bone in his body, but he knew how it felt to be both submerged and elevated by a passion. For him it was a pencil, or a brush, or a spray can. For Tortuga it was his timbales.

Azabache stood atop the pool table now, kicking balls out of her way. "Did I tell you boys that my mom is Brazilian?" she said. She moved her hips and her feet, dancing a samba to Tortuga's fast taps and crashes, her small breasts bouncing with each thrust of her hips.

Everyone stared at her except Tortuga, still in his rapture, and Eloy. Topo and Coquito hooted and slapped the pool table. Wili leaned on a wall, his face at once stony and hungry. Melody stood by his side. She had removed her panties and bra but still wore the mesh dress. Eloy could see her full breasts, the speckling of brown freckles on her chest, her round belly just slightly plump above her shaved sex, razor bumps visible beneath the mesh. Melody caressed Wili's wiry arm, whispered something in his ear. What is she saying to him? Eloy wondered. He wanted to be a part of whatever they were planning.

Some desire was waking in him, but it had nothing to do with Azabache dancing for them, or with Melody, or with Tortuga's fiery solo now reaching a climax, sweat flying from his brow and splashing onto the timbales.

It was Wili's sadness. It was Wili's hunger. It was Wili. It always had been.

And then Wili and Melody were clapping, and so was everyone else, and Eloy was the only one standing dumb. The only one not looking at Tortuga. Not celebrating his talent. But he was caught out only for a second. Then he turned and clapped, and placed his fingers in his mouth to let out a piercing whistle. Tortuga raised his drumsticks in the air in triumph.

Azabache and Tortuga had been in the bedroom for half an hour. Eloy played pool with Coquito and managed to teach him a few things, even though he was seeing double. Wili and Melody danced. She had asked for "something in English, something slow," and Eloy had found, in the jumble of discs, a compilation of Whitney Houston's greatest hits. Whoever had burned the disc had also added Mariah Carey and Aretha Franklin and Tina Turner and Gloria Estefan and others into the mix, cramming every single byte of American divas they could onto the thing.

Melody was barefoot, her chin perfectly atop Wili's shoulder as they swayed near the TV, close to the stereo. Her small hands clasped his waist. He smelled her hair as the unintelligible ballad poured over them. From the couch, Topo stared at them through a chemical haze of crack smoke. When he stood up, it was as if something had snapped. He took a step toward Wili and Melody, instantly casting a shadow over the dancers.

"Mind if I cut in?" Topo's voice sounded as if it were coming from somewhere deep underground: a well, a sewage pipe.

How quickly things could turn here. One moment, nothing; the next, everything. Eloy and Coquito stopped their pool game, and Eloy's knuckles whitened on his cue.

"I do," Wili said, still holding onto Melody. "I *do* mind."

Topo sucked his teeth and looked away, at Eloy and Coquito. Then he grabbed Melody's wrist and yanked her from Wili. She flew backward onto the floor, her head narrowly missing the sharp corner of the coffee table, now overrun by spent black rock and charred aluminum foil, beer cans, rolling papers, and half-empty liquor bottles.

"Do you mind now?" Topo said. He was gigantic. Giant face, his brow projecting blankets of dark hair over his eyes. Giant neck, bulging veins. Giant shoulders, accustomed to the weight of violence. Even his breathing was giant—steady but giant puffs, into and out of his giant lungs. "Don't forget who's boss, niño," said Topo, towering over Wili. "You're a baby here. Know your place."

But Wili was Wili. A man made of woven steel cable, cold and unflinching. He didn't move, didn't so much as blink. His eyes were blood and sour milk.

Topo huffed and turned to Melody, still on the ground, tears on her cheeks. He helped her up. "C'mon," he said. "Let's go to my place." He pulled her along by the wrist and walked past Wili, a statue, then led Melody out the door.

Wili walked to the couch and found a piece of piedra with demons still living in its crystals. He stuffed it into a pipe and lit up.

68

STANISLAVO HAD INVITED MARÍA twice for dinner before this, but each time she had canceled last-minute. Too nervous. Too afraid. His letter had been both a gift and a weight around her neck. On one hand it was beautiful, and María believed that Stanislavo genuinely regretted leaving her mom, letting her go. On the other hand, the letter was a written reminder of Stanislavo's broken promise. Oh, how their lives would have been different if her father had kept it! Eloy wouldn't be in prison. Her mom might be alive.

With Stanislavo occupied by election coverage and María working with Eloy's new lawyer, it had been easy to delay this get-together. But Chávez had won, narrowly, and the country was recovering from its collective hangover. The opposition was angry, calling fraud, but that was always the case, even if it might have been true. Things had also progressed with Eloy's case, and she wanted to share the exciting news with Stanislavo.

Tonight, upon arriving, she had looked through one of his book-cases. The books gave the apartment a technicolor hue—no matter where you looked there were rainbows of book spines, in Spanish, English, French, and Russian. Being surrounded by all this color was strange. It was almost antithetical to her father, who, she had learned, was so serious. Even in his goodness—which she could tell moved him to action—she could feel a frost. Requests came out of him like barks, and jokes never quite landed. Smiles were hard to get, apart from ones deployed by virtue of politeness and routine. Maybe his mustache had something to do with it, always dour and drooping, like walrus whiskers. Maybe he was smiling behind it all the time and María never saw it.

They sat together now at his dining-room table, where Stanislavo had spread the food he'd ordered from a nearby Chinese restaurant. "Apologies," he said. "I'm no cook, but these are the best lumpias in Caracas."

As they ate, the crunch of the egg rolls giving way to warm cabbage and pork, he told her his side of the story, beginning to end. From meeting her mom in Mochima to the way things had ended before he left Casa Finlandia for Abastos Beirut and the tunnel. And all that had happened afterward, with Nassim and Kashir and the bomb. His time in Mexico City and Bogotá, his search for her mom and her in those first years after his return to Caracas.

When he'd finished—the remaining food around them growing cold in its various containers—he said, "Who was she?—your mom."

It caught her by surprise, the way the question was delivered. In some ways Stanislavo knew her mom better than she did. He had known her in the prime of her powers, when she still believed the world could be good.

"I never saw her back down from anything," María said. "I think that was her most distinct trait. But she was also angry. I think she wanted more out of her life. Even though, to me, she was gigantic. You should have seen the way she moved people, when she was organizing in Cotiza. She was a hurricane. A tough mom to have, though."

"How so?"

"She wanted me to be like her. Maybe like you, I don't know. But I could never do it. I was bullied in school and didn't have it in me to stand up for myself. I liked to blend in instead of speaking up. It really disappointed her."

Stanislavo sipped his coffee. The ends of his mustache foamed. His eyes were glassy and more gray than green now, with a depth that felt ancient. María sensed pain there. Regret.

"I brought you something," she said, digging into her purse. "It felt right, after you gave me the letter."

"Oh, María, you shouldn't have, please."

María handed him the old Polaroid. It showed Stanislavo and three other men in front of a backdrop of green banana trees, everyone dirty and ragged and happy. From Stanislavo's story she could finally put names to them: Nunzio, the Italian, tallest of the three; Molina, the jovial prankster, round and sweaty; and Tucán, the only brown boy of the four, with a nose worthy of his nickname.

Stanislavo held the picture, his hand trembling. And if she had doubted what his smile looked like before, she didn't anymore. It was so wide, beaming so powerfully. It reminded her of Eloy's smile as a boy. Stanislavo had become, for a split second, the man in the photo: twenty-something, strong, with a life ahead of him brimming over with possibility. And then, as if the weight of all those years had coursed into him at once, his smile disappeared, and he startled María with his sobs.

She stood and came to his side. She hugged him from behind, he rested his head on her arm, and it felt as if she were comforting both her son and her father. She was a mother again, and, for truly the first time in her life, a father's daughter.

"Thank you," he said.

"It always belonged to you," María said. "Maybe in her heart of hearts, Mom was waiting to see you again, so she could give it to you."

Stanislavo settled himself, his crying abated. His hand came up to her face. "I'm sorry I stopped looking for you," he said.

The apology seemed to break forth from years of imprisonment, a malnourished and broken thing, with mangled limbs and singed hair and missing fingernails. It hobbled out. But it was alive. It was hungry for nourishment.

"I know," she responded. "But I forgive you."

He was calm now. Both of them were exhausted from crying.

"All right, Stanis," said María, pushing her chair from the table. She stacked the remaining plates and silverware and walked to the small kitchen.

"I've got the dishes," he said. He joined her and hipped her out of the way.

It felt good, this familiarity that she had never thought would fizz between them, that she had thought Stanislavo would never be capable of.

"How's the new job?" he asked.

Stanislavo had offered María an apartment, had told her that he'd be happy to cover her living expenses until she settled into whatever was next for her. But something inside her still couldn't accept such an offer from him. She needed to be her own person. And she still found comfort from being in Jacinto's rancho. "Let me at least put you in touch with a friend who might need help," Stanislavo had insisted. Finally, she'd relented and had started cleaning the offices of a consulting firm belonging to a good friend of his. That had turned into another cleaning job for the man's wife, an engineer for a big construction company in Las Mercedes. María had since hired two cleaners to help her.

She told Stanislavo how well the job was going. How Mr. Loaiza had started to pass her name along to other people. There was a sense of opportunity rising that she'd never felt before.

"Can I ask you something?" he said. "And we don't have to talk about it if you don't want to."

"Sure."

"How did it feel, reading the letter?"

María didn't want to start crying again. Stanislavo handed her a wet plate, suds still dripping off the rim, and she wiped it dry with a dish towel.

The sound from the open faucet was as loud as a waterfall.

"I wish you'd found us," she said. "Maybe if you had, my mom wouldn't have gotten sick. I can't stop thinking about it. I might be a different person too. Not so weak. So…useless."

His face was astonished. "How could you ever think that about yourself?"

"I'm not my mom," she said. "I'm not you."

Stanislavo set down the plate he was rinsing and hugged her, wet hands and all. "You don't have to be," he said. "You never did."

And for the first time in her life, María believed it. "That part in the letter?" she said, from deep in their embrace. "Where you wrote that you didn't have to change the country, or the world—that it would have been enough for you to be together?"

"Yeah?" Stanislavo said, gently releasing her.

María looked up at him, a head taller, still strong despite his age. "I think it would've taken a weight off my mom to know that. When I wasn't as big as her, as big as you—when I couldn't be—she took it upon herself to be bold for the both of us. She wanted to change the barrio, its schools, its clinics, and for our representatives to actually do something. She couldn't stop fighting for that. But I think if you'd been there, if it had been the three of us, she would've settled."

"Maybe," Stanislavo said. "But your mom was never one to settle."

"Ha, true," María agreed. "She was a tough old bird. But she would have forgiven you. I truly believe that."

"I think so too," he said. He seemed lost in remembrance, with half a smile on his face. "She was tough, but she had a fluffy center."

María snorted, the way she did when laughter caught her completely unawares. Then Stanislavo started too. Their laughter rolled together, uncontrollable, like stones falling off a cliff.

After they had caught their breath, after the plates were dry and put away, after Stanislavo had poured each of them a little bit of rum and they were both sitting, comfortable and quiet in his living room, he asked if there was anything new with Eloy.

Adriana had left her a voicemail yesterday, she said. They would probably get a sentence for Eloy this week.

"What? Way to bury the lede, María! That's excellent news!"

"By the end of the week, Adriana said." María was both elated and afraid. Maybe that's why she hadn't said anything. The risk of jinxing it was terrifying.

"This is a good thing," Stanislavo said. "We can't do anything, fight anything, change anything, until he's sentenced."

"I know. It's just…what if they just leave him there to rot?"

"They won't."

María's lawyer, the public defender recommended by Adriana, had visited the newspaper last week and sat down with both Stanislavo and María to go through the case. The judge was known for handing out fair sentences, she said, especially for first-time offenders. But all it took was for him to have a bad day and years would be stolen from Eloy's life. And any random day in prison, María knew, could turn out to be a death sentence.

"You don't know that," she said.

"No, you're right, I don't," he admitted. "But now we have a way forward."

Somehow that admission felt better — more honest — than his fake certainty.

Stanislavo asked if the lawyer had said anything about Wili's case.

This was the question María hated. Part of her — most of her — didn't even want to utter his name. But lately she'd been having trouble sleeping, her mind always going back to Wili as a kid. She dreamed of him all the time. And she knew how important his case was to Eloy. So she had brought it up with the lawyer, even though she'd told Eloy that she refused to — that Wili was dead to her and that she wouldn't lift a finger to help him.

It wasn't looking good for Wili, she told Stanislavo. The lawyer didn't even want to move his file along to the judge. "I wasn't sure what to do," María said. "I told her I would decide soon."

"He's a bad man," Stanislavo said. "You know that. It could even hurt Eloy's case. If the judge sees the two cases side by side, he could decide to give Eloy a harsher sentence."

María felt like she was betraying something—not only Wili but a part of herself. Despite that, she would have Adriana back-burner his file: "I'll tell her to forget it," she said.

"It's the right decision, María."

Perhaps. But then why did she feel hollow inside?

69

"Cover it with something," Tortuga had told Eloy in front of the mural. "We need to do this the right way. With the ceremony it deserves."

So Eloy had commandeered a few sheets from Topo's storage and rigged them to cover the mural. Everyone had already seen it, of course. He'd been working on it in the yard for weeks now, and in the boredom of prison life every single prisoner had at some point chatted with him, even helped with the mural. Robin would bring him snacks on long days. Pecueca would come say hello and hand him paints and brushes. Wili kept him company — he'd always enjoyed watching him draw, and Eloy was glad that was still the case. Even here.

Things with Wili had been strange since the party. Eloy felt uncomfortable around him, even though all he wanted was to be close to him. He couldn't look him in the eye. Wili had started to notice, Eloy was sure of it, which made every interaction between them even more awkward. And then there was the rift between Wili and Topo. Wili was still one of his enforcers, but things between them were strained. He was certain Topo was going to kill him the first chance he got, he'd confided in Eloy.

"Por mi madre, that guy's gonna get me," he'd said just a couple of afternoons ago, making the sign of the cross.

Wili had retreated into crack, hard. He reeked of the plasticky smoke of perico. Although he still functioned, Eloy could see it coming. It was a common story in Cotiza. Wili had asked Eloy for money twice already, and Eloy was preparing for the third.

It was five o'clock, and prisoners started to arrive. Eloy leaned on the wall, still in his overalls, every piece of clothing a canvas. Tortuga's men had spent the afternoon preparing people for the unveiling.

One of the prison's varones came to Eloy. "Tortuga wanted me here," he said. "To bless the mural." He wore the uniform of evangelical priests in El Penal: white button-down short-sleeved shirt, brown pants, tie, good shoes. He was clean and smelled of sandalwood. "¡Alabado sea el señor!" he said, and then repeated it. His voice carried through the yard in front of Robin's restaurant, to the hundreds assembling.

The religious ones raised their hands to the air.

When things quieted down, the varón addressed the crowd. "Even in prison," he said. "Even here where Jesus Christ's lost sheep come to herd. There's space for beauty and for goodness. In each one of us there's the possibility of something great as long as we work and strive to be closer to Him, our Lord. And as the King of kings guides us, He tells us: *Listen to the wise among you, to those who put justice and truth above all things.*"

As he said those last words, Tortuga walked among everyone gathered, and they parted for him as he advanced. Topo followed close behind. Eloy was accustomed by now to Wili being Topo's shadow, but he didn't see him. He scanned farther back, searching for Wili's bony face, for his long fingers balancing a cigarette. Nothing.

"And here with us," the priest continued, "we have a wise man. One who keeps light and order and safeguards our well-being. May our Lord Jesus Christ bless him. May He bless all of us and lead us on the path of righteousness. May He bless this place and this mural." The priest looked back at the sheets blowing in the wind, then to Eloy. "And may He bless the hands that made it." He turned to the masses and raised his palms to the sky. "¡Alabado seas, Jesús!" he yelled. And people yelled back: "¡Alabado!"

Then Tortuga spoke. "Gracias, Guillermo. Wise words. You all know me as a good man. A fair man." Tortuga measured each word carefully. "And I truly believe that prison is a place where we can find ourselves again. Learn the value of hard work, of contributing to a common cause, all with order and purpose."

There was something familiar about the way he spoke. The cadences of grandiosity and self-indulgence. It took Eloy a few lines to realize that Tortuga was channeling Hugo Chávez's intonation, a little trailing high note at the end of a phrase, small audible pauses here and there.

"Prison is a place of banishment, of darkness," Tortuga said. "We are all here because society is afraid of us, and with reason. It is my job here to cast light. In the light there is order and there is peace. In the darkness things rot, things are taken, things die. So I call all of you to the light with me, so when we finally get out of this place we are accustomed to it."

As Tortuga spoke, moving among the crowd, Topo approached Eloy. "The man of the hour," he whispered. "Enjoy it while you can. The boss loses interest in his little side projects quite quickly."

Eloy just kept staring out into the sea of people.

"Before the grand reveal," Tortuga continued now, "let us have a moment of silence, of prayer, for the health of our president, Hugo Chávez Frías. So he can recover from his cancer and lead us for another fourteen years." Tortuga lowered his head, as did the rest of the prisoners.

"You haven't seen Wili, have you?" Topo said, even closer to his ear.

The words opened a void where Eloy's stomach usually was. He searched for Wili again, but nothing.

"So let me present our latest art project," Tortuga resumed.

"Eloy Rodríguez, the artist of El Penal, worked very hard on this as a tribute to us and to what we have accomplished, and as a reminder that we are still alive, that we are still a part of this world."

Tortuga moved next to Eloy and pulled the sheets from the wall. The wind caught them and they danced beautifully, swelling and billowing. Tortuga's portrait smiled at those who called El Penal their home. Blessed them with joy. And in cursive letters he had this message for all of them: *Don't let four walls steal away your smile.*

Tortuga hugged Eloy as the crowd applauded politely. "Good work, Eloy! I'm very proud of you, young man."

"Thank you, sir," Eloy said, trapped in the embrace. But his body was already running, searching for Wili. Praying he was alive.

Eventually Eloy found him. He wasn't dead. He wasn't even hurt. He was dead-eyed, though, smoking perico with another prisoner — a reggaeton artist everyone called Cochino, because he was an ugly version of Chyno Miranda, the famous singer. It smelled like they'd been on at least a two-day bender. Not even the chemical smell of the drugs could mask the sourness of their bodies.

"Let's go, man," Eloy said, pulling Wili's hand. And even with the state Wili was in, the touch felt electric.

Wili slapped his hand away. "Get out of here, chamo. Leave me alone," he said, and sat back down on the stained twin mattress.

"Dale, Wili, let's grab a bite at Robin's. My treat."

Wili looked at Cochino and started laughing. Cochino laughed too.

"What?" Eloy asked.

"This guy," Wili said to Cochino, pointing his thumb at Eloy. "This guy pretending he's my friend."

Cochino glanced at Eloy, catching his breath, then exploded with laughter again.

"I heard about your sentence," Wili said. "Congratulations! You've only got a year to go!"

The sarcasm stung, but worse than that was the guilt shackling Eloy, paralyzing him.

"Did the old lady tell you if she's been able to help *me* out?" Wili pursed his lips, contorting his face into puppy-like sadness. A mockery of his real pain. "*Pfft*. Of course not."

"That's not fair. She tried. She told me she—"

"Stop. *Stop*. I don't care. Good boy Eloy gets in trouble and his mamita comes and helps."

Cochino was still laughing in the background, making Eloy's bones rattle.

"Don't worry," Wili said. "She's not my mom. You're not my brother. You don't owe me shit."

"Fuck you," Eloy said. And he meant it.

"You'd be dead if it wasn't for me," Wili said. "This place would have eaten you up."

"I wouldn't *be* here if it wasn't for you!" Eloy screamed.

Cochino was no longer laughing.

"Please, Wili." Eloy extended his hand again.

"Just leave, huevón. I don't want you here. Cochino doesn't want you here. I'm not hungry. Go lick Tortuga's balls or something. Faggot," he said, stabbing him with that last word.

It seemed that Wili was accusing him of something, revealing a crucial secret. Did he know? Eloy felt ashamed. Wili lay down on the mattress and put his hands behind his head as if he were sunbathing, and Eloy couldn't hold back the burn bringing tears to his eyes. But he left before Wili could see.

70

WORD CAME that Chávez had died—for real this time. Or at least the government was ready to announce it. It had been the word since Christmas. And then through the New Year, and then during Carnaval, all through the long weekend of beach parties and children dressed as policemen, construction workers, and even Chávez himself. But the words had been soft; when you chewed them, they gave too easily, like ripe plantains. The word now, in the first days of March, was fibrous and had provenance. There was infighting between Nicolás Maduro and Diosdado Cabello, Chávez's two main lieutenants. Even though Chávez had made it clear that Maduro was the heir apparent, plenty of people, especially the military, believed Cabello was the right choice. Already the country was testing the lasting power of the dying (or already dead) caudillo's request.

The country was, of course, divided. Half in mourning, half in celebration. Most of Stanislavo's friends—some who had supported Chávez at some point but no longer, most who had never liked him—were full of hope. Some were callous in their rejoicing. *Finally, he got his. May he rot in hell. Good riddance.* The overarching belief was that without Chávez his party would eventually implode. Opposition dreams were starting to float—the possibility of winning the presidential elections, which would be called once Chávez *officially* died. Henrique Capriles, who had made a good showing against Chávez in the last election, looked better and better against a divided ruling party. But El Chavismo had spent fifteen years building a system guaranteed to give them victory, where the deck was stacked against the opposition and where a few percentage points here or there always mysteriously switched sides.

Meanwhile, fringe conspiracies were starting to surface about the US somehow injecting cancer cells into the president's body. A serum created by the CIA to stop Chávez from fulfilling his dream of uniting Latin America under the banner of twenty-first-century socialism. It was hogwash, of course. That dream had long since rotted on the vine. Chávez had failed on his own account to get Venezuela on the right track, even with almost a decade of an oil boom, resources that he had squandered on gifting oil to other countries, financing elections in Bolivia and Ecuador and Argentina, and sending billions to Cuba (mostly in exchange for military advisers and spies, who now led Venezuela's intelligence agencies). What Chávez hadn't wasted, the people around him had stolen. The missions that he had created—to educate, to heal, to reinvigorate popular neighborhoods, to farm, to feed—had all become money-laundering operations for their leaders, making them wealthy. In the last decade, a new class had been created to rival any magnate of the Saudi-Venezuela days of the '80s: The Boligarchs now had mansions in Miami and penthouses in Manhattan. They owned horses that ran the Kentucky Derby. And Chávez's own family had billions. After his death, if it hadn't happened already, his youngest daughter, María Gabriela, would become the richest person in the country. A billionaire many times over.

Graciela yelled from her desk: "Stanis, Adriana Vila on line one!"

He hadn't talked to Adriana in a while. Eloy had been sentenced. In eight months María would be able to see her son again, and Stanislavo would be able to meet his grandson. Stanislavo had spoken to María about that moment many times, sitting at his dinner table with her, sharing the meal she'd cooked for them. It had become a ritual, one he now cherished. Weekend evenings, which María spent in Cotiza, were often lonely for him. He'd started to reach out to friends to fill the María-shaped void. That hour or two of sharing, of company, reminded him of his jungle days with Nunzio and Molina, of his tunnel days with Nassim, of his newspaper days before he'd become this old and mean, back when he'd had more patience for the hunger in young journalists' expressions.

"Stanis," Adriana said, and he could hear the tumult of tribunales behind her.

"Adriana. ¿Cómo está todo? How can I help?"

"I'm actually calling to help you. Well, to help María and Eloy." She lowered her voice to a whisper. "If I can."

"What's going on?"

"The National Guard is going to raid Patria y Próceres in the next few days. We're making a push to take back control of the facilities from the pranatos. Finally."

Stanislavo wondered if it was his paper's photos that had done it. They had released pictures of Iris Varela, Minister of Prisons, posing cozily with Wilmito, an infamous pran from Tocuyito Prison, in his luxurious "cell." It had embarrassed the government and made international news. That, and the leaked images of swimming pools being built with public funds and bank branches opening inside penitentiaries, plus the leaked video of a massive orgy: famous reggaeton stars mixing with drug lords and prostitutes, and one or two high-ranking officers, for an all-night party in Maracaibo Prison.

"I'm planning on a final round of transfers before we go in," Adriana said. "Some prisoners I want to move before we raid. It's not going to be pretty. They're stocked for a war in there."

"Please get Eloy on that transfer list," Stanislavo said.

"He's already on the list, Stanis. That's why I'm calling. Wili as well. But they need to get on the bus."

"Why wouldn't they?"

"There's no way news of the raids won't leak to the pran there. The Ministry is divided on this—bitterly so—and there's real money at stake for some. The pran is going to find out, and his men will be prepared. They might not let anyone leave the premises. We've had hostage situations before."

"When are you sending the bus?"

"The one to Patria y Próceres is in two days," Adriana said. "Have María call Eloy. Tell him to make sure he presents himself to the guards by noon. They won't wait. And once the bus leaves, that place is marked."

71

It was true what Topo had whispered to him months ago, during the mural reveal: Tortuga had lost interest in Eloy as a project. There had been no more party invitations, no more long conversations at Robin's. But Eloy got to keep his private room. And Tortuga's blessing on him remained. If anyone hurt him, they would be held accountable. As long as he kept himself out of trouble, he could coast to the end of his sentence. Eight more months. He was pretty much halfway. Even his financial commitments to La_Causa were taken care of. Topo had honored his billiards losses: "By word or plomo," he said, "I make sure people pay me what they owe. That means I pay what I owe too. I don't mess with that." Plus, Eloy's mom, who'd found a new job, had been sending a bit extra.

Wili was a different story. He had fallen, stain after stain, from the good graces of Topo and, ultimately, from those of Tortuga. Eloy rarely saw him anymore. Wili had moved to a different side of the prison complex, where the Gandules lived. The people who didn't contribute to the Cause. Who lived outside the light. Whenever Eloy did see him, he barely recognized the skeletal Wili. Now he was together with Cochino, always. They talked in whispers and laughed in yelps. They looked at everything with the frantic eyes of rabbits. And even though Wili was so different now, had become a crust of what he used to be, it was impossible to escape the pang of pain, regret, and, yes, love anytime Eloy saw him.

Eloy paused the movie he'd been watching in his room and went outside. It was almost time for roll call, which he was still getting used to. Apparently, the guards had done it regularly a few years back, but Tortuga had ended it. They had resumed the practice last week. Every morning Los Verdes would yell a number and last name from the other side of the prison fence, and prisoners would call out *¡Preso!* in turn to make their presence known. Though Eloy didn't know why, Tortuga had begun enforcing the prisoners' compliance with zeal.

As he waited for his name to be called, Eloy sat in the morning sun next to Mongo, a crazy-looking kid with burn scars that grew from his neck into the left side of his face. Mongo had been teaching Eloy how to tattoo, and Eloy had been creating designs for him and his customers. Mongo could draw but not as well as Eloy, so they were helping each other.

"I got you some more oranges," Mongo said. "Just pick them up from the stand when we're done here. And come by this afternoon. We're doing the snake and dagger you drew."

Mongo had given Eloy one of his ink guns, and he'd been tattooing fruit for weeks. Orange peel had a similar thickness and feel as human skin. Eloy's whole room smelled of citrus, and whatever he didn't eat he would sell to Pecueca, who used the fruit as a mash for some of the worst alcohol Eloy had ever tasted.

"Gracias, hermano," Eloy told him. Then his number was called, followed by his full name, *Andrés Eloy Rodríguez*, and he stood up. *"¡Preso!"* he yelled, making sure the guards saw him. "See you later, brother," he said, then lifted his hand in farewell and went to the fruit stand for his oranges.

"Here you go, Eloy," said Toño. "Mongo left these for you."

Eloy thanked him and looked through the other produce: a couple of large avocados, some bruised tomatoes. Toño was expertly peeling a pineapple and dicing it, separating the large cubes in plastic containers.

"Déjame probar," Eloy said, pointing at the golden piña with his chin.

Toño balanced a pineapple cube on the tip of his knife and Eloy plucked it off. The fruit was sweet and tangy, maybe a bit over-ripe with that bubbly rot at the end of it, at once off-putting and delightful.

"Okay, give me some," Eloy said, and handed him a few bills.

From there he walked past the other market stalls to the cell-phone stand, which was empty for a change, though most pris-oners were still waiting for numbers to end.

"Your mom called yesterday, Artista." His nickname had stuck. "She said to call her immediately. Sounded urgent." He handed Eloy a flip phone, secured to the table by a cable. "You can call her back on the house as long as you're still up for helping me with my shop sign."

Eloy apologized for not having gotten to the sign yet and prom-ised he would start it today. The cell-phone vendor nodded and Eloy grabbed the phone and began dialing. His mother would be at her job right now, cleaning. But as he pressed the third numeral, he was distracted by a *"Hey!"* coming from the other side of the market. Across the yard, Wili was nonchalantly walking away from one of the stalls, his hands stuffed in his pockets. His body appeared to be little more than a collection of reeds now. His head was shaved to the scalp, unevenly so, and pocked with scabs. He looked across the yard and met Eloy's eyes for a moment.

"¡Epa, coño 'e tu madre!" the vendor said, and it was clear he was addressing Wili.

Other vendors and prisoners turned their attention to Wili, who was getting away. Cochino stood waiting for him by an open-ing in the yard that led to the shantytown where they lived. But the opening was far away; Wili still had to get through most of the market, and people were realizing that he'd stolen something and gotten caught. Cochino retreated out of the plaza into the safety of the shantytown.

Eloy put the phone back on the table—the green screen with

three pixelated numerals going dark—and stepped into the yard, closer to Wili, who was now surrounded by other prisoners.

"What?" Wili protested. "I didn't do nothing." His diminished muscles tensed. He looked at Eloy, and it felt like getting pierced by something sharp. "I didn't do nothing," he repeated, fooling no one, least of all Eloy.

"That's enough, puto," the vendor said. Eloy recognized him as one of Topo's buddies who sold rock and perico and weed. Exactly the people you couldn't steal from. The man took the gun from his belt and put it to Wili's forehead. "Empty your pockets."

Eloy shoved his way into the circle of prisoners around Wili and the gunman. Wili removed his right hand from his pocket and pulled out a small baggie. Just a few bolívares worth of piedra.

Eloy had the amount of money it cost in his pocket. "It's okay," he reassured the gunman. "He must've just forgotten to pay. Here." He grabbed all the money he had—enough to pay for three times the amount of crack Wili had stolen.

"Nah," the man said. "We're past all that. You're nothing more than a bruja. Escoria. Enough of this shit."

"Here," Eloy insisted, shoving the bills in the man's face. "Here you go. Take the money."

"Artista, mind your own business, okay?"

Eloy was sure the man was about to pull the trigger. That this would be the last time he saw his oldest friend alive. He wanted Wili to look at him once more. But he didn't turn. Eloy couldn't be sure Wili even knew he was there.

He held his breath and waited. But the shot didn't come.

"I'll let El Carro deal with you," the man said. Meaning Tortuga and his men would settle this.

Wili spit on the ground. A few prisoners grabbed him by his shoulders and led him away. Eloy followed, knowing they would go straight to Topo.

"Fuck, Wili. Fuck," Eloy said, keeping pace with the men dragging his friend.

"Like you fucking care, bro."

"I'll see what I can do, okay?" Eloy left Wili and sprinted to the prison administration building and up the stairs. Past the old offices used as homes for El Carro. "Tortuga!" he yelled.

Others came out of their rooms, guns in hand.

"What the fuck?" Coquito said, his long spidery legs sticking out of red boxer briefs. "What are you doing, Artista?"

"I'm looking for Tortuga. It's urgent."

"He's not here, man. He's in the yard, doing the numbers. You know how it is these days."

Eloy ran back down, out into the main yard. The guards were done with the roll call. Prisoners had already scattered about, going on with their business. Eloy scanned the population, searching for Tortuga, or Topo, or Wili. He spotted Topo first, the biggest of the three; then Tortuga, hand on chin, pondering something; and next to him, still held by the two men, Wili.

He felt a collapsing. As if his body were a piece of paper being crumpled into a smaller and smaller ball. He raced up to Tortuga. *Wili will be my responsibility,* Eloy promised him, offering both money and labor.

"Eloy, don't humiliate yourself," Tortuga said. "Your friend is a walking stain. An achicharrao. People like that don't learn, and they don't change. I like you, but don't press me on this. I make the choices here."

After a wave of his hand, his men pushed Eloy away.

Later that day the population gathered in the yard. Tortuga, Topo, Coquito, and Ternera, the older lucero with the pockmarked face, stood together in front of Wili, who was tied to a chair. The pran and his three luceros were ready to conduct another trial.

"¡En tela de juicio!" Tortuga yelled into the crowd.

The prisoners settled, chatter dying like the rustling of leaves after a gust of wind.

"We're not the savages society makes us out to be," Tortuga said. He paced as he spoke, always measured, always slow, paying homage to his nickname. "There is light here. Our rules are light. Our norms. Those who follow the light have our protection. Our gratitude. And then there are those who eat light. They go against what we're trying to build here." He raised his arms and spread them wide. "Those who eat light are punished. Ternera," he finished, and extended a hand to the older lieutenant.

The only thing in question was the severity of the punishment, not the punishment itself. Eloy placed himself in Wili's sight line, wanting him to see at least one friendly face. And in case this was it — Wili's last day — he said a silent goodbye.

Ternera stood up and spoke. "These are the facts. Wili stole yesterday from one of our market stalls. It's not the first time he's done so. He's a known malandro, una bruja más, contributes nothing to El Penal. Has not given to La Causa in months."

"Do we have anyone here to second these words?" Tortuga asked.

The vendor from whom Wili had stolen stepped forward and raised his hand. Toño, who had witnessed the whole thing from his fruit stall, also stepped forward and raised his hand. Cochino was there on the other side of the crowd, as thin as Wili. As dirty. Even from here Eloy could imagine how he smelled, the sourness of him. And now Cochino, too, stepped forward and raised his hand. Eloy wanted to murder him. He had never felt that desire for anyone. The deepness of it. The dankness.

"Does anyone contest these words?" Tortuga said. And here he looked straight at Eloy.

Eloy thought about what he could say. What defense he could mount for his childhood friend, for the man he loved. He found nothing. Or his courage failed him. He didn't know which. He knew only that this moment — this silence in which he was trapped for what seemed an infinite time — would haunt him.

"Well, then we find him guilty," Tortuga said, finally breaking eye contact with Eloy. "Guilty of eating the light that keeps us all safe."

The prisoners cheered, shouting out "Fifty-fifty!" and "Un manero!" and "The hole!" Possibilities of pain being hurled forth like song titles at a concert.

Eloy sought Wili's eyes. He wanted his friend to see the face of one who loved him. But Wili was so scared. His eyes were closed tight.

"Fifty-fifty!" Tortuga yelled.

Fifty-fifty. That was the chance a person had to survive a bullet to the gut. If you died, you died. If you lived, then you had learned your lesson.

Topo moved for the first time since the trial had begun. He took out his gun and planted himself in front of Wili. Eloy felt shackled again. Wanting both to run to Wili and to run away. Wanting to scream and finding something stuck in his throat. In the commotion and bloodlust of the crowd, Topo singled out Eloy and smiled, his gold tooth sparkling and proud. He leaned down and whispered something in Wili's ear. Some cruelty, no doubt. Then he stretched up to his full height, pointed the gun at Wili's stomach, and fired once.

The blast muted the crowd. Eloy's ears rang in a flat, long tone. The sound of a red line stretching ahead forever with no end. Carving him in two, starting at his sternum and ending at his belly button. Nothing else made a sound. Not the prisoners cheering and jumping in place. Not their mouths forming profanities as spit flew from their lips. Not Tortuga, still talking to the masses, surely proselytizing about the laws of light and the punishment that awaited those who swallowed it. The only thing that didn't move was Wili, still tied to the chair but now toppled over on his side, his life draining into the rough cement beneath him.

Quiet. So quiet. Because the ringing had become part of Eloy. Indistinguishable from silence. The same thing as it. All Eloy could do was see. And he saw everything.

72

"I CAN'T GET to him, Stanis!" María was crying in his office.

"What do you mean?"

"I've been calling and calling—the number I always call. Yesterday the man said he would tell Eloy to call me back, but he didn't. And then this morning he said there's been some stuff happening in El Penal and he hasn't seen Eloy."

"Did you tell him it was urgent?"

"What do you think?" she snapped.

"María, the bus will be there in just a few hours."

"I know, I know. Can we call him together?"

Stanislavo picked up the phone and María pressed the buttons. Stanislavo hit the speaker function. The phone rang a couple of times and went to voicemail: "You've reached Teléfonos Plus, the voice of El Penal. All lines are busy, but please try again later. Messages are not monitored. Thank you."

Stanislavo hung up. "What does the lawyer say?" he asked.

"There's nothing she can do. She already left a message with the guards, trying to talk to someone to make sure they don't leave without Eloy, but she hasn't been able to reach anyone who can do anything."

"Today's the worst day," Stanislavo said. "The whole country is paralyzed."

"What?"

"Chávez died, María. They announced it last night."

Graciela barged into the office. "Sandra and César are on their way to Miraflores," she said.

Stanislavo asked her if they had a statement from the American ambassador yet.

And suddenly María felt like a nuisance. Like nothing. What did Chávez matter? He was already dead. Eloy, her son—Stanislavo's grandson—was alive.

"Yes, we have something," Graciela said. "I'll send it to your email ASAP."

María waited for her father to come back to the world where Eloy lived. But he wasn't ready.

He stood up from his chair. "I'm sorry," he said, "I really am. I don't know what I can do. Adriana isn't picking up—I'm sure all the ministries are scrambling right now. People aren't even going in to work. Half the people are mourning, the other half are about to go celebrate in the streets. There might be violence, riots—"

"Nobody cares," she interrupted. "Nobody cares except me."

Stanislavo shook his head. "That's not true," he half-whispered.

"It's okay, Stanis," she said, wiping her tears with her sleeve. "You've done enough. Really." She stood up.

"Wait, María. Wait."

"No, I understand. This is big. This country. Chávez. Our patria. This newspaper. All this shit." Her whole body shook in frustration. "My son is just one person."

Stanislavo closed his eyes—whether in vexation or denial or shame, she wasn't sure.

"He means so little to everyone. He's meant so little his whole life. Just one boy in Cotiza. That barrio is so fucking big, and he was just one boy in it. And when he was shot, he wouldn't have made the news if he had died. Not in Chávez's Venezuela, not in the Venezuela before Chávez, not in the Venezuela after the president is buried six feet under. Because Eloy means nothing."

Stanislavo rested his old hands, freckled and hairy, on his desk.

"And now he's a man in a Venezuelan prison. He's worth even less. He's nothing to no one. Except to me. Yes, you've helped. It's true. I'm thankful. I am. I'm so thankful. But you have no idea."

"You forget I have a daughter," Stanislavo said.

Bile boiled in her gut. "And you left her, remember?"

He was stung. María could see it. She could imagine how he felt, being confronted at this moment by his failures, today of all days. But she couldn't hold back.

"I did," Stanislavo acknowledged. "But then we found each other."

"That's not enough. Now you've got to be a father. To me. And a grandfather to my son. You aren't a young man. You've got, what? Ten years left? Five? Less, if you're unlucky. And you're here wasting them on Chávez. Who fucking cares that he's dead! He ended up being just one more politician like all the others. *Worse*, because he made us believe that he wasn't. Fuck him. And fuck you!"

María felt her breath almost as another person. It had a body, red and swollen and electric. She wanted to hold that breath. Call it back into her, where she could protect it. Mother it into submission.

"I'm so sorry," Stanislavo said.

And María could see he meant it. And that there was nothing he could do. "It's okay, Stanis," she said, but everything was hazy, the tips of her fingers tingly. "You've done what you can. I know that. I really do."

Stanislavo looked beyond his office door, out into his newspaper. If the customary sight was chaos, it was now pandemonium.

"I'll go with you to the Ministry," he said. "See if we can find Adriana. Anyone who can get us a line into the prison."

Her body went soft with relief. She knew what this gift meant. The paper was his life, and this moment would define generations of Venezuelans.

"Eloy isn't nothing," her father said. "He's never been nothing. And he's not nothing to me."

And then she remembered the first time she had met Adriana Vila, in tribunales. Adriana had given her that Post-it note with the number of a pastor in Eloy's prison. She hadn't called him because Eloy had called her before she had to track him down through the priest.

"Wait," María said. She cleared space on Stanislavo's desk, pushing some papers aside, and rummaged through her purse. "Where is it? Where is it?" And then she lifted the Post-it note in the air like a torch, bright pink, its corners bent, the adhesive strip on the back lined with dirt and hair and lint, but bearing the all-important number that might rescue her son.

73

ONLY ELOY had dared run to Wili when he lay bleeding on the ground. To press against his wound with his shirt and, when that was soaked through, to beg someone for another. And only after Tortuga and his men had left did others help. A few evangélicos came bearing water and rags and a bottle of pills that could do nothing, because how could pills close this hole?

The young men moved Wili to the crumbling church, to a room used as an infirmary. But they had nothing there to treat a wound like this. Eloy wondered if they were even allowed to, or if there was a rule against administering aid to someone punished by the "justice" of this place. The evangélicos did what they could. Cleaned Wili and wrapped him. In a couple of hours, it was night and everyone else was gone. Just Wili, sweaty and in pain, muttering nonsense to the one lightbulb in the room, and Eloy, holding his hand.

With his other hand, Eloy touched the scar beneath his shirt. So old. Wili's wound was so new, so furious. It hadn't decided yet if it would ever become a scar. If it would harden into a story for Wili to tell—or if it would remain the wet, red thing it was now.

Then, suddenly, the feverish fog that had kept Wili away seemed to clear. And he looked at Eloy, then at their locked hands.

"¿Eloy? Hermano."

"Sí, Wili, estoy aquí," Eloy said and managed a smile.

He wondered if he would be able to hold the smile: even with Wili's gray skin; with the wet bandages wrapping his midsection; with the dirty room whose walls were peeling paint that must have been older than the two of them. But he needn't have worried about that. It was so easy to smile at his friend, to peer into him and find the real Wili. He saw Wili as a child, lying next to him on his mother's bed, saying, "It's time for your pills." He saw Wili standing next to his mom in the kitchen while she pressed down on the empanada dough, the edges of which he loved to mark with the fork. Wili running to the sandlot, both of them gathering the empty beer bottles, the plastic refuse, the bullet casings into a large plastic bag so they could have a clear field to play in. Wili behind him in class, saying, "Psst, psst!" until Eloy shifted in his seat enough for Wili to copy his test. He saw Wili pimpled and dirty, arriving at the rancho after four days away, smelling sour, like spilled beer left in the sun: María and Jacinto angry with him, and afraid for him, and glad for him to be back. He saw Wili kissing a girl on the steps up to Cotiza, remembered feeling both excitement and loss, like a thing going away forever. He saw Wili loading his first gun, how softly he touched it, how much reverence could be paid to so cold an object. He saw Wili's body tense up the day El Portu found La Loca Juana's body in the ravine behind his store, her hair tangled in weeds; recalled how Wili had looked at him then and how Eloy didn't have to say anything to his friend, not one thing, just be there so their eyes could find each other's. He saw Wili's hand on his mother's back as they all stared into Jacinto's casket, his body lying there diminished, no longer the man Eloy had called *Father.* No longer a man at all, just a carcass.

Eloy remembered Wili at the bottom of Manicomio hill, sitting on the sidewalk, waiting to be picked up that night of the robbery; remembered Wili handing him the gun he would carry into the house that had landed them here. "It'll be in and out, I promise," Wili had said from the passenger seat and flashed a wicked smile that filled Eloy with both dread and delight, a feeling like the one in his stomach the time they'd gone up on that rollercoaster: *clickety-clack, clickety-clack, clickety-clack,* up and up and up, hoping at once that the fall would never come and that it would happen right away and be over.

And then Eloy saw other Wilis, impossible ones. Wili graduating high school. Wili holding down a job at the cell-phone store. Wili at the Tiburones game bringing two cold beers to their seats. He saw his hand in Wili's hand, felt its softness, brought it to his mouth to kiss. They were old now, Eloy and Wili, playing dominoes in the plaza. Wili was bald, he was fat! Wili had never been fat, would never be fat. He would never be anything again.

Someone shook Eloy awake. He was still lying with Wili, still holding his hand, but Wili was so cold. Stiff. He had been dead for some time. Eloy had felt him disappear a few hours earlier but had not let go of his hand.

"Wake up," he heard, as if from a distance. "Wake up."

It was one of the young evangélicos who'd helped Wili yesterday. Next to him stood the pastor, the same one who'd blessed the mural months ago.

Eloy sat up. Wili's body was frozen in a fetal position, his eyes closed as if he were merely asleep.

"Eloy," he heard.

Still the sound was coming from far away, like words traveling down a long corridor. Like someone calling to him from the other side of a big house. Perhaps Casa Verde, those few times he'd been there as a boy, when his mother would admonish him to stop playing with the Romeros' toys.

The pastor shook him again. "Eloy!"

"Yes. Yes," Eloy said.

"I spoke to your mother, Eloy. Are you listening to me?"

"Yes," Eloy repeated, and looked at Wili again.

"Mírame." The pastor clapped his hands before Eloy's face, and the sound snapped him back into the world. "Your mother just called me. You have to get ready. You're being transferred."

"What? My mother is here?"

"No. Listen to me very carefully, okay? Change into these clothes." The pastor pointed to a small table beside Wili's bed, next to his face. "I'm taking you straight to the guards' office. I don't want you to grab anything, say goodbye to anyone. You're going to change and you're going to come with me. ¿Entendido?"

Eloy reached for the clothes. His pants, his bare chest, were covered in blood. He was still so confused. "What about Wili? Is he coming too?" But Eloy knew that Wili was dead even as he uttered the words. He knew it like he knew anything else. Like he knew that he was alive. That he was in prison. That this man in front of him was a pastor. Why had he said it, then? But now he repeated it. "Is he coming too?"

"No, Wili isn't coming. I'm sorry."

The evangélico helped Eloy take his pants off. They were crusted brown. Flakes of dried blood fell off like caked dirt.

Eloy tried to put on the short-sleeved button-down shirt but couldn't find the holes for the plastic buttons. The evangélico and the pastor assisted him with the shirt and even gave him new shoes, though they were too big. Eloy felt like he was dressed in Jacinto's clothes.

"We can't let Tortuga see you," the pastor said. "If he doesn't want to let you leave then you're not going anywhere."

They walked him away from the bed.

"Wili's not coming," Eloy said, no longer a question.

"No," the pastor agreed. "You can tell him goodbye, though."

But Wili's dead, Eloy thought. "I already did," he said.

They moved through the prison yard, slowly at first. The men had to prop up Eloy, as if he were a child learning to walk or a drunkard being steered home. But then the steps came easier. He began to belong to his body again. And his mind too. Things came a bit more into focus. The sun was bright in the middle of the sky, flaming down on all of them, alone in all that blue. Bodies gathered under shade. La Tasca was slammed for lunch, prisoners' necks red and sweaty, and Robin worked the burners like a man on fire. They went past Tortuga's soldiers, two men holding AKs who looked out at the guards' post, the receiving room, and then, past that, the rolling blue metal gate through which Eloy had walked with Wili so many months ago, when they were different men. When they were both alive.

"He's got an appointment with Los Verdes," the pastor said.

Tortuga's men nodded, unworried.

"Number?" the guard said on the other side of the fenced gate.

"What's your number?" the pastor asked Eloy.

Three-two-three? Or was it four? His head was still gone.

"¡Número, coño!" the guard snapped.

The pastor intervened. "Sorry, sir. He's a bit slow, you know? He's set for a transfer? Andrés Eloy Rodríguez."

Tortuga's men paid attention then. "Transfer?" asked one of them. "We've already sent out all authorized transfers. The pran hasn't authorized anyone else."

The pastor ignored him. The uniformed guard looked through his paperwork, scanning for Eloy's name.

"Hey, go get Topo," one of Tortuga's men said to the other, and the soldier strode off. "Father, I said no one else is authorized to go."

"He's authorized," the pastor said. "Is he on the list?" he asked the guard on the other side, who was still flipping through a folder.

"I'm looking," the guard said. "Relax. Yeah, here it is, Andrés Eloy Rodríguez." He lifted a sheet of paper. "Show me your face," he said.

And Eloy could do that. He complied.

The guard compared whatever was on the paper with Eloy's features and seemed satisfied. "Okay, bring him through."

Other guards fiddled with the locked gate.

"Hey, Father," Tortuga's man said. "You have to wait for Topo to get here and confirm." He grabbed the pastor's arm, holding the AK in his other hand.

The pastor turned back, and for the first time Eloy saw him as an imposing man. A man of size. He was a pastor, but he was also a prisoner. He was capable of violence. Or remembered enough of it to pretend.

"Don't touch me, hijo," he said, and the young soldier let go of him, immediately.

The pastor pushed Eloy toward the guards, and he walked through the gate. The guards locked it behind him.

"May God go with you, Eloy," the pastor said, and he made the sign of the cross.

One of the officers took Eloy's thumb and pressed it against an ink pad, then placed his thumb on a sheet of paper containing his name and photograph and some other information he couldn't make out. Unable to recognize the boy in the photo, he had trouble understanding how Los Verdes had seen in him the same person.

"The driver had to go to the bathroom," one of the guards said. "It's the only reason the bus didn't leave without you, coño. You're pretty lucky."

Eloy looked back into the yard, still just a few feet away, with only a fence dividing him from those buildings, those people. Topo rushed angrily to his soldiers, to the pastor and his young acolyte. But Eloy couldn't hear what Topo said. He was already being led away from all of them. Away from Wili, still lying on his side in that crumbling church. The sun would be shining through its cracked walls, painting him in glittering hues of gold.

74

ONLY ONE WEEK IN and Eloy's body already expected the opening bars of the national anthem. He woke up at 5:58 a.m., two minutes before the chorus of voices intoned "Gloria al bravo pueblo" through the prison speaker system. He lay in his bunk, eyes closed, waiting for it. By the second line, he sat up. Looked at Ricardo, his cellmate, on the other bunk, stretching himself awake. Ricardo was twenty-two, from Petare. Another artist, actually, a grafitero who'd tagged half the walls in Caracas with *Slomo*. By the second verse they were standing at attention, as the guards expected them to be.

The first couple of mornings, as he lay in his bunk with the blanket still wrapped about his legs and his eyes still crusted over, the guard for his section had rattled the cell bars with his baton. "¡Reo Fifty-Six!" the guard had shouted, his number here. "We stand for our nation's anthem."

After the himno nacional they both focused on their bunks. Ricardo had shown him how to pinch, fold, and tuck until the surface was as flat as a plank of wood. Then they waited for their turn at the bathroom and showers. A daily shower. With water pressure. That you didn't have to pay for.

The first day, Eloy had been mortified. He had left his small stash of savings, every bit of cash, in his room at El Penal. The

idea of starting from zero here—of falling into debt immediately with whoever was in charge, of having to figure out what
he could do to make money, how he could have his mother send
him money—had made his skin itch. And all without Wili as his
guide. When Ricardo had told him that things were different here,
he hadn't believed it. A week in and he was still waiting for the
moment when someone would come and exact whatever tax he
owed for existing here.

But under the warm spray of his five-minute shower, he forgot
most of these worries. The needles of water erased Tortuga, Jacinto,
Topo, his mother. Five minutes wasn't enough to erase Wili—there
wasn't enough water in the whole prison for that—but Wili at least
receded while Eloy washed his face, breathing in the clean tang of
the blue soap, his skin slick with it even after rinsing it off.

By 6:30 a.m. Eloy was dressed in his fatigues and black boots,
his white shirt tucked in. He sat next to Ricardo in the mess hall
at a long table with eighteen other prisoners. Four other tables like
this fit in the white institutional room. They were fed two arepas
with white cheese and beans, orange juice, and an apple every morning. Before they ate, they thanked the revolution: *New men. Strong
men. Revolutionary men. The past doesn't define us. It is what we do with
the life we have left that counts.* He was still learning the words. Still
mouthing most of it, studying Ricardo for cues.

Everyone looked at the large portrait of Hugo Chávez that
hung on the far wall, next to the Venezuelan flag. Even though he
was dead. Had died the same night Wili died. One week ago. One
week without Wili in the world, and unlike Chávez no one would
ever know who Wili was. No one would really care that he'd died.
Except Eloy, of course. He could already see years into the future,
on the anniversary of Chávez's death, how sullen and taciturn he
would become. And everyone would assume that Chávez had meant
so much to him, as he had to so many. They would wonder what
connection he had to Chávez, what the former president might have
given him to make his passing still so painful after all those years.

But the only thing Chávez had given Eloy was the same thing every other politician had given him: nothing at all.

After breakfast the inmates cleaned the facilities, then moved to Military and Ideological Instruction. Three hours of marching drills, exercise, and dogma. They were bathed in the boring, rote light of the holy trinity: Simón Bolívar, Karl Marx, and Hugo Chávez. With all the instruction coming from the mouth of a drill sergeant who desperately wanted to emulate Chávez — the way he spoke, the way he moved — but could barely string together two sentences without contradicting himself.

Then lunch, usually chicken and rice, efficiently made by other prisoners. Always lacking salt. Then working crops in the field — Eloy's favorite part of the day — with the heat here in the Central Valley so much more manageable, and a breeze coming in from the west. Then another shower, and then dinner. And then his bunk bed and Ricardo's gentle snoring, which Eloy didn't even mind. The sound made him feel less alone.

Every Sunday he was granted a one-hour phone call, and for his first one he had spoken to his mother, of course. He told her about Wili's death. As she cried on the other end of the line, he considered coming clean to her — about how he had grown to love Wili, not as a friend but as something else. Something more. How Wili's death had cut him in two, placing another scar on top of the one he already had. But no sutures, no ointments, no antibiotics could heal this one. There was no Vargas Hospital to save him. No amount of sweet mothering could soothe the pain. So Eloy said nothing. But he also knew that he would tell her at some point — when he was ready. There was comfort to be found in that thought.

The first week turned into the second, and the second into the third. And in the third week he heard what had happened at El Penal. He heard about Los Verdes going in with an army, grenades first. How Tortuga and his men had tried and failed to mount a defense, being unable to reach their weapons cache in time. The army had taken that building first, cutting them off from their guns.

The newspapers carried the photo of Tortuga's dead body: THE PRAN OF PRANES DIES IN TAKEOVER OF PATRIA Y PRÓCERES. Another photo in the same article featured Eloy's mural, littered with bullet holes from the attack. Dozens were dead, Topo and the rest of Tortuga's luceros among them. The final paragraph talked about the animals Tortuga kept, most of which the soldiers released. They took the cunaguaro, Azúcar, to the zoo in Parque del Este, in Caracas. Eloy wondered if he could go see her once he was out. If she'd remember him.

But that week also passed, and eventually it became routine to do the things that were expected of him in this place. So easy not to think about El Penal. So easy to see the calendar days falling. So easy to stop counting.

75

Stanislavo heard Graciela's voice over the furious *click-clack* of his keyboard. He was so close to his computer screen that his nose almost touched it.

"Of course. He's just fighting against his op-ed. Per usual. I'm sure he'd appreciate a break."

It was María, bearing a gift. "¿Cafecito?" she asked.

"Hmmm," he said, still half-thinking about the paragraph he was working on. Did he want to use *feud*? Or *battle*?

María placed the mug of coffee, black and steaming, on the lone unoccupied patch of desk. "Hey, look at me," she told him.

His daughter and the aroma of the coffee snapped him out of the op-ed's spell. He unpeeled from the screen and slid his reading glasses from the bridge of his nose up to the top of his messy head of white hair.

"Don't you have anything to say to me?" María asked.

He thought about it for a second. "¿Gracias?" When she just kept staring at him, he ransacked his brain. Then he remembered. "Oh, María! I'm so sorry I forgot. It's Eloy's day. His release!"

She grinned at him, clearly happy that he'd remembered without her having to tell him.

"It's the protests," he said. "They're getting worse. Definitely don't come back through downtown tonight, okay? How's your driving going? Are you feeling ready?" He couldn't help it—though she'd had the car for a while now, he was still concerned about her driving. But then he abandoned the worried-dad routine, knowing she would deflect the questions anyway. He stood up and approached her with arms open.

She landed on his chest and it was like hugging her mother, beautiful Emiliana. María had never set foot in the jungles of Mochima, yet she still transported him there, to the joy of pure feeling. His knee didn't hurt. His hands felt strong, his fingers limber. His hair was red. It was only temporary, of course. Soon enough he diminished back into his old bones. But every time he hugged his daughter, something flickered ahead. The future, alight again with possibility. Maybe not a full beam, as it had been when, hand in hand with Emiliana, it seemed like Venezuela was theirs to mold. But there was a candle, and as long as he walked toward it gently, carefully, it would remain lit. How glorious it felt to hold his daughter, and to be held by her, on such a good day. Soon he would get to meet his grandson. What an inconceivable, ridiculous, fantastical thing it was, all of a sudden to have a family.

And what a year it had been. Chávez was gone and buried. His chosen successor, Nicolás Maduro, had been declared winner of the special election, this past April, by the slimmest of margins. The election had been stolen. Again. And the country was still out on the street, seven months later. Venezuela vibrated around him, hot and angry, like a dropped hornets' nest. Sandra exploded into his office often with the latest updates on the protests (the largest he'd seen since 2002), or Maduro's fresh blunders, or the new lawsuit Cabello had lobbed at the newspaper. It all mattered.

But it was not what mattered most.

María sat in front of him and crossed her legs. Sipped her coffee. It was as if Emiliana herself was there.

"You remind me so much of your mom," he said as he sat. "Sometimes I can't believe I didn't recognize you instantly the day we met at the hospital."

"I look almost nothing like her," María said, though the pride on her face was apparent.

"Yes you do. You move like her, you sit like her...your voice is hers. And you have a way of seeing inside people. Deeply. You understand them. That's all your mom."

María gazed down at her coffee and smiled. "You've never told me about *your* mom," she said.

Stanislavo realized she was right. He'd talked with her about Ludmil, about the accident that had killed his twin brother, but he'd never talked about how, after Ludmil's death, with his parents it had been as if he had died as well. "At first I thought my mom would cling to me after Ludmil," he said now. "That I would remind her so much of him that she'd want me close. But it was the opposite." He described his mother's complicated relationship with death: his Jewish ancestors in Europe, the family members who'd disappeared during the Holocaust.

And then he related one of the only good things that had come from his years in exile, after the tunnel. His parents would visit him in Mexico City, he said. It was there that they really processed everything together: Ludmil, their estrangement, his time in the Movement. The way he'd felt around his mother, every bit as dead to him as Ludmil was.

"Did she understand?" María asked.

"She asked me to go for a walk one night. My dad was feeling ill and stayed back at my apartment. We found a bench in Alameda, by one of their beautiful fountains, and finally she told me she was sorry." Stanislavo's eyes grew glassy at the memory.

"How did it feel?"

"I felt closer to her, of course. And it also brought my brother back to me a little bit. Because of everything that happened after he died, I'd never been able to think of him without the weight of how damaged things were with my parents—with my mom, especially. But from then on I could remember my brother...I don't know... more purely. Does that make sense?"

María nodded.

He had never told anyone this story. Gratitude—for María, for what it meant to have someone he could talk to like this now—overwhelmed him, and he went on. "Years later, after my father died, she told me that her apology had allowed her to start dreaming about us as children again."

"My mom and I had a similar conversation," María replied. "The night of Chávez's election. It was the first time she ever really talked about you. It made such a difference, to be let into her world in that way." María paused and sipped her drink. "We're so far away from our children sometimes. Then at others it's like we're the same person. Don't you think, Dad?"

It always touched him when she used that word, and it still caught him off guard. He nodded a quiet *yes*. A sudden desire rose up in him then, so unexpected that he questioned voicing it out loud. But he didn't want to be a person who kept things like this from María. He'd wasted so many years that no time was left for that kind of withholding. So he risked the question.

"Is your mom buried somewhere?" he asked.

María's face told him she hadn't anticipated the question.

"It's just...I would like to visit her," Stanislavo said. "If that's okay with you."

She came to him and hugged him again. "Of course," she said.

And after sharing directions to the grave at Cementerio del Sur, she told him about her funeral, about how it seemed all of Cotiza had turned out for her mother. El Portu had brought food for everyone. One of her mom's organizer friends had his guitar and sang Pablo Milanés and Silvio Rodríguez and Alí Primera songs. Such a crowd had gathered that the cemetery director ultimately had to break up the party, politely asking everyone to leave. There had been such a profusion of flowers that people had decorated the headstones near her mom's grave as well. She had only just arrived, and already she was the heart of the neighborhood.

76

It took María longer than she expected to reach the prison. For a time, she was stuck behind a bus on a one-lane highway, and she was afraid of passing it, even on long, straight stretches. Even when she knew no cars were coming from the opposite direction. She'd been practicing for months, ever since she bought the car to help with her cleaning business, but it was still nerve-racking. How absurd it would be if she died in a crash on her way to her son.

Her mind ran to other worries. What if she had the date wrong, or had forgotten her ID, or something happened and Eloy couldn't get out today? It hardly mattered that she had talked to the lawyer that morning and confirmed that everything was in order. That Eloy had been processed, that everything was ready, that she didn't even need to go get him; he had enough money in his account to take the bus into the city on his own. The lawyer was obviously not a mother.

She looked at the empty passenger seat of her Corolla. At the gray dash, eroded from years of its previous owners' shoes against it. The torn cloth on the ceiling. The peeling fabric of the seat. And, perched upon it, the tin that housed the quesillo she'd baked. Eloy's favorite dessert. The creamy flan protected inside the circular metal vessel, free to jiggle every time she hit a pothole, of which there were many on this road. She could smell the caramel, even through the metal lid—the light burn of it, its dark sweetness.

Her dad would be going to the cemetery now. To visit her mom. They'd be close to each other for the first time since before she was born. A reunion almost fifty years in the making. And suddenly María wasn't alone in the car. She felt her mom there, as sure as her hands touched the wheel. She felt how proud her mother was of her. Of the woman she'd become. Was still becoming.

Finally, María took the set of turns that led to the prison. A stern white building. It didn't even look like a prison. She parked her car and handed her ID to the guard, who said Eloy would be out momentarily.

She waited. And those six minutes seemed longer than the almost two years since she'd last seen her son out in the world. Since that morning when he'd told her he planned to go out with Wili for a beer after work.

"You boys behave," she had said. "Tell Wili I love him."

And now here Eloy was, walking toward her. He was taller than she remembered. Straighter, somehow? His hair was cut so short. Military-style. His chest was broad, and he moved differently. With more purpose, maybe. And then another ghost came to her: Wili lived within her son. She could see them both so clearly. One dead, one alive. She mourned for one and celebrated the other. She feared that Wili had taken over. What if Eloy was no longer there?

But then he smiled. Her son. Her beautiful boy was in front of her.

Eloy lifted her up like María weighed nothing. Like she was the child and he was the mother. Like he had been on the outside all this time and she had been the one in prison.

EPILOGUE

STANISLAVO DROVE DOWN to Cementerio del Sur. He thought about María—his daughter—making her own pilgrimage. To Eloy. It felt right for both of them to be going on a journey of their own at the same time. Apart but together.

Flower vendors lined the street leading to the cemetery. Stanislavo bought lilies and chrysanthemums, but his mind was on all those wildflowers, all those orchids and bromeliads, that had been the backdrop of his relationship with Emiliana in Mochima. He thought of the araguaney tree, up in the mountain, of the yellow flowers it gifted them as they talked.

Once in the cemetery he had to defend against the assault of his journalist brain. The place was in complete disrepair. The economic crisis had marked the return of grave robbing as a possible profession for the poor. The bronze from older graves and mausoleums had started to disappear, and a few months back the paper had published a story about bodies being exhumed for jewelry and gold teeth. He shook it off as he searched for Emiliana's grave amid the labyrinth of plaques and headstones.

And then, there it was: Emiliana Rodríguez. Right where María had said it would be. The humble grave was dusty, overgrown with weeds. Stanislavo knelt and cleaned it off as best he could. The stone read simply: *Mother. Warrior.* He placed the flowers gently on the ground before it and stood.

He wanted to say so much, but in the end, the man who had spent a lifetime crafting words could summon only four of them. "I'm sorry, mi amor."

The feeling that seized him then was immediate. At long last, Stanislavo was truly free.

ACKNOWLEDGMENTS

Thank you to my parents, Manuel Antonio and Emilia, who taught me always to be kind first, and to be proud of my country and all that it has given me and gives me still.

To my sister. My best friend and my guiding light. When in doubt, I always ask: *What would Emiliana do?*

To my brother, Manu, whose power and resilience astonish me. Thank you for lending me a dark part of your past so I could tell this story.

To my family and friends from Venezuela, especially all the primos and the Santiagueños, always at the front of my mind and at the root of my affections.

To Emily Forland, my agent, whose sweet and steady guidance gave me confidence every step of the way.

To Ben George, my editor. We figured out this riddle of a book together, and in the process I've become a better writer. Thank you for being both the novel's toughest critic and its most stalwart believer. And to the rest of the team at Little, Brown: Maya Guthrie, Bryan Christian, Lena Little, Sabrina Callahan, Lauren Roberts, Pat

Jalbert-Levine, Allan Fallow, Cecilia Molinari, and everyone else, thank you.

To the Michener Center for Writers in Austin. The three years I spent there were the most creative, fertile, exciting, and fulfilling of my writing journey so far. What a dream to be taught by Bret Anthony Johnston, Elizabeth McCracken, Amy Hempel, Oscar Casares, Peter LaSalle, Laura van den Berg, Kevin Auer, Maya Perez, Cindy McCreery, among many others. But it was my time spent working with my contemporaries at the Michener and the New Writers Project that taught me the most. Thank you to Rickey Fayne, Molly Williams, Zack Schlosberg, Emmie Atwood, Fernando Villagómez, Ellaree Yeagley, Colwill Brown, Bev Chukwu, Amanda Bestor-Siegal, Maryan Nagy Captan, Megan Kamalei Kakimoto, Stephanie Macías, and so many more. Special thanks to Billy Fatzinger and Holly Doyel, who kept the fellowship running through the pandemic years.

I'm proud to say that this book has been touched by Venezuelan hands in all stages of its production. Michu Benaim and Lope Gutiérrez, my dear friends, designed the beautiful jacket. Boris Muñoz, journalist extraordinaire, proofread a late draft of the book; his keen eye for historical detail identified some very important holes in my research. Luis Bernardo Suárez, childhood friend and heart surgeon, answered all my questions about medical procedures. Federico Vegas, one of Venezuela's great writers, read some pages of this book and gave me much-needed advice. And my madrina, Maitena de Elguezabal, always encouraged my creativity and was a voice in the back of my head that told me I could do this. Thank you.

This novel is indebted to many books and documentaries. The series of books about the Venezuelan left by Agustín Blanco Muñoz and the documentary *Venezuela: Los guerrilleros al poder*, by Miguel Curiel, gave me the colors I needed to paint the 1964 section of this book. *El acertijo de abril* by Alfredo Meza and Sandra Lafuente and *The Silence and the Scorpion* by Brian A. Nelson helped me navigate the complicated days of the April 2002 coup d'état. Finally, Pavlo Castillo kindly screened for me the documentary he was working on, *La Causa* by Andrés Figuredo Thomson, on a rainy afternoon in Caracas many years ago. This documentary, paired with hundreds of pages of excellent journalistic reporting—especially *El gobierno de Wilmito* by Alfredo Meza—helped me construct the Patria y Próceres prison in the novel, as well as its pran, Tortuga. Many of these books were put in my hands by Garcilaso Pumar, whose bookstore in Caracas, Lugar Común, was an oasis of knowledge. He's a testament to the nobility of booksellers, especially those operating in the toughest of conditions.

Becoming a writer would not have happened without three specific teachers. Thamara Hannot, one of my sociology professors at Universidad Católica Andrés Bello in Caracas, was the first person who read any of my stories seriously—they were not good, yet she found encouraging words to say. Michael Noll read my stories and essays and pushed me to keep going and to put my work out there. S. Kirk Walsh, and her workshop, allowed me to sharpen my skills and really start sinking my teeth into work that mattered. Kirk's mentorship has been a steady companion for more than eight years now.

Thank you to the 2017 Tin House Summer Workshop, specifically the James Hannaham crew, where I first let anyone read any of these pages.

My community in Austin throughout the years has been a refuge. It's what made me fall in love with this city and call it home. Patricia and Adriana Salerno, Sam Scarpino, Laura Beerits, Rafael Guerrero, Genevieve Smith, Emily McTavish, Catalina Cuellar, Gabe Díaz and Emily Smallwood, Mariska Brady and Igor Holas, Tinisha Hancock, Gayle Burstein, Liz Milano, Nic Bennett, Pam Willis, Mendy Black, Pete Weiss, Lacey Gordon, Taylor Cumbie, Jessie Hunnicutt, Joshua Cullen, Aaron Charlston, Erin and Scott Augustine, Julie Wernersbach, Mike Bartnett, Adeena Reitberger,

Juli Berwald and Keith Fern, Mary Pauline Lowry. All the Kirk-shoppers. Everyone at The Grand Billiards Room, the Krieg Softball Fields (Go Chron!), and various tennis courts across the city. And to so many others in the almost twenty years I've been in Austin: I could fill another book—maybe not as long as this one—with y'all. Thank you.

Gracias to my work family at MAP, i2i, and Picturebox Productions, especially James Aldrete and Margie Becker: We spent ten years in the trenches of progressive politics, and at times managed to make a small difference. Thank you.

A good portion of this book was written and conceived at the Austin Central Library. What a gift that building is to the city! Thank you to all the librarians, staff, and patrons who keep the Austin library system strong.

To my Minneapolis family by way of Mississippi and Ohio: Karen and Steve Sonnenberg. Thank you for your unwavering support and for being such great grandparents. And to Bonnie Marshall, a true friend. Thank you!

Finally, to Brittani Sonnenberg. My love: I'm the luckiest person in the world because I got to marry my favorite writer, and I get to read your stuff before anyone else does. Thank you for what you brought to this book. I learn from you every day, and I'm so thankful we're in this together, with Ona and Penny and Logan by our side.

ABOUT THE AUTHOR

Alejandro Puyana, who came to the United States from Venezuela at the age of twenty-six, received his MFA from the Michener Center for Writers at the University of Texas. His work has appeared in *Tin House, American Short Fiction, The American Scholar,* and elsewhere, and his story "The Hands of Dirty Children" was reprinted in *Best American Short Stories.* He lives with his wife (the author Brittani Sonnenberg) and their daughter in Austin, Texas.